Chariots of Glory

By
Carl Baxter

PublishAmerica

Baltimore

First printing

ISBN: 1-4137-1537-0
PUBLISHED BY PUBLISHAMERICA, LLLP
www.publishamerica.com
Baltimore

Printed in the United States of America

To my wife Gail for her persistent encouragement ("Honey, why don't you get out of the kitchen and go over to the library and worry them half to death?"); to my daughter Carmen, the computer programmer for her continuous help with a balky computer ("Daddy, did you ever think about using the Help Program?"); to my son Will, a good writer in his own right, and to my mother, Miss Ida Bell, who was there in the beginning and in the middle, and is still there.

***

I wish to thank my brother and sister-in-law, Warren and Karen Baxter for their reading of my initial draft and for their honest and valuable opinions.

PROLOGUE

Daylight was breaking over the Ozarks in Southern Missouri, as Private Homer Adkins turned to look out of the east window of the cabin of the C-47 paratroop carrier. From his preflight briefing, he recognized Dove Mountain twenty miles in the distance. It was only a few minutes now to the drop zone.

Private Adkins was in the lead airplane, in a squadron of 16 transports that had departed in the middle of the night from Fort Benning, near Columbus, Georgia. The squadron's destination was a drop zone on the Fort Leonard Wood U.S. Army Reservation in South Central Missouri.

When the squadron had passed over North Central Arkansas, Homer had taken a long look out of the cabin window of the little transport plane, affectionately dubbed the Gooney Bird, by the U.S. Army Air Force. He had tried in vain to locate some recognizable landmark near his Izard County home. He had been in the army for only 16 weeks, but he was more than ready to go home. The bravado that he had felt when he had first visited the recruiting station in Batesville, Arkansas, in October 1942, had long since vanished and had been replaced with the fearful realization that to remain in a paratrooper organization for any length of time would more than likely result in serious injury or his getting killed outright. He had already given thought as to how he might remedy the situation.

After several weeks of intense training, two companies from the Twenty-Second Regiment of the famed 82 Airborne Division would soon be making their first actual parachute jump from an airplane. The paratroopers had been briefed that upon reaching the ground, they should gather up their parachutes and proceed to the designated assembly area where they would be met by a fleet of trucks to carry them to the base mess hall for breakfast, after which they would repack their parachutes and re-board their airplanes for a return trip to Fort Benning. They would make their second jump of the day at their home base. If all went well the troopers would sleep that night in their own bunks.

The lead pilot was heading for Mansfield, Missouri, where he would visually pick up the Gasconade River and use it as a navigational aid, following it northeast to the western edge of the Fort Leonard Wood Reservation. There, he would make a right turn and lead the squadron over the drop zone at 3000 feet.

Each trooper had packed and was harnessed to two parachutes. The backup chute provided a degree of safety as well as what the army thought was a source of confidence and a sense of well-being. The larger primary chute was harnessed to the front of each trooper and a smaller reserve chute was harnessed to the back. The primary chute was opened automatically from the static line when the trooper exited the aircraft, but it was not uncommon for the novice trainee to panic and unnecessarily deploy his reserve chute on his first jump.

The aircraft commander's voice came over the cabin speaker announcing the close proximity to the drop zone. The jump master moved to the side exit door of the aircraft and admonished the troopers to remember their training and to form in single file and hook up to the static line that ran the length of the plane, ending at the side exit door, which the jump master slid to open position; a rush of cold air filled the cabin.

A red light came on at the front of the cabin while simultaneously a loud clanging bell rasped out the signal that the jump was to begin. The troopers moved in single file to the exit door and leaped into the breaking dawn. Homer moved stoically forward with his eyes closed and felt the jump master's hand on his shoulder as he pushed him into space. A blast of icy air momentarily took Homer's breath away as he plummeted toward the landing zone.

Several seconds passed with Homer waiting for what should have been the shock and jerk of the opening parachute. He opened his eyes and looked upward making the horrific discovery that his parachute had candled partially open with shroud lines entangled. He reacted quickly to deploy the reserve chute only to have it entangle with chute number one; his descent hardly slowed.

One of the earlier jumpers had panicked and deployed his second chute and was slowly descending with both chutes open, to an anticipated controlled soft landing, when Homer suddenly plunged between his two open chutes and landed squarely astride his neck. The startled trooper looked up into the shocked face of his unexpected rider as the pair suddenly accelerated toward the landing zone below. Homer looked down into the panic-stricken face between his legs and yelled out, "I bet them durned trucks won't be waiting down there neither."

CHAPTER 1

It was a spring-like Northeast Arkansas morning, in mid-March, 1943. The Scott and Adkins family members were at work clearing more ground for planting. They were cutting down trees with a crosscut saw, dynamiting the stumps and piling and burning brush a half-mile south of the Scott farmhouse, in the Horse Island community, off eastern Lawrence County.

Ellis Scott was handling the dynamite. He used a pair of pliers to clamp the black-powder-fuse into the dynamite detonator cap that resembled the casing of large caliber pistol shell. The interior of the cap was packed with a very sensitive explosive nitroglycerine compound. One false move, one slip of the fuse against the interior of the cap would cause it to explode with the force of a giant firecracker or cherry bomb. There were a number of people walking around with mangled hands caused by the careless handling of dynamite caps.

After the fuse was clamped into the dynamite cap, Ellis took a steel rod the size of a pencil and punched a hole to a depth of two inches into the top of a stick of dynamite. The stick was a tube eight inches long and one and one-quarter inch in diameter, packed with an explosive compound. It was wrapped in heavy dark red paper and coated in paraffin. The dynamite explosion was the result of pressure caused by the exploding cap inside the dynamite stick. A cap exploding prematurely while the fuse and cap were being inserted into the dynamite stick could result in death for the handler or at least an incapacitating injury. Ellis Scott had been lucky so far.

Ellis Scott was paying Hazel Adkins a dollar a day to help clear the ground. While Ellis was preparing the dynamite, Hazel took a heavy five-foot steel rod and with a sixteen-pound sledge hammer, drove the rod at an angle as far as he could underneath the stump creating a hole for the stick of dynamite to slide down. He then removed the rod and moved to a safe distance as Ellis placed the dynamite, using a slender willow pole, to gently slide the dynamite, with fuse in place, down the hole under the stump. Once the dynamite was in place, Ellis cut the fuse at ground level leaving thirty inches or so attached to the dynamite. A fuse that length usually allowed sufficient time for the thirty-five year old sharecropper to get safely out of range by the time it burned down to the dynamite. Ellis always yelled, "Fire in the hole," as soon as he lit the fuse, a habit left over from his days as a coal miner in Izard County, Arkansas.

"Daddy, can I light the fuse on the next one?" asked Bud Scott, after the muffled underground explosion blew the debris from the shattered stump in a high arcing, umbrella-pattern flight over one hundred yards from ground zero.

"Yeh. I guess so. I'm gettin' too damned old to keep runnin' across this field anyway," replied Ellis. "Once I git the dynamite under the stump and the fuse cut, come over and bring the box of matches. But Bud, as soon as you see that fuse begin to burn and sputter sparks and smoke, you git the hell outta there."

"Can I do one, too?" asked the thirteen-year-old Joel Adkins, who was a year older than Bud, and two inches taller.

Ellis Scott always said that Joel could run like a turkey. It was not uncommon to see Joel run down a cottontail rabbit in a cleared open field. "Damdest thang I have ever saw," Ellis said in admiration after witnessing one of Joel's rabbit chases. "Better'n any dog I ever had."

"It's up to Hazel," Ellis said in reply to Joel's question.

"Well, I guess so," said Hazel. Joel was a big part of the Adkins family meal ticket and Hazel didn't want to risk his getting injured, but there wasn't much risk to just sticking a match to a dynamite fuse, as long as you didn't linger too long admiring your work.

Ellis Scott was sharecropping the Houston Johnston farm, on the Egypt-Bono county road. Mr. Johnston had recruited Ellis out of the coalmines of Izard County, in 1940, to work as a day laborer for seventy-five cents a day. The labor situation had improved in a wartime economy. A good hand could command a dollar for a ten-hour day in 1943.

Ellis Scott had brought his family of three, to live in a four-room cypress-log pioneer cabin at the back of the Johnston 120-acre farm. The old cabin was originally built in 1880, or so legend had it. Over the years, various occupants had added a log smoke house and a cypress-board outhouse and had attempted repairs of one kind or another. The cabin and outbuildings sat within twenty-five yards of the west bank of Cache River Ditch, on a quarter-acre plot carved out of a field that was sometimes planted in corn, sometimes in cotton. The rows of the crop under cultivation ran right up to the back door of the cabin. Ellis had moved from a life of digging a living from under the earth as a coal miner in Izard County, to a new life of scraping a living from on top of the ground as a day laborer on a cotton and corn farm in Lawrence County.

Ellis was an even six-foot in height. He was slender and sparsely built with raven-black hair and an olive complexion that darkened in the summer sun. Ellis was a descendent of Irish immigrants on his father's side of the family. He had picked up a Cherokee Indian gene from his mother's side of the family.

According to family legend his great-grandfather Carter married a full-blooded Cherokee maiden – Nellie Ray – shortly after the American Civil War. Grandma Nellie Ray was a descendant of the Cherokees who had passed through Northern Arkansas, on the Trail of Tears, during their trek from Alabama to the Oklahoma Indian Territory before the Civil War. Some Cherokee families dropped off along the route to establish homesteads in northern Arkansas. Ellis was fond of saying that his great-grandfather was an old Indian fighter, and his great-grandmother was an old Indian.

Bud Scott wanted to look like his father, like an Indian, but he didn't. Bud took after his mother, Inez. Inez Durphee Scott was a tall, five-foot, ten-inch, raw-boned, red-haired descendant of Irish immigrants, on both sides of her family. Bud was perpetually skinny, with dark red hair that tended to curl when it grew too long, which it was most of the time. He only got haircuts three or four times a year, when his mother would set him down in a straight-backed cane bottom chair and cut his hair with horse shears and a heavy steel comb. Bud hated the abundant large brown freckles on his face and arms that darkened as the summer passed. He had just reached his mother's shoulder in height, and could eat twelve times a day and still be hungry.

The physical characteristics of the Adkins family were in sharp contrast to the Scott family. They were of Scandinavian ancestry. They tended to be above average height. Their hair was reddish-blonde and they were light complexioned, and tended to sunburn easily. Hazel and his wife Dovie were both forty years of age. Both their ancestors were Swedish immigrants that had settled in the State of Minnesota in 1840. Both their great-grandfather's families had survived the great Sioux Indian uprising in Minnesota in 1862, during the American Civil War, and shortly afterward both families moved to the Ozark Mountains of Southern Missouri.

Like many of the Ozark hill people, Hazel had moved his family to the east bottom lands of Eastern Arkansas, near Crowley's Ridge in Northeast Arkansas, to make his fortune with King Cotton. The Adkins family currently occupied the same pioneer log cabin that the Scotts had lived in prior to their moving up to the main farmhouse on the county road. Since coming to the delta cotton country, Hazel had moved Dovie and their three children from farm to farm, trying to catch lightning in a bottle, but instead had become trapped in a cycle of poverty. Hazel was on the bottom rung of the ladder and had lost the will to try to climb higher.

Joel Adkins was the middle child of Hazel's three children. Joel had an older sister, Betty, fifteen, a thin, rustic blonde beauty, and a younger brother, Little Claude, four. Joel had been a field hand since he was seven years old. He had never lived in a house with electricity or running water and never expected, too. The Adkins family did not have an animal of any kind, not even a chicken. "Can't feed no animals," said Hazel. "Barely kin feed our own selves."

Ellis Scott was clearing thickets and hardwood land on the Johnston farm, in an attempt to reclaim more land for cultivation. The Johnston farm bordered on over a half-mile of the west bank of Cache River Ditch. The man-made drainage ditch, which could be described as an inferior river or a superior ditch, originated as a government drainage project in Clay County about 1930, just south of the Missouri border. The ditch, dug with giant draglines, cut northeast to southwest, through the Horse Island community, and through the eastern edge of Lawrence County, Arkansas, eventually emptying into the White River, over a hundred miles to the south.

A blue smoky haze hung over the bottomland throughout the spring months. Bud loved the acrid smell of powder and wood smoke, and he loved to watch the big piles of stump pieces and brush burn. Bud knew that when he started smelling black powder, mixed with the smell of wood smoke and freshly plowed ground that summer was not far behind.

In the spring of 1943, Ellis Scott and Hazel Adkins would plant sixty to seventy acres of cotton, and twenty acres of corn with two one-row planters pulled by two teams of mules. The rest of the farm could not be cultivated until it was cleared, and drained.

A few days after planting, the budding young cotton and corn plants would have to be thinned, chopped out by hand with a goose neck hoe, to promote a better growth and yield, and to clear the planted rows of grass and weeds.

The work was hard and the hours were long—daylight until dark. Bud hated chopping cotton and corn, or anything else with a passion.

Nineteen forty-three was the middle year of World War II. There was excitement in the air. Men, women, and some underage boys, passing themselves off as older, were leaving the fields of the delta and enlisting into the various branches of the armed forces. They were being sent to strange and exotic places, with names like Guadalcanal and Anzio. Great land and sea battles were being fought on and around the islands in the South Pacific and in the desert sands of North Africa. Delta sharecroppers shared in the scraps of war information from sources such as local small town newspapers that occasionally made their way out into the rural countryside. Occasionally, there were radio broadcasts by war correspondents directly from a battleground. There were newsreels to be viewed at an occasional picture show, with actual battle scenes. Metal coffins containing the war dead were sometimes shown stacked for shipment in the Movietone Newsreels, usually to a foreign burial ground.

It was a common sight for people along the county roads to see big green U.S. Army sedans passing by, driven by grim-faced men in military uniforms. They were coming from local military installations into the farm communities to deliver a dreaded telegram from the War Department, informing sharecropper families that their sons, daughters, husbands and wives would not be coming home, or would not be coming home in one piece.

Squadrons of fighter planes from Army Air Corp, and Naval Air training bases, scattered throughout Northeast Arkansas, Southeast Missouri and Western Tennessee, were daily practicing aerial maneuvers around and over Ellis Scott's farm. Sometimes daredevil pilots would buzz low, just above the tree tops, and they would take a good look at the dynamite explosions, which Bud and Joel thought, must have made them feel like they were really in a war zone. Sometimes the pilots could be seen waving at them, and the boys wondered if they were going to wave at the Japs and Germans too, when they got the chance. The Army Air Corps referred to the aerial maneuvers going on overhead as "dog fighting." On any good day for flying, smoke trails from a variety of aircraft could be seen crossing in the sky. Sometimes the crossing smoke trails looked like giant checkerboards or tic-tac-toe games.

"You boys don't need to be standin' 'round with one finger up your ass, and one in your mouth, changin' ever little bit," admonished Ellis, when Bud and Joel got caught up in the aircraft action overhead and forgot about loading stumps and brush on the mule-drawn sled.

It was Saturday morning and a good day for flying, when without warning, the pilot of a single-engine plane picked a most inopportune time to drop down for a closer look at the activity in the field below. "That's a Grumman Hellcat," said Bud. He was proud of his ability to identify most of the aircraft that were flying overhead from pictures he had seen in newspapers and magazines. The pilot made a pass at treetop level over the field just as Ellis Scott set off a dynamite charge, blowing a stump out of the ground. A large piece of the stump broke away and spiraled upward smashing into the aircraft propeller. Part of the propeller broke away and fluttered to the ground like a wounded duck.

The pilot immediately made an attempt to climb higher so that he could safely make a parachute jump and he seemed to be making some progress, when the engine began to belch smoke and flames. The pilot brought the airplane around and began an angled gliding descent, passing almost directly overhead where the men and boys were watching from the field below. The pilot seemed to have the plane under control, when the engine quit altogether. The pilot was clearly visible as he quickly climbed out of the cockpit and onto the wing, and then slipped off into the air.

"He's got a parachute on!" yelled Joel. "He's gonna land right in this field!"

The pilot had a parachute on all right, but it didn't open. The pilot fell like a rock and crashed into a small patch of timber a few hundred yards from where they watched. Joel and Bud ran toward the downed pilot, who had fallen through a big oak tree; Ellis and Hazel were close behind. "Damdest thang, I ever saw," said Hazel. "Ellis, you shot him down with a stump." Ellis Scott, white as a sheet and out of breath, stood looking down at the pilot, not saying a word.

The pilot was lying on his unopened parachute that was still strapped to his back. He was bleeding from the nose and ears and was lying on his back with one leg doubled up under him. His eyes were wide open and death had frozen a look of terror on his face. The youngster didn't look much older than the two boys who were looking into his cold dead eyes. The pilot's leather flight helmet had been torn off by the tree branches and was hanging from a limb several feet above the ground. Joel Adkins, barefoot, dug his toes into the rough bark and scampered up the tree to retrieve the helmet. The pilot had left deep scratches in his heavy brown leather flight jacket in a frenzied attempt to find the parachute release handle—the rip cord—as he plummeted to earth.

whom   Later, when the Army Air Corp officers, from the Walnut Ridge Air Station—fifteen miles north of the Scott farm—came to collect the body, one of them said that the parachute had been packed incorrectly, and by the pilot himself. The parachute release handle was positioned on the opposite side of his body from where it should have been. The pilot had panicked when he had reached with his right hand for the release across his body and couldn't find it.

Ironically, the plane glided to a crash landing, in a cow pasture on the Cecil Smith farm about a mile away. The plane received little damage except for a broken wing and landing gear. If the pilot had stayed with his plane, he more than likely would have survived.

Ellis told Joel to stay with the body and keep the bugs and ants away. He told Bud to go up to the Scott house, and wait for the army people, who Ellis assumed would soon be coming down the county road, once the other pilots radioed the position of the accident back to their base. The Scotts did not have a telephone, or any other method of notifying authorities. Ellis and Hazel went back to clearing ground.

Bud ran all the way home and told his mother about the accident. Inez Scott was a raw-boned, hard, stoic Irish woman, three generations removed from the old country, and she had received a lot of bad news in her 35 years. Her thoughts went immediately to the young pilot's mother and what she was going to have to endure. She fought back tears, but was not entirely successful. She knew that she could just as easily be getting the word that it had been Ellis, or Bud, blown up by dynamite.

Bud, meanwhile, found a big cathead biscuit left over from breakfast and a slice of fatback bacon. He poured himself a large glass of cold water from a gallon jug in the icebox and then went out on the front porch. He sat down on the porch steps to eat his biscuit and bacon sandwich, and to wait for the authorities to arrive.

He finished his sandwich and soon became tired of waiting on the porch, so he climbed high up in a large catalpa tree in the front yard. He began pulling himself up through the heavy branches, with the elephant ear leaves, to his favorite perch, from where he knew he could see down the county road a mile in either direction. On the way up the tree, he disturbed a nesting blue jay. The jay, sensing danger, began to dive at him, sometimes nipping the bill of his cap, in an effort to drive him back down the tree. Her cries attracted her mate, and soon Bud had two jays with which to contend. He straddled a large limb and lay back against the trunk of the tree, so the jays could only come at him head on. He sat quiet for a while, while the jays squawked and fluttered through the upper branches of the tree. They finally got tired of harassing him, and one returned to the nest, while the other sat on a limb staring intently at Bud to see if he was going to make any false moves.

Little Blue, one of the Scott's two blue tick hounds, moseyed out from under the house to see what all the commotion was about. The hound looked up in the tree, and quickly spotted Bud far up in the branches. He had seen all of this before and soon lost interest in the arboreal proceedings. He sat down under the tree, and with remarkable flexibility, twisted around and began to lick his own rear end, like young dogs can. Bud watched the dog and laughed out loud remembering something his father had said one time to Buell Smith, a farmer from back toward Egypt, who had stopped by for a brief informal visit, while walking to Turner's Store.

Ellis and Buell sat down on the front porch steps, took out their tobacco pouches and rolled themselves smokes. Bud sat quiet on the porch behind them in an old caned-bottom rocking chair, listening to the two men talk. Little Blue came out from under the floor to investigate the visitor. After taking a good look at Buell, and seeing that there was nothing in it for him; he sat down in the yard just in front of the two men and performed his contortionist act by twisting around to lick his rear end.

The men sat quietly watching Little Blue perform his own peculiar brand of hygiene, when Buell broke the silence. "Boy, I wish I could do that," he said, obviously impressed with the dog's physical dexterity. "Well, go ahead if you want too," said Ellis, with a straight face, "but, if I was you, I'd pet him first."

An hour passed before Bud, from his high perch, finally spotted a small caravan approaching from the west. The caravan included a Lawrence County Deputy Sheriff's car followed by a big green sedan with U.S. Army stenciled on the side in large white letters, and behind it, a white military medical vehicle with a big red cross on the side.

Bud quickly climbed down out of the tree, exciting the jays again, and went out into the road and flagged down the caravan. Looking at the four uniformed occupants through the open window of the army sedan, he told them where the pilot was, and added with just a touch of pride, "My daddy shot the plane down."

"He what?" exclaimed the officer driving.

"Shot him down with a stump," replied Bud.

"Get in and tell us about it son," said an older officer riding in the back seat. Bud squeezed in between the two officers in the front seat and by the time he had directed them down into the field where Joel was watching over the body, the officers had finally sorted out from their young guide that the pilot had carelessly flown directly into the path of a dynamite explosion.

"I'm awful sorry 'bout this," said Ellis Scott, as he came over to where a knot of officers had gathered around the body. He was still visibly shaken at the turn of events of the past two hours.

"It is not your fault, Mister," said the older officer. "We're getting these damn fool kids from all over the country and we're trying to make pilots out of them so they can kill Japs and Germans, but a lot of them are killing themselves." And turning to one of the officers, continued, "Make a note— Major—at our next briefing, tell them to stay the hell off the deck, where farmers are using dynamite. We can ill-afford to lose men or airplanes to anymore of this foolishness."

Bud was still excited that night, and at supper he kept up a steady stream of chatter about how Ellis had shot down the plane with a stump, and how the pilot had fallen through the oak tree, when his parachute didn't open.

Ellis who had remained silent through Bud's exuberance, finally had enough. "Bud, it ain't nothin' to be proud of, and I want you to shut up about it, and right now!"

"Teddy Bud," interjected Inez. "Death is a terrible thang. It was a terrible event, what happened today."

As memorable as the event was to those who witnessed it, it paled in comparison with events that were soon to follow. Events that would make the year, 1943, the most memorable year, for anyone that lived in that time and place.

CHAPTER 2

Bud was sitting on the front porch steps early the next day—Sunday—waiting for his parents to get ready for church. The Scott family did not own a motor vehicle. The family would travel by mule-team and wagon, a mile-and-a-half northeast, to the Little Brown Freewill Baptist Church that was situated within a quarter-mile of the west bank of the Cache River Ditch.

Bud was thinking about the plane crash the day before, and the way the young pilot had spiraled down through the oak tree. He planned on giving his eyewitness account at church, but out of earshot of his parents. He stepped off the porch and wandered across the yard and out into the gravel road in front of the house. Deep in thought, he began to throw rocks at fence posts and dragonflies. Ellis Scott had already harnessed a pair of mules to the wagon. Bud always felt sorry for the mules because they had to work hard all week and then had to go to church on Sunday. When Mr. Johnston left his farm, in Ellis Scott's care, to move to Jonesboro, he left Ellis with two teams of mules as well as all of his farming equipment. If there was a need for Ellis to use only one team, he swapped them around, so that one team did get to rest from time to time. Bud thought about that, and wished he had someone with which to swap work.

Ellis Scott appeared on the front porch, dressed in clean freshly ironed overalls with galluses snapped over a once white long-sleeve cotton shirt that had grayed from age and repeated washings. He was wearing a soft-gray felt hat that he called a fedora. Ellis did not attend church on a regular basis, finding it repetitious and boring, but he was going today. Bud wondered if it had anything to do with yesterday's tragic mishap involving the airplane.

Ellis had been informed by the Lawrence County Draft Board that he would not be drafted into military service, because he was thirty-five years old, and was a farmer with two dependents. The Draft Board officials said that the war effort needed farmers as well as soldiers. Bud knew that his

16

father felt extremely fortunate to be a sharecropper and not subject to be drafted. He knew that his mother felt that way, too.

Bud wondered what had gone through his father's mind as he looked down into the dead pilot's bleeding face and horror-stricken eyes. He wondered if perhaps a little shame may have crept into his father's soul, not so much because of the accident, as senseless as it was, but because others were having to go off to war and were dying in foreign lands so that he could be a sharecropper. But, Ellis Scott was a quiet man when it came to discussing his innermost feelings. Bud knew that his father would never say out loud what he felt inside.

Ellis was a hard worker. He was considered to have good common sense by the people who knew him. He was not a profane man, but neither was he into religion like his wife, Inez. He wanted to believe that there was a heaven. He already knew there was a hell, because he felt like he was in it and had been for some time. Ellis went to church on occasion, usually because there wasn't any pressing matter that had to be taken care of around the farm. When he went to church, he liked to go early because it gave him a chance to visit with his fellow farmers. The men liked to gather in a group in the churchyard prior to the service, and discuss crops and the weather, their two favorite subjects. The women liked to gather in a separate group and discuss the offerings of the newest Sears and Roebuck Catalog.

Inez Scott had been baptized in Polk Bayou when she was thirteen and became a member of the Polk Bayou Free Will Baptist Church, in Izard County. She sometimes referred to herself as a God-fearing woman, and she said she loved God's son, Jesus, who she told Bud, was one and the same. Bud never could reconcile himself to that way of thinking. He couldn't comprehend that someone could be the son and the father at the same time, and he could not understand how you could love someone and be afraid of them at the same time.

Inez read her Bible as often as she could, and she knew it well for someone with a fourth-grade education. Bud, thought it unusual, that at twelve years of age, he already had two more years of formal education than either of his parents; however, he was careful, not to let on that he thought that he was smarter. Flaunting his educational superiority around his parents could be dangerous to his health and welfare.

The Scotts would leave home at 9:30 a.m., for the ride to church in a wagon with iron-rimmed wheels. They would arrive at the Little Brown Freewill Baptist Church at 10:00 a.m., where they would spend the rest of the morning in a Sunday school class, and a lengthy church service. The service would last sometimes until one o'clock in the evening, especially when Roscoe Gilmore preached. "Seems like he repeats hisself a lot," said Ellis Scott, after enduring one of Roscoe's marathon sermons.

Preacher Gilmore could drone on, for what seemed like forever to the members of the congregation who had to endure sitting on the hard wooden church pews. He could preach incessantly about the end of time and chariots from glory, his two favorite sermon topics. There was no doubt about it, he repeatedly said, the end of days was in sight, and "Jay-sus," as he called Him in his sermon chant, would soon be coming for the believers, in a chariot of glory pulled by two white horses.

Bud knew something about wagons, and he had seen a picture of a chariot that to him was nothing more than a two-wheeled wagon. He wondered just how all of the believers were going to get on board. To Bud's way of thinking, there was going to have to be several trips made or there weren't going to be very many riders.

Bud never thought much about Roscoe's sermon. What he thought most about, when he wasn't thinking about Joel Adkins' fifteen-year-old sister, Betty, was what he was going to have for dinner when he finally got back home.

Inez occasionally teased Bud about being "struck" on Betty. Bud didn't know exactly what struck meant, but he thought that the ashen-blonde was real pretty and he knew that he liked being around Betty, especially when she had on a new flour sack dress with lots of red and blue flowers on it, and he liked the way Betty smelled when she dabbed herself with vanilla flavoring. Betty smelled like a big sugar cookie to Bud, and being around her always made him hungry.

Inez Scott usually prepared dinner before leaving for church, and left it on the kitchen table. She covered everything with an oilcloth to keep the sand and flies off of the food. The dinner this Sunday would consist of fried chicken, potato salad, cornbread, onions, corn and white navy beans. For dessert, there would be chocolate cake with a hard cocoa fudge icing.

After the hog killing in late November when the temperature reached the freezing point, fresh pork chops, bacon and liver, often showed up on the Scott's table, throughout the winter months. The Scotts did not raise cattle, keeping only a milk cow, and rarely ate beef.

It was one of Bud's chores to feed the three hogs destined for slaughter, and the thought often crossed his mind when he was mixing the wheat shorts and corn and pouring the mash in the trough, if the porkers would make such pigs out of themselves, if they had an inkling of what awaited them in November.

Bud was absent-mindedly throwing rocks while waiting for his mother to make her appearance so that they could get on the road to the church house, when he happened to look down the road and saw a very tall man approaching from the west. The man was wearing blue jeans and a long-sleeve white shirt, and military brogans with no socks. He had on a broad-brimmed planter's hat, a hat not often seen in the delta country where straw hats were usually the head covering of choice along with baseball caps. This hat was light brown in color and had a six-inch brim that stuck straight out, and the crown was short, and it was round like a coffee can. He was carrying a dark green, military canvas duffel bag, slung over his shoulder. The name "Adkins," was stenciled in one-inch white lettering on the side followed by a military serial number.

"Hello, I am Homer Adkins. Could a man get a drink of water? I'm awful thirsty," he called out as he approached. Bud immediately took him up on the front porch, while at the same time trying hard not to stare at Homer's extreme light color and pinkish-red eyes that seemed to be glowing from the shadow under the brim of a hat that covered a shock of shoulder-length hair the color of new fallen snow. Bud wondered, with those eyes, if Homer Adkins could see in the dark.

Bud went into the house and told his parents that there was a very strange-looking man standing on the front porch, and that he was getting him some water. Ellis, who had gone back in to hurry Inez along, went out on the porch to see for himself, and Inez eased up to peek through the screen door. Bud went to the kitchen, took a pitcher of cold water out of the icebox and poured a glass for the visitor. He went back out to the front porch with it in time to hear the visitor make a remarkable speech. "I am Homer Adkins," he said. "I have walked all the way from Izard County on a mission from God. I have come to this God-forsaken territory to preach the gospel, save the wicked, and in general do good, but first I am in need of baptism. I am lookin' for a preacher in this here wilderness named Roscoe Gilmore. He is a relative of mine. His mama and my mama, Helen Adkins, are first cousins." Homer paused to take a long drink of water, and then continued. "I am an albino, as you can plainly see." Then with both arms stretched straight out in front of him with fingers widened, he went on, "As y'all may have already noticed since y'all have been starin' pretty hard at me, I have webs between all the fingers on both hands, but what'cha can't see is that I got webs between all ten toes as well. The people where I come from thank I may have supernatural powers because of my webbed fingers and toes, and that I may be divine. Some have gone so far as to say that I may be the Messiah, because my mama got knocked up by divine intervention, or so she said. I can't rightly speculate on that."

When Inez Scott heard Homer refer to his possible divinity, she inwardly bristled but politely deferred a challenge. However, in the privacy of the Scott kitchen, just prior to boarding the wagon for church, Bud overheard his parents discussing Homer's ancestry, or lack of it.

Ellis, Inez and Homer had exchanged enough information while standing on the front porch, to allow the Scotts to come away knowing that Homer was the fatherless child of Helen Adkins of Izard County, and also that he was a distant cousin to the Adkins family that was currently working for Ellis.

Evidently, Homer did not know that he had relatives, other than Roscoe Gilmore, in the area. Ellis Scott thought better of letting Homer know about the Adkins family, until he could talk to Hazel. Right now, Hazel Adkins couldn't afford another mouth to feed, and it did not appear that Homer had any visible means of support.

Ellis said that he knew about Helen Adkins. He had met her some years before, when she was cooking at a large mining camp near the little town of Cushman, in Independence County. Ellis said, that Helen having gotten herself pregnant by divine intervention or otherwise hardly qualified as real news, for she had been known to have been "loose" even as a teenager. "A regular Jezebel," Inez Scott said in agreement. She had known Helen, too.

Inez Durfee Scott and Helen Adkins, as young girls, had grown up in the same community in Izard County, near the headwaters of Polk Bayou. There had been a rumor among the hill folks that Helen's baby sister, who was born when Helen was twelve, was actually Helen's daughter. Ellis Scott said that he felt fairly confident that Homer was not divine, just severally strange, and Ellis went on to say, "That simple bastard is the skinniest and the whitest person I have ever saw."

Of course when Inez Scott became aware that there was a potential preacher of the gospel on her front porch, she immediately looked past Homer's introductory remarks and invited him to ride in the wagon to church. Homer was glad for a ride anywhere, and was elated when he found out that the preacher at the Little Brown Freewill Baptist Church was none other than cousin Roscoe.

They got started with Inez and Ellis sitting on the driver's seat that was nothing more than a wide board nailed across the sideboards of the wagon. Homer sat on his duffel bag with his back to one sideboard of the wagon. Bud sat across from him. Everyone was quiet for a while and there was nothing but the sound of the mules' steel-shod hooves and the iron-rimmed wagon wheels clattering along the gravel road. Bud was trying his best not to stare at Homer, but it was a difficult proposition, because of Homer's whiteness and particularly his pink eyes and snow-white shoulder-length hair.

Homer knew that Bud was inwardly struggling with his appearance. "I was born without any skin pigmentation," he said. "And I sunburn real easy. That's why I always have to wear long sleeves and a hat in the sun. When I was small, my mama always made me wear a bonnet."

Bud didn't know what to say, so he didn't say anything. He was mulling over the word, "pigmentation." It was the first time he could remember having heard it. They didn't teach words like that at Egypt Elementary. Inez broke a prolonged silence and asked Homer how he came to decide to go into the ministry.

When people went into the ministry in those days, they were said to have received a "calling." God, Jesus or somebody, perhaps an angel, spoke to them and they were told to go to preaching the gospel. Seemingly, anyone regardless of education or occupation who got the call just dropped whatever they were doing, picked up their Bible and hit the glory road. Bud hoped that he never got the call because it looked like a dead-end road to him. The worst part of being a preacher to Bud's way of thinking was that a preacher had to work Sundays.

One hot summer day the year before, Bud thought that he had gotten the call. It was in August, and it was 105 degrees on the thermometer in the shade on the Scott's front porch. Bud was chopping cotton with his parents and the Adkins family in the field right behind his house, when he thought that he had begun to hear voices calling him to the ministry. He said as much to Inez, but she said—no—that it was the heat and for him to go up to the barn and pump water on his head and rest for a while in the shade. Anyway, Bud thought that he was too young to preach. Bud thought that to be a preacher, one had to be old enough to have experienced misery, and a lot of it.

It was in answer to Inez's question, that the Scotts learned that Homer had been in the United States Army. That was where he said he had gotten the call to preach. He said the army had recently discharged him because of his calling, and had classified him as a Conscientious Objector. That statement would be found out later to not necessarily be true. It was true that he conscientiously objected to being in the Army, but he had not been discharged because of it. In fact, he had not been discharged at all. Homer had deserted and was on the run from the military authorities.

It would become an enduring mystery to the people of the Horse Island community that Homer, a web-footed and web-fingered albino, who was so white as to practically glow in the dark, could have possibly passed a military physical examination; but it was wartime. The fact that he was six-feet-four-inches tall would seem to have disqualified him from being a paratrooper. However, his height was evidently offset by the fact that he weighed no more than one hundred fifteen pounds, about the same, more or less, as most men a foot shorter.

A serious discussion, by a number of ignorant people, about military eligibility requirements would sometime later be conducted down at Turner's Store. The discussion involved Homer's height and weight, and the fact that he had webbed fingers and toes. Those physical oddities caused one callous person to say that he wondered why the army hadn't just used Homer as a one-man glider. Bud thought it was an unfair jousting of a man who was evidently patriotic and had received the calling to boot. Homer had been a paratrooper in the famous 82nd Airborne, and was a hero in Bud's book.

Members of the congregation of the Little Brown Freewill Baptist Church were proud to say that their preacher, Roscoe Gilmore, was once the biggest sinner in the whole State of Arkansas, that is until he had received the call to preach. Some continued to say that he was still the biggest sinner in Lawrence County.

Roscoe had impressed a lot of people with his conversion to Christianity, or at least his version of it. There seemed to be at that time a direct relationship between the magnitude of sin and the degree of impression made on most people when a person converted. A real sinful man like Roscoe made a huge impression when he got saved, while most women and children converts made almost no impression at all.

What led to Roscoe's conversion was his near-death experience caused from drinking his own moonshine whiskey that he made at his camp on Horse Island, north of Turner's Store, near the Cache River Ditch. The batch was still green when he had gotten into it, and he was seriously poisoned, some said because he was running the batch through an old automobile radiator that he used as a condenser. The doctor at Walnut Ridge, where Abe Turner took him in his pickup truck, said he thought lead salts from the radiator poisoned Roscoe. At any rate, he nearly died.

Roscoe was slow to recover from his brush with death. However, it didn't keep him from continuing to make moonshine whiskey. He found a copper condenser, and he was real careful afterward, to let the batch mature and ripen a bit before sampling it.

It was reported that six members of an eight-member family up near Sedgwick, had died from drinking green moonshine whiskey in the summer of nineteen forty-one, and some said it was Roscoe's whiskey that had done it. Bud thought that it was to Roscoe's credit that he always denied it.

After his conversion, Roscoe had approached some members of the Little Brown Freewill Baptist Church—many whom were his paying customers— about the need to find a platform for his religious views that he had developed while in an alcohol induced coma. The church was in between preachers at the time, and welcomed the converted sinner into their midst, if for no other reason than he might have something interesting to say.

Roscoe's conversion was a surprise, but his baptism was even a greater surprise to most people, and Roscoe most of all. He had been sampling a fresh batch of his moonshine, and decided to walk down the ditch bank to Turner's Store. It was a Sunday afternoon, although, time and date was immaterial to Roscoe. Roscoe arrived at Turner's Store, to find a baptismal service in progress, in the blue hole, just downstream from the one-lane wooden bridge spanning the ditch. Roscoe, in a state of almost perpetual inebriation and without invitation, marched right down the path to the water's edge, during the singing of, "Onward Christian Soldiers." He waded out to where the preacher, from the First Baptist Church of Bono, was baptizing his converts.

Roscoe waded right up to the preacher, who first became aware of his approach by the strong smell of alcohol and body odor. The preacher without the formality of introduction grabbed Roscoe and dunked him under the water.

"Have you found Jesus?" asked the preacher, as he brought Roscoe up.

"No. I ain't," sputtered Roscoe.

The preacher dunked Roscoe a second time. "Brother, have you found Jesus?" the preacher asked again as Roscoe surfaced.

"No, I ain't," sputtered Roscoe.

The exasperated preacher dunked Roscoe for the third time and this time held him under water for several seconds. Bubbles came to the surface.

"Brother, have you found Jesus, this time?" asked the preacher.

Roscoe gasping for breath, and blowing water, replied, "Are you sure this is the spot where He fell in?"

That Roscoe Gilmore was a preacher of the gospel was in itself a modern day minor miracle, for one would normally expect a preacher of the gospel to spend hours studying the Bible, and this is where Preacher Gilmore stood out among his peers; Roscoe Gilmore could neither read or write. Never had time to learn was all he ever said, when pressed about it.

The mystery as to how he acquired his sermon material, which did vary somewhat, was finally solved when someone from the community spied Roscoe coming out of a Saturday worship service of the Seventh Day Adventist Church near the town of Bono. It seems that Roscoe rode his little gray mule over there on most Saturdays when those people went to church and memorized enough material from their preacher's sermon to add to his central theme of "Chariots from Glory," which he evidently considered to be a winner. This kind of undercover acquisition of preaching material allowed him to make presentations in his Sunday services that would seem to have come from a much more learned individual.

It seemed to Bud that before church services began people greatly enjoyed congregating and visiting while keeping an eye out for friends and acquaintances. Little kids chased one another around the church house, and threw water on one another at the outdoor pump, and the way Bud looked at it, everyone just had the best time, then the service began. The people of the Little Brown Freewill Baptist Church were no different than any other church group, when it came to visitors, and visiting before church. So when the Scott wagon pulled up in the church yard, the Scotts and their rider had already been the object of attention for some time as people were trying to determine who was in the Scott family wagon, and as the wagon drew closer, they began to openly stare. Bud knew it was because of Homer. Bud thought it was rude and said so to Inez, but Inez said that was the way of people. "They stare at things they don't understand." There was a group visiting with Preacher Gilmore just outside the church house door. They stopped talking and began to point and look toward Homer. Roscoe, Bud thought, was probably expecting to welcome a new sheep into the fold—so to speak.

Ellis parked the wagon in the shade of a large oak tree, and tied the mules to a hitching rail and loosened their harness. He then put down two big buckets of shelled corn, one for each mule. The mules were not going to have it all that bad, Bud thought. They would get to stand in the shade and eat corn for the next three hours, which was better than what he was going to be doing.

The Scott family, with Homer in tow, went on up to the church house, and as they approached Roscoe's group, Roscoe detached himself and came forward staring intently at Homer. Then he made an unusual statement. "Are you the one, or should I look for another?"

"I have come in search of a baptism, and I wish to assist you in spreading the gospel, and saving the heathens in this wilderness," replied Homer. "We are related I believe."

"I am not worthy of this blessing," said Roscoe. Then Roscoe beckoned the congregation to come inside. When Bud heard the exchange between Roscoe and Homer, he thought that there was something here that didn't quite meet the eye, or either Roscoe was drunk again. The congregation broke up into different age groups for Sunday school. Bud wanted Homer to come with his group but Homer went with an adult group that included Roscoe Gilmore, and was taught by the dapper Deacon Johnny Abbott. Bud went to a class taught by Abe Turner.

Abe Turner was something special. Everybody said so. In addition to running the big country store on the bank of Cache River Ditch, with his wife, Ruth, Abe taught Sunday school, acted as a deacon and elder, and as usher helped take the collection. He also acted as secretary for the church, and filled in for Roscoe, as preacher, when Roscoe forgot what day it was. Abe was a good preacher in his own right, but Bud didn't believe that Abe had Roscoe's flair for the dramatic.

Abe and Ruth Turner had not come from the hills as most everyone else, whom had migrated to the east delta country. Abe had volunteered the information that he and Ruth had lived in Jonesboro, Arkansas, for seven years before building the country store on the east bank of Cache River Ditch. However, neither he nor Ruth would talk about their life prior to that.

Someone had gotten a letter in their mailbox by mistake, addressed to Abraham Turner. That bit of information led to the speculation that Abe was a Jew. That and the peculiar argument he made one time during a game of checkers down at the store when Jesus' name came up in idle conversation, as it often did.

He had said that he believed that the Jews had been unwitting participants when Jesus committed political suicide. He said Jesus didn't have to come riding into town on the back of an ass. He didn't have to call attention to himself by throwing the moneychangers out of the temple. He didn't have to send Judas to the authorities, and he didn't have to hang around and wait for them to show up. Jesus and his disciples could have simply walked out of Jerusalem in the night and could have been miles away by daylight. Also, when Pilate had asked him if he was King of the Jews, he could have simply said "no" because he wasn't.

Abe said that the reason the Jews didn't recognize Jesus as being the Messiah, was simply because Jesus did not meet the ancient beliefs of the Hebrew people as to what a Messiah was, that in the Hebrew way of looking at things, the Messiah was a military or political figure, like a king—not a religious figure.

When Inez had heard about that conversation from Ellis, she said it was blasphemy to talk that way. However, Ellis seemed to think that Abe had made a good point. Bud didn't know what to think. Bud thought that Abe could preach the gospel with the best of them, and he knew the Old Testament better than anyone. Abe was never directly asked about being a Jew, and he never volunteered the information. Bud couldn't figure out what there was to worry about anyway. His thought was, what you don't know, won't hurt you.

After Sunday school, the church service began and everything went well with Roscoe seeming to reach down deeper than normal within for words of inspiration. Ellis Scott said that Roscoe was always at his best when he had been in the "shine" prior to the service. Bud always looked forward to Roscoe mentioning the chariots from glory, and he was not disappointed. Roscoe had the chariots coming and going and made it sound like the day of glory was going to be a real three-ring circus.

When church let out, Homer let the Scotts know that he appreciated the ride over and said that he would be going home with Roscoe to study the ministry under his guidance. It would be several days before Homer was seen again, and that was when he ventured off Horse Island to begin his ministry in the wilderness.

CHAPTER 3

Roscoe Gilmore was living in a one-room cypress-log cabin that he had built on Horse Island. Horse Island was not found on any map, and was known to only a few local people. It was a high wooded ridge surrounded on three sides by a swamp, about a mile north of the Egypt-Bono road, and one hundred yards from the east bank of the Cache River Ditch.

During the great Arkansas flood of nineteen twenty-seven, the tree-covered ridge was one of the few places between the towns of Egypt and Bono that rose above the flood plain. Several farm animals, mostly horses and mules and some hogs, along with wild inhabitants of the swamp, found refuge on the high ground and survived the flood. Their owners probably never knew what happened to their stock, so after the floodwater receded, the animals were left to grow wild. Most of the domestic animals eventually died or had been killed by hunters and wild cats by nineteen forty-three, but a few horses and hogs were still in the area.

There was a narrow causeway-like-ridge that ran off the bank of Cache River Ditch out to the island, so that it was possible in dry weather to drive a team and wagon from Turner's Store up the east bank of the ditch and onto Horse Island. However, most of the time the only way to get to Horse Island was either by foot or on a mule. Roscoe Gilmore usually traveled back and forth on a little gray saddle mule.

Roscoe had sought refuge from federal revenue agents, who were looking for him because of his whiskey making in Izard County. He fled to the Horse Island community in 1935. Most farm people never understood the revenue law and why taxes had to be paid on something that most people seemed to enjoy so much, and was so plentiful. Even the devout Inez Scott kept a quart jar of Roscoe's whiskey in the kitchen cupboard. She said she kept it for medicinal purposes. When any of the Scott family members came down with a bad cold, Inez would mix some of the whiskey in a cup of hot water with sugar and honey, and she would add lemon juice, if she could find a lemon. She called it a hot toddy. Bud liked it so much that he sometimes made one for himself when she wasn't looking.

After Roscoe had his religious conversion, he decided that Horse Island was the perfect place from which to launch his ministry, and not incidentally, the best place to hide a whiskey still. He idolized John the Baptist of the New Testament, who he first heard about as a child. He had never forgotten the story about John living on locusts and wild honey and dressing in animal skins. So it wasn't long after he arrived in the community, that he appeared at Turner's Store wearing a coonskin cap, deerskin jacket and trousers with matching moccasins, proposing to trade Abe Turner out of some groceries with a fresh batch of moonshine whiskey, which many of the local experts thought was the best whiskey that had ever graced Lawrence County.

Roscoe preached his first sermon at the Little Brown Freewill Baptist Church, dressed, in what Inez Scott called his Davy Crockett outfit. No one could remember a word of the sermon because of their amazement at this stout, bushy red-haired Irishman who dressed like a frontiersman. The women of the church finally persuaded Roscoe to wear more conventional clothes as they felt his style of dress was too distracting to the youth of the community, many of whom began to wear coonskin caps and to hold contests to see who could eat the most and greatest variety of insects.

Roscoe willingly accepted the ladies' solicitations, and he went to Turner's Store where Abe Turner kept a selection of work clothes. Thereafter, Roscoe showed up to preach wearing a clean pair of blue denim overalls and a matching denim long-sleeve shirt. The congregation approved of the new look even though he still wore deerskin moccasins.

In addition to his moon shining expertise, Roscoe was adept at making a beer commonly known as "home brew". He made the beer by mixing a concoction of water, yeast and sugar, along with cornmeal in a number-three steel washtub that he covered with a clean linen cloth. As the yeast and sugar worked off, he would remove the scum from the top of the amber liquid, add more yeast and sugar and keep it working until the alcohol content reached about ten percent. He then strained out the impurities through a white linen cloth.

Roscoe furnished gallon jugs of the amber beer to Abe Turner, who took clean empty cola bottles and filled them with the beer. Abe recapped the bottles, and kept them in the back of an icebox behind the regular soft drinks. He discreetly supplied his favorite customers with an ice-cold bottle of brew, usually at the late Saturday night checker and card games at the store. Ellis Scott had come home from playing checkers a little wobbly, more than once, and Bud heard his mother say that he had been in the brew again.

Bud could tell when his father was drunk. He came into the house singing and took the old fiddle and bow down off the wall, and began sawing off an Irish jig, and he tap-danced at the same time. He was actually better at playing the fiddle when he was a little drunk, more so than when he was sober.

Bud made an attempt to learn how to fiddle when he was nine years old. Neither parent discouraged him, but his mother made him practice outside on the front porch. The Scotts' two coon hounds would come around to see what all the screeching was about and would howl along with the fiddle music. Then the three cats could be seen easing around the corner of the house to determine if there was a need for them to attack something. Bud finally became so distracted by his audience that he gave up the fiddle as a lost cause.

Bee trees were plentiful in the swamp so that an abundance of wild honey was available to Roscoe and anyone else that wanted to try to take it away from the bees. Grasshoppers, which Roscoe called locusts, were everywhere. The big green hoppers were in abundance and easy to catch. Roscoe caught several dozen at a time and roasted them in a cast iron skillet over a hickory wood fire until they turned black and crispy. He salted them and dipped them in honey, and then dried them on a cypress board after which he put them in sealed fruit jars. He brought the jars of honey locusts up to Abe Turner's Store. Abe kept several jars of the roasted honey locusts on hand that he labeled, JOHN THE BAPTIST HONEY ROASTED LOCUSTS, and sold them for a nickel a jar. They were a community treat. John the Baptist, in Bud's book, really didn't have it all that bad in the wilderness.

Roscoe's greatest possessions were his "recipe" and his whiskey still that he had brought by wagon from Izard County. The recipe, a heavily guarded family secret, and still had been his father's and his father's before him— family heirlooms. Only a few people ever had the opportunity of seeing the still in action on Horse Island.

Roscoe had two guard dogs. One was a blue tick hound and the other was a redbone hound, which doubled as hunting dogs as well as guard dogs. Their names not surprisingly were Old Blue and Old Red, and they were two of the best coonhounds in the county.

Roscoe supplemented his whiskey income from selling coon and possum skins in the winter months. He caught the animals, skinned them and dried the skins on boards. A fur buyer from Jonesboro came out to Turner's Store twice a month during the winter, and he paid two and sometimes three dollars for a good coonskin, and a dollar for a possum. Mink skins could bring as much as ten dollars or more, a lot of money for the nineteen thirties and forties. Ellis Scott and Hazel Adkins made extra money that way, too.

Roscoe took Homer to Horse Island, and it was there that Homer's ministry had its grounding. In too short a time, Homer ventured off the island in a muddled attempt to spread the gospel throughout the Cache River Ditch swamp country, or as it was referred to by Roscoe and Home: the wilderness.

No one had seen anything of Homer for more than two weeks after his arrival in the community. When asked about him at Turner's Store, Roscoe said that he was in the wilderness being tempted by the devil, and that he expected Homer to come out in a little while secure in his faith. Roscoe said he had baptized Homer in the Cache River Ditch, which he had begun to call the River Jordan.

Bud and Joel were fishing on the ditch bank, close to Joel's house, early on a Saturday morning. It had rained heavily during the night delaying work in the fields. Inez told Bud that he had better take advantage of the wet conditions and go fishing, as he wouldn't have many chances once school was out and cotton-chopping season began. Carp was the only fish biting and the boys had caught several using red worms. Most people didn't like carp that well but the way Inez Scott fried them in cornmeal, flour and bacon grease, it wasn't the worst thing that Bud had ever eaten, especially when she served the fried fish with dill pickles, cornbread and sliced onions and fried potatoes. It was at these times that being a sharecropper's son wasn't all that bad.

Joel mentioned that Homer had been to their house for supper the past couple of nights. The Adkins family had made the discovery that Homer's great-grandfather and Joel's great-grandfather were brothers. So Joel and Homer were indeed cousins, a few times removed, although Joel was not bragging about it. Joel seemed to lack the same respect for Homer that Bud had. Bud figured that Joel would come around though, once he got to know Homer better. After all, they were cousins.

Joel said Homer had disappeared after supper both nights, and wasn't seen again until late the next day. He never said where he had been, but Joel said he had looked across the field in the night and thought he had seen a light in the old Thompson barn.

There had been a Thompson family that had a forty-acre homestead close to the ditch. The family of ten had built a fairly big house with a dogtrot, and when the oldest Thompson boy got married, he and his bride moved into the log cabin that was currently occupied by the Adkins family. The Thompson family also built a nice barn by the main house.

The Thompson family had come down out of the Ozark Mountains from Southern Missouri in nineteen twenty-nine, and had acquired one forty-acre block of land through a government program called the Swamp Lands Act, but Mrs. Thompson had missed her Missouri home and was never satisfied with living in the delta country.

The Thompson house burned mysteriously in nineteen thirty-one. It was rumored that Mrs. Thompson burned it on purpose when everyone but her was in the field. The loss of the house was all the incentive that the Thompson family needed to move back to Missouri. Mr. Houston Johnston then acquired the Thompson family forty-acre plot by paying the back taxes. So it was that Mr. Johnston found himself in possession of a rich new ground that had already been under partial cultivation, a nice apple and pear orchard and a good barn, with a good supply of fresh water from a pitcher pump. He then added the newly acquired plot to the eighty acres that he already owned.

Bud and Joel were having a discussion as to what the light could mean in the Thompson barn, when suddenly Homer appeared walking down the path leading from the top of the bank to the water's edge. "How'd you boys like to be my disciples?" asked Homer.

"What'd we have to do?" asked Bud.

"Follow me, and I'll make you fishers of men," stated Homer matter-of-factly.

"I thought you was supposed to be fastin' forty days and forty nights in the wilderness, like Jesus," said Bud.

"I couldn't take the skeeters," replied Homer. "I stood it for as long as I could. I stood it for three days. I still got welts all over me," and he rolled up his sleeves to display his arms that had large red splotches all over them. "I had to take a bath in Calamine Lotion. I was itchin' to death. I think I know why Jesus spent most of his time in the desert and the hills and didn't do no baptizin' down on the Jordan River—no skeeters."

Having attended church on a regular basis, Bud recognized something out of the Bible, when Homer made the "fishers of men" statement. However, Joel, who had seldom been inside a church, was stumped and he just stared at Homer, whose pink eyes were aglow from under the brim of his planter's hat as he stood in the shade of a willow tree scratching himself.

"Well, before we go fishin' for men," said Homer, "I first need to perform a miracle or two, to gain attention to myself and get my ministry offen the ground. I can't walk on water and I've danged near drowned twice tryin' it, and so far I ain't figured out how to heal nobody, and I ain't been able to turn water into wine, although, I believe I come close one time. However, I do believe I've figured out how to fly, and as fer as I kin tell, Jesus nor any of the disciples ain't never flew around the sky and landed agin and lived to tell about it; Roscoe don't think so neither. Boys come help me with some pigeons. I am goin' to fly."

The mystery of the light in the old Thompson barn was then revealed. It had been Homer down there at night with a miner's carbide lantern blinding pigeons with the light, catching them, and putting them into wire cages that he had made out of wood strips and chicken-wire fencing. He had caught well over one hundred.

There were a lot of pigeons in those days, and at sunset every day large flocks could be seen heading for someone's barn to roost for the night. Since the Thompson barn was vacant it was the ideal roosting place.

The pigeons were all colors. There were black, white, red, blue, gold, shades of green and brown, and it was a sight to see the setting sun glinting off a flock of a hundred or so beginning their descent to a roosting place. It looked something like a moving rainbow.

A lot of people said that these were passenger pigeons and that passenger pigeons had been used in World War I, to carry messages on the battlefield. Bud and Joel caught two pigeons out of the Thompson barn, the past December, after they had heard about the message carrying business. They decided to send a Christmas list to Santa Claus by pigeon, so Bud wrote out his list and tied it to his pigeon's leg with sewing thread, and Joel did the same. It was the middle of December when they released the pigeons, pointing them north. The pigeons took off in the right direction, but the boys never heard anything from it. Joel said he never got anything on his list, and as a matter of fact, he never got anything at all, and all Bud got was some apples, oranges and nuts in an old sock that he had tacked to the wall in the front room by the potbellied stove. The fruit and nuts had not been on Bud's list. Bud had asked for a Schwinn bicycle or at least a Red Ryder BB rifle, preferably both. The boys lost interest in pigeon communication after that.

Homer's idea, which the boys thought he must have picked up from his army training, was to take one hundred pigeons and tie fifty to each arm with nylon fishing line, and then he, aided by pigeon propellant, would launch into space from the highest point on the roof of the Thompson barn.

The Thompson barn was a two-story affair that was built to house animals in stalls on the lower level with a heavy-planked wood floor built above the stalls. The old barn had never been painted and had a light gray weathered look. The second story was a hayloft that extended across the width and depth of the barn. The roof was covered with sheets of tin that overlapped at the edges and was rusty with age, and it was sharply sloped. The edge of the barn roof was only about seven feet off of the ground but it sloped sharply upward to a peek of about thirty feet. The pigeons roosted in the rafters of the hayloft. There was a long ladder in the loft that was used during haying season when bales of hay were stacked there. A few bales still in the loft were covered with pigeon droppings. Homer had been sleeping up there the past few nights, and he had some of it on him.

When Homer was drafted in nineteen forty-two, he had been given a choice as to the branch of military service he entered. Homer had asked for the Army Air Corps because he had always wanted to fly in an airplane. A sergeant in the military personnel classification system obliged by sending him to the 82nd Airborne Division as a paratrooper. Homer arrived at Fort Benning, Georgia, thinking he was going to be a mechanic or a loadmaster on a C-47 aircraft. Unfortunately, Homer's limited education had not prepared him for the ability to adjust his thinking to align with reality. Even when he was jumping from the one hundred foot practice tower at Fort Benning, did he little realize that he was a paratrooper in an airborne division.

Homer was down at Turner's Store one day when the subject of his military service came up and someone asked him how he had liked being in the Army Air Corps, which of course most everyone knew by then was actually the 82nd Airborne. Homer said he thought it was all right, "except for having to jump out of them durned airplanes."

The first thing the boys had to do was to get Homer and the two crates of pigeons on top of the barn. They got the ladder down out of the loft and with some effort got both pigeon coops up on the lower edge of the barn roof. It was early morning, and fortunately the tin roof was cool as they were all barefoot. All of the other pigeons had already left the roost for the cornfields east of the ditch where they went every day.

The Wilson family had planted several acres of corn east of the ditch, and Elmo Wilson had been coming into Turner's Store buying shotgun shells with which to shoot pigeons, complaining that the birds were scratching the freshly planted grain out of the ground and were eating their early corn crop.

The pigeons in the crates were quiet. Homer had the foresight to cover the cages with burlap bags so the pigeons were being kept in the dark. The boys set about cutting one hundred, three-foot lengths of fishing line and tying a loop on each end. The idea was to take a pigeon and loop one end of the line around both of its feet and then loop the other end around Homer's arms.

The plan was put into motion by getting both coops up to the very highest point of the roof. The coops were placed close enough together so that Homer could sit down on the peak of the roof while Bud, working out of one coop, and Joel out of the other, tied fifty pigeons to each of his outstretched arms. After a length of line was looped around both feet of each pigeon, and the other end looped around Homer's arms, the pigeon was placed back into the covered cage. The pigeons were kept under cover until all the tying was accomplished and Homer was ready for lift-off. Bud was impressed by the way Homer had figured out this complicated procedure, and Bud believed Joel was too; although truthfully, Joel hadn't said much up to this point.

The barn faced due south which meant that the roof sloped from its peak to the east and west. Homer had chosen to make a running takeoff down the west slope into the breeze that was coming that morning out of the southwest. He said that was what airplane pilots always tried to do—that is take off into the wind to get the maximum lift. Bud, and Joel too, was impressed with this bit of information.

A nagging thought invaded Bud's mind: namely, when the pigeons left the roost at sunup, they always went east, back across the ditch toward the Wilson's cornfields. Homer said that he had not fed the pigeons for three days and had given them nothing but water. He said he wanted to reduce their body weight somewhat, as they were all pretty fat and plump. The pigeons were hungry.

Bud and Joel finally got through with tying the pigeons to Homer's arms. Homer had removed his shirt and shoes to reduce as much weight as possible.

"How fer do ya thank you'll fly exactly?" asked Joel.

"Well, I've calculated that the pigeons will take off at about tree-top level, and will fly me about half-a-mile before givin' out and goin' to ground. Now I want you two disciples to come a runnin' to where I land and bring your pocket knives so's you kin cut me loose, once I've made a touchdown."

Homer suddenly stood, tall and erect. Bud and Joel moved away as far as they could, and what a view they had from on top of the barn. It was possible to see miles across the flat lands in every direction. Bud could see his house a half-mile to the northwest, Joel's house a quarter-mile to the south. Just across the river from Joel's house was the Claxton house. Bud could see smoke coming out of the stovepipe. He wondered to himself what they were having for breakfast. He could see the top of Turner's Store a mile to the north, and across the river a mile to the southeast was Bull Taylor's farmhouse. History was in the making, and Bud and his best buddy were in a perfect spot to witness man's first pigeon-powered flight. Bud suddenly wished that he had brought his mother's Kodak Brownie, because he didn't believe anyone would believe this, unless they saw it in black and white.

"I'm ready. Stand back and let her go boys!" yelled Homer.

Homer yanked both arms up and straight out simultaneously, springing the pigeons out of the coops and into the bright sunlight. Homer began to wave his arms up and down and was yelling at the top of his voice. The pigeons were startled. The pigeons went wild, and the pigeons went east.

Homer was caught off balance expecting a westward movement, and began to furiously backpedal down the east slope of the barn roof. The pigeons were thrashing the air and some of their lines became entangled around Homer's neck. Homer was trying to get the pigeons out of his face while floundering backward down the sharp incline of the barn roof. He finally lost his balance and landed flat on his back just before he and the pigeon flock went off the east edge of the barn roof—Homer, head first. The last thing the two boys saw of Homer in flight was the bottom of his bare feet as they disappeared over the edge of the roof.

Homer let out a high-pitched squall as he went over. The shriek of terror was immediately silenced with a loud thump that was followed by a mushroom cloud of dust and pigeon feathers that rose slowly and drifted out over the barnyard fence.

The boys sat on top of the barn for a moment stunned into silence by this unexpected turn of events. "Well, we'd better go see if that durned fool is dead," said Joel, and they eased down the roof to where they had left the ladder and climbed down to the ground.

"Knocked out, cold as kraut," said Joel, when they got around to where Homer lay on his back, with the pigeons kicking up a fuss. The boys took their pocketknives and cut the birds loose. Most of them, that were able, flew toward the river. Some just walked around the barn lot stunned. Bud was as stunned as any of the pigeons and was speechless.

Homer was still alive and began to make twitching moves and began to groan. Joel went to the horse trough over by the barnyard fence where there was a pitcher pump and an old bucket. He pumped the bucket full of water and threw it all on Homer's head. Homer's eyes fluttered open but he didn't speak, couldn't speak most probably.

"He's all right I guess, just landed on his head," said Joel. "Let's go back to the ditch and get our fish and go home."

That sounded good to Bud as he was already getting hungry and he could almost smell those fish frying in the pan. So off they went, leaving the pioneer pigeon-aviator and holy man in the barn lot, lying in a puddle of mud and water.

CHAPTER 4

Two days after the pigeon fiasco, Bud was in Turner's Store. "Abe, seen Homer lately?" asked Bud.

"He come through here yesterday goin' back up the ditch to the Gilmore camp. Said he had a sore neck. I gave him a bottle of horse liniment to rub on it."

"He say what caused it?"

"No. Never said. I didn't inquire."

"Fell off of the Thompson barn on his head."

"What was he doin' on top of that barn?"

"Tryin' to fly."

"Fly?"

"Yep."

"Did he fly?"

"Yep."

"How far?"

"About seven, eight feet, I reckon."

"Up?"

"Down."

Abe chuckled to himself, at the thought of Homer trying to fly off of the Thompson barn, and he didn't know about the pigeons, yet. Bud Scott was not one to do a lot of talking, so unless you knew what questions to ask, you were not going to get a lot of information out of him.

"Did he flap his arms, or what?" asked Abe.

"Nope."

"Well, just how was he supposed to fly?"

"Pigeons."

"Pigeons?"

"Yep. Me and Joel tied a bunch of pigeons to his arms on top of the barn, and they was supposed to fly him out in the field aways."

Abe was about ready to burst out laughing, from Bud's droll verbal expression, but the seriousness of Bud's demeanor was holding him back. He wished Ruth was out front to hear this.

"Me and Joel is his disciples," said Bud.

"Disciples?"

"Yep."

Abe was about to lose all semblance of composure. "Just exactly what are y'all's duties?"

"We're gonna help him fish for men."

"Any luck, so far?"

"Nope. I think we need better bait."

Abe collapsed behind the counter, and Bud, who was sitting next to the wall of the store on a nail keg could hear, what sounded like muffled sobs, and coughing, as Abe thrashed around on the floor. Abe finally raised himself above the counter. He had a straight face, but tears in his eyes, from choking back gut-wrenching laughter spasms.

"Whatsa matter, Abe?"

"Swallowed a hairball, I guess."

It was early April. Ellis Scott and Hazel Adkins had worked up most of the farm's cultivatable land with the two teams of mules. The cotton had been planted and the cotton stalks were just beginning to break the dry crust of the ground.

Ellis and Hazel would begin plowing the cotton in a day or two, when the stalks reached about four inches in height. The cultivator plows would push the dirt against both sides of each row of cotton plants, helping to support the young plants, and keep them from being knocked over by wind and rain. Chopping would begin after the first plowing.

Everyone that could, went to the fields when it was time to chop cotton. All members of the Scott family would go, as well as all the Adkins, even little four-year-old Claude. All farm kids went to the fields, many before they could walk. Inez Scott had put Bud on an old blanket at the end of a cotton row, when he was just six months old. Bud had to fend for myself while Inez chopped to one end of the field and back. There were bugs, chiggers and spiders, and one time when she got back to where she had left him, she found a black chicken snake coiled up on the blanket beside him. Of course Bud would crawl out of the shade into the sun sometimes and would get terribly sunburned, even with his bonnet on.

The summer before, Little Claude, received several stings when he got into a red wasp nest in a fencerow. He had come running down through the field, screaming at the top of his lungs, as fast as his little chubby legs could carry him. The field hands were scared at first. Everyone just knew that he had been bitten by a snake for someone had mentioned seeing a copperhead in the fencerow a while back, but luckily it was just wasp stings.

Hazel Adkins and Joel, too, their teeth perpetually yellowed with tobacco stain, always carried a twist of tobacco in their overalls. They chewed up some and put gobs of wet tobacco on the stings. The wet tobacco poultice had a soothing effect, but the poor little fellow cried and hung around his mother's feet the rest of the day so that she could hardly work. Bud felt sorry for him for the same thing had happened to him when he was too young to know better.

Ellis decided it was time to begin weeding and thinning the cotton. There was Johnson grass, Bermuda grass, cocklebur and lamb's quarter to contend with, plus several other species of weeds and grass. The kids were still in school, so he decided to start on the third Saturday in April. Kids and adults would all be available on Saturday. Ralph Claxton, his wife, Irene, and their two teenage sons, from across the ditch, waded across a sandbar, to chop for a dollar a day.

Ellis started in the cotton patch directly behind the Scott house. In addition to the four members of the Claxton family, four Adkins family members were available, as well as the three members of the Scott family. There were eleven people in all, more than Bud could ever remember seeing chopping cotton at one time, in the same field.

Everything went well throughout the cool spring morning. However, Bud's hands began to form blisters by noon, so during the noon meal break he found a pair of cotton work gloves, and was managing to hold his own with everyone else, even though at twelve years old, he was the youngest worker in the field. When Inez Scott came out to work in the afternoon, she brought a roll of white cloth tape and a small pair of scissors. She taped the fingers of several of those that had blisters formed on their hands during the morning, and that didn't have gloves to wear.

Anyone old enough to chop cotton usually carried a heavy file in their pocket so that when they stopped for water they could take some time to sharpen their hoes. Bud was pretty good at it, and he usually sharpened his mother's hoe as well as his own, and if he could, he would sharpen Betty Adkins' hoe. Betty usually gave him a little pat on the head, to show her appreciation, which kept Bud motivated in keeping Betty's hoe as sharp as possible. Inez Scott was amused at watching Bud cater to Betty. She smiled inwardly and never said anything. She looked over at Ellis, and caught him with a twinkle in his eye and a little smile, as he watched Bud's attention to Betty.

At two o'clock, a greenish-blue cloud moved in with rolling thunder from the southwest, lightning danced across the top of it. It looked like it was going to start raining any minute. The air had turned cool and moist. It was fairly comfortable, considering the work being done.

"May be some wind in that," said Ellis. It was spring and tornado weather. Every spring the Scotts spent several hours in the storm cellar in the back of their house. The cellar had not been there when they moved into the house. Inez insisted that it be built right away. Ellis, Hazel and their two boys had taken shovels and dug a hole in the orchard, eight feet by eight feet square and six feet deep. They lined the walls with cypress logs and put logs across the top. Then they took the dirt that had come out of the hole and packed it on top of the logged roof. They made a sloped entryway into the cellar with wooden steps and a heavy oak planked door. A piece of heavy trace chain was nailed to the inside of the door. The chain could be fastened to one of the interior wall logs to hold the door against the sucking wind. It was a top-of-the-line storm cellar. Ellis was proud of it and having it available made Inez less anxious when the thunder rolled.

Inez was deathly afraid of any storm and particularly one that looked like it might contain a twister. When she was a child, she saw one up close that ran through the hills by her family's Izard County homestead, sweeping a clean path a hundred yards wide completely clear of large rocks and boulders. It looked like a giant had swept the hillside with a broom.

A tornado had not hit the Scott farm yet, but Bud had already seen three twisters cut across the fields close to the house. They didn't look so bad in daylight. Bud thought he might actually outrun one if he had to, but nighttime was another thing. They could slip up on you in the dark.

"Ellis, reckon we ought to go to the cellar; looks pretty bad?" asked Inez.

"We'll be up to the barn in a little bit. Take a look at it then," replied Ellis.

Bud had drunk an extra tumbler of iced tea during the noon dinner break, and he suddenly felt the need to relieve himself. He dropped his hoe and took off in a trot for the barn two hundred yards away. "Son, can't you wait till we get these rows out?" asked Ellis, as Bud went by.

"No sir, I reckon not, lest I ruin myself," answered Bud. Bud heard Irene Claxton chuckle at his remark as he passed her. She was a few yards ahead of the rest.

Bud was in a stall in the barn, when he heard the lightning strike. He knew it was close because he could hear it sizzle before the sharp clap of the strike. Bud left the barn and was on his way back to the field, when he saw his father walking up to the barn looking very serious. He knew something was wrong.

Ellis' hands were shaking, and he was having difficulty rolling a cigarette. "Bud, help me git the team hooked up to the wagon," he said. "Irene Claxton has been killed by lightnin'." Bud was dumbfounded, having just left her alive and laughing in the field.

Ellis, with Bud sitting on the wagon seat beside him, drove the wagon to the place in the field where Irene lay. Everyone was in shock, some standing, and some sitting on the ground, their hoes lying on the ground. Ralph Claxton was sitting on the ground with Irene's head nestled in his lap. He and his sons were crying. Inez, along with Betty and Dovie Adkins, were shaking and crying, too. A light rain began to fall.

Irene's hair had caught fire and was wet from where Joel Adkins had poured water on it from one of the water jugs. She seemed to have turned darker all over. She had bad burns on her hands where she had been holding the hoe and her leather shoes, which had been blown off her feet by the force of the strike, lay a few feet away, still smoking. She was wearing a western-style long sleeve shirt with metal snaps instead of buttons. The metal snaps had all burned out of the shirt, leaving a row of small smoking holes where the snaps had been. She had not suffered. She was dead before she hit the ground.

Ellis finally got Ralph Claxton on his feet and helped him load Irene's body in the wagon. "Y'all go on and get undercover at the barn," Ellis said to the hands. Inez led the rest of the hands in a fast trot toward the barn.

Ralph, and his two sons, got into the wagon with Ellis. "Thet cloud is movin' slow. I thank we kin stay away from it, if we go on," said Ellis.

Ellis started the team and wagon down the county road toward Turner's Store. One of the boys was cushioning his mother's head in his lap, tears running down his face. Ralph Claxton turned on the wagon seat and looked back toward the southwest. "Ellis, I believe it's gonna miss you. Probably won't get rained out after all." Ellis didn't know what to say so he didn't say anything. They arrived at the store in a light rain.

Ellis stopped the wagon and went into the store to inform Abe Turner about the accident and asked him to call the authorities in Walnut Ridge. Inez Scott later called the accident, an "act of God." Bud didn't believe it. He didn't think God would just strike down, an innocent woman like Irene Claxton for no apparent reason, while she was chopping cotton. What great sin had she committed to justify something like that?

While at the store, Ralph Claxton asked Ellis to buy a sack of nails. "We're gonna need to build a coffin," he said. Ellis always kept a few tools in the wagon, including a claw hammer and a buck saw. The Claxton house was a mile south down Cache River Ditch behind Abe Turner's store. It backed up to the east bank of the ditch. When they arrived at the house, Ralph and his sons, carefully lifted Irene's body from the wagon bed and gently laid it on the front porch, "One of you boys, go inside and bring a bed sheet. We need to wrap her up," said Ralph.

Ellis stayed at the Claxton house long enough to help Ralph put together a coffin out of cypress planks that had been left over from the construction of the house. After the coffin was completed, he asked Ralph if there was anything else he could do.

"I would 'preciate it, iffen you could settle for the work today," said Ralph.

Ellis kept a few single dollar bills in the bib pocket of his overalls during the cotton-chopping season so he could pay the workers at the end of each day.

"Here's four dollars," said Ellis, handing the money to Ralph.

"Ellis, that's too much. We ain't worked a full day," said Ralph.

"No. It's the right thing to do. Take the money," replied Ellis.

Ellis drove the wagon back home, unharnessed the mules, and then walked back down in the field. The worst part of the cloud had missed the farm, and the rain had stopped. All the hands were at work as if nothing had happened. Ellis picked up his hoe where he had dropped it, and without saying a word to anyone went back to work.

Sunday afternoon, after church, Ellis, Inez and Bud took the team and wagon and went to the Claxton house, carrying a basket of food. When they got to the house, they found the front door wide open, but no one at home. The Claxton family didn't have any animals or chickens. Some pieces of furniture were still in the house. There was no food of any kind to be found except a pair of partially filled salt and pepper shakers. There was an abundance of cockroaches in and around the kitchen stove, and several mice that had been playing on the floor skittered out of sight into holes in the baseboard.

There was no sign of the coffin, or a grave.

"I wonder what they've done with pore Irene," said Inez. She never expected a response, and never got one. They spent some time looking around the house, and Bud went over the ditch bank and looked up and down stream, but there was no sign of anyone. After a few minutes passed, they climbed back in the wagon to return home.

Abe and Ruth Turner were out on the front porch of their store when the Scotts drove back by on their way home.

"Y'all seen anything of Ralph and the boys?" asked Ellis.

"No. Ain't they there?" answered Abe.

"No one's there. Nobody. No grave. No nothin'," said Inez.

"Musta went south then, toward Egypt," said Abe.

"Wonder what they done with the body?" asked Ruth.

"Musta floated it down river in the coffin. They couldn't a carried her fer," replied Ellis. "And I don't believe they woulda buried her in Bull Taylor's family graveyard. Bull wouldn't allow it."

Bud and Joel kept a watch on the house off and on for the next few days. The boys waded across the ditch a couple of times and went over to the house, but they never found a sign of anyone. The Claxton family disappearance became one of the great mysteries in the Horse Island community. What happened to Irene Claxton's coffin and the Claxton family? No one ever knew.

After the Claxton family tragedy, Bud approached Homer Adkins, whom he found at Turner's Store one day, about the possibility of Homer helping the Scott family chop cotton. Bud knew that his dad would hire almost anyone, who could sling a gooseneck hoe.

"No, I can't do that," said Homer. "It is my belief that an evangelist should not do manual labor."

When Bud later told his dad what Homer had said, Ellis replied that Homer probably thought *manual labor* was the name of a Mexican.

Homer said, "Accordin' to the Bible, Jesus just walked round the countryside with a bunch of His disciples talkin' with people and preachin' the gospel, and the best that I can tell, the whole group just sponged off of people for their room and board, wherever they happened to be when the sun went down. Jesus seemed to spend a great deal of time eating, and drinkin' wine with Republicans, and that is exactly what I plan on doin'; although, my family is mostly Democrats."

When Inez Scott heard what Homer had said, she laughed, and said she thought Homer had probably gotten confused. It was probably Publicans that he was talking about, which she explained to Bud, were probably tax collectors, among other things.

Bud dreaded cotton-chopping season with a passion, and not just because of the work, but because it was the time of year—spring—when Inez thought his system needed cleansing. She did that with liberal doses of castor oil. Castor oil was a clear foul-smelling fine oil that was made from castor beans, and Bud thought it must have been bottled by witches.

The castor bean extract, undiluted, is as poisonous as cobra venom, although, sharecroppers didn't know that in nineteen forty-three. Castor oil, which had most of the poison processed out of it, was used during the war for lubrication of engine parts. It was never fit for human consumption, but it was fit for Bud, and he was not alone in getting the cleansing every spring. Most of the people who migrated to the east bottoms from the hill country believed in various old-time herbal remedies and castor oil seemed to have risen to the top of every mother's list. Most farm kids who had hill people for parents got the castor oil treatment.

Inez Scott, to her credit, did her best to disguise the castor oil taste. She tried stirring it into a cup of coffee, but it wouldn't mix and came right to the top in a greasy blob. Then she tried stirring it into orange juice, and it wouldn't mix with it either, but in this case the orange juice separated and came to the top.

The first time Bud tried it mixed in orange juice, he drank the orange juice right down, thinking he was home free when he didn't taste the castor oil, only to find the greasy blob waiting for him at the bottom of the cup. By the time the cotton-chopping season rolled around Bud was usually so weak that he could barely walk, but his system had been cleansed, and that was what was important to Inez.

In addition to castor oil, there was sassafras tea made from boiling the roots of the sassafras tree. Sassafras tea wasn't all that bad when mixed with sugar and hot water. Inez Scott said it was good for the blood.

Also, there were Carter's little liver pills, which were not little, but as big as a quarter and couldn't be swallowed whole, by anything except a horse. Then, there was Black Draught that was heavy black syrup with high alcohol content, and it had the same affect on most people, as did castor oil. Bud spent a good portion of the early spring puking, or as Ellis Scott said, 'shittin'' like a tied coon."

Bud spent so much time in the family outhouse during the "cleansing" that he became intimately familiar with the previous year's edition of the Sears and Roebuck Catalog, that is what was left of it. It was during one of the cleansing cycles that he really set his mind to eventually acquiring a new Schwinn bicycle.

CHAPTER 5

Nineteen forty-three was, among other things, the year of the bobcat. Bobcats seemed to be everywhere and they were traveling in packs. They were mysterious creatures. You seldom saw one in the daytime, but as soon as the sun went down, they could be heard calling to one another, in a high whistling cry. After the bobcats, and the red and gray foxes cleaned out most of the field rabbits and quail, they were driven by hunger to come to farm houses in the middle of the night looking for a meal. It became necessary to protect young calves, pigs, pups, cats, and especially chickens from these predators.

The bobcats were bobtailed long-legged wildcats. Just a smaller version of the lynx, and some people argued that some of these cats were indeed, lynx. Some male bobcats weighed as much as thirty pounds, and they could be dangerous even to small children, especially when they were traveling in packs.

Joel Adkins counted seven bobcats drinking out of the horse trough at the old Thompson barn late one evening as he was passing by the barn on his way home from Turner's Store. Joel was downwind from the cats and he spotted them at the trough before they detected his presence. He stealthily passed by the barn down the dirt road leading to his house. When he got a hundred yards past the barn, he took off for home as fast as he could run. He was barefoot of course, and Ellis Scott always said that Joel could run like a "stripped-assed ape." Joel was in full flight, and he said later that he was thinking, *feets don't fail me now*. There were stretches of the dirt road where he didn't remember his feet actually touching the ground. He said later that he believed he might have set a new overland speed record for man.

Bordering the Scott house place that included the barn lot and orchard, to the southeast was seven-acres of uncultivated land. One third was in pasture; the rest was divided by a wooded ridge and a slough. The slough had some water in it all of the time, even though it was reduced to a large mud puddle in the heat of summer. The Scott's hogs went down to the slough every day, to feed on the fish that had been trapped when the Cache River Ditch overflowed into the slough, and later receded leaving the fish behind.

The fish were mostly carp, catfish and a few grinnell. The slough was a dangerous place. In addition to fish, it was full of cottonmouth water moccasins, some as big around as a man's arm, and extremely poisonous. The hogs didn't care, though; they ate the snakes along with the fish, if they could catch them.

Bud and Joel would go down to the edge of the slough sometimes to watch the hogs in action. The hogs could be seen running down the fish in the shallow stagnate pools. The cottonmouths would be hanging on limbs just above the water, and if a hog spotted one he would head for it, knock it into the water, grab it in his mouth and crunch it. Of course the hogs got snake bit a lot but it didn't seem to bother them very much. Large lumps the size of a baseball, would appear on the hog's head or shoulder as a result of being bitten, and the animal would seem to be off its feed for a day or two, but then it was right back to the slough again for more fish and snakes.

The bobcats wouldn't bother baby pigs during the daytime when they were in the woods. A bobcat would not go into a slough for a pig or anything else. The adult hogs, particularly the old five hundred pound sows with pigs, would kill a bobcat with one crunching bite if they could catch one. The big sows were particularly dangerous when they had a litter of pigs, and Bud and Joel gave them wide berth. However, the bobcats would raid a barn lot after dark and steal a pig right out from under a sleeping sow. A cat would jump the barn lot fence with a squealing pig in its mouth and carry it back into the woods and eat it.

The wooded ridge in that seven-acre woodlot ran up to within 200 yards of the Scott barn lot. The Scott house was on the west side of the barn and the chicken house was thirty yards farther west of the house, situated in a small apple and pear orchard, in back of Inez Scott's vegetable garden. At twilight, the Scotts could sit on their back porch and listen to the bobcats calling to one another from just beyond the barn. The cats made an eerie whistling sound, and they always seemed to be fifty to a hundred yards apart. Bud learned to distinguish calls from as many as five different locations.

In addition to the bobcats, the great horned owls would start calling just after dark. One night a big owl flew down and tried to carry off one of the baby pigs, but the old sow caught the owl on the ground and killed it. Ellis had heard the ruckus and rushed to the barn, gun in hand, and carrying a flashlight, only to find the old sow making hash out of the owl.

Between the bobcats, the great horned owls and the smaller screech owls, there was enough noise made in the night to scare the living daylights out of Bud, and he would not go into the woods at night by himself, even with Ellis' old Greener shotgun, for all the big orange drinks in Turner's Store.

The Scotts had a big yellow tomcat named, Old Tom. Old Tom was almost as large as a bobcat, and during the time of the bobcat invasion, he disappeared for two or three days. Tomcats have a mind of their own and one could never tell if Old Tom's absences were intentional or accidental.

Old Tom was found on the backdoor step one morning, ripped and bleeding. Ellis Scott said he had fought a bobcat and appeared to have gotten the worst of it. Tom was a tough old rascal though. After appearing to be on death's door for a couple of weeks, he pulled out of it. The Scotts noticed that he didn't leave the yard much after that. Inez Scott said that cats were supposed to have nine lives and it appeared that Old Tom had used one or more of his allotment.

One of the big white Poland China sows had a litter of ten pigs that weighed about five pounds apiece and they were all solid white even though their daddy was a solid red Duroc boar. Bud couldn't understand how that could happen.

One night there was a terrific commotion down at the barn. The Scott family was awakened about midnight by pigs squealing and the low growling sound that an old sow makes, which means that if you are nearby it is time to climb a fence or tree, but just get away and quick. That old sow meant to kill something and it didn't matter to her what it was.

Ellis jumped out of bed in nothing but his flour sack nightshirt, slipped into his brogans and headed for the barn, grabbing his Greener twelve gauge that he kept loaded with a heavy number four shot. He had begun to leave the shotgun propped just inside of the door on the screened-in back porch.

Ellis had taped a flashlight underneath the double barrels, so that he could switch it on with his left hand, and quickly light his target as he brought the gun up to firing position against his right shoulder.

Ellis ran for the barn with Bud right behind. They could hear a little pig squealing but the squeals seemed to be going away from them. A bobcat had stolen one of the pigs and had already jumped the fence and was headed for the woods. Ellis climbed on top of the wooden gate of the barn lot and shined his light toward the woods, in the direction of the pig's squeals, but the bobcat was already outside the range of the flashlight. Ellis couldn't see anything but he shot one time anyway toward the squealing pig, hoping that he might by chance hit the bobcat, but he didn't. The little pig's squealing grew fainter and fainter and finally stopped.

The old sow was beside herself. She could smell the blood of one of her babies and she was extremely dangerous. Ellis and Bud spent an anxious hour trying to get the sow and the remaining nine pigs inside a bobcat proof wooden stall in the barn. It was no easy task, but they finally managed. Everyone finally got back to bed in the early morning hours. Bud felt sorry for the little pig and lying in bed, he felt a few hot tears running down his cheeks and falling on the pillow. He couldn't sleep the rest of the night for thinking about the little pig, and wondering too, if a bobcat could get through the screen of his open bedroom window.

After the attack on the hogs, Ellis started penning up the old sow and pigs every night inside the barn. Then the bobcats became even bolder and started coming up around the chicken house. This led to a small family tragedy that was serious at the time but as years went by became comical with the repeated telling of it.

Inez Scott had raised a rather large flock of chickens. She had about fifty hens of all ages and one old rooster and two younger ones. One of the roosters was a pedigree Rhode Island Red, but the other two roosters and the hens were without pedigree.

Some of the chickens were for eating, and some for laying eggs, and then she had her favorite setting hens that she would sit on large nests of eggs and hatch out baby chicks. Inez loved her hens and had even given names to some of her favorites, names such as Margaret, Louise and Jezebel.

She was extremely proud of her chicken house that had been built by Mr. Houston Johnson when he had lived on the place. It was built of heavy cypress planks that still had a golden glow in the sunlight. It had a single heavy chicken-wire screened-in opening that was four feet high, with the bottom edge of the opening being four and one-half feet above the ground. This large "window" ran across the complete length of the twenty-five-foot-long chicken house, or "my hen house," as Inez called it.

The opening could be completely covered by four, side-by-side wooden hinged doors that could be propped up to let air in during hot weather, or could be let down to keep the air and rain out in cold weather. There was a row of ten box nests along the front wall just underneath the window for the setting and laying hens. There was a cypress plank walkway that went the length of the chicken house directly in front of the nesting boxes, and across the walkway was a rack of poles about four feet off the ground where the majority of the chickens roosted at night.

The chicken house faced to the south and was ten-feet from front to back. The roof was nine feet high, slanted slightly from front to back and covered with cypress shingles. There was just a tiny narrow opening where the roof and wall joined. The single solid wooden side door of the chicken house was visible from the back porch, a distance of about thirty yards. Every night Inez made sure that her chickens were inside and that they were in their proper positions either in their assigned nesting boxes or on the roost, and that the chicken house was properly secured. It was bobcat, fox and owl proof. There was no question about it—it was a top-of-the-line chicken house.

Bud didn't share his mother's enthusiasm for all of the chicken operation. He liked scrambled eggs on toast smothered with sausage gravy as well as anyone, and he liked fried chicken as well as any preacher, but he didn't like having to shovel chicken manure out of the chicken house with a scoop shovel into a wheelbarrow, and then spread it on the garden. Bud had that chore to do three or four times a year and he hated it, and he despised one of the roosters, the black one, the one Inez called "Blackie".

Blackie appeared to give Bud special attention and watched for him to come out of the house so he could attack him with his terrible spurs. Blackie would charge, and jump up in the air with his long spurs flashing in the sunlight. The spur was a hard bone-like appendage that extended from inside each ankle of the rooster's foot, and it cut like a knife. Blackie succeeded a few times in hitting Bud around the upper-thigh and brought blood even through his heavy denim overalls. The rooster made Bud nervous and kept him on edge all of the time.

When Blackie made his charge, Bud tried to get to the safety of the back porch or he would make a run for the barnyard and jump over the gate. He couldn't outrun Blackie because the rooster could fly faster than Bud could run, and Blackie would sometimes hit Bud in the back or on his head. Bud could tell that Blackie purely enjoyed harassing him, and the rooster seemed to know that he was immune from any retaliation.

Inez often witnessed the confrontations between Bud and Blackie, and she would always take the rooster's side. She would yell at Bud to, "Leave that rooster alone!" Then one day, she happened to look out just as Bud took a swing at Blackie with his fist and missed. Inez came out on the porch and yelled to Bud, that he had better not hurt that rooster, if he didn't want a whipping; a whipping usually with what Inez called a switch – a limb cut from the nearby plumb tree and trimmed to about four-feet in length, which to Bud, was nothing more than a thinly disguised club.

What really got Bud's goat though, was when Inez would go out in the back yard and yell out, "Come here Blackie, come here sweetie, come to mama," and the rooster would come running up to her preening and prancing and making clucking noises and acting pretty much like a pussycat. Inez would reach down and pet him and give him a handful of ground corn. Blackie thought Inez Scott had hung the moon.

Bud noticed that his dad didn't have any problem with Blackie. Ellis just ignored Blackie and the rooster ignored Ellis. It is a difficult task to assess a chicken's ability to think, but it seemed that the rooster knew that if he messed with Ellis that Ellis would kill him. But Blackie had his bluff in on the other roosters, the two hounds and the two old mama cats. However, he gave wide berth to Old Tom, the big yellow tomcat. Old Tom did not cotton to fowl of any kind, particularly sassy roosters.

Early in his chicken career, Blackie had challenged Old Tom—once— when the cat had ambled out through the orchard. Tom saw Blackie coming on a run toward him. The old tomcat watched for a moment and then just sat down on his haunches facing the rooster and waited. Bud stood by and watched with interest at this development. Tom looked around at Bud with an expression that said, "What does this damn fool think he's doing?" Blackie followed through with his charge and leaped at Tom, and Tom made his leap at Blackie. They met in mid-air, with Tom grabbing the rooster with both front feet and came down on top of him. It was difficult to imagine a more surprised chicken.

Tom was savaging the rooster pretty good when Bud finally got them separated. This was at the time before Bud and Blackie were having their problems. Later on, Bud had wished that he had let Old Tom kill the rooster. That would have saved him a lot of future tongue-lashings from Inez, and finally a thrashing.

Relations between Bud and Blackie worsened over time and matters finally reached an impasse one day when Blackie chased Bud down to the barn and Bud had to jump the barnyard gate, yet again.

Bud had an old broom handle that he had left at the barn that he used to bat bumblebees with. They were playing a little baseball at school, and there is nothing better to sharpen your batting eye than swatting bumblebees with a broom handle. But, this day, Bud had something else in mind to swat.

Bud retrieved the broom handle and headed directly to where the chicken flock was feeding in the orchard, where Blackie had returned to stand guard. Bud intended to have it out with the rooster once and for all, regardless of the consequences. Blackie had his eye on Bud from the time he climbed back over the barnyard gate. Blackie lowered his head and extended his neck low and forward and extended his wings out and downward, like roosters do when they assume the attack position. He charged as soon as Bud got within fifty yards, but this time Bud stood his ground. Blackie was on Bud as quick as a whip. Bud thought that he detected at the last moment a slight hesitation in Blackie's movements. The rooster seemed genuinely puzzled that Bud hadn't tried to make a run for the backdoor. Chickens are dumb creatures. Their brains are not large. They operate pretty much on instinct and habit. Blackie's instincts were too great for him. He made his attack and Bud, with perfect timing and a hefty swing with the broomstick, broke his neck.

Inez came out on the back porch just as Blackie was in his death throes and Bud was standing over him with the broom handle. Bud was, at the moment, trying to think of how he was going to explain the rooster's demise to his mother. The thought of grabbing Blackie up and hiding him somewhere was crossing his mind, when Inez yelled out, "Theodore Scott, what have you done to my rooster?" Inez had a way of getting formal when she was upset.

There was only one thing for Bud to say. "I killed the old sonuvabitch," Bud replied, bold as anything.

Inez had Bud cut her a good switch off the plumb tree and after she had whipped him for a while, she made him get the big cast-iron pot that was used for a multitude of outdoor activities, fill it with water and build a fire under it. Bud was still stinging from the switching when he grabbed old Blackie by his feet and begin to souse him up and down in the boiling pot to loosen his feathers. Bud had to pluck his feathers, then hold the rooster close to the fire and singe the remaining feather stubble. Blackie was to tough to fry, so after Inez finished cleaning the chicken, she cut it up and then boiled the pieces in a large pot on the kitchen stove. She then made dumplings.

Bud couldn't remember when he had enjoyed chicken and dumplings more. He thought that his mother might tell his dad about the rooster, and then Ellis might decide to add a special touch to his punishment. Bud detected that his dad sensed something wasn't right, when Inez served chicken and dumplings in the middle of the week, but Ellis didn't say anything and neither did Inez, and Bud certainly wasn't going to bring the subject up.

Inez's hens were producing more eggs than the family could use, so she worked out a deal to sell eggs to Abe Turner for a penny apiece. Abe had a big electric cooler in the store and he could keep several dozen eggs in it for some time. Abe sold eggs to his local customers for two cents each, or in bulk to merchants in Jonesboro and Walnut Ridge, for three cents each. No one was going to get rich off the eggs, and everyone was satisfied with the arrangement, including Bud, because Inez would usually let him have a dime out of the egg profits every time he made an egg delivery to Turner's Store.

Inez used her egg money for odds and ends such as buying yards of cloth that she made into dresses for herself, or shirts for Ellis and Bud, which she was good at. She also used the money to pay for the family's new electric bills, or "light bills," as everyone called them. The Rural Electrification Association (REA) had brought electricity down the county road early in nineteen forty-three, putting up high-line poles and stringing electrical wire. Electricity was new for the west side of Cache River Ditch, and the new recipients were amazed by it. Abe Turner's Store was on the east side of the ditch and the REA had run electricity out of Bono to the store almost a year before, so the Scotts had been able to see the possibilities.

The availability of electricity was a blessing. The Scotts now had light bulbs hanging from the ceiling in every room of the house. Inez could put away the smelly kerosene lamps. But it had been a shock when she found that these little conveniences came with a price tag. She was mortified when she got the first light bill out of the mailbox for one-dollar and fifty cents. She was disturbed even more after Ellis arranged to have a small electric icebox delivered, along with two electric fans and an electric steam iron, to see the light bill rise to almost three dollars.

"How in the world are we going to pay for this?" she would always say, when she looked at the light bill, but then she cajoled Abe into giving her one-and-a-half cents per egg. This caused Abe to have to adjust his prices all the way around, but everything worked itself out eventually. Everyone loved having a glass of ice tea with real ice cubes, and Bud, particularly, loved the homemade ice cream that Inez made in the ice trays.

Everything was working fine with the chickens and the egg production until the bobcats started coming up to the chicken house and scared the hens nearly to death. Most of them quit laying. An unhappy hen does not lay eggs. The hens were not in any danger while locked in the hen house at night, but they didn't know that.

Part of the fault lay with the Scott's two redbone coonhounds, Big Red and Little Red. The two hounds were as good as any two dogs in the county when it came to running a coon, but they were scared of bobcats. A hound would not normally be scared of one bobcat, but bobcats traveling in packs were another matter. A dog that blundered into a pack of bobcats could get mauled badly, if not killed outright.

When the bobcats started coming up around the barn and through the orchard to the chicken house, the dogs would whine, but would not come out from under the house, which is where they spent the majority of their time. The dogs failure to show a little courage and at least come out from under the house and bark like they could, might have kept the bobcats at bay, but as Ellis said, "Except for coon huntin', them hounds is as useless as tits on a boar hog."

The weather had turned hot and steamy as it usually did around the first of June, and the fieldwork was becoming more difficult. The Scotts found themselves getting little sleep because of having to get up every night to chase away bobcats. Ellis never could get a clear shot at one. He did spot one on top of the chicken house one night prowling around trying to figure how to get through the roof to the chickens, but the bobcat heard him before he could get a bead, and leaped off the roof and made his getaway. Ellis shot anyway, hoping at least to scare him off, as well as any others that might be lingering about.

The Scott family had a growing crisis on their hands. They couldn't work in the field from daylight till dark, and then stay up all night fighting bobcats. They were all becoming exhausted. Ellis was desperately trying to figure out what to do, when what they thought was to be their savior appeared on their doorstep late one afternoon at suppertime. It was Homer Adkins in his prophet's robe and rubber-tired sandals, come to solve the bobcat problem. He said he had heard about it through the grapevine.

Of course Inez invited him in for supper, and it was during the meal, which Homer seemed to enjoy immensely that he outlined his bobcat plan. He said if the Scotts would let him sleep on their screened-in back porch for a few days, that he would keep alert at night for the bobcats, and would sleep during the day. He said the mosquitoes were just eating him alive up on Horse Island, and he needed a break. Ellis and Inez went for the proposition immediately, since it was not going to cost anything but a few meals.

Inez provided Homer with one of Ellis' flour sack nightshirts. He welcomed the gift even though it only reached to the middle of his thigh, and barely kept him decent. Homer, like Bud and Ellis didn't wear underwear in bed, just nightshirts, and having an electric fan blowing up under a nightshirt during hot humid nights made a world of difference.

The Scotts didn't have an extra bed, but they did have several fifty-pound bags of cottonseed left over from the spring planting stored in the barn. Ellis and Homer carried half a dozen or so of the bags and laid them out side by side on the back porch, making a comfortable bed. Inez offered Homer one of her spare sheets for cover, but the heat and humidity was such that Homer declined. He chose to sleep in the cotton nightshirt on top of the cottonseed sacks.

Ellis' twelve-gauge shotgun with the flashlight taped underneath the double-barrels was propped just inside the screen door of the back porch. Ellis warned Homer about the old Greener's sensitive nature regarding the external hammers and double triggers, because when both hammers were cocked at the same time, even though only one trigger was pulled, both hammers would release, firing both barrels simultaneously, with a shoulder-breaking recoil.

Homer said not to worry; he had been in the army and knew his way around firearms. After all, he had been in the vaunted 82nd Airborne, if only for a little while. Homer convinced Bud that he knew what he was doing, although, Ellis remained skeptical.

Homer said that he didn't expect to stay long, as he figured that he would have the bobcat problem fixed in a few days. Homer had become a prophet and didn't know it. It is safe to say that everyone was surprised just how short his stay would be, Homer most of all.

Ellis usually tuned the radio to a St. Louis Cardinal baseball game every night after supper, except on Friday night, when the radio was reserved for the *Gillette Friday Night Fights* from Madison Square Garden in New York City. This night the Cardinal's game had been rained out, and Ellis tuned to a station that was carrying a broadcast purported to be coming live from an overseas battlefield. Ellis, Homer and Bud drew close to the radio. They could hear guns firing and people in the background cursing and yelling. An unidentified war correspondent or soldier was heard yelling over the gunfire, "Here they come again!" Men were screaming in the background, "Kill the bastards, kill the sons-of-bitches!" There was a cacophony of sound in the background from rifle and machine gun fire.

It was all very exciting but at nine o'clock Ellis brought the evening to a close, saying it was time for bed. Homer, using some army lingo, said that he would "secure the perimeter." The lights were turned out, and everyone went to bed, except Homer.

Bud slept in the back bedroom with a window that opened directly onto the screened-in back porch. He was still awake when he heard Homer returning from his security patrol, and heard him settling onto his cottonseed-sack bed. Bud felt secure with Homer on guard and he soon drifted off to sleep. The last thing he remembered was Ellis snoring in the next room, and thinking that he was happy that his dad was finally going to get a good night's rest.

About midnight, an awful ruckus from the chicken house awakened Bud. He got out of bed and went to the bedroom window that opened onto the back porch and looked out. Homer was a white marble statue sound asleep on his bed of cottonseed sacks. About that time Bud heard Inez, from the front bedroom, say, "Ellis, somethin' is after my hens."

Bud stepped through the screenless window onto the porch and shook Homer awake, and told him something was after the chickens, which was now evident with all of the racket coming from the direction of the chicken house. Homer jumped up and without a word eased through the screen door, in his bare feet, collecting the shotgun as he went by.

Bud eased out of the screen door and sat down on the backdoor steps to take in the action. It was a moonlit night. Homer was so white in his white flour sack nightshirt and long white legs and white hair that he practically glowed. Bud heard two audible clicks. Homer had cocked both hammers on the old Greener.

Both redbones began emitting low growls, and had not taken to whining like they generally did when a bobcat was in the area. Bud began to suspect that whatever was after the chickens was not a bobcat. Then out from under the floor of the porch, right beside where Bud was sitting on the steps, came Little Red. Little Red just turned his head toward Bud to acknowledge his presence like dogs do, and then began to trail along after Homer, confirming what Bud had already suspected: no bobcat.

But something was in with the chickens. The chickens were cackling and squawking, and Bud could tell that they were falling off the roost. The chickens were blind in that dark chicken house and they were scared.

Bud noted Ellis' presence behind him. Ellis looked out over Bud through the screen door just as Homer began the last few feet of his stealthly approach to the chicken house. Bud knew that he was looking at a trained killer, and he saw enough in the moonlight to tell that Homer's finger was on the shotgun's trigger and that he was ready to flip the switch on the flashlight as soon as he opened the hen house door. The tension was such that you could have cut it with a knife.

Little Red seemed puzzled by Homer's whiteness, like he really couldn't figure out what he was. Bud noted Little Red's interest in Homer and the thought crossed his mind that perhaps it was a sign that Homer was indeed divine. Animals seemed to be able to sense the supernatural more so than humans. While Homer was intent on opening the chicken house door, Little Red seemed more intent on Homer's legs. Homer didn't know Little Red was behind him.

Homer eased open the chicken house door and in a crouched position stepped into the open doorway and switched on the flashlight, and at the same time pointed the shotgun into the interior toward his intended victim. At precisely this moment, Little Red, who was always the more inquisitive of the two hounds, ran his head up under Homer's nightshirt and cold-nosed Homer right in the rear end. Homer, rightly startled, squalled out, leaped in the air, and let go with both barrels.

Homer's head hit the top of the doorway just as the shotgun went off. The lick on the head knocked him cold as a wedge, and the kick from the shotgun knocked him backward leaving Homer stretched out to his fullest in front of the chicken house door.

Homer's surprised yell at being cold-nosed and the subsequent shotgun blast at such close quarters scared Little Red so bad that he squealed and headed for the house with his tail between his legs, like something was after him, and he kept yelping in a high pitched voice even after he had gotten to relative safety underneath the floor of the porch.

Inez came rushing out on the porch practically hysterical, thinking Homer had shot Little Red. It was then that she spotted Homer's prostrate body lying in front of the open chicken house door from which a small cloud of dust and chicken feathers had begun to emerge. She became even more hysterical, evidently thinking that Homer had shot himself. Ellis was trying to get her to quiet down, in order to explain what had happened which was a difficult matter, because one would have to have seen it to believe it.

Possums love eggs. It was at this moment, in the dim glow of the flashlight, taped to the shotgun that Homer had dropped, and the soft glow of the moon that a half-grown possum, with an egg in its mouth, was seen moving sprightly through the chicken house door. The little possum evidently had gotten into the open hen house during the day and had been inadvertently locked in for the night when Inez secured the building before going to bed. It ran directly over Homer, made an abrupt left turn, and exited through the garden fence to disappear into the night.

Inez said that she was going to get her kerosene lantern. She told Bud to go get a washcloth and get some ice out of the icebox, wrap the ice up in it and put it on Homer's head to see if he might be revived.

Homer was beginning to stir a bit when Bud finally got to him with the ice. Homer with some difficulty had managed to sit up, flat on the ground, with his legs stretched out. Bud couldn't see anything in the dark but he felt around on Homer's head and discovered a large knot directly in the top center. He gave Homer the ice and told him to hold it on the swelling knot, while he collected the shotgun.

"Where am I at? Is this heaven?" asked a dazed Homer.

"Nah, it ain't heaven," replied Bud, who had picked up the shotgun with the flashlight still on, and had taken a quick look at the carnage inside the chicken house. "But I'm afraid it might be hell, in a minute or two."

Ellis came up and took the shotgun and flashlight from Bud and stepped inside the chicken house. After a quick review of the devastation, Bud heard him say, "Good God Almighty! Seventeen hens and a rooster." Then Ellis said, "Bud, I believe it would be a good idea to get Homer back to the porch before Inez gets out here, and make sure that you put away the shotgun and hide the shells. We don't want your mama gettin' her hands on it right at this time."

Bud knew first hand just how sensitive his mother was about her chickens. He was on his way back to the porch with Homer leaning on him when Inez passed with her lantern heading for the chicken house.

"What's the matter with him?" Inez asked, as she approached, in what Bud took to be an overly gruff tone.

"Hit his head on the door frame," Bud replied.

"Hope it didn't hurt the door," Inez said, in passing.

Bud finally got Homer through the screen door and onto his bed of cottonseed sacks on the back porch. He then returned to where Inez had joined Ellis standing silently in front of the hen house door. Inez had not uttered a word even after viewing the destruction of her beloved hens. She had a look on her face though, that Bud had seldom witnessed in his young life. It was death and hell, rolled into one.

The last time Bud had seen that look was when Ellis had come home late one night after being in the brew while playing checkers down at Turner's Store. That was the night when Inez stood by the door on the back porch waiting with a cast iron skillet in her hand. When Ellis opened the door to come in, Inez stepped forward and hit him full in the forehead with the skillet knocking him backwards into the yard, cold as a cucumber, as they say in the country.

But Bud knew his mother to be a tolerant Christian woman, most of the time. He knew her to be kind to strangers, to be gracious in the most trying of circumstances, to be steadfast in times of trouble, to be charitable and forgiving of the most grievous physical and spiritual onslaughts.

"Ellis, I want that squirrel-headed, albino sonuvabitch out of my sight by the time the sun comes up," she hissed. Then she continued in a more resigned tone, "It looks like we're goin' to be cleanin' chickens the rest of the night."

CHAPTER 6

Ellis told Bud to get Homer out of the house and on the road and point him east toward Turner's Store. Ellis said to tell Homer that they would not be needing his services any longer. Bud watched as Homer's thin ghostly figure staggered off barefoot into the moonlight down the gravel road toward Turner's Store. He was still wearing the flour sack nightshirt and he was carrying his prophet's robe, planter's hat, and rubber-tire sandals. The Scott family turned to the task at hand and spent the rest of the night cleaning seventeen hens and a rooster.

It was daybreak when they finished with the chickens. Three of the chickens were shot all to pieces, but Inez managed to salvage the hearts, livers and gizzards. Four of the chickens didn't have a mark on them, probably dying of fright. The others were in various states of injury.

Inez quickly cut up three of the chickens. She took some flour and seasoned it with salt and pepper and put it in a large paper sack. She put the chicken parts in the sack and shook it, making sure all of the parts were well coated with the seasoned flour, and then she told Bud to take the chicken to Dovey Adkins. She told Bud to hurry, as they would be getting ready to go to the field. Inez said that Dovey would have to fry up all the chicken as the Adkins family didn't have electricity or an icebox or any other way to keep uncooked chicken for long. They would have to cook it and eat it right away.

"Bud, there'll be fried chicken waitin' when you git back," Inez said. "And I'll have some biscuits and milk gravy made fer' your breakfast. When you git through with breakfast, I want you to take the eight whole chickens we got left, down to Abe's, and ask him to give you fifty cents apiece fer 'em. Do you think you can remember thet?"

"Yessum, I kin remember thet much," replied Bud.

Bud made the round trip to the Adkins house, and back home, in nothing flat, feeling that he was near starvation. He had to pause briefly at the Adkins' house to explain what he was doing on their doorstep at dawn with a paper sack full of chicken ready to fry. It was Betty Adkins that met him at the door and took the sack of chicken. She was ready for the field, dressed in blue jeans, with a flour-sack blouse on. She smelled of flour and vanilla. Betty, 15, a slim five-foot, six-inch blonde with a slightly turned up nose, above full lips rosy in color without lipstick, was a pretty girl by any standard, and she always reminded Bud of a big sugar cookie when she splashed herself with vanilla extract. Bud made a hasty exit from the Adkins house and ran all the way home drooling, thinking about fried chicken, sugar cookies, and Betty.

After breakfast, Bud set off on foot for Turner's Store, with eight whole cleaned chickens, in four large brown paper sacks. Inez tied the sacks with heavy twine, and she tied them all together so they could be draped across Bud's shoulders. When Bud arrived at the store, Abe naturally wanted to know why he was on his porch at just after daybreak, with eight bagged chickens since Abe knew how Inez prized her hens. Bud related the whole affair including the part about Homer being cold-nosed by Little Blue and the resulting shotgun blast and chicken slaughter.

A casual observer might have thought that Bud had told the funniest story in the world. Abe started laughing so hard that he had to sit down on the store porch. Tears came into his eyes. Abe's wife, Ruth, who seldom smiled and always seemed to carry the burden of the world on her shoulders, came out to see what all the hilarity was about. Abe then had Bud repeat the story to Ruth. As the story unfolded, Ruth began to smile inwardly. Bud could see the mirth building, and when he got to the Little Blue cold-nose part, Ruth cackled out pretty much like a hen herself. Bud didn't have any trouble getting fifty cents each for the chickens.

Inez told Bud that he could take ten cents of the chicken money and get what he wanted at the store. He opted for his usual: a big orange soda pop and a bag of salted peanuts. Bud had just got settled onto the front porch steps with his treat, when he heard singing coming from across the road. He looked up to see the preacher, Roscoe Gilmore approaching, riding bareback on his little gray mule.

Roscoe was holding two burlap bags, tied across the mule's withers. The bags contained several quart fruit jars of moonshine whiskey and some home-brew beer that had made him famous. He had come to trade with Abe. He was already drunk, and the day just beginning.

Bud enjoyed hearing the stout little Irishman sing his song, which Roscoe had evidently made up himself. No one else was ever heard singing it before

Roscoe, although over time a number of people, including Bud, could be heard singing or humming Roscoe's tune.

Bud memorized the words of the little song that could be sung to any number of tunes:

> I've got an armadillo for my pillow
> And a raccoon on my head.
> I've got a coat made out of fox skin,
> And a possum in my bed.
> I ain't never gonna be lonely,
> Even though all my friends are dead.
> For I've got an armadillo for my pillow,
> And a raccoon on my head.

Roscoe would always finish the little refrain with an old Jimmie Rodgers' blue yodel. Bud thought that it was about the best song that he had ever heard.

Roscoe was barefoot, and dressed in blue denim jeans and a denim work shirt. He was bareheaded, and his shoulder-length bright red hair and abundant beard were glistening in the sun. He presented a remarkable sight in the early morning light. Roscoe rode right up to where Bud and Abe were sitting on the porch and promptly fell off his mule.

"Well, I'll be damned!" said Abe. "Fell of his ass, and landed on his head. Here old fellow let me help you."

Abe, with Bud's help, managed to get Roscoe upright, and dusted off. Ruth had heard Roscoe's approach and came out on the porch. Abe asked Ruth to fix Roscoe a cup of strong coffee and a plate of eggs and ham. She returned to the kitchen. They all followed, with Bud holding up one side of Roscoe and Abe, the other. They marched him through the store back to the living quarters at the rear, and set him down at the kitchen table, in what could best be described, as a befuddled state of mind. Ruth soon had a cup of hot black coffee in front of Roscoe, and in a jiffy she dished up fried eggs and sugar-cured ham and biscuits.

She looked at Bud, who always appeared underweight and scrawny, and without a word put another cup of coffee on the table and another plate of eggs, ham and biscuits. Bud was tempted to tell her that he had already had a full breakfast of fried chicken, gravy and biscuits, not to mention that he had followed that with a big orange drink and a package of peanuts, but the smell of the sugar-cured ham overcame his desire to confess. It was turning out to be a pretty good day for Bud, after all.

Abe was standing in the doorway of the kitchen, when the sound of an automobile could be heard rattling across the wooden bridge spanning the ditch.

"The centurions have arrived," Abe said, as he looked toward the front of the store.

Bud got up from the kitchen table to see who it was, and looking through a front window of the store, he could make out a late-thirty's model ford car with a big star on the front door, and "Lawrence County Sheriff," lettered underneath it. The car stopped in front of the store. Two very large deputy sheriffs got out and stepped upon the porch. Both were wearing big hats, big boots, and big pistols.

Abe, in a low voice, told Bud to go out the back door, and go around to the side where they had left Roscoe's mule with the burlap bags of whiskey and home brew still tied on, and lead the mule around behind the store and tie him to a tree. "Take the sacks off the mule and hide 'em in the weeds," said Abe. Bud eased out the back door of the living quarters, as Abe went out to the front of the store to greet the deputies, and distract them from looking at the mule too closely.

After the deputies went inside, Bud led the little mule around behind the store. It was with some difficulty that he finally managed to get the heavy bags of quart fruit jars full of moonshine whiskey and home brew beer off of Roscoe's mule. He finally succeeded without breaking anything. Bud dragged the sacks into some high weeds. He then eased back through the rear door, to finish his ham and eggs.

Roscoe sobered quickly, from either the strong coffee or the sight of the deputies. When Bud got back to his second breakfast, Roscoe had pushed away from the table and was savoring a third cup of coffee while keeping his eyes on the front of the store. He seemed nervous and ready to bolt out the back. Ruth left the kitchen and went out to the front of the store. At the moment, Bud and Roscoe were doing more listening than eating.

They heard one of the deputies say that they had gotten word that there was some moonshine whiskey being made somewhere up north along Cache River Ditch, between Abe's store and the town of Sedgwick. The deputy asked Abe if he knew anything about it. Roscoe and Bud listened intently as Abe said that he had heard the same thing, and that someone at the Little Brown Freewill Baptist Church, just the past Sunday, had mentioned it. Abe went on to say that there was a discussion as to how sinful such a thing was, but Abe continued, no one seemed to know who the culprit was.

"I guess you boys are thirsty after that drive out from Walnut Ridge," Abe said, and went to the drink cooler.

Abe reached way in the back and pulled out two soda bottles containing an amber-colored liquid, and popped the caps off, handing one to each deputy.

"This is some new stuff I just got in from Jonesboro that I believe came from the Nehi Bottling Company. Its ice cold and refreshing," continued Abe. "Let's see how you boys like it."

It was later discovered that Roscoe had made an addition to his home brew recipe. He had obtained a box of malt – the same ingredient that was used in making ice cream malted milkshakes, and started mixing it into his beer. The mixing of the malt in with the yeast, sugar and cornmeal created a chemical reaction that caused the brew to work off faster and produce a drink that was about fifteen percent alcohol. According to what Bud had heard his dad say: You could drink three quick bottles without effect, but about thirty minutes later it hit you, and "you got shit faced."

The day was building to being hot and humid as usual. Not a breath of air was stirring. The deputies no sooner had finished their first bottle of brew, and with some gusto, than Abe had a second bottle in their hands.

"Well, I wish you boys some luck, for the last thing we need in the presence of a God-fearing community is moonshine whiskey," Abe said, as the deputies started for their car. Abe quickly pulled out two more ice-cold bottles of brew and wrapped them in a paper sack, and as the deputies got into their car and were ready to drive away, Abe reached in through the open window on the passenger-side of the car and placed the bag between them on the seat.

"One for the road," said Abe. "Why don't cha'all go up to Sedgwick. It seems logical to me that if a moonshiner is operatin' on the upper part of the ditch that his contacts would be along the Jonesboro-Hoxie road, and what better place than Sedgwick?"

"What better place indeedy," replied the deputy from the passenger side, who had started to giggle for no apparent reason. "Lets head for Sedgwick. Co-pilot to pilot, set a course for the north country."

"Roger that, over and out," replied the deputy who was driving, and who was also having a problem with maintaining his composure. The deputy doing the driving put the car in motion, and the two law officers started back west, the way they had come. The car was weaving when it crossed the narrow one-lane bridge, but it was safely navigated, and the sound of the car soon died away. Abe came back in the store to where Ruth, Roscoe and Bud had now gathered. Abe was laughing.

"Them ole' boys will never make Sedgwick today," he said, as he was looking back out the front window of the store in the direction the car had gone. "Hello," said Abe. "Here comes the prophet."

They all looked out of the front window of the store and sure enough, from underneath the river bridge limped a disheveled Homer Adkins.

"What are ya doin' under the bridge, Homer?" asked Abe, as Homer entered the front door. Abe had begun to chuckle at the remembrance of the past night's activities, previously described by Bud. Ruth, standing behind, could be heard smothering a chuckle.

"A prophet is totally without honor except in his own county," replied Homer, which didn't make any sense at all to anyone. Roscoe, who had not heard the story of the chicken disaster, just looked on in puzzled befuddlement.

"The skeeters have about et' me alive," said Homer. "Abe, I need another bottle of Calamine Lotion. Put her on my account."

"On account of what?" asked Abe.

"On account of I ain't got no money," said Homer.

Bud finally realized that he needed to get along to the field. He left it to Abe and Ruth to sort things out with Roscoe and Homer, and he took off across the bridge and turned south to follow the ditch down to where his folks and the Adkins family would be at work. He was already thinking of what he would be having for lunch, and he figured it would be cold chicken and biscuits, and perhaps egg custard pie, which Inez was so good at. It just seemed to Bud that he stayed hungry.

CHAPTER 7

The day passed pleasantly enough, if you can call working in ninety-five degree heat along a ditch bank where there was no breeze—pleasant. Bud and Joel jumped, fully clothed, into the ditch several times during the day, to cool off. They became caked and gray with mud as the day wore on, but their mothers didn't seem to care. Bud asked Betty if she would like to join them because he wanted to see what water might do to her flour sack blouse, but she was not inclined.

While they were chopping along, Inez Scott and Dovie Adkins fell slightly behind the rest, but they were within earshot of Bud, who overhead Inez quietly say to Dovie that Betty needed some kind of clothing under her blouse—for support, she said. Bud dropped back a little closer to see if he could hear the gist of the conversation, because where Betty was concerned, he was concerned.

Mrs. Adkins seemed to agree, but she said that right now there just wasn't anything. Bud overheard his mother say that she would look through her things tonight and see if she could find something for her. She said that she would bring it to the field tomorrow. Bud was getting to the age where he hated to hear that Betty's appearance might be altered in some way.

At the end of the day, the Scotts were so tired that they were staggering. They had not slept from the time that they had gotten out of bed the previous day. They laid down their hoes at sunset and started the long walk home. Ellis finalized the day's proceedings, as he usually did, with the statement, "God willin', and the creek don't rise, we'll finish this patch tomorrow."

As the Scotts plodded through the cooling dust, Inez and Ellis began a conversation about the bobcats and what to do about them. Bud rummaged through the remains of their tin dinner bucket, and found a chicken wing, and half a biscuit that had been overlooked. He wasn't inclined toward conversation right then.

As they approached their house, they saw Preacher Roscoe Gilmore's little gray mule tied up to the barn lot fence by the watering trough. Roscoe was sitting under an apple tree out in the orchard. There was a half-gallon silver bucket by his side.

"Ellis, I have heard about your bobcat problem, and have come to fix it," said Roscoe, as a way of introduction and his reason for being on the premises.

"How's zat?" replied Ellis.

"I've brought some sour mash, I've been cookin' off. It's fresh and ripe and it smells good," Roscoe said, as he reached in his pocket and produced a small bottle of clear liquid. "And I've brought a bottle of strychnine. Cats love sour mash. Before it gets real dark, why don't we go down to the edge of the woods where the cats make their approach and see if we can find a trail or two and we'll bait it with strychnine."

"Bud, go get a flashlight and catch up," said Ellis, and without further delay, he and Roscoe set out through the barn lot toward the darkened woods beyond.

Bud ran inside the house and quickly retrieved a flashlight, and made a dash after his father and Roscoe. He caught up with them just as they reached the edge of the woods beyond the pasture. It wasn't hard to spot animal trails passing through heavy stands of weeds and through thickets even in the gathering darkness. Bud and Ellis had been in the woods several times hunting for bobcats so they already knew the trail locations.

Roscoe produced a hatchet from his belt, when he found a trail that led out over a log with bobcat droppings on it. He took the hatchet and with just a few licks cut out a bowl- shaped depression in the log. He took his pocketknife and pried the lid off of the bucket of sour mash and poured about a half-cup or so in the depression, and then he opened the strychnine bottle and shook a few drops of the clear liquid onto the sour mash. This process was repeated at a half-dozen other trails that ran out over logs.

"Ellis, you'll need to keep your animals up for the next seven days, including the dogs. Hogs, and dogs too, will eat sour mash, and whatever eats this will be killed graveyard dead." And as was his habit, Roscoe added for emphasis, "and I don't mean maybe."

They left the woods and walked back across the pasture to the barn. As they approached the barn, the unmistakable sound of the bobcats calling could be heard drifting up from the woods behind them. It wouldn't be long before the cats were at the poisoned bait.

Ellis asked Roscoe to stay for supper, but surprisingly for a preacher, he declined. He said he and the mule had to head for home. He had a miner's hardhat with carbide lantern tied to the mule's bridle. He untied the lamp, lit the carbide lamp that was attached to the front of the hard hat, and adjusted the hat on his head. He straddled the little gray mule bareback, and with a slight nudge of his knees, off they went down the road, toward Turner's Store.

When Ellis and Bud went into the house, Inez had already fried some fatback bacon and had made biscuits, along with a pitcher of fresh tea. She had already checked her hen house, making sure that it was secure, and she had already run a number-three washtub full of water for herself on the back porch. She was getting ready for bed.

Ellis and Bud fixed themselves a big cathead biscuit and bacon sandwich with a slab of white onion. They washed down their sandwiches with a tumbler of iced tea. It was so good that tears came into Bud's eyes. He and Ellis, both, went for seconds and thirds.

After supper, Bud and Ellis fed the dogs and locked them in the smoke house, where they would be confined for the next seven days while the Scotts were at work in the field. Then they went to the barn to feed and secure the stock. The mules, hogs and the jersey milk cow would be kept in the barn lot until there was no further danger from the poisoned bait, but the stock would fare well since there was plenty of hay in the loft and corn in the crib.

"Bud, get yourself cleaned up and git to bed. I'm goin' to stay up an watch a while."

"Do ya thank the poison'll work?"

"I thank so. Hope so, anyway."

Everything was quiet for the present. Bud went to sleep as soon as he laid his head on his goose-down pillow.

The next thing Bud knew it was just breaking day, and Inez was shaking him awake. Breakfast was ready. Ellis was already at the table and had already eaten his breakfast by the time Bud got into the kitchen. Ellis was savoring a third cup of strong black coffee. Inez had fried up several eggs and some fatback bacon, and of course the Scotts always had on hand maple-flavored syrup that was made by the Craft family over at Bono. Craft maple-flavored syrup stirred into warm butter and spread on a hot cathead biscuit was to Bud's way of thinking, one of the world's great treats.

"Any sign of the cats last night?" asked Bud.

"I don't thank any come up round the house or barn," replied Ellis. "About nine o'clock, I heerd some loud screechin' and whining down in the woods, like the cats was a fightin'. Everythin' got quiet all of a sudden. I stayed up till midnight. It was the quietest night we've had round here in some time. I didn't hear nothin' at all up around the house."

The poisoned bait worked, and in three or four days buzzards began circling over the woods behind the barn. Bud and Joel, made a search of the woods, and by watching where the buzzards were flying as well as noting where some were perched in trees, they were able to find the remains of six bobcats and two red fox. One bobcat was found on top of the fence that separated the woods from the county road. It looked like it had died while attempting to jump the fence. The Scotts had few problems with critters during the remainder of nineteen forty-three, except for the occasional fox or possum that would come by, but never again that year did they know of a bobcat that came around the house or barn.

After word got out, that it was Roscoe who had come up with the solution to the Scott's problem, it seemed that people began to look at him in a little different light. They seemed to consider him more of a preacher and less a drunk.

CHAPTER 8

The war was heating up in Europe and in the Pacific. The Scotts followed the progress of the war primarily by radio broadcast. They learned to identify some of the broadcaster's voices, such as H.V. Kaltenborn, Drew Pearson and Edward R. Murrow. They did occasionally receive some war news from magazines and newspapers that were dropped off at Turner's Store by produce salesmen. Abe had obtained a recent copy of Life Magazine from one of his trips to Jonesboro. Life Magazine had run a story about President Roosevelt, and there was a full-page color photograph of the president with the article. Inez asked Abe if she could have the photo and he cut it out for her. She brought it home and tacked it up on the wall in the front room. It was the only picture she had on a wall. She did have one other picture. It was a portrait of what someone thought Jesus must have looked like. It was on a calendar that she hung on the side of the icebox in the kitchen. Bud would occasionally stare at the portrait of Jesus and think to himself that Jesus probably would not have so pleasant an expression if he had to endure one of Inez's castor oil cleansings.

President Roosevelt had become like God to many people in the delta country, and people during church services often prayed for him, if not directly to him. Bud asked his father one time why it was some people seemed to think more of President Roosevelt than they did of Jesus, and Ellis said that President Roosevelt had done more for the poor people of the country than Jesus ever would.

The airplanes were still dog fighting above the fields. Smoke trails were always forming patterns in the air, blown by the wind into unusual shapes. Bud and Joel had fun trying to make out what the patterns looked like. Sometimes they might look like an animal, sometimes a bird. Ellis said if Bud and Joel spent as much time watching what they were supposed to be doing as they did watching airplanes, that maybe the cotton might finally get chopped out.

One day the field hands heard the low droning sound of a motor. Everyone began to look around in an attempt to discover the source of the noise, when suddenly a huge oblong balloon appeared just above the treetops. It was approaching from the east passing over Cache River Ditch and directly overhead. There was a little glass pod hanging underneath, with people clearly visible inside. The occupants in the glass pod waved at the field hands, and everyone in the field waved back, except for Bud and Joel. The two boys had picked up some hard gumbo clods and were throwing them at the aircraft in a futile attempt to bring it down. It was beyond their range.

They were all dumbfounded. It was the largest moving thing any of them had ever seen with the exception of a train, and they couldn't be sure about that, and this thing was flying through the air. It was bigger than the Scott's house or barn. It was bigger than the Thompson barn. Inez Scott said she thought that it might be one of those zeppelins that she had read about in a magazine. Everyone dropped their hoes and watched, not saying a word, until the flying machine went out of sight, low over the trees to the west.

Ellis was behind in getting his cotton chopped. There had been several rain showers and with the rain came new grass. He would get one field of cotton chopped and plowed, and then the field would have to be reworked. It wasn't going to be long until school would take up for the summer session, and Bud, Joel and Betty would only be available after school. Ellis began to look around for help.

There was an elderly couple named Dement that lived about a mile west of the Scotts. Mr. And Mrs. Dement were both more than sixty years old and both were disabled. Their daughter-in-law, Francis, had come to look after them while her husband, Ed Dement, was overseas fighting in the war. Francis was just eighteen and Ed was nineteen when they married in the spring of nineteen forty-two.

Francis was pregnant when Ed was drafted, but she didn't know it at the time. She made the discovery after he had gone to California for basic training, but she never said anything about it then, because she didn't want to burden him with the information. Ed was shipped overseas directly from basic training, not knowing that he was going to be the father of a little girl. He had been overseas several months, when Francis finally broke the news to him by letter, enclosing a Kodak snapshot of her holding their baby girl. It was not long after that when Francis started receiving a small army allotment that Ed had made to her.

Francis told Ellis Scott that she could chop cotton for a few days as her in-laws were doing fairly well at the present time and that they could take care of themselves and her little girl during the day, and besides she could use the extra money.

Francis said she wanted to save as much money as possible so that when Ed came home from the war that they could go to California. Ed had written that there were all kinds of things to do in California, and that was where he wanted to settle down when the fighting was over. Ed had grown up on a cotton farm and he didn't want any more of it. Francis said she was really looking forward to going west, where it was always sunny and warm, even in the wintertime.

Bud thought Francis was pretty, and he daydreamed while he was working in the field beside her that he would marry someone like her, someday. Maybe it would be Betty Adkins, and maybe Betty and him would go to California, too. Bud already knew one thing for sure: he was not going to be a sharecropper for the rest of his life.

Ellis Scott found the Fisher brothers unemployed as usual. The two boys were in their early twenties, but were too stupid to pass any kind of military examination, and that was saying a lot, but they had been classified "4-F," or unfit for military duty, because not only were they, "a few bricks shy of a full load," as Ellis said, but both had at least one finger missing, lost to dynamite caps exploding in their hands. They would not be going to war, which was just all right with both of them.

The Fisher brothers were simply lazy. Their father had kicked them out of the house more than once because they wouldn't earn their keep. They would usually just camp out somewhere on the ditch and fish, but when they got hungry, they would slip up to their back door late at night and their mother would feed them. Old man Fisher finally found out where all his food was going, and just resigned himself to the fact that he couldn't overcome a mother's love for her children, and he let them back in the house.

Ellis told the boys straight off that he didn't expect them to, "stand round with one finger up your ass and one in your mouth, changing ever little bit." Bud was always amused by the way his father would come straight to the point. Ellis told the Fisher brothers that as long as they chopped the cotton like it was supposed to be chopped, and they stayed up with the rest of the hands, that they would get paid like everyone else, which was a dollar for a ten-hour day.

The first day with the new help went as well as could be expected. The Fisher boys drank a lot of water and kept running over the ditch bank to relieve themselves in the brush. At the beginning of the work day, the brothers had kept a close eye on Betty Adkins' thin flour sack blouse, but by noon, the heat and humidity had begun to take its toll, and by one o'clock, they were just plodding along, fighting the fatigue, heat and dust with everyone else. Betty Adkins had been forgotten.

Inez had gotten the message however, witnessing the Fisher boys attention to Betty's bosom. The next morning she packed one of her old brassieres in a large paper sack with the dinner bucket. When she got to the field she gave it to Dovie Adkins, and Dovie took Betty over the ditch bank, and helped her put it on. Things just weren't the same after that, for the Fisher brothers or Bud either.

The day was hot and humid as usual. They were still chopping out the patch of cotton down by the ditch bank. At about nine o'clock in the morning, an approaching car could be seen coming down the field road from the direction of the Scott house, trailing a cloud of dust. A big green army sedan was driven right up to where they were working.

Francis Dement was the only one in the group that had a relation in the war, so it wasn't any question whom they had come to see. Two military officers got out of the dusty car and out of the corner of his eye, Bud saw Francis slowly sinking to her knees. She seemed like she wanted to stand but her legs wouldn't hold her.

The officers came up to Bud first as he was nearest their car. The older one said to Bud, "I am Chaplain King. Is there a Mrs. Francis Dement here?" Bud just pointed to Francis kneeling on the ground, tears were already cutting trails through the dust on her face. The Chaplain walked up to Francis and said, "Mrs. Dement, I have a telegram from the War Department, and I am sorry to have to inform you that your husband Private First Class Ed Dement has been killed in action, fighting the Japanese, on or about June, fifteenth, nineteen forty-three, somewhere in the South Pacific. For security reasons, we are not allowed to say exactly where."

The Chaplain bent down and tried to hand the telegram to Francis, but Francis suddenly jumped to her feet and started running across the cotton rows. She screamed out, "It's got blood on it! It's got blood on it!" and she kept yelling like that until she was out of hearing.

Everyone stood there, stunned for a moment. Inez Scott recovered first.

She went to the officers and told them to give her the telegram. She said she would give it to Francis, and she asked if there was anything else that Francis needed to know. The other officer, who had remained silent, spoke up and said for Inez to tell Mrs. Dement that some official from Jonesboro would be in touch with her in a few days in order to settle Private Dement's affairs. He said to tell Mrs. Dement that due to the distance and the circumstances involved that Private Dement's body would not be shipped back to this country. In all probability, burial would be in the military cemetery in Hawaii called the Punchbowl.

Chaplain King again expressed his regrets, and said that they had to be on their way as they had more telegrams to deliver. He said there was a lot of fighting in both the European and Pacific Theaters of War, and a lot of boys from Northeast Arkansas were involved, and a lot of them were not going to be coming home. Then the two men got back into their car, and turned back toward the Scott house and the county road. Inez started across the field in an effort to try to catch up with Francis who was now several hundred yards across the field and was wandering aimlessly in a circle. Everyone else stood quietly, trying to understand what had just happened. Bud could see tears in Dovey's and Betty's eyes. They soon turned to the task at hand and without a word went back to work. The rest followed, one by one. Ellis Scott, who remained silent the whole time, stood for a few minutes watching the army car until it went out of sight.

They never saw Francis Dement again. She took the baby and returned to the little town of Egypt that afternoon and stayed with her folks for a while. It was later learned, that after receiving some life insurance money from the army, she bought a car. She packed up the car with what little belongings she had, and she and the baby set out for California. She wanted to go where it was always warm, she said, even in the wintertime.

CHAPTER 9

It rained the day after the army officers brought Francis Dement the telegram. The rain was heavy enough to halt work in the field. Ellis, Bud, Joel, and Hazel went to Turner's Store about mid-morning. Inez gave Bud a dime from her chicken money. Joel had some change in his pocket, too. Bud could hear it jingle. Bud would like to have known how much Joel had, but Joel didn't volunteer the information and Bud was too polite to ask.

Bud had bought his regular treat: a big orange soda pop and a package of salted peanuts. Joel bought a big orange drink and a banana moon pie. The boys were out on the store porch, enjoying themselves, when Mr. A.D. Adams came walking up. "Howdy boys," he said, as he went inside.

Mr. A.D. Adams was known as a "character," in the Horse Island community. He had survived the great Mississippi River flood of nineteen twenty-seven, after being stranded for seven days on top of a farmhouse near Monette, Arkansas, near the border of Craighead and Mississippi Counties. He had nothing to eat but a slab of raw bacon and a pone of cornbread. When he told that story, which he often did, someone would usually ask, "Well A.D., what did you have to drink when you were on top of that house?" His answer was always, "Water, and plenty of it."

The flood waters got so deep in the spring and early summer of nineteen twenty-seven, that it was possible to travel by boat from Crowley's Ridge at Jonesboro, sixty miles—all the way to Memphis, and never see dry land. Someone in a motorboat finally spotted Mr. Adams waving his shirt from on top of the house. After his rescue, he was taken to the nearest dry land, twenty miles east, to the hill country of Crowley's Ridge, near Jonesboro.

Mr. Adams was now over seventy years old, and currently lived alone in an old log cabin about two miles east of Turner's Store, down the county road toward Bono. His wife had been dead for five years. Mr. Adams walked everywhere he went unless he was lucky enough to catch a ride. He didn't have a wagon and team, or even a mule to ride. However, he did ride a mule at one time, but the mule died about the same time as his wife, and he never got another wife or mule. People said that he walked them both to death. Abe Turner said that one time Mr. Adams came to the store riding his mule, while his wife followed walking several yards behind. Abe said he asked Mr. Adams, how come he rode while his wife walked? Mr. Adams replied, "She ain't got no mule."

Mr. Adams always had something interesting to say, so Bud and Joel went back into the store. Ellis Scott and Hazel Adkins were playing checkers in the back of the store and Mr. Adams was watching. Abe Turner got Mr. Adams a can of Prince Albert smoking tobacco. Bud loved to watch Mr. Adams roll a cigarette. He placed the cigarette paper in one hand and poured the tobacco in with the other, and then he rolled the cigarette with only one hand. Bud wanted to learn to do that but his mother was dead set against smoking, and Ellis, who did smoke, wouldn't let him practice with his fixings. Bud felt like someone was against everything he wanted to do.

Bud was going to be thirteen years old on the fifteenth of August. His mother said that she wanted him baptized as soon as he turned thirteen, because he would then be accountable for his actions, at least according to what she understood from the Bible. However, Bud thought that before he was baptized and received forgiveness for his sins, which was part of the deal according to the Baptist way of thinking, that he ought to start smoking since it didn't make any sense to get baptized unless one had sinned in some way and he hadn't so far, at least as far as he knew; nothing significant anyway. Everyone knew smoking was a sin, all of the preachers said so. Undergoing baptism after smoking, to Bud's way of thinking, would at least have a purpose.

The conversation around the checker game finally got around to the Scott family's recent problem with the bobcats and the loss of several chickens. Mr. Adams said he could appreciate a woman's love for her hens. Chickens had always been a valuable commodity to farm folks. He said that back in "twenty-seven," he was living near the Dell Community over near Blytheville, and was working on a cotton farm. In the early spring before the floods came and ran everyone out of the area, there was a great tornado that cut a swath near a half-a-mile wide across the country all the way from Monette, to the Mississippi River, crossing into Tennessee.

There was a farmer who had a homestead directly in the path of the tornado, and the farmer's wife had a large flock of hens and only one rooster. The tornado was bearing down on the farmer's house, when through divine providence it rose in the air and passed over to drop down on the other side. The farmhouse and outbuildings were spared.

However, when the tornado passed directly overhead, it created such a vacuum that most of the chickens were picked clean, including the rooster— left naked. The farmer's wife was very distraught as she knew her only rooster would not survive long once the sun came out; he would surely sunburn and it would kill him. A good rooster was hard to find. She had to do something.

Her husband had worked some as a carpenter at Blytheville, and he had an old pair of worn out carpenter's overalls. The overalls were the kind that was white with tiny blue pinstripes, with a loop on the side, where he hung his hammer. She cut out a pinstriped pattern to fit the rooster, which was no easy task since a rooster doesn't have a waist or shoulders. However, she was resourceful and developed a bib over the leggings with cross galluses that was sufficient for the rooster to keep his britches up. The rooster was sufficiently covered and would be protected from the sun until his feathers grew back out.

Mr. Adams said, "It was a sight for sore eyes to see that rooster dressed up in pinstriped britches, especially when he ran down a hen and caught her. The rooster would hold the hen down with one foot and try to get his britches off with the other."

Well of course that story got a big laugh from everyone around the checker game. Bud didn't know whether to believe the story or not. Ellis Scott said simply, "A.D., you're as full of shit as a Christmas turkey."

Just then, Roscoe Gilmore came riding up to the store on his little gray mule. He was carrying a dozen or so handbills upon which an advertisement had been printed with the message that the ALBINO PROPHET AND HOLY MAN, HOMER ADKINS would be preaching the coming Sunday, and it gave the time and date.

It was entitled, "THE SERMON IN THE SWAMP." Roscoe was on a circuit ride from Turner's Store, to Bono, and then to Sedgwick and Egypt. He would be placing the handbills at several locations. Abe let him put one of the handbills in the front window of the store. It was going to be Homer's coming out, so to speak.

Roscoe said Homer had been studying his bible and had been working on his delivery. Homer's voice, to Bud's way of thinking, was not really of the preaching caliber. It was kind of high-pitched and didn't carry like Roscoe's. Roscoe had more of a baritone voice, and it only got into the higher ranges when he got excited and began to shriek about the chariots of glory, which he often did.

Ellis Scott told Bud not to tell his mother that Homer was scheduled to preach. Ellis said if she found out, after what happened with the chickens, she might not go to church, and too, he thought it might be a nice surprise. Well, it did turn out to be a surprise.

Ellis and Bud kept Homer's debut as quiet as they could. Inez Scott seldom went to the store, and no one outside the family came around the Scott house the rest of the week, so there was no way that she could have found out before actually getting to the church house.

Sunday dawned hot and humid. It was ninety degrees in the shade by the time the worship service began. The first thing Bud spotted of interest, upon arrival at the church, was Betty Adkins standing in the churchyard. It was the first time he had ever known her to go to church. Betty had on a pretty white cotton dress and black shoes. Her short blonde hair was combed straight down all around, and she had parted it a little left of center. Her glistening hair was combed in such a manner that it swept back over her left ear which was exposed but covering her right ear. Betty was beautiful.

Joel was there too, standing off to the side by himself, and looking uncomfortable and a little embarrassed. He had on shoes.

"Well, will wonders never cease, it's the Adkins kids," said Inez.

"It is a wonder," replied Ellis, as he and Bud suppressed little smiles.

Bud's first thought was to make sure that he got seated next to Betty, so he went directly to her. She appeared relieved to see someone she knew so well. Joel strolled over and stood looking uncomfortable, not saying anything. Bud usually took a seat on a back row bench so he could doze off unmolested, if the need arose. However, he wasn't going to be dozing today. The handbills had evidently done the trick. The excitement was building, and a large crowd was growing by the minute. There were a lot of people present that Bud had never seen before. Evidently, a six-foot-four, albino prophet and preacher was a hot topic on a hot Sunday.

Mrs. Alma Carter came over near where Betty, Joel and Bud were, to a group of people that Ellis and Inez Scott had walked up to, and had engaged in conversation. Bud overheard Mrs. Carter say how excited she was about getting to hear Homer's first sermon. At this announcement, Inez had the look of a possum caught in the glare of a carbide light. She seemed momentarily like she wanted to run, but didn't know where. She took a deep breath and steadied herself while staring intently at Ellis for his reaction to this news. Ellis was a sly old bird. He didn't give any reaction at all, like he hadn't heard.

He simply went on talking about the hot weather and crops and the usual farmer conversation. For farmers, the weather was always too hot or too cold, or too wet or too dry. Out of the corner of his eye, Bud could see Inez shoot a hard glance in his direction, which he deftly dodged by taking a close-up look at Betty's white cotton dress, while moving in close to smell the vanilla.

Preacher Gilmore appeared on the front steps and announced in a loud voice to those gathered, that due to the heat and the size of the crowd, there would not be any Sunday school, and that the church service would start at the normal eleven o'clock starting time. The announcement was met with some shouts and hand clapping, and Bud thought he heard an amen or two.

Joel motioned for Bud to look over to the edge of the gathering crowd, and there stood the whore, Mary Margaret Miller. Mary Margaret was well known in the Horse Island community as well as several others, and was in Inez Scott's words, "a soiled dove." If Mary Margaret's name came up in conversation when Ellis Scott was present, he would simply say, "Mary Margaret Miller is a whore." Ellis Scott did have a way of getting to the point.

Mary Margaret, was twenty years old and had already been married four times, and it was said that she had broken up that many more marriages. The first time she married, she was only thirteen, the same age as Joel Adkins was now. Bud couldn't imagine being married that young.

Bud eased over near where Mary Margaret stood talking to the Morgan boys from Sedgwick. They were identical triplets, tall, thin, black haired, and handsome young men. Most people could only tell them apart because each one usually wore a different colored long-sleeved shirt under the galluses of his overalls, but you still had to connect a name with a color and remember it. Mary Margaret was often seen in the company of the three twenty-year-old brothers. "She has hit another triple," was a common expression, when the four were seen together. Bud had heard someone say that Mary Margaret Miller had hit more triples than the entire Gashouse Gang put together, a reference to the early nineteen-forties' St. Louis Cardinal baseball team.

Bud heard her say that she had come to see the albino preacher. She seemed sincere when she said that she had considered mending her ways and that she thought religion might be the answer. Bud thought he saw an expression of severe disappointment, mixed with disbelief, spread across the Morgan boys' faces at this announcement, but being in the close proximity of a church, they were reluctant right then to voice an argument against what they had just heard.

Bud collected Betty and Joel, and told them that they had better go on in and claim their seats in the coolest place they could find, which Bud intended to be on the last bench by the back door. However, Betty said she wanted to be up close, and as smart as anything, she walked right down to the front row bench, just like she had been going to church her whole life, and she sat down directly in front of the pulpit. What could Bud do? He followed Betty.

Bud, Betty and Joel, each picked up a cardboard fan off of the stack near the front door. The fans had been donated to area churches by a Walnut Ridge funeral home. The fans had a head and shoulders picture of Jesus on them, and the funeral home's name and telephone number—like they expected someone was going to call. No one that Bud knew, but Abe Turner, had a telephone. Bud and Joel had never talked on a telephone and neither had any intentions of ever doing so.

The church house was hot and was going to get even hotter when the crowd all came in. The church had twelve benches down either side with a narrow side aisle and an aisle down the center. Each bench would seat about eight people. During regular Sundays, the church never was more than a third full.

There was no electricity in the church, but there was sufficient light that came through six large side windows, three on either side, and the large front door that was left open during the summer months, and then there was a side door to the left of the altar area that was also kept open in hot weather.

When there were church services at night or there were special singings, kerosene lamps were placed in the windows and in the altar area. It was a fairly modern church for its day. The side door off the altar area wasn't there originally. It was more or less an accidental creation by Deacon Johnny Abbott, a couple of years before, during a snake-handling mishap on one of those "special" Sundays.

Sometimes good Christian people get carried away by what they find in the Bible, and try to apply to themselves something that Jesus meant only for His disciples. Jesus never said that he meant for just anyone to go around picking up snakes, to prove their faith, but sometimes it seems like everyone wants to be a disciple.

Jesus also said that anyone that had as much faith as a grain of mustard seed could move a mountain. Bud once asked Inez had she known anyone who had ever moved a mountain by just thinking about it. She said that she only knew of one person who had tried, and that was an eighty-year-old man, by the name of Brother Silas Snow, in her home church in Izard County.

One Sunday, during services, old Brother Silas had gone into a trance, after announcing that he was going to move Puberty Mountain, a budding hill, two miles west of the church. Inez said that the small congregation had gone to the windows and watched the hill intently as he had prayed and strained, and strained and prayed. Suddenly Brother Silas screamed out and fell down holding his stomach. He had given himself a hernia, and had to be taken home in a wagon. He finally recovered, but he never again tried moving anything bigger than a water glass, and then, only when it was empty.

There were some good-meaning people at an Assembly of God Church, near Sedgwick, who literally interpreted the Bible verse: "They shall pick up serpents, and if they drink any deadly thing, it will not hurt them; they shall lay their hands on the sick, and they shall recover."

There is nothing in the verse that says the serpents have to be poisonous, or for that matter, the serpents have to be snakes. Bud thought that the Assembly of God people might have gotten carried away by a false assumption. Bud thought if he was to test his faith with a snake, that he would do it with a garter snake or perhaps a chicken snake, but he was not about to test it with a copperhead or a rattlesnake. Those things can kill Christian and pagan alike. But there are a lot of foolish people in the world who in their attempt to reach the highest level of discipleship, reach the highest level of all: martyrdom.

Deacon Johnny Abbott was a dapper little man, five-foot, six-inches, in height, and weighed no more than one hundred twenty pounds soaking wet. He had coal black hair and a thin black mustache. He loaded his hair with Rose Hair Oil, and combed it straight back. Deacon Johnny was a member in good standing of the Little Brown Freewill Baptist Church. He had become a legend in his own time because of his eccentricity, or as some in the community said, because he didn't have all his oars in the water. His legendary status was assured when he bought a military flamethrower from the Army-Navy Store, in Jonesboro, for the purpose of burning off the Little Brown Freewill Baptist Church Cemetery during the annual church-sponsored Cemetery Cleaning and Dinner on the Ground Day.

The flamethrower had not come with instructions, so after fiddling with it for a while, he yelled for everyone to stand back and he pulled the trigger. The recoil knocked him down, destroying his aim. A fifty-foot stream of fiery napalm blasted out and incinerated the women's outhouse.

Deacon Johnny had gone to Sedgwick to witness one of the snake handling exhibitions, and although, he had not personally participated, he came back and convinced the leadership of the Little Brown Freewill Baptist Church that the congregation ought to have the opportunity to witness really true Christian faith. He wanted to bring a box of snakes to the Little Brown Church.

Inez Scott was dead set against it. She hated snakes and killed every one she came across. Ellis Scott's idea was not to test your faith by handling a snake; he said why not simply test it by drinking a deadly thing, like it says in the same Bible verse. Why not get a jug of strychnine, and then anyone who wants to take the faith test, just take a nice swig out of the jug, and wait for the pass-fail test results. Ellis said he thought that might rid the country of a lot of stupid people. Ellis wasn't against bringing the snakes into the church; in fact he wanted to see it. He said he wished that one would bite Deacon Johnny on the ass, because he wanted to see who would volunteer to suck the poison out.

Well, everything was arranged with the Assembly of God's people and four men showed up one Sunday with a wooden box containing about twenty copperheads and rattlesnakes. It was hot in the box and the snakes were mad. One could hear the rattles buzzing and there was a bumping noise coming from inside the box; the snakes were attacking each other. Bud thought that he would not have stuck his hand down in that box for all the orange soda pop that had ever been bottled in the United States.

Deacon Johnny who was directing this particular service, started with a prayer. Roscoe Gilmore said he didn't want any part of it, and was sitting on a backbench near the door. Deacon Johnny concluded the prayer and went right to the meat of the program. The congregation was too nervous to sing a hymn or take a collection. Deacon Johnny called the visiting delegation forward. Three of the visiting snake handlers came up to the pulpit area, which was a raised platform about six inches in height. Deacon Johnny moved over to the side of the pulpit area, a look of sublime contentment on his face, as the fourth member of the delegation carried the box of reptiles up the center aisle. It was quite noticeable that most people in the congregation had moved away from the center aisle and close to the side windows.

When the man with the box reached the raised platform, he either didn't see it or just didn't step high enough, because he tripped, lost his grip, staggered over toward Deacon Johnny, and spilled the entire writhing contents of the box right at Deacon Johnny's feet. There were a number of expressions that passed across Deacon Johnny's contented face, terror being chief among them.

The Deacon let out a babbling scream, bringing the congregation to its feet. It appeared for a moment that he was trying to speak in tongues, which normally wasn't attempted in the Little Brown Freewill Baptist Church. The Deacon made several high leaps in such quick succession that it seemed like his feet never touched the floor, and that he was suspended in mid-air. His arms were whirling like windmills and it seemed that there was the distinct possibility that he might actually fly. There was not an exit between the spreading pile of snakes that were striking in every direction, and the left rear corner of the church where Deacon Johnny was trapped. Deacon Johnny made one.

He lowered his head and made a leap of faith completely through the wall of the church, bursting between two supporting upright timbers and the outer cypress planking. The members of the congregation also made fast exits, including the visiting snake handlers. The more agile ones went through the windows. The rest stampeded through the front door and out into the churchyard. The church service was over almost before it began.

It wasn't altogether a lost cause. There were some pretty fair carpenters in the community and a couple of them got together and framed out the hole in the wall where Deacon Johnny had butted through. They constructed a nice door there that was always later referred to as The Deacon Hole.

It was time for the service to begin. The church was packed to the rafters. Betty was sitting on the front-left-bench next to the center aisle, which placed her directly in front of the pulpit. Bud was sitting on Betty's left, and there was a small space on his left caused by Joel suddenly getting up and walking out of the church. Either the excitement was too much for Joel, or his shoes were hurting his feet.

There was a hush that went over the crowd, and just as Bud turned his head to see what was happening, a strong scent of toilet water, shampoo, hair spray, lipstick, rouge, talcum powder and lye soap, washed over him, as the whore Mary Margaret Miller passed in front of him and sat down in the space just vacated by Joel Adkins.

When Bud first sat down next to Betty, he thought that he could hear the angels singing. Now he realized, to his great embarrassment, that it was just nervous indigestion, and that he had gas. Bud was completely bewildered by this sudden turn of events. He didn't know what to do with his hands, so he sat on them. Ellis Scott said later that from where he sat near the middle of the church, that he could see the back of Bud's neck and ears and that they turned so red that they practically glowed.

Preacher Gilmore and Homer Adkins entered the church through The

Deacon Hole. They took their seats on cane-bottomed chairs on either side of the altar area, facing the congregation, Homer on the left, Roscoe on the right. Abe Turner came forward and led the congregation in singing a hymn. He followed the hymn with a short prayer, mentioning President Roosevelt twice, but through nervous anticipation of what was to come, or something else, forgot to mention Jesus at all, and he sat down.

Roscoe came forward to the pulpit, and the first thing he said was, "Well it's hotter'n a goat's butt in a pepper patch," and then he made some complimentary remarks about Homer, calling him, "my apostle." He then referred to Homer as a "prophet and seer," and then he sat down. Homer, in all his albino-pink-eyed-whiteness, came to the pulpit. Bud heard a man sitting directly behind him, exclaim under his breath, "Well, butter my butt and call me a biscuit!"

Bud remarked later to Ellis, how calm Homer had appeared standing before such a large crowd for the first time. Ellis said that a pint of good moonshine whiskey would calm your nerves like nothing else will. Bud thought his father's remarks were uncharitable, but Homer was indeed calmer than one would have expected under the circumstances.

Homer had on a gray robe that appeared to have originated as a light woolen blanket. The skirt of the robe reached halfway between his knees and feet. His feet were encased in rubber sandals that he had fashioned from a worn out automobile tire. The sandals were tied with woven rawhide cords. Bud noted later that when Homer walked where the ground was soft, he left tread marks. The robe had sleeves that reached between elbow and wrist, and it was tied with a broad sash of the same material.

Sometime later it was revealed that the robe was made for Homer by Mary Margaret Miller, which may have accounted for the reason that she wanted a front row seat. She probably wanted to get a good look at her creation in action. One of the ladies of the community was overheard to say—after being made aware of the robe's seamstress—that she had known Mary Margaret had aspirations toward the fashion arts from the first time that she had ever laid eyes on a Sears and Roebuck Catalog.

Homer, his pink eyes, framed with snow-white, shoulder-length hair, glowing in the unlit church and his beardless face shining, began his sermon:

"Oh m'God, The heathen are all around us.
We have become mocked by our neighbors.
Shunned by those around us."

His opening statement was followed by a chorus of amens—so far, so good. Homer's eyes swept the congregation. His piercing pink eyes momentarily locked on Bud. Bud cringed in his seat.

"Then the Lord awoke as from sleep. Like a strong
man shoutin' because o' wine and lively spirits. And he put his
enemies to route; He put 'em to everlastin' shame."

Another chorus of amens. Homer's pink eyes again swept across the assemblage. Bud heard audible gasps.

"He sent among 'em skeeters which devoured 'em.
He destroyed their cotton crops with hail, and weevils. Then they
remembered God was their rock. The most high God –
their redeemer."

Homer went on in this vein for several minutes, and then Bud noticed that his horrific gaze had quit sweeping over the congregation. Homer appeared to focus his attention to the front row bench only, and more specifically on the trio of Betty, Mary Margaret, and Bud.

The heat in the church was becoming unbearable. Bud noticed that both Betty and Mary Margaret had eased the hem of their skirts well above their knees and were fanning down low with their little cardboard fans. Bud cut his eyes sideways and down at Betty's bare left knee and noticed that several little beads of perspiration had formed their own little congregation, and then in single file they slid down the inside of her leg to only the Lord knows where. Homer suddenly seemed to have mentally changed gears:

"Behold beauty is only skin deep.
Yore the roses of Sharon, lilies of the valley.
Bright and shinin' stars.
Arise my lovlies, my fair ones and come away, for lo,
the rain is over and gone and the ground is dry."

Homer paused for emphasis. There were no amens this time. The congregation had grown deathly quiet, and clearly confused at the sermon's change of direction. But, Bud picked up on it right away. Homer was trying to quote from the Old Testament from memory and he wasn't doing a very good job of it. Bud thought that it must have been the Song of Solomon, but he wasn't sure. That was the one book in the Bible that Inez said that she didn't want Bud to read. She said it wasn't fit for young minds, so naturally he had read it anyway, when she wasn't looking. He really didn't understand any of it, but he thought the words were pretty. Bud thought Old Solomon sure could write a good song.

Homer's eyes were now so intent on Betty and Mary Margaret's exposed secrets that he seemed to began having speech problems. His voice became hoarse and raspy, but Homer bore down:

"Oh pretty maidens, how purty are yore feet and other things.
Yore thighs are a work of a master potter's hand.
Your navals are like round bowls of muscadine jelly.
Your'alls breasts are like unharnessed hillocks.
Your'alls necks are like two birchbark saplings.
Lord, it's hot in here."

You could have heard a pin drop. Homer had begun to lick his dry lips. A heightened tension could be sensed throughout the congregation. Bud had a sudden desire to get up out of his seat and ease to the rear of the church. He was pretty young, but he thought he recognized that Betty and Mary Margaret were being verbally molested, and right out of the Bible, too. But what could he do?

In the midst of determining what his next move was going to be, the tension was dramatically broken. Mary Margaret suddenly stood and pointed to the left of the pulpit.

"I see Him! I see Him!" she yelled.

Homer appeared to suddenly awaken from his trance. He had the look of a person trying to determine what the light was at the end of the tunnel, only to discover that he was about to be run over by a freight train.

Roscoe Gilmore, who had been as mesmerized as anyone else by Homer's sermon material, stood up, and said, "Who do you see, Mary Margaret?"

"I see Jesus! He is standing by the pulpit and He's looking straight at me!" replied Mary.

Homer seemed to slightly recoil to his left away from the spot where Mary Margaret had centered her gaze. The congregation sounded uncomfortable; benches squeaked, feet shuffled.

"I see Jesus! I see Jesus!" exclaimed Mary Margaret, and then she fainted dead away and collapsed in a heap of ruffles at Bud's feet. Betty, to her credit, reacted quickly. She sat down on the floor and pulled the hem of Mary Margaret's skirt down to a more modest level. She cradled Mary Margaret's head in her lap and began fanning her. Bud sat like a rock, his entire body momentarily paralyzed.

Homer looked around wild-eyed, and then he regained his senses, and made a brilliant recovery:

"Thus says the Lord keep His commandents, and do right
fer soon salvation will come like a whirlwind, like a fiery
chariot from glory, and the Lord's deliverance will be revealed.
Blessed are those who does this. You may get a ride in
the chariot. Keep the Sabbath. Keep your hand from doing evil.
Hold the reins tight. Keep the mules in check.
Heaven is afar off. Pace yourselves. It is not how soon you
git there. It's the gittin' there that counts. Amen."

Homer then looked directly at Bud, and said, "Bud, go to the pump and bring a dipper of water. We've got a sinner down for the count."

CHAPTER 10

Bud's thirteenth birthday was on the fifteenth of August . Egypt School had been in split-term summer session since the first week of July. The summer session would last for six weeks, then school would let out for six weeks for the cotton harvest.

When school started in the summer of nineteen forty-three, the school kids on the Egypt-Bono county road were transported in a genuine yellow twenty-nine-passenger school bus for the first time. In the previous five and one-half years that Bud had gone to school, Winslow Dexter had always transported the children on the Egypt-Bono road, to and from school, in his nineteen thirty-six Ford pick-up truck. Winslow had a contract for several years with the Egypt school district to haul students because the school district didn't have money for buses, and, too, there was a shortage of buses because of the war. Winslow had constructed a wooden cab over the bed of his truck to protect his riders, but it didn't keep the occupants from nearly suffocating in summer and getting frostbite in winter.

Joel and Betty Adkins usually walked up through the field to the Scott house to catch the ride to school. Joel was there on the first day of the summer session, but Betty wasn't. Joel said she wasn't going back to school. He did not give a reason. Bud was naturally disappointed, but he never said anything. A lot of kids never attended school past sixth grade, so someone quitting school was not a surprise. Most parents didn't care, because it meant that the kids were available for work all year long. Bud wanted to go to school, because that was his only vacation time.

Joel told Bud that Elmo Wilson and his older half-wit brother Charlie, from across the ditch, had cut down the tallest cottonwood tree on the east bank of Cache River Ditch, near the Adkins' house. They had felled the tree directly across the ditch and trimmed the branches; and except for high floodwaters, the ditch could easily be crossed on this very large foot log. Elmo had been crossing the ditch lately and coming over to the Adkins' house around suppertime for no other reason than to do a little sparking with Betty; although, according to Joel, he would always say he had just been in the neighborhood and thought he would drop by.

Bud was more than a little disturbed by this information. He knew that Betty was almost three years older than him, and he knew at sixteen that she was getting past marrying age, and that one day she must marry, and in all probability would leave the community – but, Elmo Wilson? Bud had higher hopes for Betty.

About the middle of August, Joel and Bud were at Turner's Store on a Saturday morning. Ellis Scott had gone with Hazel Adkins to Cord, Arkansas, in Independence County, to recruit field hands for the fall harvest. There were not enough hands just among the Scott and Adkins families, to harvest all the cotton on the farm before winter. The cotton bolls were beginning to open, school would soon be out, and the cotton harvest would start the last week in August. Extra help was needed.

Abe Turner loaned his truck to Ellis for the trip. Ellis had found two families near Cord, the year before, who had picked cotton for him, and he hoped that he could talk them into coming back this fall. Ellis planned to let them camp out in the old Thompson place.

Joel and Bud were sitting on Abe Turner's store porch enjoying a couple of big orange drinks and banana moon pies, when Abe came out and asked them if they would like to make some easy money.

"How's zat?" asked Joel.

"Castratin' some cats," replied Abe.

"Castratin'?" Joel was confused by the word.

"Cuttin' some tomcats," replied Abe.

"Cuttin'?" said Joel, still confused.

"I need the balls whacked off of about twenty tomcats that's hangin' round this place," stated Abe, quite clearly and to the point.

"Well, why didn't you say so in the first place?" exclaimed Joel.

Abe went on to explain that he was having problems with so many tomcats hanging around the store. They were fighting over the three or four females, and were keeping Ruth and him awake at night with all their caterwauling.

"Well, why don't you just take a shotgun and thin 'em out?" asked Joel.

"Because, I need the cats around to keep the rats and mice away from the store. When is the last time you saw a mouse or rat around here?" asked Abe, not really soliciting an answer. Because the answer was already known and had been stated publicly more than once by people who frequented the store. Abe didn't have rats and mice because he had a bunch of cats. Everyone in the county kept a cat or two for the same reason.

Abe said he would give twenty-five cents for every pair of tomcat balls that the boys could deliver. He even presented a plan. He evidently had been thinking about the proposition for some time.

There was a weather-tight shed behind the store that was currently empty. The building had only one door and no windows. Abe usually kept a supply of dry goods in the outbuilding that he sold in the store, including sacks of cornmeal and flour.

Abe said that before he replenished his supplies for the fall harvest, would be a good time to lure the cats into the empty shed where the toms could be hemmed up and caught and their balls whacked off. It made perfect sense to the boys.

Bud and Joel had participated in the castration of hogs. Bud had never really understood the need, but evidently being relieved of the source of their sexual anxieties and frustrations had some effect on their ability to gain weight. "You had rather have a fat shoat than a pore' boar," Ellis Scott was fond of saying.

Bud had helped hold the young hogs that weighed about fifty pounds or so at the time the castration took place. Ellis would usually do the cutting, and the hog testicles would be put into a bucket. There wasn't much bleeding, but Ellis would take a stick wrapped with a cloth that he dipped into a mixture of grease and yellow sulfur powder, and he swabbed it on the hog. It must have worked because no one could ever remember a hog getting infected from the operation. Ellis said that there were a lot of men who needed that operation. He was talking about those that had a house full of kids and couldn't feed them.

Hazel Adkins always took the bucket of testicles home to eat. He called them mountain oysters. The Scott family had never eaten them, but Joel Adkins said that they were better than a mess of catfish, especially when they were cut into thin slices, dipped in an egg, flour and cornmeal batter and deep fried, and especially when served with wild poke 'salet' greens and fried green tomatoes. Joel said that the taste and texture of the testicles was somewhat like chicken gizzards, which was a food that Bud really liked, and he was tempted. However, he just couldn't get used to the thought of eating something that a hog had been carrying around in a sack on his backside. Bud had been hungry enough at times to eat almost anything, but he drew the line at eating two things: rattlesnake and hog balls.

Abe said that he would open a couple cans of sardines and the boys could tie a piece of string onto each can and drag them around the store and through the weeds, and other places where the cats usually laid up during the daytime. Abe said he figured that the scent of the sardines would liven up the cats and they could easily be drawn out and would follow the scent trail that the boys would leave, right through the door of the shed and to the inside back wall, where they would leave the cans. After the cats were inside and occupied with the sardines, they could shut the door on them and go to work. It sounded easy enough, and the boys became excited about the prospect of earning several dollars.

Abe provided Joel and Bud, each, with a heavy pair of leather welder's gloves that had cuffs that came up to their elbows. He also let them have a miner's hardhat with a carbide lamp on it. Joel would be the first to wear the hat since he was going to be the first cutter. Both boys were already barefoot and after they removed their shirts, they were left with wearing only their overalls, except for Bud, who had on an old St. Louis Cardinal baseball cap that he had found in the county road. Inez had washed the cap for him and now it was his greatest treasure.

The first part of the project went like clockwork. Once the cats got a whiff of the sardines, they started coming from everywhere, mewing and making cat sounds, and some of them were huge. A couple of the bigger toms looked like they might have been mixed with bobcat, as they were larger than usual, with long legs, and had a shorter tail than the other cats. Bud and Joel immediately began to have doubts. But a fellow could buy an awful lot with a few quarters in nineteen forty-three.

As soon as they dragged the sardine cans inside the shed, the cats rushed through the door, mama cats and all. The boys never got an accurate count. Joel estimated at least twenty. The boys could see dollar signs dancing before their eyes. Bud could tell that once Joel and him got their hands on all that cat castration money, that a period of inflation would be created right there in Turner's Store, on the banks of Cache River Ditch.

Joel thought that the first thing they needed to do was catch the mama cats and throw them out the door so they wouldn't be in the way, so they started. There were four of them. It took a little while to catch all of the female cats, and one had some kittens with her, and they had to catch them too. The heavy gloves paid off, as the mama cats couldn't bite nor scratch through them, although they gave it their best effort.

The first problem they discovered was that Joel couldn't operate with the heavy gloves on which meant that once they caught the big toms, Bud would have to hold the cats by himself while Joel removed his gloves and administered the knife. Tomcat testicles are not easy things to get a grip on. First of all, they're awful small and secondly, the tomcat objects to it. Joel was right handed and would have to try to get a grip on the cat's testicles with the fingers of his left hand, and cut off the testicle sack, using his right hand to grip his razor-sharp Barlow pocket knife. An empty fruit jar was kept handy to put the testicles in for accounting purposes, and the subsequent financial reward.

There was one other problem: lack of ventilation. Abe had made the building air tight by insulating the inside walls in order to keep the air and moisture out, but unfortunately it kept the stink in, and there was soon plenty of it.

They caught the first tomcat. Joel said that they might as well start with the biggest cats so that it would get easier as the work progressed. They hemmed up one of the big bobcat mixes in the corner, and got their gloves on him, but they soon found out that catching the cat was going to be a lot easier than holding him or turning him loose. The cat turned on them with a vengeance. The boys were down on all fours and Bud had what he thought was a pretty good grip on the cat's head and front quarters and Joel had the rear, but Bud lost his grip and the cat turned on Joel, and with a vicious swipe knocked Joel's hat off extinguishing the carbide lamp. The room went pitch black, and the cats went wild.

The cats began to scamper and jump through the air and of course when cats get scared they begin to piss and crap all over everything, and their natural instinct is to climb anything that is handy, and Joel and Bud were the only thing that was handy. They got climbed.

All of the cats seemed to be trying to get on the boy's heads at once, and neither of the boys had shirts or shoes on, and Bud soon lost his baseball cap. They had cats on their heads and shoulders and they could feel claws all over them as the cats were jockeying for a position at the top. Joel and Bud were yelling at the top of their voices. The boys were trying to find the door, but they had gotten turned around in the dark. They were grabbing cats off of their head and shoulders and slinging them off the walls and ceiling, while trying to find the door handle, and it was getting difficult to breathe. There was a lot of screaming and yelling, and it wasn't just the cats. Bud knew real fear for the first time.

What saved the boys from getting hurt worse than they already were, was that in the dark, Joel and Bud accidentally collided and fell down. The cats miraculously got off of them, as their height advantage was temporarily lost. Joel was smart enough to recognize this and said, "Bud, lay quite a minute, and let's try to figure out where the door is. We've got to get the hell out of here."

Bud lay as quite as he could, but he was burning from a hundred scratches and he could taste blood among other things in his mouth. The cats could smell the blood, too. There was some of the loudest and most vicious growling going on all around them that they had ever heard. The commotion was so great that Abe Turner had heard it from inside the store, and he came out to the shed to see what was happening. "How are you boys doin' in there?" Abe called out.

"Abe open the door!" yelled Joel.

"You sure?"

"Has a cat got an ass?"

"I guess that means you're sure."

"Damn right, I'm sure!"

Abe opened the door, and as soon as they saw daylight, Joel, Bud and the cats all made a break for it at the same time, and all seemed to have gone through the door together. Abe just barely got back out of the way in order to keep from getting trampled in the stampede.

Joel and Bud got outside and were trying to get their breaths while gagging at the same time. They heard Abe whistle. "You boys look like you have been through a sausage grinder."

"Tell me about it," said Joel.

Joel and Bud were looking at one another. Joel's left ear was rimmed full of gray cat shit and his hair was plastered down with cat urine. He was bleeding from scratches all over his body and including his face and head, and Bud was a mirror image. The boys headed for the bridge. The ditch was low, but there was a clear pool with a sandy bottom that had washed out on the down-stream side of the bridge, that was about five feet deep. Without consideration for snakes, turtles or alligator gars, they leaped off the bridge, twenty feet above the water, feet first into the pool.

To Abe's credit, he soon appeared on the bridge with two cakes of lye soap and tossed them down to the boys. They began to scrub themselves all over with the lye soap that burned like fire when it got into the cat scratches. They even washed their overalls without taking them off. After several minutes of this, the boys climbed the ditch bank and went back to sit on the store porch and dry out. Several of the deeper scratches were still bleeding. After looking them over, Abe went into the store and soon came back out with two bottles of Calamine Lotion. He gave one each to the boys, who immediately began to treat their wounds. He went around to the back of the store and looked into the empty shed observing the mess left inside. Returning to the front of the store where Bud and Joel were still busy with their self-medication, he said, "Boys, I believe I over simplified the cat-cuttin' operation, but I'll tell you what I'll do. If you boys will take a bucket of water and some lye soap and a couple of mops, and go in thet shed, and mop it down real good, I'll give y'all a dollar a piece. I'll have to figure something else out about the cats."

Well, a dollar was better than nothing, so they got a bucket of water and the mops and cleaned the inside of the shed in about an hour. Not only did Abe give them each a one-dollar bill, he, also threw in two big orange drinks and gave each a banana moon pie. The sting of the cat scratches eased a bit and the bleeding finally stopped by the time the boys polished off their treats. They followed Abe's treats with two-nickel cups of ice cream mixed with grape soda that they financed themselves out of their earnings. The boys were alive and well, and looking to fight cats another day.

CHAPTER 11

Excitement was building in the Horse Island community. It was almost time for the cotton harvest to begin. A lot of strangers were coming into the delta to pick cotton. Turner's Store was a beehive of activity, particularly at night, and on Saturdays. Farmers could never be sure what they were going to get when they started letting people come onto their place, but most itinerant farm workers were decent hardworking people. Occasionally, a bad apple showed up in the barrel.

Most transient workers that came to the east bottoms in the fall came out of the hill country of Izard, Independence, and Stone counties. They were decent hardworking people for the most part, but had little opportunity to earn money during the year. A family that came to the cotton fields in the fall could make enough money to buy their winter clothes and shoes, and enough food staples to last them through the winter months.

For a few days the previous year, the Scotts had an attractive young woman from Chicago, Illinois, in their field trying to pick cotton, and "trying" is the word, because she "couldn't pick a lick," as Ellis Scott said. She did manage to pick seventy-five pounds one day.

It was never known for sure what brought her to the Horse Island community. Some speculated later that she didn't come for the sole purpose of earning money, but that she was actually conducting research for some purpose, perhaps for a newspaper or maybe she was writing a book.

She said that she had relatives in the Bono area, but she never said who they were. She just showed up one day driving a black nineteen forty model Ford Sedan, with Illinois license plates. She drove right out into the field where the pickers were at work, and stepped out of the car with a new canvas, nine-foot pick-sack and asked Ellis if she could pick cotton for him. Naturally, he said yes.

It was a pleasant diversion to have someone from Chicago, picking cotton

95

in the field, when there was so much interest by most young people and many older people, in getting off of the farm and going to places like Chicago and Detroit. Bud tried talking to her one day while he was helping her weigh a sack of cotton at the wagon, but she spoke a different kind of English than he knew, so he finally gave up trying to decipher it. She picked cotton six straight days, Monday through Saturday, hung her pick-sack on the wagon, and drove away, never to be seen again.

Ellis and Hazel Adkins had been successful on their recruiting expedition, and they managed to get the same two Milligan families, whom had picked cotton for Ellis the previous year. There would be eight in all, adults and teenagers, and since the two families were closely related, it meant that they should get along, or at least that is what Ellis hoped.

Brothers, Vaughn and Cauly Milligan, headed the families. Vaughn brought his wife, two teenage daughters, and teenage son. The teenagers, who were to play a large part in Bud and Joel's "fall" experience, were Maxine, sixteen; Sherry, fourteen; and Cody, thirteen. Cauly Milligan brought his wife and his sixty-year-old mother.

Vaughn Milligan's two teenage daughters were pretty by most country standards. However, Bud didn't think that they were in Betty Adkins' class, but he thought that he just might be visiting some down at the Thompson barn after work.

The two families would camp in the Thompson barn, which meant that it had to be cleaned. Inez, Ellis and Bud, had already taken buckets, lye soap and some brooms and mops and had spent the better part of a day, cleaning and fixing the place up. Ellis had taken rolls of tarpaper that they tacked up on the inside walls to help keep out the chilly drafts that would come with the autumn nights, and too, the dust and dirt.

The loft was large and it had some hay on the floor, which made it easier to get rid of the pigeon droppings. The pigeons would have to find another place to roost. There was good water at the pump, and Ellis had built two new privies that he put beside the barn. He found two outdated Sears and Roebuck Catalogs, down at Turner's Store, and put a catalog in each privy. He also bought four new number three washtubs from Abe Turner, and put them into the barn. The individual stalls would provide sufficient privacy for bathing, and the water pump was close by, an added convenience.

The Milligan family had acquired an unusual pattern of speech, even for hillbillies. All of the Milligan family members had the habit of using the letter "h" in the way they pronounced certain words, particularly "it" and "ain't".

Instead of saying, "That ain't it," the way the better educated person would, they would say, "that hain't hit." Bud was amused at their manner of speaking, and passed it off as ignorance, or lack of "school housin'," as he put it. Bud once asked thirteen-year-old Cody Milligan what his favorite letter was, and Cody had replied, "Z." Bud, thinking it would be the letter, "H" went into a spasm of laughter at the unexpected answer. Cody just stared at Bud for the longest, trying to understand what was so funny.

The previous year, before the cotton harvest had even gotten underway, Bud had gotten into a corncob fight with Cody Milligan down at the Thompson barn, and had hit him in the eye with a corncob. Cody ran squalling to his mother. The mother then confronted Ellis Scott, seeking retribution on a grand scale. Bud, faced with a severe thrashing, had pleaded innocent, stating that he had actually been throwing the corncob at a bumblebee that was chasing Cody around the barn, and Cody had run into the line of fire. Cody said that he had not seen a bumblebee and doubted that there was one within a mile of the place.

Ellis had let Bud off easy because of his ingenious answer, but told him in no uncertain terms that he better not have a repeat, and to leave Cody alone. Cody was underweight and sickly in appearance. Inez Scott said that she thought he was "wormy," and that all he needed was a good dose of castor oil, her cure-all for most ailments.

People began coming into the community by foot, mule and wagon, or horseback, and a dilapidated vehicle or two. They were looking for a farm that they hoped had a decent house or barn that they could occupy during the cotton harvest. Some people brought their own shelters in the form of canvas tents. In wet weather they slept in the tent. In dry weather, they might just sleep in a wagon or on a truck bed.

Bud was sitting on the front porch of Turner's Store late one afternoon, looking into the setting sun across Cache River Ditch, and thinking about getting up and following it home, when across the bridge walked two people with the biggest and blackest dog Bud had ever seen—a middle-aged man, and a young girl about Bud's age. The man was walking slightly ahead of the girl. The girl was walking next to the dog with her right hand on the dog's head.

The man and girl were both dark complexioned with hollow eyes, prominent cheekbones and nose, and coal-black hair. They both were very thin, average height, and walked slightly stooped. They appeared near complete exhaustion. They were dressed in nothing but rags. The old man had on overalls with holes in each knee and a dingy blue cotton shirt, and he was wearing a straw hat. He was wearing worn-out brogan shoes. The girl had on torn and patched overalls, with the same kind of blue shirt and she was wearing a bonnet that hid most of her face. Her hair was woven into a single braid that was protruding from under the bottom edge of her bonnet down the middle of her back. She was barefoot.

The top of the dog's back appeared to be higher than the girl's belt, and its head was nearly as high as her shoulder. The dog's head was as big and square as a twenty-five pound block of ice. Its eyes were blood red, and were already glowing in the gathering twilight. There were twin saddlebags slung across its back.

Bud got to his feet as they crossed the bridge and approached the store porch. He didn't know if he should go inside, or if he should try to go around the group and start for home, but he decided that he wasn't getting off of the porch with that dog anywhere near, so he nonchalantly pretended he had further business in the store and went inside. Bud eased over to the shelves along the wall and pretended to be looking for something. Abe was in the back of the store near the meat box.

The old man came in and left the girl and the dog outside on the porch. Abe came up to greet the old gentleman. Bud eased over to the front window to get a better look at the girl and the dog. Abe, also, moved up near the front window and casually looked out to see what had Bud's attention. Abe gave the girl and dog a long look, especially the dog. The girl looked very tired. She didn't look like she weighed ninety pounds. She had sat down on the porch steps and had rested her head on her knees, dropping her hands to the ground. The dog stood directly in her front, facing her.

The old man addressed Abe. "My name is Blue Duck Smith, and thet's my gurl outside with the devil dog. Her name's Sally. Me and her 'ere looking for a place to pick some cotton this fall. Do ye know of anybody thet's a-needin' hands? We'all's hungry, too. We hain't 'et nothin' since this time yestiddy over near Black Rock."

"How'd you get this fur since yesterday?" Abe inquired, knowing Black Rock was thirty miles to the west.

"Walked."

"Walked all the way from Black Rock?"

"Yep. We're of Cherokee blood. We walk a lot."

"You got any money?" asked Abe.

"I got a quarter s'all," said the old man.

"Cotton ain't gonna be ready to pick for another week. How do you expect to live on a quarter for thet long?" Abe asked, straight to the point. He had heard this same story every fall, since he had been in the store business.

"On the kindness of the white man," Blue Duck replied, his black eyes flashing like fires in a cavern.

"Well, kindness don't pay the bills," said Abe. "But, I'll make you and the girl a baloney sandwich, and give you a drink, and then y'all have to go on down the road. There's a lot of sharecroppers lookin' for some fall help. Y'all just have to stop at some houses along the road and ask."

"Well, hit's gittin' dark now. I reckon we'll have to camp out som'meres, and start in the mornin'," said the old man.

"Well, you kin stay under the bridge or you can stay on my front porch, if yore a mind too, but y'all need to stay quite. How about thet dog?"

"The dog'll take care of hisself, I reckon," replied the old man. "You got cats?"

"Yeh, I got a bunch of cats round here," replied a puzzled Abe.

"The dog likes cats," said the old man.

"To eat?" asked Abe.

"There hain't no tother reason for a dog to like a cat, fur as I know. I've 'et cat myself," Blue Duck replied, with just a hint of a smile creasing his thin lips, revealing darkened and missing teeth.

"I've never had a cat roast myself," responded Abe, now caught up in the humor of the conversation. "How does it taste?"

"Purty much like skunk," replied Blue Duck, his face a dark blank.

Abe suddenly realized that the conversation with Blue Duck was not going to have any intelligent outcome, and that Bud was still in the store, and it was dark, and there was an awful big dog standing out front. "Bud, hadn't you better git on home?"

"Well, I was thinkin' bout it, but I didn't know bout thet dog," Bud replied.

"Thet dog'll not hurt ye, iffen you don't git to close to thet gurl," said the old man, in a voice with just a hint of malice.

Bud eased out the front door, and moved to the end of the porch nearest the ditch bridge. The girl never raised her head off of her knees, and Bud never did get a good look at her face. The dog never moved and never took his eyes off of her, and seemingly paid no attention to Bud at all, as he eased toward the bridge. Bud walked quietly across the bridge, trying not to attract any undue attention. When Bud got across the bridge, he looked back into the light coming from the store's front windows. The girl still hadn't moved from her position on the porch steps, but the dog had moved to the right of the porch and it was now staring intently into the darkness toward the sound of some quarreling tomcats.

Bud was barefoot, and the road was gravel, but he made the mile home in record time. Bud hit his front porch out of breath, and found Inez and Ellis at the supper table. Ellis never paid any attention to Bud, but Inez sensed his excitement.

"Where have you been, Teddy Bud?" Inez asked, as she employed the double nickname that only she used.

Bud related his recent encounter with the old man and the girl at Turner's Store, and he described their dog, and the fact that they were Cherokee Indians, or so the old man said.

"How old was the girl, Bud?" asked Ellis, suddenly interested.

"Bout' my age, I reckon."

"I've heard about 'em. The girl is his wife. He bought her from another Indian family when she was nine or ten years old. They come from around the Lafferty Creek area, up on White River, some thirty miles or so above Batesville."

"That little thing is his wife?" Bud asked, incredulously.

"Reckon so. Don't you have nothin' to do with 'em. The old man is dangerous, and so is thet dog."

The conversation ended on that note, because Inez had placed in front of Bud a plate of fried green tomatoes, fried okra, biscuits and white flour milk gravy, and a slice of sugar-cured ham. He wouldn't have time to talk for a while anyway.

The next morning Inez sent Bud back to Turner's Store, for a loaf of light bread and some bologna and brick cheese. When he got to the middle of the bridge spanning the ditch, he stopped and surveyed the scene. He was looking for any sign of the Cherokee couple and their dog. Then Bud saw Abe Turner standing on the west end of the store porch looking toward the near ditch bank.

"They're gone," Abe called out, when he spotted Bud standing on the bridge, anticipating his concern. Bud went on over the bridge to the porch.

"Have you noticed anything unusual?" asked Abe.

Bud looked around a moment; there wasn't a cat in sight. Usually, at that time of day one could see ten or so cats anywhere you looked. "Where are the cats?" Bud asked.

Abe chuckled and pointed toward an enormous cottonwood tree that stood on the bank of the ditch. The Cache River Ditch was nothing but a large man-made ditch, engineered for flood control back in the nineteen thirties, and when the construction crew dug through the area with the big draglines, they had cut the bank close to the cottonwood, but left it unharmed. The tree must have been close to a hundred-years-old. When the evening sun began to set, the big tree completely shaded the store.

The first limb on the tree was twenty-five feet up and was as big around as Bud was at the hips, and it hung perfectly horizontal. That one limb was lined with eighteen extremely nervous cats. They were apparently keeping a sharp eye out for the dog, which was long gone. Some were searching the brush along the ditch bank below. Some were looking toward the store and others were looking in every direction. One was even looking further up the tree, as if it expected the dog to somehow come from above. They showed no inclination to want to come down anytime soon. Abe said later, that they stayed in the tree for three days.

"I ain't seen the two big short-tail hybrids. I'm purty shore the dog got 'em. They wouldda been the ones to put up a scrap. I heard a couple of screams durin' the night and then bones crunchin'. I thank it's dog: two – cats: zero," said Abe.

Bud discovered a few days later that the Cherokee couple had settled in an abandoned shack at an old sawmill site, called by locals, the "peckerwood sawmill," about a half-mile south of Turner's Store. The Wilson family had operated the sawmill. The Wilsons had moved their operation about a mile east, and had set up a new camp. Bud was hoping that the Wilson family would move their logging operation even further east and make it harder for Elmo Wilson to get to Betty Adkins.

The shack was in the edge of a heavily wooded and swampy area. The Wilson family had cut roads into the woods in all directions, in order to drag the logs back out to the sawmill with their eight-mule teams. There was still a pile of sawdust at the sawmill site and a lot of wood pieces left lying around, even an outhouse. Bud and Joel had been in the vacant shack while hunting in the area the past winter. It had one room, about ten by ten feet, and there was an old cast-iron heating stove, with a flue that went through a sidewall. The shack was made of cypress, with a cypress-slab roof, and it appeared to have been watertight when Bud had looked inside. It wouldn't be a bad place to spend the cotton harvest.

The Wilson family, also, owned the half-mile of cultivated cotton ground between the northern edge of the woods and the Egypt-Bono road. Evidently, the Cherokees were going to pick cotton for old man Wilson.

Bud thought of the little Cherokee girl and old Blue Duck, and wondered how they were going to survive until they were able to earn some money picking cotton. Though great as his concern was for the girl, it did not equal his fear of the dog. Bud knew that he was not going anywhere near that sawmill shack while that dog was around. It was not Bud's nature to wish evil on anyone, but deep down he hoped that before the cotton harvest was over that the Cherokee's dog would maul Elmo.

Harvey Winkles, the movie man, was returning to Turner's Store. He would again show movies like he had the past fall. A movie theater company from Missouri was bringing in a large tent on a big flatbed truck, and Abe Turner would give them permission to set the tent up on the east side of the store in a grove of trees. Harvey Winkles, the company projectionist, would hook up a long electrical cord to one of Abe's outlets and plug in his projector, and he would show films at night for several weeks during the cotton harvest. It was something all of the community was excited about.

For ten cents, on any given night, one could see Tarzan, Lash LaRue, Hopalong Cassidy, Roy Rogers, Gene Autry, Charles Red Starrett, Bill Elliott, and horror films such as *Dracula, Frankenstein,* and *The Werewolf.* There were, also, newsreels, serials and cartoons. You could get world, and particularly war news from the *Movietone Newsreels* that alone was worth the ten-cent price of admission.

Harvey would also set up a full-size movie-house popcorn machine, and sell small white paper sacks of popcorn for a nickel. Abe Turner liked that aspect of it, because Abe knew that people who bought popcorn had to have a cold drink to go with it. Abe's drink sales soared during the picture shows, and too, the grownups bought Abe's groceries on their way home, and they paid cash. There soon would be a lot of jingle in everyone's pockets.

It was common practice for Harvey to do some practice runs after getting his projectors and sound equipment set up, so if someone happened to be present when he was checking everything out, they just might see a film for free. Bud found out from Abe what night he was going to do that, and Joel and Bud made sure that they were down at the store at the proper time. Bud didn't know if Homer had advanced notice, or if it was a coincidence, because he was present, also.

Harvey did a practice run-through of a movie, *Tarzan of the Apes.* It starred Johnny Weissmuller, a former Olympic swimming champion. They got to watch the whole thing, and were all impressed by how Tarzan could swim and whip crocodiles and such, and they were particularly impressed with the Tarzan yell, and after the movie, Homer, Joel and Bud got out on the road in front of the store and tried to imitate it, to the point that Abe Turner came out on the store porch and told them to shut up. He scolded Homer for carrying on so, saying it wasn't seemly for a man of the cloth. Homer, although, a self-ordained prophet and holy man, was just a big kid at heart.

Before they broke up and went their separate ways, Homer, sitting on the store porch, related information that the harlot, Mary Margaret Miller, was going to be baptized sometime soon, before the weather cooled. She was currently in residence on Horse Island with Homer and Roscoe, studying the Bible, and preparing for baptism and the assumption of the responsibilities of the Christian faith. Joel and Bud sat down next to Homer at this revelation, in startled anticipation of hearing more.

"What's a harlot exactly?" asked Joel.

"Same as a whore, but more biblical," replied Homer. "Me and Roscoe felt like since Mary Margaret had seen Jesus durin' my sermon, and had a religious conversion, that we should upgrade her title to one more fittin' a Christian woman."

Well it seemed to Bud and Joel to be the right thing to do. Homer went on.

"The thang that puzzles me, is how a harlot was able to see Jesus, but me, a holy man, and a prophet, among other thangs, was not able to see nothin'. Did y'all see anythang?" asked Homer.

"I never saw nothin' for the steam risin' off of Mary Margaret and Betty. They was on the floor in front of me. My eyes was burnin'," Bud replied.

"I was out at the horse trough soakin' my feet," said Joel.

"Well, Roscoe didn't see nothin' neither," continued Homer. "And he was more disappointed than I was, and he's got a right to be, cause he has been in the preachin' business longer. Roscoe said that it seems like people who try to see Jesus, never do, but there are others when not expectin' it, has Jesus step up and slap 'em right in the face."

"Where's the baptism goin' to take place?" Bud asked. He, for one, didn't want to miss it.

"I suspect that if the water in the ditch is as low as it is now, it will be right out there in that sandy hole just below the bridge," replied Homer, motioning toward the place where Joel and Bud had bailed off the bridge to wash away the results of their big cat caper. "We will want to make it convenient for the congregation."

They all just sat a moment in silence. A slight breeze was rustling the trees along the ditch bank. There was a half-moon, which meant rain, to the superstitious. The older Irish people leaned toward superstitions, Inez Scott more than most. When Bud was just a baby, she had wrapped him in a blanket and put him on the ground in front of the chicken house door and had run the chickens out over him, supposedly to ward off the chicken pox. It didn't work.

Bud always felt that the older Irish folks were superstitious because they had little education, and it was just ignorance on their part. Bud knew from his schooling, that the different phases of the moon were from shadows on the moon caused by sunlight passing the earth, and the shape of the shadow on the moon was dependent on how much sunlight got past the earth to reach the moon during the night. Bud noted that Homer was studying the sky intently.

"Whatcha lookin' at Homer?" Bud asked.

"Well, you know as a prophet, I need to be up on all the signs, and I've been readin' bout' the zodiac in a nineteen forty-one copy of *The Old Farmer's Almanac*, and I've got it down pretty good. The sun will rise at 5:30 a.m., and tomorrow will be a beautiful day. What does it say to you, Joel?" asked Homer.

"What it says to me," replied Joel, "is that any durned fool can tell that tomorrow is probably goin' to be a beautiful day, since there ain't a durned cloud in the sky."

"Well, I don't want to get in a battle of wits with you about the weather," replied Homer. "It's against my nature to fight an unarmed man." Joel did not respond immediately, wondering if he had been accidentally or intentionally insulted.

Bud heard a hoot owl call from down the ditch bank behind the store, and he heard the deep voice of a hound echoing up from the woods, to the south, in the direction of the Cherokee camp. It was time to head for home.

Homer had the same thought. "Well, I got to be goin'. It's almost time for Mary Margaret's next catechism class," said Homer, and he got up and walked across the road, north, toward Horse Island.

Joel and Bud got up and headed across the bridge for their homes. Bud was mulling over in his mind what a catechism class could be. Any word that had a cat in it couldn't be all that beneficial. Joel simply didn't care one way or the other, and began to whistle Dixie.

One of the hardest rains of the year fell during the night and all the next morning. It was still showering lightly as Bud made his way down to Turner's

Store, in the middle of the afternoon. So much for zodiac signs, he thought.

When he got to the ditch, he wasn't surprised to see that the water level had risen at least three feet from the day before. The water was rolling and muddy. The sky began to clear and a hot sun came out and the rain stopped, just as Bud crossed the bridge. Joel and Homer were already at the store sitting on the porch when Bud arrived. Joel was smiling, and he nodded toward Homer and winked at Bud. "Shore' is a purty day," drawled Joel.

Homer's mind was on other things at the moment and he ignored Joel's slight. "Boys, I've been thinkin' 'bout that Tarzan fellow and how he could swim, and I believe I kin beat him," said Homer.

"Well, you got an advantage," replied Joel. "You got more webs on your fingers and toes than a duck."

"Well, that is true I suppose. It's a God-given physical attribute, and I mean to use it to its fullest today. Boys, I intend to swim from here to the Egypt bridge!" exclaimed Homer, as he looked searchingly at both Joel and Bud, for any appearance of disbelief.

Bud remained stoic and noncommittal, having been through the pigeon fiasco. He didn't want to encourage any further acts of stupidity on Homer's or anyone else's part.

"How fur is it to the Egypt bridge?" asked Homer.

"Five miles," replied Joel.

"Well, the water should warm up with the sun comin' out like it has, and with the current, I believe I kin make it before dark."

"I believe you kin, too," replied Joel. "It'll give you a well-deserved reputation...if you kin do it."

"If I kin do it! Hell! I know I kin do it. It's just a matter of getting started," exclaimed Homer.

"Don't let us keep you," replied Joel, and he winked at Bud like he did the time he had talked Wally Owens into eating some dried chicken droppings, telling him that the white part of the chicken dropping tasted like vanilla, and the black—like chocolate. Wally had sampled both parts.

"What does it taste like, Wally?" Bud had asked.

"Tastes purty much like chicken shit to me," replied Wally.

Homer, without further discussion, went to the ditch, down the bank and under the bridge, and began to remove his clothes and rubber tire sandals. Homer was as naked as a jaybird and white as a Canada Snow Goose, when he slipped into the water and began long pulling strokes down stream. Joel and Bud watched from the bridge.

Both banks of the ditch were overgrown with large oak, willow, mulberry and cottonwood trees. In some cases the largest trees almost overlapped in mid-stream. It created a shady tunnel-like effect, and it wasn't long until Homer was just a white blur in the shadows, well down stream. It was then that Homer gave his first Tarzan yell. The high-pitched yodel echoed along the water and was just dying away, when off to the right the boys saw an airborne covey of quail and a prancing white-tailed deer that had been flushed off the ditch bank and out into the adjacent cotton patch.

Joel and Bud sat for a moment with their feet dangling off the edge of the bridge just savoring the moment. Joel, who was fourteen now, had taken out a can of Prince Albert tobacco and some cigarette papers and was rolling himself a smoke. He was pretty good at it, but he had to use both hands. He offered to roll one for Bud, but Bud declined. Bud was afraid that he might be seen by Abe, who might report it to his mother.

Bud wanted to smoke and chew tobacco like his buddy, Joel, but Inez had told him that if she ever caught him with tobacco in any form, which she considered to be the prime cause of consumption that she would use a switch on him in such a manner that the seat of his britches wouldn't hold corn shucks. Bud had been down that road a few times and he wasn't anxious to begin another trip.

He would occasionally sneak out to the grape arbor that grew along side the Scott garden, and cut off a piece of dried grapevine to smoke. He would light one end with a match and pretend he was smoking a cigarette, but all he got from smoking grapevines was smoke in his eyes and a blistered tongue.

Homer was now out of sight. They had not heard anymore Tarzan yells.

"Do you reckon Homer'll git to the Egypt bridge a-fore dark?" asked Joel.

"Well, I reckon so," Bud replied. "With the current being like it is and all."

"Bud, do ya know whut Homer is a-goin' to discover when he gits to the Egypt bridge?" asked Joel, with a chuckle in his voice.

Bud thought a second. "No, don't reckon as I do."

"He's gonna discover that he left all his clothes under this here bridge," replied Joel. "And he shore as hell ain't gonna be able to swim back upstream. He's gonna have to walk five miles back up here, in his birthday suit."

Rumors started surfacing in a day or so about a large white ape traveling north along the west bank of Cache River Ditch. No one got a real close look at the creature, although, Don McElrath, who farmed about three miles down stream, said his two beagle hounds, Shorty and Bully, had been hot on the trail of something along the ditch bank about sundown. Then there was a God-awful screeching, yodeling sound that came out of a growth of timber along the ditch that just about scared the two beagles to death. He said the dogs came back to him whimpering with their tails between their legs and refused to go back into the woods.

Speculation ran high around the county as to what the creature might be. Some said it was probably some type of big ape that had escaped from a circus somewhere. Don McElrath gave an exclusive interview to the Walnut Ridge newspaper, and an article appeared in the paper with a drawing of the creature as Don described it. The drawing depicted some sort of skinny long-armed, and long-legged alien creature, that Don said, "…was as white as the driven snow."

Don was guest speaker for several area church groups, and was interviewed on the radio by KBTM in Jonesboro, and KRLW in Walnut Ridge.

Bud went to one of his talks at the Little Brown Freewill Baptist Church, along with Inez, Ellis and Betty Adkins. Don told an interesting story. He was very animated and liked to describe how the creature bounded along at the edge of a field by the ditch bank. He even brought his two beagles into the church evidently in an effort to further liven up his demonstration of show and tell, and the poor little things had to endure an awful lot of cooing and petting from a bunch of total strangers, and when Don tried to imitate the creature's yell, the dogs began to whimper and ran under a church bench, and could not be coaxed out. When Don forcefully dragged them out by hand, Inez and Betty went up to Don and without a word, picked up both beagles and came back to their seats and held the dogs on their laps, and petted them, until Don's talk was over. Bud thought, what he wouldn't have given right then to have been Betty's beagle.

Joel, Homer and Bud were the only ones that ever knew what or who the creature was, and Homer swore the boys to secrecy upon the pain of their going immediately to hell, for revealing the shenanigans of a holy man. And when people gathered in Turner's Store and speculation began as to the origins of the creature, Bud and Joel speculated right along with everyone else.

CHAPTER 12

Roscoe Gilmore announced the date for the Harlot Mary Margaret Miller's baptism during the Sunday worship service at the Little Brown Freewill Baptist Church. It would take place the following Sunday afternoon. The prophet and seer, Homer Adkins would perform the baptismal ceremony.

Joel and Bud got a part in it. Homer asked them, as his disciples, if they would go to the blue hole right below the bridge at Turner's Store, just before the three o'clock start time and clear the water of turtles, snakes and particularly alligator gars.

Most folks and particularly kids had not previously been that concerned about jumping in one of the blue holes until word spread about what happened to old man Moses Collins.

Moses Collins was among a small group of local men, including Ellis Scott that got together the past summer to seine out some of the deeper holes along the ditch. In one deep blue hole, they trapped an alligator gar between the seine and the bank. The men all saw the fish close to the top of the water and knew it was large. Ellis said he believed it would have weighed close to seventy-five pounds, a monster by Cache River Ditch standards.

The gar has a bill that protrudes out several inches, resembling an alligator's jaws, and around the bill is a row of teeth as sharp as any knife. Gars are dangerous to handle in or out of the water because they throw their head from side to side and slash anything that gets in the way.

Moses had on a pair of overalls, with no shirt or shoes. The others in the fishing party were similarly dressed. As the men pulled the seine toward the bank, the big gar, which was poised close to the surface near the bank, clearly visible, and facing the incoming net, suddenly made a dash for freedom toward the center of the seine that was being held by Moses. The gar knifed through the mesh of the seine, right between Moses' legs, tearing the straddle out of his blue denim overalls, and removed some pretty important body parts that

Moses had not expected to lose on such short notice.

Moses leaped into the air and screamed like a panther, and then he made a mad dash out of the water, and up and over the ditch bank. When the other fishermen finally caught up to him, he was found standing out in a cotton patch next to the ditch, holding his bleeding privates and according to Ellis Scott, "Shaking like a dog shittin' peach seeds."

The crowd had already begun to gather at Turner's Store, seeking refreshments, when Joel and Bud took some long poles down on either side of the ditch and began to yell and beat the water in the blue hole, where in the deepest part, towards the middle of the ditch, the water was chest deep on the average person. The hole was about thirty feet across, and about thirty feet long, running from just below the bridge to a sand bar that ran completely across the ditch, so that the water passing over the sand bar was no more than a foot deep.

There seemed to be very little marine life in the blue hole. Bud saw a couple of turtles exit through the shallows over the sand bar down stream. Joel said he saw some kind of water snake and a few minnows over where he was, but nothing significant.

There was a trail leading down the bank on the west side of the ditch to a broad sandy bank. Joel and Bud went right over and staked out a spot next to the water so they would have a front row seat, so to speak. The bridge, twenty feet above, and without any protective railing, was beginning to line with spectators, mostly older boys and men. The Wilson brothers were there as well as several strangers. Some came from Bono, others from Egypt, and the Morgan triplets were there from Sedgwick. The word of Mary Margaret's baptism had evidently been passed along to a lot of her friends and admirers.

A couple of cars eased by the spectators on the bridge and parked over by the store. Some wagon teams parked along the road on the west side of the ditch, and presently a number of members and friends of the congregation of the Little Brown Freewill Baptist Church began filing down the bank and lining up behind Joel and Bud. Inez and Ellis Scott had chosen not to attend. Betty Adkins attended, but viewed the proceedings from the top of the ditch bank, to the rear of the congregation, the point from where Mary Margaret would make her appearance.

Abe Turner came down to the edge of the water and faced toward the congregation. He would lead the hymn singing. Preacher Roscoe Gilmore came down and stood next to Abe. He would lead the congregation in prayer. Homer came down to the water's edge wearing the same robe that he had worn the Sunday that he had preached; the day that Mary Margaret had her religious conversion, or as Ellis Scott put it, "religious convulsion." Homer stood beside Roscoe. Homer would perform the baptism.

There was some hushed whispering that elicited giggles among the congregation. One woman was overheard to say in a fairly loud whisper, that she didn't think that there was enough water out there to do the trick, and that she thought Mary Margaret probably needed to be anchored under water overnight.

Upon a signal from Abe, the crowd hushed. Then Abe led the congregation in a hymn. Some of the boys on the bridge joined in and kept time by slapping the bridge with their hands. Bud thought that they all did an admirable job, even though Abe kept casting scolding glances upward over his right shoulder toward the distant drummers.

A prayer from Roscoe Gilmore followed the hymn. Roscoe mentioned Mary Margaret's name several times, and the fact that a chariot of glory was coming for her soul and would be arriving any minute. Upon the cessation of the prayer, and as if the movement had been rehearsed, Homer began backing out into the water toward the middle of the blue hole. When he got to what he thought was the proper depth, he held his arms up towards the crowd and said in a loud voice, that caused Bud to involuntarily flinch, "Mary Margaret Miller, come forth and be baptized in the bosom of Jesus!" Bud and Joel turned and looked back up the bank, in anticipation of witnessing the appearance of Mary Margaret.

The crowd parted as if upon command, and then Mary Margaret became visible standing on the top of the bank, dressed in a white shroud. Actually she was wrapped in a thin white sheet held together with a single safety pin over one shoulder, the other shoulder was bare. The evening sun had dropped to a point to where Mary Margaret was standing between it and the congregation below. Mary Margaret was not wearing any underwear, which was made fairly obvious when the sun X-rayed her through the thin sheet. Bud and Joel stood in unison at this revelation.

"Holy Mary, Mother of God," said Roscoe in hushed tones of astonishment and admiration. He involuntarily crossed himself. "My God, he's Catholic," said a female voice in the congregation. Murmurs ran through the crowd. The women cast knowing glances at one another. A smattering of applause, and some hoots were heard coming from the spectators on the bridge. The rapture that everyone talked so much about in church, but which no one could ever explain, had evidently overtaken most of the men present, for they just stared and appeared stunned, like a duck that had been hit on the head with a stick. Mary Margaret made her way slowly down the sandy bank and through the crowd. You could have heard a pin drop.

"Come to me my child," rasped Homer.

Mary Margaret stuck a tentative toe in the water and seemed momentarily to recoil, but Homer with outstretched arms and pleading pink eyes, beckoned. Mary Margaret eased into the water and out to Homer, who took her by the hand. The water was just up to her ample chest.

There was a sharp contrast between the baptiser and the baptisee. Homer, six-feet, four inches tall, extremely thin, with shoulder-length white hair, and snow-white , pink-eyed features, stood tall over the five-foot, four inch, dark haircd and voluptuous Mary Margaret. Mary Margaret had fairly large and well-developed breasts that were the envy of many of the half-starved, flat-chested sharecropper wives. Her complexion was creamy and smooth. She spent a lot of time in bed and out of the sun. "Every time I seed her, she allus seems well-rested," said a woman in the congregation.

Mary Margaret was well fed too. On her dates, she usually required that her companion of the moment escort her to Main Street in Jonesboro, to Chuck's Cafe. Chuck's Café was a narrow, long, shotgun establishment that served tasty cheeseburgers, good chili, and a variety of malted milks, of which Mary Margaret was so fond. At Chuck's, she was known as a "regular."

Mary Margaret reached a depth in the water so that her buoyant breasts were pushed by the water up and out against the restraining sheet. "Floaters," whispered Joel, loud enough to elicit giggles from some women parishioners, sitting behind Bud and him.

The Baptist Church ritual of baptism varied somewhat from preacher to preacher. It seemed to Bud that the main objective of baptism was not to get yourself drowned. Homer put his left arm around Mary Margaret's waist. The she put her left hand over her mouth, while pinching her nose together with thumb and forefinger. She then placed her right hand over the left for additional support. Homer then placed his right hand over both her hands, which was the standard Baptist baptismal grip.

The standard method of baptism at this point was for the preacher to offer a short prayer, the length dependent upon the coolness of the water, and then to lay the convert back into the water for a short dunk three times, once each, for the Father, Son, and Holy Ghost. Some preachers just dunked once for all three. Preacher Gilmore was of the triple-dipper school of baptism, and Homer was his prophet.

Homer omitted the prayer and went straight to the dunking. "I baptize you in the name of the Father," intoned Homer, and he laid Mary Margaret back into and under the water. When he brought her back up, her shroud had been pulled off her shoulder, so both of her shoulders were now bare. Mary Margaret nor Homer appeared to have noticed.

"In the name of the Son," said Homer, for dip number two.

When Mary Margaret came up the second time there was no sign of the shroud.

"She's nekkid as a jay bird," whispered Joel.

A murmur ran through the crowd. Homer with his eyes shut, and Mary Margaret with her eyes full of water still hadn't noticed her naked state of affairs.

"And in the name of the Holy Ghost," said Homer, and he dipped Mary Margaret for the third time. The rising of a new soul from baptism was probably never so greatly anticipated by so many.

When Homer pulled Mary Margaret up for the third time, he looked down and suddenly realized the naked truth. Some, in attendance, said later that several expressions crossed his face. Bud and Joel weren't looking at Homer.

Mary Margaret stood bare breasted facing the congregation. Both nipples had acquired a bluish hue. The golden globes with a single blue eye were bobbing in the water, winking at the congregation on the bank.

"Wouldja lookit thet," said Joel.

"Amazin'," replied Bud.

It was when she began blowing water out of her nose and was wiping her eyes that Mary Margaret looked down to discover her shroud was missing. She let out a shriek that echoed along the ditch and energized Homer who had been frozen in shock. Elmo Wilson fell off the bridge.

"For God's sake, sing somethin'!" shouted Homer, and then he baptized Mary Margaret a fourth time, and he went under with her. He would say later that he was groping for the shroud, although Mary Margaret said that he was groping something else.

Mary Margaret who had been caught by surprise by this last unscheduled dunking had neglected to take a breath. The water was boiling and occasionally a body part would surface and go under again. Mary Margaret was being drowned by a panicky preacher, while the congregation on the bank had broken into a rendition of, "Down by the Riverside."

Miss Ava Goodman was a big woman. Six-foot-three inches tall and weighed in at an estimated two hundred-forty pounds. She was the only woman in any church that anyone could remember, ever having attended, who sang bass. She had never married for obvious reasons.

"Best man in the county," Ellis Scott said of Miss Ava, but making sure she never heard him. "She is as ugly as sin," someone once remarked. Someone else had remarked that, "She fell out of the ugly tree and hit every branch on the way down." Inez Scott, who was more charitable, than most, once said of Miss Ava, "Bless her heart, she can't help being ugly, but she could've stayed at home."

Suddenly, above the singing of the choir, Miss Ava's basso boomed out.

"That fool Homer is a-drownin' that gurl!"

And without further hesitation, Miss Ava stormed off the bank and into the duel going on under the water; Mary Margaret trying to surface, and Homer trying to keep her under until he could find the lost shroud.

Miss Ava reached down in the water and grabbed hold of Homer with one hand, and Mary Margaret with the other, and with a heave stood them both straight up. She held on to Mary Margaret with her left hand and then hit Homer with a beautiful right-cross to the jaw, dropping him like he had been poleaxed. He went down and under for another unscheduled dunk.

"There it is!" someone yelled out in the congregation, and everyone looked around where some people were pointing toward the shroud that had washed up on the sand bar a few yards down stream.

"I'll get it," said Joel. He was barefoot anyway. He ran down to the sand bar, pulled up the legs of his overalls and waded out to retrieve the sheet. He then rolled it up into a ball and threw it out to where Miss Ava was holding on to a sobbing and blubbering Mary Margaret and was trying to shield her from hundreds of prying eyes that was focused on her from both sides of the river and from the bridge above.

Bud was embarrassed for Mary Margaret because of all the heathen laughter and hand clapping, and whistling that was coming from the boys on the bridge. Bud was disappointed that Elmo Wilson, who had fallen into fairly shallow water wasn't hurt. Elmo was now climbing up out of the ditch toward the opposite bank, and was getting hoorawed by the bridge party. Miss Ava finally got the wet sheet wrapped around Mary Margaret and with one arm around her, walked her back toward the congregation.

Roscoe, who now seemed suddenly energized, and wanting to be helpful went into the water toward Miss Ava and the struggling Mary Margaret.

"Get away from me, you drunken sot!" shrieked an obviously distraught Mary Margaret. "And go drown yourself with that feeble-minded, albino bastard!"

Roscoe knew how to take a hint as well as anyone, and he veered off down stream where Homer, face down, had washed up in the shallows of the sand bar.

Miss Ava, upon reaching the ditch bank, took Mary Margaret by the hand and led her through the crowd and up the path to top of the bank. She told some of the ladies as they passed by that she would take Mary Margaret home with her, as none of Mary Margaret's family were in attendance.

The crowd began to break up and head for Turner's Store for refreshments. Bud and Joel were the last of the gathering to leave, and when they had walked up the path to the top of the bank, Bud looked back to see that Roscoe had managed to pull Homer upon the sand bar and had him sitting upright. Homer was gagging and spitting water, and he was shaking his head like he was trying to get his bearings. Homer, it seemed, would live another day, to continue his service to the people in the wilderness.

CHAPTER 13

Joel and Hazel Adkins, and Bud and Ellis Scott were going to town. Abe
Turner asked if they wanted to ride to Walnut Ridge with him in his pickup
truck. He was going to go to a wholesale market to pick up some grocery
items for his store and conduct other business that would take a few hours.
During that time Joel and Bud could take in the afternoon one o'clock movie
at the Main Street Theater. Ellis and Hazel were going to a hardware store to
look for some of the new-fangled spring-operated cotton scales, hoping to get
away from the old-fashioned balance scales that used a combination of peas,
or iron weights.

Inez had made up a sack of fried bologna sandwiches, with mustard, dill
pickle and a thick slice of white onion. It was a fifteen-mile ride on rough
gravel roads all the way to town, and would take about an hour to get there.
Ellis and Hazel rode in the cab with Abe. Joel and Bud rode in the back. The
sandwiches didn't last halfway to town. Even Abe joined in on the treat.

Main Street in Walnut Ridge, and a couple of cross streets were paved
with red bricks. The other side streets were mostly gravel. There had been
some articles in the local paper suggesting that after the war, perhaps some
of the main county roads might be paved, but nobody believed it, because
nobody believed it was possible to make that many bricks.

Abe let everyone out on Main Street near the theater. He said to watch
for him in about three hours, and then he left to conduct his business. Ellis and
Hazel walked down the street toward a hardware store. Ellis told Bud and
Joel not to wander off when they came out of the movie, but to hang around
the front of the theater so they could be easily found when Abe was ready to
go home.

The town was bustling with activity. People were wandering up and down
Main Street, which was the longest street in town. Walnut Ridge also had a
courthouse square, which was typical for southern towns that had originated

in the last century. The founders of new towns usually built the courthouse first on a square lot. The main thoroughfare usually ran in front of the courthouse, and streets were laid on both sides and rear; then businesses lined up around the square. Main Street in Walnut Ridge ran east and west, passing in front of the Court House. The post office was also on Main Street just west of the courthouse.

Also, on Main Street, past the post office was the funeral home that had passed out the cardboard fans to the area churches. There was a heavy black power line that ran off a pole into the funeral home. Bud supposed that was the line to the telephone that they had bragged about in the advertising on the fans.

Joel and Bud were just standing gawking around at everything waiting for the movie to start, when they looked down the street and saw several people lined up at a wooden barrel on the sidewalk. The boys meandered down to have a look. The barrel had a canvas cover over a hole at the top, and there was a seedy looking fellow who seemed to be in charge. A hand drawn sign stated: LOOK AT RARE RED BAT FROM SOUTH AMERICA, 10 CENTS.

They watched as a man gave a dime to the man in charge, who then carefully pulled the canvas cover back, and let the man look down into the barrel. The man stared down in the barrel for a couple of seconds, wiped his eyes and looked a second time, and then with a strange little smile walked away without a word. The boys watched as one after the other paid their ten cents, looked in the barrel, and without a word to anyone walked away.

Joel and Bud had fifty cents apiece, which was just enough to get them into the movie and have enough left over for a drink and a bag of popcorn. Bud didn't feel like he had an extra dime to waste on looking at a bat, but he sure would like to have seen it. According to a large clock in the front window of a drug store it was about time for the movie to begin, so Joel and Bud scurried back to the theater to buy their tickets.

There were some Negroes, who got in line with them to buy tickets. Now it was a rare thing for Horse Island boys to view a Negro up close, as there weren't any black folks out in the county. No Negroes went to any of the county schools or churches as far as anyone knew, and the only time Bud or Joel saw a black person was when they went to town. Their teachers never said anything about the Negroes, and there was nothing in any of their books about them. Although, one of the teachers had mentioned that a black man from Alabama had invented peanut butter. Bud liked peanut butter and he had been curious about black people ever since he was five years old. That was when his mother had given him a *Little Black Sambo* coloring book. That was the book that showed Little Black Sambo being chased around a tree by tigers so fast that the tigers eventually turned into syrup and the syrup was then poured on pancakes and eaten by Little Black Sambo. It was one of Bud's favorite books, and he still had it.

Bud wanted to talk to a Negro boy his own age just to see how he sounded. Joel said he had heard a black shoeshine boy in Jonesboro one time talking to a barber in the doorway of a barbershop. Joel said the barber carried on a conversation with him just like anyone else, and seemed to understand him all right, but Joel said he didn't seem to speak the same language as everyone else.

Joel said that the shoeshine boy, who was really a grown man, owned his own car, and Bud had seen one other black man driving an old truck down Main Street in Walnut Ridge. But no one that Bud knew ever saw any of the black folks working in the fields, and he thought it strange that they didn't seem to have jobs, but they owned cars. The sharecroppers that Bud knew couldn't afford an automobile. Only the farm owners or store owners, like Abe, was able to afford one.

Joel and Bud bought their tickets and went into the theater lobby and there was a side door that read: "COLORED ONLY," leading to the balcony. Beside the door was a water fountain that had the same "COLORED ONLY" sign. Bud wanted to go up into the balcony and said something about it to the girl selling popcorn, but she said—no, that the balcony was reserved for only colored people.

The boys bought their popcorn and a fountain drink at the concession stand in the lobby, and went down towards the front of the theater. The lights in the theater were still on and Bud looked back around towards the balcony, which was only about half full of colored men, women and children. Bud said something to Joel about the fact that there seemed to be plenty of room upstairs, but Joel said he had rather sit closer to the screen, so Bud dropped the subject.

The movie was a cowboy and Indian shoot-em-up, and they had a colored man as a cook on a chuck wagon, and he had a couple of funny scenes, particularly when the mules pulling the chuck wagon had a runaway during a stampede. Bud heard laughter and hand-clapping coming from the balcony, and it got him to thinking about why coloreds were so privileged. They didn't have to work in the fields, they owned cars, they had their own water fountains, they had good parts in movies, and they had the best seats in the theater from

117

which to watch the movie. Not only that, but as he found out later, they had their own bathroom upstairs, and that was the best deal of all. Bud couldn't get used to the bathrooms in the theater. He loved to go in there and flush the toilets and urinals. It just didn't seem fair to Bud that the colored and city folks had so much more than his family did, but he thought that must be the price one had to pay for being a sharecropper.

The newsreel, cartoon and movie lasted about an hour-and-a-half, so it was two-thirty, when they came out of the theater. Bud had heard that Homer's picture was on a wanted poster down at the post office. So since they had about thirty minutes to kill, the boys ran down there to see if it was true.

Sure enough, hanging on the wall was a poster with a real good likeness of Homer. It was just inside the front door in a little lobby. The picture on the poster showed Homer in an army uniform. The poster was hanging right up there with several other criminals, wanted for bank robbery, murder, and of all things, robbing a post office.

Homer's poster gave his description, to include the fact that he was an albino, and that he was a deserter from the United States Army, and that there was a thirty-dollar reward for information leading to his capture. It went on to relay that if anyone knew his whereabouts to notify the Lawrence County Sheriff's Office.

"I wonder, how come nobody has turned him in?" asked Bud.

"Well, I suspect not to many people on Horse Island know about this reward business for one thang," answered Joel. "And too, I don't thank to many people are goin' to turn in a holy man—someone connected to a church. If they was too, I thank they'd live to regret it—continually."

"Or more'n likely, not live long to regret it," stated Bud.

Joel and Bud started back to the theater. They stopped momentarily in front of the courthouse and continued the discussion as to what would happen to Homer if he was caught. Somewhere Bud had read, or seen in a newsreel or newspaper, that deserters in time of war were executed usually by a military firing squad. In the ensuing discussion as to whether it would be better to be shot or hung, Bud remembered hearing about an old gallows that was in the attic of the Walnut Ridge Court House, and that it was around nineteen twenty-nine, when the last man was hung up there. The boys decided then and there that they had to see it.

They went inside the courthouse and walked down a hallway to the center of the building and climbed the stairs up to the second floor. They were walking up and down the hallway, peering into some offices and into the courtroom itself, when finally a man came out of one of the offices, and Bud asked him about the gallows and the possibility of their seeing it. He was very helpful, and told them where to look for the door to the attic stairs, and then he said with a sly little smile that it was a well-known fact that the ghosts of those having been hung up there were still—and he paused—hanging around. He chuckled at his own little joke and then he went on down the hallway. His revelation that ghosts, "were still hanging around," had somewhat of a dampening affect on the boys' enthusiasm for seeing the gallows up close. Joel said that he wondered if they had time since Abe would be along any minute.

The possibility of seeing something grisly overcame any trepidation that Bud might have been experiencing at the time, so he headed for the door to the attic.

"You lead the way, since you thought of it," said Joel.

"You ain't skeered are ye?" asked Bud, in his best bravado.

"No, I ain't skeered. They ain't no sich thangs as ghosts, no way," replied Joel, with a voice tinged with anger at the suggestion that his courage was being called into question.

Bud was leading the way when they reached the top of the stairs and stepped out onto the heavy wooden planked floor of the attic. In the center of a large room that ran the width and length of the courthouse, stood the gallows, just like they had seen in the cowboy movies. It had thirteen steps going up to a platform that was eight feet above the floor of the attic. The gallows had a heavy crossbeam from which to hang the noose, but the rope was missing. There was a trap door hanging down from the floor of the platform—the trap thrown. The air was heavy with dust particles. There was some light coming through two small side windows, the windows being heavily coated with cobwebs and dust. The attic was full of shadows and was more than a little spooky.

"I wish they'd left the rope," said Bud. "I'd like to see how they tied it. It's supposed to have thirteen loops in the knot."

"Bud, we'd better go meet Abe," said Joel, who was hanging back close to the stairwell.

"We've got a little time. Let's climb up on the platform," Bud replied jauntily. "I'd like to look out on what the condemned man sees just before they drop him through the trap."

Bud was trying to steady his own nerves that suddenly surfaced in the form of goose bumps on his arms. He could feel the hair begin to stand up on the back of his neck. He tentatively placed his right foot on the first of the steps leading up to the gallows platform. It creaked slightly.

Suddenly, there was a rustling movement that froze Bud in his tracks. Joel standing behind Bud, attempted to make a run for the stairwell, but found that he was unable to make his legs work. An apparition suddenly set bolt upright on the platform and swung its legs over the side. It was an old black man, who looked to be a thousand-years-old in the dim light. He had snow-white hair, and in the dim light all the boys could see was his outline, and the whiteness of his teeth, hair and eyeballs.

"Can't an ole' niggah' git some rest?" said the apparition.

Joel was facing the gallows platform and was standing between Bud and the top of the stairwell leading down to the second floor. He couldn't get turned around before Bud squalled out and ran over him and plunged down the stairs. Bud was clawing at the doorknob at the bottom of the stairs when Joel, who had received a sudden burst of energy, crashed into him, knocking him down and away from the door. Joel clawed the door open and ran out, leaving Bud behind, still inside the stairwell. Bud leaped to his feet and scrambled through the door into the rear of the second floor. Joel was nowhere in sight, having already passed down the next flight of stairs to the first floor. By the time that Bud could get outside the front door of the courthouse, Joel was already across the street and down in front of the theater. He was bent over trying to get his breath.

Ellis Scott and Hazel Adkins were standing with Joel, and had broken into laughter at Joel's blubbering about a ghost that was on the gallows in the attic of the courthouse. Bud arrived just in time to hear Ellis say, "That was probably old Uncle Henry. He's the janitor at the courthouse, and he's been known to slip off up in the attic during the day to catch a little nap. Nobody usually bothers him up there. You boys didn't have no business up there no way."

Abe came driving up right on time, parked and got out of the truck. He looked back down the street to where there were still a few people lined up at the barrel that supposedly contained a South American red bat. People were still handing the seedy-looking fellow a dime for a peek at the creature. He would cautiously pull back the canvas cover. They would take a quick look into the barrel, sometimes doing a double take, and then walk away without a word.

"You fellas get a look at that bat?" asked Abe.

None of them had, or didn't admit to it.

"Well, it's just as well that y'all ain't wasted your money," said Abe. "'Cause

I got a good look at it when he had the thang over at Jonesboro. It's just a loose brick out of the street. It's a red brickbat. Now it might be from South America, I don't know, but that's the way that fellow makes his livin'. He goes from town to town sittin' up on a street corner, usually on a Saturday. The sheriff'll prob'ly be after him before sundown. He'll leave here tonight and go set up in Pocahontas or Newport or some other town where he ain't been before. He says it beats choppin' cotton."

Ellis and Hazel crawled into the cab of Abe's truck, and Joel and Bud squeezed into the back among the boxes of wholesale goods that Abe had bought. They got home after a bumpy ride of about an hour, to find Dovey Adkins and little Claude at the Scott house, standing on the front porch with Inez. Dovey Adkins immediately came off the porch toward the truck, a worried look on her face. Betty was missing she said.

CHAPTER 14

Abe had put the truck in gear and was about to go on to his store. However, when Dovie Adkins stated loud enough for all to hear that Betty was missing, Abe cut the engine and got out of the truck to hear the details.

Dovie said she had missed Betty early in the morning just after Hazel and Joel started to the Scott house for the trip to Walnut Ridge. Her first thought, she said, was that Betty had gone fishing, but after a while she went into Betty and Little Claude's bedroom and discovered Betty's clothes were missing along with an old cardboard suitcase. Betty's little black purse was gone, too, and Dovie said she knew that the purse contained fifteen dollars or so that Betty had saved from money earned chopping cotton. Little Claude said that he had not seen Betty since he woke up. Dovie said that she went to the ditch, walked up and down the bank calling out to Betty, but got no response. "I believe she has run off with that Elmo Wilson," she said.

Abe said, "Hazel, why don't you get back in the truck. We'll go by the store and unload, and I'll take you on over to the Wilson house and see what they know about it."

Mr. Adkins told Joel to come along, too, and they loaded back up and drove off. Bud would have liked to have gone, because he couldn't bear the thought of Elmo Wilson running off with Betty. Bud hoped that Mr. Adkins would catch Elmo and give him a sound thrashing. However, Bud thought that it really wasn't any of his business, and anyway about the time that they were leaving, Bud caught a good whiff of what he thought to be the aroma of vegetable soup coming from the kitchen, and he, also, correctly identified the vague aroma of freshly baked yeast rolls of which he was so fond. Bud really couldn't have gone anywhere right then, anyway.

Inez invited Dovie Adkins and Little Claude to stay for a while and have some soup and rolls. Little Claude ate six of the big yeast rolls and that aggravated Bud, because he only got two, and it meant that there wouldn't be any left for later. Dovie Adkins was embarrassed about it, but Inez laughed and kept encouraging Little Claude to eat all he wanted, and evidently Little Claude wanted them all.

After supper, Dovie and Little Claude started back down through the field to their house. Bud was chagrined to observe that the four-year-old was holding his stomach, and he thought to himself that it wouldn't bother him a bit if Little Claude came down with a really bad belly ache.

Ellis and Bud went to the barn to feed and water the stock and milk the cow. Inez went out to tend to her chickens. As they were approaching the barn, Ellis stopped suddenly and stood still—listening. Bud stopped to listen, too. There was the faint sound of baying from a running hound about a mile south of the house; the sound of the deep voice wafted upon a slight southerly breeze. It was somewhat unusual to hear a hound running in daylight.

"I don't recognize that dog, but it's big," said Ellis.

People that hunted and kept hounds reached a point where they could not only identify their own dogs, but other people's dogs as well. The running of dogs at night was a joyful noise to the hunter. There was excitement about building a fire in the woods; sitting around drinking coffee from a thermos while listening to the dogs baying; debating as to what game the dogs were running, because the tempo and beat of their baying changed according to whether they were running a coon, possum, fox or deer. It was also a matter of pride among hunters as to whose dog was leading the pack. It was the music of the hounds that caused normally sensible people to spend hours in the dead of a winter night, braving sub-freezing temperatures, lolling about a campfire while melting ice and snow pelted down from the tree limbs above.

"I wonder if that's the Cherokee Devil Hound." Bud ventured. Bud thought that he was the first to give the dog that name, and it stuck. When the subject of the hound came up in conversation afterward, whether at Turner's Store or any gathering, it was always referred to as the Cherokee Devil Hound.

"I think yore probably right," replied Ellis, and he knew immediately to which dog Bud was referring. "I don't like the idee of thet dog bein' on this side of the ditch. You and Joel, and anybody else, for thet matter, had better be careful when yore down round the ditch with thet dog on the loose. If he comes up close to the house, here, I'm goin' to have to kill him. May have to anyway."

Ellis didn't elaborate, and Bud didn't need to ask. Bud knew all to well the reason for his statement. Dogs as big as the Cherokee Devil Hound, running loose, could be a danger to man and beast, especially if it happened to get into a scrape with another dog mad with rabies, and there were a lot of mad dogs running loose in that country. Ellis always vaccinated his dogs against rabies, but a lot of people who kept dogs didn't. If a dog like the Cherokee Devil Hound became infected, the whole community would be in danger.

Once when Bud was walking home from Turner's Store, he had met a mad dog in the road. He saw it coming toward him from a quarter of a mile away, walking to the side of the road. It was stumbling and weaving, like it was drunk. Bud had been told that rabies made dogs go blind, and if you saw what you thought was a dog mad with rabies, to move to the opposite side of the road and stand very still until it passed.

Bud did better than that. He jumped a five-foot wire fence with a single strand of barbed-wire across the top. The fence separated the adjoining cotton field from the county road. The strange thing was—that later—he couldn't remember how he had gotten over the fence. Bud stood in the field and watched from behind the fence as the dog came on. As it drew near, he could see that it was foaming at the mouth, and he could hear it making low growling sounds. It had all the signs of being blind and mad. The dog carried its head low, and it seemed not to have seen or smelled Bud, as it passed on down the road toward Turner's Store. Bud had never known such fear. He only hoped that the dog couldn't smell it.

Abe, Hazel, and Joel, upon arriving at the Wilson house, were met on the porch by Mr. Wilson, and his oldest son, Charlie. Charlie Wilson had been described by uncharitable people as being "crazy as a bat," since being kicked in the head by a mule when he was three years old. Mr. Wilson sent Charlie to school at Bono, until he was sixteen, but the parents of the other third grade students complained so much about the older boy being in class with their children that the principal was given an ultimatum by the school board: "Either Charlie goes up, or you go out." The principal went to Mr. and Mrs. Wilson, and asked them about taking Charlie out of school, because letting Charlie just sit in the back of the classroom and whittle on a stick all day was not gaining anyone anything. So Charlie left school and became a full-time hand, working in the Wilson's cotton fields and peckerwood sawmill.

The Craighead County Selective Service Draft Board, had long ago given up on the twenty-two-year-old Charlie, but according to Mr. Wilson, Elmo had received a letter two weeks previous, telling him to report for an induction interview. Elmo, who did not possess the patriotic fervor of many the county citizens, had stated publicly that, "I ain't goin' in no army!"

Mr. Wilson said that he thought he had persuaded Elmo to change his mind. He appealed to him to do the right thing and enlist, if he was eligible. So before sunup that morning, Elmo had saddled up the Wilson's little smoky-gray mule, indicating that his intention was to ride the mule to Bono, a distance of about four miles, tie the mule up behind the bus station, and catch the bus coming through from Walnut Ridge, or catch some other ride into Jonesboro, and report to the draft board.

Mr. Wilson said that was where he thought Elmo had gone, and he figured it would be late by the time that Elmo could catch a ride back to Bono, and get the mule and come home. But, Mr. Wilson said, he didn't know anything about the whereabouts of the Adkins girl, and had in fact never, to his recollection, ever laid eyes on her.

Abe loaded up Hazel and Joel, and started for Bono. Abe said that he figured if Elmo had gone to the draft board that they would meet him on the road on his way home. But there was no Elmo to be met. They went straight to the bus station, and the little mule was tied up where Elmo said he would leave it. On a hunch, Abe went inside and asked the lady ticket agent if she knew Elmo, and had he bought a ticket earlier in the day to Jonesboro. The ticket agent said that indeed Elmo had bought two tickets, but not to Jonesboro. He bought two one-way tickets to Chicago, and he boarded the bus with a pretty blonde girl carrying an old cardboard suitcase. Elmo had stated that they were married and that they were going to Chicago to work in a defense plant. The lady ticket agent went on to say that she hoped that everything went well for the young couple, and that they got settled soon.

"Why do you say that?" Abe had asked.

"Because the girl, in my estimation, has been pregnant for some time," replied the woman.

The countryside was a paradox of nature in late August. The cotton fields lining the county roads turned snow white as the Big Boll Rowden cotton swelled out of the drying husks and blew up into big balls of cotton candy. The smell of the ripened cotton, combined with the withered husks and the dead leaves of the cotton stalk permeated the air. There was no escaping the aroma of the cotton field. It followed you down the road to the store, it went with you to church, and it slept in your bed at night. As far as the eye could see, the fields were as white as snow. It looked like Christmas in August.

It was revival time for several churches in, or near, the Horse Island community. The beginning of the fall season and the cotton harvest was the perfect time to rejuvenate the spirit, to commune with nature and God, outside, in a beautiful arboreal setting.

Starting back in nineteen thirty-eight, an annual revival, not restricted to any particular church, was held in a grove of trees about fifty yards east of Turner's Store. Usually, different preachers from around the county would alternate leading services for the six nights the revival would be conducted.

Before electrical wires were strung along county roads, kerosene lanterns hung from tree limbs produced light for the revival. Several local churches provided pews or wooden benches for the congregation. The Little Brown Freewill Baptist Church provided the lectern or pulpit.

Roscoe Gilmore, Little Brown's preacher, would speak at one of the services. Roscoe did not feel Homer was ready, after his initial offering, to conduct a multi-denominational service. However, Homer would assist Roscoe, and possibly offer some guidance on the meanings of certain words as well as geographical references, because Roscoe was seriously geographically challenged. That became apparent, when, during one sermon, he placed the Jordan River on the Continent of Africa, with Alexandria, Egypt, on its banks. When he was politely asked by one of the parishioners, after the service, if he didn't mean the Nile River, Roscoe had replied, no, that the Nile River, he believed ran into the Mississippi, just north of St. Louis. He said that he had heard somewhere that a man named Lewis Clark had traveled up the Nile early last century in an effort to find the Pacific Ocean, and that he had been assisted in that effort by some Indians with black feet.

Events were coming together. Some farmers near Bono had already started picking cotton. The arbor revival would begin on the following Sunday night, and run for six nights, ending on Friday. Ellis Scott would start picking cotton the following Monday.

The revival would run nightly beginning at eight o'clock, and would hopefully finish by ten, so that Harvey Winkles, the movie projectionist, could run a late movie for the revivalists, and anyone else who wanted to attend.

It would be an exhausting week for Abe and Ruth Turner. They would have to be up past mid-night every night. However, the Turners were advantaged that during the day when the workers were all in the field, it was possible for Abe to watch the store while Ruth napped and vice-versa.

Bud had already received some disappointing news from his mother. He could go to the revival, but he could not stay for the movie except on the last night of the revival, which was a Friday night. Joel, on the other hand, did not have restrictions placed on him. He probably would not attend the revival at all, but would attend most of the late shows.

Bud would have Joel keep him informed about the escapades of Gene, Roy and Hopalong. Bud would, also, be sure to quiz Joel about any of Joel's late night adventures. He would especially want to know if Joel made any · stops at the Thompson barn on his way to the store, and what, if any conversation, he might have had with the Milligan sisters.

There was some disturbing news that filtered up out of the Cherokee sawmill campsite. Old man Wilson, whose cotton field abutted the fence that separated the field from the woods and the old saw mill camp, had reported to Abe Turner, that he had been to the camp late one afternoon to check on the condition of the cotton, and to advance the Cherokee couple twenty dollars for food.

Abe later told Ellis Scott, that Mr. Wilson, upon coming to the wire gate that opened from the field into the camp site, had heard some banging around inside the shack and he could hear the young woman scream out, followed by loud sobbing. Mr. Wilson said that he had gone up to the door and knocked. Blue Duck opened it looking a little disheveled, and he could see the girl huddled in the corner with her face in her hands, a slight trace of blood coming from the corner of her mouth.

Blue Duck seemed to be in a belligerent mood at first, but he became more agreeable when Mr. Wilson handed him a twenty-dollar bill, and told him that it was an advance on future earnings that would be deducted from the couple's wages once picking began. Mr. Wilson, who knew about the hound, took the precaution of carrying his shotgun with him, but there was no sign of the hound's presence at the camp. However, from the woods to the south, he had heard its unmistakable deep baying echoing up, "like the voice of hell," as he put it.

"Anything wrong with the girl?" Mr. Wilson asked.

"Tripped, and hit her head, I reckon'. She'll be alright," Blue Duck responded.

Mr. Wilson said that he didn't challenge Blue Duck about it, but as he told Abe, he knew "it was a damned lie."

Mr. Wilson said that he had gotten a good enough look at that girl's face to know that she had been getting a regular beating.

"It ain't really my business, how a man treats his family," said Mr. Wilson. "But I sure as hell can't hardly stand for a grown man to beat a little woman."

And—no! Mr. Wilson, had replied to Abe's inquiry. He had not heard anything from Elmo, and——no! Abe, had replied to Mr. Wilson's inquiry——the Adkins family had not received any news from Betty. Abe had not passed on what the lady ticket agent had said about the possibility of Betty's pregnancy to Hazel or Dovie Adkins, or to the Wilson family. He didn't see any reason to worry them with unconfirmed hearsay, and further to the point, they couldn't do anything about it anyway. Elmo and Betty's future was in their own hands for the time being.

Even though the Adkins family had lost Betty, at least temporarily, Ellis Scott believed that with his family and the remaining Adkins family members, plus the two Milligan families, he could put enough pickers in the field to get out a full bale of cotton every day, and maybe more. That would be very satisfactory if that were to happen, because if the weather cooperated it would mean that they could get the cotton picked by the last week in October, which was always Ellis' annual goal.

The first revival meeting started promptly at 8:00 p.m., on Sunday night. There were more than one hundred people from the surrounding countryside attending. The weather was perfect. There wasn't a cloud in the sky and the temperature was a comfortable seventy-five degrees. Electrical cords were strung from the store out to the meeting ground, and through the trees around the worship center. Bare one-hundred-watt light bulbs were hung from tree limbs in several strategic locations.

Bud liked attending the revival, if for nothing else, to watch the flying squirrels as they glided from tree to tree above the congregation. He sat on a rear bench and kept a close eye on the little creatures, which were numerous. He was trying to determine where they hid out during daylight hours. He and Joel had talked about trying to catch some of them for pets. Joel had declined to attend the first service, but chose to sit on the store porch, some seventy-five yards from the arbor setting, and watch from there while indulging in a big orange drink and a banana moon pie.

Bud's mind was not on the service. In addition to watching the flying squirrels, he kept thinking about the preacher from Bono, who participated the previous year, and had brought a picture that was supposedly taken in Philadelphia, Pennsylvania, of snow on a coal pile. Some people, including Bud's mother, said that if you looked at it in just the right way, you could see the head of Jesus, made by the pattern of the whiteness of the snow against the blackness of the coal. The preacher said that a woman who had once viewed the photograph, and had apparently seen the image, made the statement, "Now! I see the old buzzard!" and had immediately fallen dead.

Bud had looked at the black and white Kodak photograph several times, but he had not been able see anything but snow on a coal pile, and he took that as a sign that perhaps it was time that he was baptized. The repeated discussion about the woman having fallen dead, after a verbal insult to Jesus, stuck with Bud, and he had made up his mind that if he ever did see the image, he was not going to say a word that might be construed by anyone, holy or otherwise, that he was anything less than a good Christian boy. He was too young to die.

The Reverend Alva Stroud, of the Big Brown First Baptist Church, near Sedgwick, won the right in draw poker to be the lead preacher in the revival. All of the preachers for the revival had gathered in Turner's Store for a planning session. When it came time to pick the preaching rotation, Abe Turner had produced a deck of cards. The preachers all drew cards, and the highest card won the right to lead off. The Reverend Stroud had drawn the Ace of Spades. The rest of the schedule was determined by the value of the card picked from the deck by each preacher, except that Roscoe Gilmore, Pastor of The Little Brown Freewill Baptist Church, was hosting the revival and would preach the final night.

The Reverend Alva Stroud's Big Brown Church was sort of a sister church to the Little Brown Church, but the Big Brown Church members were "hard-shell" Baptists, who tended to interpret scripture more literally than did the Freewill Baptists. This led to at least one program every year where they washed each other's feet, based on Jesus' example with his disciples. Bud and Inez Scott had attended, and Inez made sure that Bud had scrubbed his feet before leaving home, and that he wore shoes.

The foot-washing ceremony, which didn't seem a bit religious to Bud, led to some humorous conversation among the participants. One man was overheard to say, "You'll never catch a Methodist washing his feet." And a woman said, "This is the first time I've had my feet washed since last year."

A young girl about Bud's age washed his feet, and he in-turn washed her feet. Everything was going well, until he ran out of foot, and started moving up above her ankle. Either because it tickled or because of her concern for modesty, she had squealed out suddenly and kicked over the dishpan full of water. There was no great harm done, but Bud was embarrassed because everyone looked at him to see what he had done, and Bud thought that in the future he might have to reconsider this foot-washing business.

Bud and Joel, met up with Homer, at Turner's Store on Wednesday night, and Homer told them that he and Roscoe were going to hold the revival's final service on Friday night, as they were the home team, so to speak. Homer said that he and Roscoe wanted the service to be special, something to remember; something for the congregation to take with them into the winter months; something to remember back on, in times of trials and tribulations.

"How 'bout turpentinin' a cat?" asked Joel.

"How's zat?" replied a puzzled Homer.

Bud saw the possibilities, immediately, even if Homer didn't. By taking something abrasive like a corn cob and rubbing a cat's rear until it's raw, then splashing on a liberal dose of turpentine, the cat will go wild and run to the nearest lighted place. Why? No one knows, but it will.

"Sometime durin' yore service," continued Joel. "You give a signal, and me and Bud will turpentine that old black tomcat that hangs round here. We'll aim him for the lights, and you kin tell the congregation that the devil is about to make an appearance. When that ole' tomcat comes screechin' through, that'll give 'em somethin' to remember."

Homer immediately saw the genius in the proposal. "That's the best durned thang I've ever heard of in my life," he said. "And here's how we'll do it. You know when we git to the part of the service where the testifyin' starts, which the Pentecostals are so big on, I'll lead the introductory prayer, and when I git to the part about the devil among us, I'll raise my right arm straight up. When I do thet, you boys let her rip. I'll leave it to you boys to work out the timin' with the cat. Boys this revival is a-goin' down in history."

Bud could hardly wait until Friday night. He and Joel decided that they would get to the store early, with two empty burlap feed sacks, and that they would catch two cats. They would need one in reserve, in case something went awry. Joel said that he knew there was at least one black tomcat and there was another that was a dark gray. They would try to catch that one also. In the dark, the gray tom could pass for the devil just as well as the black one.

There had only been one mishap by the time of the revival's final service. On Wednesday night, Sister Evangeline Cox, from near Sedgwick, a member of the Assembly of God Church, suddenly began to talk in tongues and went into a trance. She was seated near the rear of the congregation. Suddenly she stood upright on a bench in the back row, her eyes focused on the sky above. Then, with her eyes locked on the sky, she proceeded to run all the way to the front, stepping on just the top of the benches while scattering some startled congregants. She reached the front row without missing a bench, but her momentum carried her forward and momentarily into space. She hit the ground, tripped over her own feet, and plowed headlong into the sturdy oak lectern furnished by the Little Brown Freewill Baptist Church. Sister Evangeline was knocked cold as a cucumber.

Bud told his parents that he wanted to attend the last night of the revival. Inez told him that he could attend the revival, and he could stay for the movie following the close of the service. She was not going to attend because she had heard that Homer had a part in it. The Friday night fights were on the radio, so Ellis Scott would not be going. With his parents out of the way, all Bud and Joel had to worry about was Abe Turner.

The boys got to the store early, having stealthily crossed the bridge, and eased around to the rear of the store, taking ever precaution to stay completely out of sight.

The boys decided to put their plan into action near the left-rear of the store, which would put them between the movie tent and the store so that they would be in dark shadows during their part of the religious exercise. They had two cats to catch.

They both had taken the precaution of bringing a pair of heavy leather work gloves, and Joel brought two empty burlap bags, that had formerly held fifty pounds of potatoes, as Bud noted with interest—from Idaho. Joel had brought a can of sardines, which he opened with his pocketknife, and they proceeded to look for the cats. There were a lot of cats, and soon the black tomcat appeared. Joel threw down the opened can of sardines in back of the store. The black tom rushed the sardines along with a dozen or so of the other cats and became engrossed in protecting his interest in the sudden bonanza.

Bud moved in with a heavy burlap bag, and before the tom knew it, he was wrapped up and couldn't move a muscle. They quickly tied up the sack, and moved in on the old gray tomcat. The sardines evidently had a mesmerizing effect on the cats, because he was just as easy to sack as the first one. They took the two sacked cats around to the shadows in front of the movie tent, and got their corncob and can of turpentine ready. Joel even took the precaution of loosening the cap to the can. Timing was critical. They didn't need any unforeseen delays, like a rusted cap, that couldn't be unscrewed.

They sat back in the shadows against the wall of the store and waited. The two sacked cats had quit their mewing, and in the darkness of their sacks were quietly contemplating their fate. The service started on schedule at eight o'clock.

Preacher Roscoe Gilmore was in full flight with his chariots from glory theme. He likened the chariots to the flying squirrels that were as busy as usual with their high jinks in the arboreal lushness. The sky was clear, a full moon was rising, and it was not overly warm—shirtsleeve weather.

Finally, at about nine o'clock, it was time for the testifying to begin. This was usually the time, when most of the adult women stood up and testified as to how much they loved the Lord, and why. The teenagers and young adults, although prompted, usually sat quiet, while some of the older men sucked up their courage and stood up and confessed their sins, which could prove to be fascinating. So fascinating in fact that in one case it led to two divorces.

Homer then took center stage. It was time for the boys to let the cat out of the bag. They carefully untied the bag that held the black tom and by careful positioning they revealed his rear end, while keeping his head and forequarters still inside the sack. Joel would control the cat. Bud would take the rough corn cob and "sandpaper" its rear end, and then apply a liberal dose of turpentine to the raw area. After about three seconds, the cat would feel as if all the fires of hell had gathered right under his tail.

There was a happenstance that the boys had not considered in their detailed plan. In their intense preparations in the final minutes just prior to sending the deviled cat out to wreck havoc with the congregation, the Cherokee couple, and their giant hound, came up the field road from south of the store and passed quietly on the opposite side, away from the revival meeting. The couple entered the store and left the big hound on the porch unattended. Blue Duck said to Abe, upon entering, "He tain't gonna bother nothin', and he won't leave thet porch with this gurl in hyar."

Of course Blue Duck could not have known, when he made that statement, of the extravaganza being planned a few feet from where the dog stood staring intently through the front store window, in an effort to keep track of his mistress, the little Cherokee maiden.

Homer was dressed in his now familiar robe, his head uncovered, and his shoulder-length silken white hair glistening in the lights from the eight, one-hundred-watt light bulbs that were hanging in the tree branches. Homer's right arm shot skyward, and he began to intone about the depth of black sin all around, and how the devil was among them, even now. That was the signal. The cat's rear had been "cobbed." Bud splashed on the turpentine and Joel pulled the cat free from the sack and held him straight out at arm's length, waiting for the turpentine to take effect.

The cat began to squall out and claw the air. Joel had him aimed for the lights of the revival. Some of the congregation stood up to look behind them at this unearthly sound. The devil was out of the bag, and then all hell broke loose. The Cherokee Devil Hound upon hearing the cat squalling knew supper was at hand, and with a deep bellow leaped off of the porch and headed straight for Joel, and the cat. Joel who had heard from Bud about the size of the dog, but had not actually seen it, looked over his left shoulder and saw what appeared to be a young bull calf, with fiery red eyes, charging him.

"Oh m'God!" yelled Joel, and flung the cat forward. The hound veered left, the cat in his sights.

The cat now had two problems: one was under his tail, and the other was on his tail. The cat as predicted headed for the bright lights, with the monster hound in hot pursuit. None of the congregation, including Roscoe and Homer had ever seen the dog, which in the dim light appeared to be Satan incarnate.

Homer had dropped his arms straight out in a horizontal position and due to his six-foot, four-inches in height and excessive thinness, did in the dim light and shadows resemble the Cross. However, the visual effect was lost on the congregation, because the entire assembly had a runaway down the county road—in both directions. The squalling tomcat scampered directly down the center aisle between the benches making straight for Homer with the big hound in close pursuit. Roscoe had hunkered down behind the lectern and was trying desperately to become invisible.

Homer, not expecting the monstrous hound, froze in shock with arms outstretched. The cat desperately needed something to climb and Homer was handy. The cat with little effort leaped on top of Homer's head, and before Homer could react to this development, the Cherokee Devil Hound, which outweighed Homer by a good forty pounds, and apparently not recognizing the shocked Homer to be human, leaped for the cat, knocking Homer flat on his back. Homer squalled out in terror thinking he was dog meat. This, in-turn, caused the dog to hesitate when he hit the ground, and he stopped momentarily to look back in what might be described as dogged amazement. This was all the break that the cat needed to make it to the nearest tree and it was up in the branches in a flash.

The hound, emitting low growling sounds, moved quickly out of sight into the darkness of the grove. He was hungry and before the night was out, he meant to kill something. The Cherokee couple came out on the porch with Abe to see what all the commotion was about just in time to witness the dog's leap that knocked Homer down. Blue Duck decided it was time for he and the missus to take their leave. They left the way they had come, down the road on the opposite side of the store, away from the lights of the revival.

Bud and Joel witnessing with some satisfaction their well-timed event with the cat, but seeing it complicated by the terror of the chase, and the scattering of the congregation, decided it was time to take their leave, before someone, and especially Abe happened to spot them in the darkness, and put one and one together.

They quickly unsacked the second cat. It hissed at them a couple of times and then ran under the side of the canvas movie tent. They gathered up their gloves and the turpentine can, and moved stealthily around the rear of the store. They had just started to move out of the shadows at the rear of the store, when the Cherokee couple stepped off the front porch and started down the road that led past their position in the rear of the store, and down through the field beyond. Joel spotted the danger and in the nick of time and caught Bud by the arm. They dropped and lay flat on the ground next to the rear wall of the store, remaining perfectly still while the Cherokee couple passed.

The Cherokees walked some twenty yards past the boy's hiding place, but were still visible in the faint light that emanated from a rear window of the living quarters, when the girl stopped, cupped her mouth in both hands and gave a shrill pulsating yelping cry. The hair stood straight up on both boys' heads. They immediately developed such a rash of chill bumps on their arms and face that for several minutes afterward, gave the appearance of a bad case of poison ivy.

Harvey Winkles, forty-five years-of-age, was originally from the Missouri Bootheel. He had never married, and had no living relative. Harvey was officially orphaned at the age of forty, when his father passed away in St. Louis, while a resident of a home for veterans of World War I.

Harvey had worked in the lead mines in Southern Missouri, and had worked at a variety of other jobs. He had chopped and picked his share of cotton and he didn't want any more of it. He had fallen in with the movie people and they had trained Harvey to be a projectionist. He traveled with the company and helped them set up the tents and then he would stay on at various locations to show the films. He was adept at splicing broken film as well as doing maintenance on the projectors. He was good at his job, and Harvey believed that he would be in, what he called, "the movie business," the rest of his life.

Harvey lived in the tent where the films were shown. He slept in a cot in the right rear of the tent, slightly behind the movie screen. Harvey obtained his food out of Turner's Store. He ate mostly sandwiches, and if he ever got a home-cooked meal, it was Ruth Turner that did the cooking.

Harvey could bathe in the Cache River Ditch as the notion struck him, which wasn't often, and his company supplied him with his own portable toilet. When the local cotton harvest was over, and winter set in, Harvey's schedule called for him to move south, to Northern Florida, and set up the movie tent near St. Augustine, in preparation for the orange harvest that would begin in January. Life just couldn't be better for Harvey Winkles.

Harvey had developed the habit of napping on his cot prior to setting up the projectors for the ten o'clock movie. He was happy that this was the last night of the revival, so he could return to the 8:00 p.m. schedule. He had developed a taste for good moonshine whiskey, and he had become especially fond of the brand that Roscoe Gilmore made. Harvey had finished off a pint of Roscoe's whiskey, which had its customary soothing effect and he was in a sound sleep when the big gray tomcat came into the tent. Harvey didn't hear the cat, nor had he heard the shrill call of the little Cherokee maiden.

The old gray tom knew that the cat-killing hound was nearby, because he had heard it as he lay helpless in the burlap bag, and he knew, as only cats can, that the hound had just as soon have a supper of cat-in-the-sack, as a poke in the eye with a sharp stick.

The other cats that hung around the store were already high up in the cottonwood tree on the ditch bank and on full alert. The gray tom found himself in unfamiliar surroundings and began immediately to look for higher ground. The best position available was at the top of one of the three, fifteen-foot center tent poles. The cat began its ascent by first jumping up on the table that held the projector and several rolls of film in round metal cases. In its haste to climb higher, the cat knocked an empty metal film case off the table. The metal case hit the ground with a bang and a rattle. The crash of the metal film case awakened Harvey out of his slumber—something or somebody was in the tent with him.

Harvey had strung a single, one hundred watt bulb from the center of the tent. He carefully eased off of his cot and groped for the string to the light switch. He finally found it and pulled the string. In the bright light, the first thing he spotted was the big gray tomcat's glaring eyes looking down from atop a center tent pole. The cat hissed at him. Harvey, in something of a fright, instinctively picked up the empty metal film case and flung it toward the cat. The cat squalled out as the missile sailed by, and it leaped off the pole to the top of a film storage cabinet. The rattle of the film case striking the ground, followed by the cat squalling, attracted the Cherokee Devil Hound, which was just in the act of passing a few yards south of the tent.

The hound, which had been in the act of catching up with his mistress, now veered toward the rear of the tent where there was a ray of bright light coming out from under the canvas. The dog pushed his gigantic square head underneath the tent to investigate just in time to see Harvey in the process of trying to knock the cat off of the film storage cabinet near the front entrance. The dog unleashed an unearthly bellow that reverberated within the confines of the tent.

Harvey turned to see a gigantic head with glaring red eyes looking right at him. All he could get out of his mouth was "nice doggie," before he bolted through the front flap of the tent and headed for the front of the store where Abe was still standing on the porch watching events unfold. The big tom was off the cabinet in a flash and was right on Harvey's heels. The monster hound seeing his second chance for supper disappear though the front of the tent, stood straight up and in doing so, pulled the corner tent-pole out of the ground. The pole fell inward, loosening the tension ropes of the center poles.

The three center poles were stabilizers. Heavy ropes stretched from the center poles to each of the four corner poles, providing support for the heavy canvas tent. None of the poles had been interred more than a foot in the ground. The falling of the corner pole and the releasing of tension at one corner of the tent created a domino effect, causing the center poles to give way and the tent to collapse, pulling down the three remaining corner poles. The tent was now flat on the ground except for the portion that was still being held up by the projector that was on top of the projectionist table, and the film storage cabinet in the corner.

Bud and Joel, who were in full view of the tent from their hiding place behind the store, had watched the collapse of the tent with severe disappointment, knowing that there would be no movie tonight. Otherwise, it had been great fun.

Another shrill cry rent the night, from further south this time. The big hound had pulled backward from under the tent, when the corner post had fallen, and now was moving silently through the darkness toward the Cherokee couple plodding through the moonlight to their camp at the abandoned sawmill.

CHAPTER 15

Abe Turner received a telephone call from a Lawrence County official in Walnut Ridge, telling him to alert the countryside to the fact that the following week, a government representative would be at the Egypt school, to pass out rationing stamps. Sugar, shoes, and gasoline were among those things that were being rationed in nineteen forty-three.

Abe had not had any fresh meat in the store for some time either, even though technically, it was not rationed. He had received some slab meat from a wholesale grocer in Jonesboro, which he thought was bacon. The meat, though, unlike bacon, had a tough hide with some hair left on that strangely enough, resembled horsehair. Ellis Scott, tired of eating bologna, and knowing it was too early to kill a fattening hog, bought a cut of Abe's meat and took it home. Inez cut it into thick slices and fried it. It didn't smell like bacon, but it didn't smell bad either. However, they soon found that the meat was too tough to eat. They could chew it, but they couldn't swallow it. Inez threw the inedible stuff out in the yard for their two hounds. The dogs chewed around on it for a while, but they couldn't eat it either. Word filtered down later to Abe, that the meat, was either horse or mule meat.

Inez had plenty of sugar, but she would go get her ration and bury it with the rest. Rumors had circulated that county officials would come to people's homes to investigate the hoarding of rationed items, so Inez had boiled out an empty lard can, and had filled it with sugar and had Ellis dig a hole out by the cellar, and bury it. However, no one from the government ever did come to any of the homes in the Horse Island community to check on hoarding.

Bud needed a new pair of shoes before school started, and certainly before winter. He had outgrown last year's shoes, but he was still wearing them. He had cut holes in the shoes in strategic places to relieve pressure on his toes. Ellis and Inez did not want to have to send Bud to school without shoes or with shoes with holes, and Bud wasn't looking forward to that either. Two years before, Joel Adkins had gone to school during the winter barefoot, even with snow and ice on the ground. Bud asked him why he didn't have shoes, and Joel had replied that it wasn't his turn.

Abe put a notice in the window of the store about the rationing stamps, and he got word to Ellis and Inez Scott, that Ruth and him were going to go get their ration stamps, so the Scotts could ride along in the truck.

Inez was able to get one ration stamp for a five pound bag of sugar, and enough ration stamps for two pairs of shoes. They would have to go for shoes for Ellis and Bud. She would do without, and hope to get by. Hopefully, by spring, things would be better.

Inez Scott had not felt well for some time. She put it off as hard work and a poor diet, but down deep she knew it was probably more than that. Inez was now thirty-six years old. Her mother had died young, at forty-one, and her grandmother on her mother's side, had died at forty-seven. For the past several months, Inez had sporadic shooting pains high up in her stomach. She had tried to convince herself that it was only heartburn, from eating too much fried food. She treated herself with hot mustard patches that didn't help, and sometimes with ice packs that did occasionally relieve the pain. She hadn't said anything to Ellis, but Bud had noticed her face contorted in pain more than once, and had asked her about it. She always gave the same reply: something she ate, she guessed.

Inez thought, too, that she was probably being poisoned by her teeth. The few she had left were all bad, and the past winter when she had gone to the dentist in Walnut Ridge, he had whistled softly at what he saw when he looked into her mouth. Inez had suffered terrible toothaches over the years and never had the money or little opportunity to get to a dentist. She used the only remedy she knew, which was to take pure lye in a teaspoon and pack it into the rotten tooth, and let the lye eat the rot out of the tooth, and eventually kill the nerve. In the process, the lye burned away part of the gum around the tooth, and blistered the lining inside her mouth. It was impossible to keep from swallowing some of the poisoned lye, and she guessed that the lye had been doing some damage to her stomach and possibly her kidneys as well.

Ellis told her that if the crops were good that she could have her teeth fixed. The dentist had told her that he would pull her remaining nine teeth for fifty cents a piece, and he would fix her up with a full set of dentures for seventy-five dollars. Ellis said he thought they would be able to afford that much.

Abe talked Harvey Winkles into staying in the community a while longer and to continue to show his films. Harvey had been scared so bad when the Cherokee Devil Hound had wrecked his tent that he went to Abe and said he wanted to use Abe's telephone to place a call to his company in Missouri, to come and get him. He said, he didn't want to go through that experience again.

Abe, looking at a large revenue loss, if the movies weren't shown, soothed Harvey's nerves by giving him a couple of ice-cold bottles of Preacher Gilmore's malt liquor. Harvey became less anxious, after downing the two bottles in quick succession. Abe asked Harvey if he would consider staying a while longer, if Abe arranged for the tent to be put back up? Abe sweetened the deal by offering to provide Harvey with all the moonshine and malt liquor that he could drink free gratis.

Harvey said he wasn't born yesterday, and that he wasn't about to let a proposition like that go by. So Abe asked Ellis Scott if he and Hazel Adkins could bring Ellis' two teams of mules down to the store, and help put the tent back up. Abe, also, recruited several other men out of the Little Brown Church to help. Sunday afternoon, following the Friday night collapse of the tent, twelve men with two teams of mules, put the tent up in short order, and had it ready for a film on Monday night.

The last Monday in August dawned hot and clear. Bud looked at the temperature gauge on the front porch just before sunup. It read "85 degrees." Bud had just finished a breakfast of scrambled eggs with a slice of salty sugar-cured ham and a big cathead biscuit. He drank a cup of coffee, and went to get his new nine-foot, canvas, cotton pick-sack.

The first thing Bud needed to do before going to the field was to mark his sack, so he went down to the barn lot fence where there were several poke salet bushes, loaded with scarlet berries. He picked several berries and squashed them in an old tin can and then took a stick, wet the end with the juice and wrote his name—BUD—in big scarlet letters across the middle of the heavy canvas sack. There was something magical that Bud could not explain about starting off the cotton-picking season with his own personalized pick sack.

Bud was eager to get to the field. He started walking down the field road to the ten-acre cotton patch that lay between the Thompson barn and the Cache River Ditch. His parents would be along shortly, with a team of mules pulling a big cotton wagon. The wagon was large enough to hold a load of picked cotton, thirteen to fifteen hundred pounds that after ginning would produce a bale weighing about five hundred pounds.

Bud walked toward the rising sun that was just topping the trees along the ditch bank. The cool dust of the field road squished up between the toes of his bare feet. He felt good now, but ten to twelve hours from now when he started the long trek home, he would be exhausted and dragging his feet.

Bud could see smoke rising from the Thompson barn lot. He knew that the Milligan families were cooking breakfast on an outdoor fire. The field road ran right by the barn, so he thought that he might just saunter over by the camp to say hello, and see what kind of breakfast they were having.

Inez Scott had made arrangements for the Milligan families to have a sufficient supply of fresh eggs at no cost. These little kindnesses set Inez apart from other more selfish people, and the ability to get fresh eggs on a daily basis was a huge motivating factor for itinerant farm families. They had a tendency to return year after year to the farms where they were well treated.

Bud got to the Thompson barn lot just as the families were finishing their breakfast of eggs, biscuits, and fried bologna. Sherry and Maxine Milligan were helping wash the tin plates and utensils in a number-three washtub full of hot water. They rinsed them off under the pump at the horse trough. One of the Milligan women was packing the leftovers from breakfast into a tin dinner bucket. Bud's mouth began to water, when he thought of fried bologna on a big cathead biscuit, but it didn't look as if he was going to have any luck getting anything from those people.

Bud exchanged some pleasantries with the girls and started on toward the cotton patch where they would be picking. Cody Milligan retrieved a pick sack from a pile of new sacks that was lying on the ground, and went along with Bud. Bud noted that Cody had simply marked his sack with a big "X", using pokeberry juice. Bud wondered if Cody could write his name, so he asked him.

"Can you write yore name?"

"Hell yes!" answered Cody, in a belligerent tone. "And, I can name all forty-eight states, and their capitols, and all the presidents of the United States. I can say my ABCs forward and backward, and I can multiply by twelve, and I can add, subtract, multiply and divide fractions. I betcha' can't do that."

Bud knew immediately that he had stepped into an academic cow pie, and he needed somehow to pull out gracefully without leaving too much on his feet. "Well," Bud said, "I saw the 'X' on your sack and wondered why you didn't put your name on it."

"I don't need to put my name on things, I know to be mine," replied Cody.

"What does that prove anyway? That's just bullshit as far as I'm concerned."

"Well, it's a nice day to pick cotton," said Bud, hoping that Cody would get off the subject of naming presidents, and particularly working with fractions. Academia was never his strong suit.

"Well, I guess so, if you say so," said Cody.

Bud felt as if he had been verbally abused by a wormy itinerant farm hand. It was not how he had intended to start his day. He began to wish that he had a heavy wet corncob handy.

Abe Turner was the acting postmaster for the community. People that lived off the main road and that didn't have mailboxes, had their mail delivered in care of Turner's Store, at Route Three, Walnut Ridge. This included most of the itinerant farm workers that came into the community during the fall. The Milligan family would have their mail posted to the Scott mailbox. Bud liked the fact that he could deliver the Milligan's mail. It not only gave him a sense of importance, but he got extra chances to be around Sherry and Maxine Milligan, who were not hard on the eyes.

Abe kept a big cardboard box in the front of the store, on which he had written "postal" in big black lettering. Anyone could come in and rummage through the box to see if they might have received mail. The Adkins family had their mail sent to Turner's Store. Joel Adkins had started to check the mailbox more often. Dovie Adkins was getting more and more anxious about hearing from Betty. There had been nothing so far. If a letter did come, it would have to be Joel who read it, as neither of his parents could read or write.

The first week of the cotton harvest season went as well as could be expected. Ellis Scott was getting out a bale or more a day. Ellis had two wagons. He kept one in reserve, so that when one wagon was full and ready to take to the gin, he would move the empty wagon into the field. He would hook a team of mules to the full wagon and head for the gin. Sometimes he went to the gin at Bono, sometimes to Egypt, and occasionally to Sedgwick. Bud couldn't understand why he went to the different gins, and Ellis' explanation didn't help to clarify the matter either. Once when Bud asked him why he varied his itinerary, Ellis said he wanted to make it hard for anyone to catch him in an ambush.

Bud appreciated his father's little humorous asides, but Ellis never did say for sure why he chose to go to different gins. The price for the cotton was the same at each gin. The waiting line was about the same, as the cotton harvest was underway all over the county. The truth of the matter was, that Ellis just got bored with traveling the same route all the time. He liked meeting farmers from the different areas. He liked to hear them brag on their cotton and, also, to talk about the same tried and true subject that all farmers had in common: the weather.

It was about the end of the first week of the harvest, when Joel Adkins discovered, what amounted to a gold mine for a teenage boy. The Milligan girls had taken to late afternoon skinny dipping in the Cache River Ditch, and to top that off they were being joined by the Taylor sisters from across the ditch; six naked teenage girls in a fairly shallow and reasonably clear pool of water. For Joel, Christmas had come early.

There were four of the Taylor girls: Christine, Justine, Willene and Pearl. The girls were thirteen, fourteen, sixteen, and eighteen years old respectively. The Taylor girls all went to school at Egypt, but none of them were in the same class as Bud and Joel. Christine was one class behind, and Justine was in the class ahead. Willene was two classes ahead, and Pearl, a senior, would be graduating the following May.

The Taylor girls were all natural red heads, which was made quite evident by the dying rays of the afternoon sun filtering through the trees onto their wet glistening bodies. Their red hair contrasted sharply with the black-haired Milligan sisters. How the Taylor and Milligan sisters all happened to end up in that pool in the ditch at the same time was currently a mystery to Joel, but it was a mystery that didn't need to be solved, only enjoyed.

Joel had discovered this momentous event entirely by accident. Late one evening during the first week of the cotton harvest, just before dark, and after finishing supper, he had decided to do a little fishing. He dug up a shovel full of dirt from under an old log, and found several night crawlers. The big earthworms were excellent bait for catfish. He had taken his cane pole and had gone over the bank to set his line in the water, when he heard female voices and laughter floating down over the water, like nature's own telegraph.

Joel made his way quietly along a well-worn path running down the top of the ditch bank, to a point where he had a clear view of the glassy pool and discovered it was full of naked girls. He could see the girls, but they couldn't see him sitting in the lengthening shadows of dusk. Joel rested.

To tell Bud, or not to tell Bud, was the nagging question that Joel struggled with the whole of the following day. Bud was his best buddy, but if he were to let something slip in the cotton field around the Milligan girls, then he and Bud would likely be in more trouble than they could shake a stick at, not only from the Milligan girl's father, but Ellis Scott as well, not to mention Hazel Adkins, and the Taylor girls' father, the six-foot-four, two hundred and seventy-five-pound, Bull Taylor, who was known to be a heavy drinker and a ruffian, particularly when drunk.

Late in the afternoon, just before the final weighing of cotton for the day, Joel and Bud were picking close together on adjacent rows. With no one else close enough to overhear, Joel told Bud about the swimming party. The question was: Did Bud want to participate in viewing this natural phenomenon? Bud did.

Joel didn't have a problem getting to the swimming hole late in the day while the girls were there, because the Adkins house was within a hundred yards of the ditch, and the swimming hole was only a couple of hundred yards or so upstream. However, Bud lived a half-mile away, which meant that he would have to go home, eat a quick supper, and then find some reason to get away from the house. He would have to run all the way in order to get to the ditch before dark.

He would have to pass through the seven-acre woodlot behind the barn, and into a twelve-acre block of corn beyond, in order to stay out of sight of members of the Milligan family at the Thompson barn. The corn had rows a quarter-mile in length that ran from behind the woodlot east all the way to the ditch bank. The corn stalks were well above Bud's head, so that he could not be seen, once in the cornfield. It was going to be physically challenging, particularly after picking cotton all day, but it was a challenge that had to be met. Opportunity to view an all-naked-girl swimming party might only come once in a lifetime, if it came at all.

Bud devised a brilliant plan of deception, while riding home in the cotton wagon with his parents at the end of the day. His plan was to eat a hurried supper and immediately head for the barn to feed the livestock. He would take a piece of meat or a biscuit to coax one if not both of the hounds to follow him to the barn, where he would quickly feed the stock. He would go through the back gate and he and the dogs would head for the woods behind the barn. As soon as he was in the cover of the woods, he would tear out for the cornfield and eventually the ditch beyond, leaving the dogs to do whatever dogs do.

Should he be questioned later by Inez or Ellis as to his whereabouts, and he most certainly would be, he would say that he had decided to take the dogs and see if he might jump a possum around the persimmon trees that grew in the wood lot behind the barn. It was a plausible enough reason, under normal circumstances because the persimmons were beginning to ripen and possums loved persimmons, but it didn't really make a lot of sense either, since Bud had not shown a previous interest in possum hunting. The plan on the whole, was pretty thin, but it was all he had, and it would have to do. But the best laid plans of mice and men sometimes go awry.

"Bud, after supper, I want you to take two-dozen eggs down to the Milligan camp," said Inez, as they rode along home in the cotton wagon.

Bud struggled with his composure. *Damn! Damn! And double damn*! he thought. "Yessum," was all he could reply. He mentally shifted gears, and began to formulate Plan B, and he wondered if Inez could hear his mind working.

Bud moved through supper quickly. He would come back later in the night for seconds. Inez put a dozen eggs each, into two heavy brown paper bags, and Bud was off in a flash back down the field road to the Milligan camp. He would make a quick delivery, then cut back north across a cotton patch toward the cornfield as if he was going back home through the woods, but once in the corn, and out of sight of the Milligan camp, he would make a right turn and run between the corn rows to the ditch. The sun was already beginning to set.

Bud delivered the eggs, having double-timed it to the camp. Cody Milligan had a Barlow pocket knife and was sitting on the ground near the barn, playing mumbly-peg when Bud arrived. A quick survey of the premises did not reveal Cody's sisters.

"Where's yore sisters at?" asked Bud, trying to be casual about it.

"Gone to the ditch," answered Cody.

"What for, to pick muscadines?" asked Bud. There were a lot of the big blue muscadine grapes growing wild along the ditch bank. That diversionary question was a stroke of genius, Bud thought.

"Gone swimming, I reckon," answered Cody. "You want to play a game of mumbly-peg?"

"How come you didn't go swimming?" asked Bud, ignoring Cody's question. Bud didn't give a rap about playing mumbly-peg; spinning a knife in the air with two blades opened, with points collected dependent upon which blade stuck in the ground. Bud had soured on that game some time back when he had inadvertently twirled the knife out of control and it had stuck in the fleshy part just inside the big toe on his right foot. It hadn't bled much, but it hurt like the devil. He hadn't told anyone, but when Inez mentioned his limp, he had said that he thought it was a stone bruise.

"Bad ears. I can't git in water without gettin' an ear infected," answered Cody. "How bout a quick game of mumbly-peg?"

"Nope, I got to get home before dark, maybe next time," answered Bud, and he set out on a dead run across a cotton patch, toward the corn field and the woods beyond. He was not out of ear shot, however, when he heard Cody yell, "Scared of the dark are ye'?" A hot flash of anger welled up in Bud, and he wished he had a heavy wet corn cob to throw, but he had other things to do, which was to get a good look at Cody's naked sisters in the swimming hole, and he wasn't about to get into a verbal contest with Cody Milligan.

Bud was soon in the corn. He turned east toward the ditch. He ran as hard as he could with the corn leaves slapping him in the face. He stumbled out of the cornfield, completely winded and went up and over the ditch bank. He turned south down-stream, toward the swimming hole. Bud could see the big cottonwood tree several hundred yards away, south of the swimming hole, where even now he imagined that Joel from high up on a limb had been privileged to view the river activities for the past hour.

He heard talking and girlish laughter, but it was not coming from the ditch. From atop the ditch bank he looked back out to the field road that led from the ditch to the Thompson barn, and there were the Milligan sisters on their way back to their encampment. Bud collapsed at the base of a big willow oak, his energy suddenly sapped. He was feeling all the weariness of the day's labor as he sat a moment contemplating his fate and the long walk home with victory just out of sight, when suddenly from just across the ditch he heard the deep baying voice of the Cherokee Devil Hound. It was trailing down the opposite bank.

Bud thought he might be in trouble if the hound crossed the ditch. He was not about to start for home back through the cornfield, because if the prey the hound was running decided to cross the ditch, it would probably head for the corn field in an attempt to escape, and Bud did not want to be in that cornfield with that dog on the loose. Bud quickly decided to run the field road from the ditch, by the Milligan camp at the Thompson barn, and hope that he wouldn't be seen in the near darkness as he passed.

Bud started his run down the field road in the gathering dusk just as an owl called from down the ditch bank somewhere near the Adkins house. The owl's call had not died away, when there was an answer from a second owl hooting from the very spot Bud had just vacated on the bank. Dueling owls,

Bud thought, disgusted with his lot in life. Even a game of mumbly-peg with Cody Milligan would have been better than this.

While they were picking cotton side by side the following day, Joel, to Bud's chagrin, gave a first-class presentation of the last evening's events in the swimming hole, not just in black and white, but also in technicolor. All six girls were there again, and Joel got close enough to overhear something marvelous: the Milligan sisters, and the Taylor sisters planned to meet at the swimming hole between two and three o'clock, the following Sunday evening.

Bud asked Joel if he had seen the Cherokee Devil Hound. Joel said from where he was in the cottonwood tree, he could see the hound running in the field along the bottom of the east ditch bank. The hound was running a deer. Joel said he was not nearly as concerned about the dog, though, as he was Pearl Taylor. For when the Taylor girls came out of the swimming hole and got dressed to go home, Pearl had picked up a double-barreled shotgun that was leaning up against a tree, that Joel, heretofore, had not seen. Joel exclaimed, "I know thet gurl. If she had caught me watchin' 'em from up in thet tree, she probably would have shot my ass outta there."

The news that the Milligan and Taylor sisters were going to have a swimming party next Sunday evening was more that Bud could have hoped for. Bud knew he would be able to make that schedule, as the Scotts seldom worked on a Sunday. Inez didn't believe in it. Ellis Scott didn't either, but not on religious grounds. Ellis had said more than once, if you can't make a living working six days a week, then you need to find something else to do.

There had been occasions in the past, when the Scotts had gone to the field on Sunday evening after church. They would work on Sunday, if they were behind because of the weather, or if it was particularly late in the season, and they needed to beat the cold weather of late fall. But now it was early in the season and the weather was excellent. Bud felt reasonably sure that he would be on the ditch bank come Sunday evening at two o'clock, with a brown bag lunch.

The coming Sunday promise of extraordinary visual delights dominated Bud's ever-passing thought. Inez Scott noted at breakfast that Bud was deep in thought. "Bud, what's the matter? You don't normally stare at your eggs that way."

Bud came out of his trance to find himself staring intently into his plate at two sunny-side-up eggs, and in his subconscious noting how much they resembled female breasts. "Well, they're staring at me," he replied. Inez chuckled, thinking that Bud had acquired his father's mental quickness and sense of humor.

Joel's detailed description of nubile delights kept playing in Bud's head, like a short film that kept repeating. He had become elated at the prospect of Sunday's adventure and at the same time despondent.

Bud, at thirteen, had already developed a mature moral awareness. He was being torn by religious training from a devout mother with deep religious convictions grounded in the Bible, and by a sinful nature; a gift from his father's irreverent and risqué character. Bud thought that there must be a battle going on over his soul by the forces of good and evil. So far "good" appeared to be outnumbered.

At noon, Bud sat a little off to the side from the others, most of whom had gathered in the shade of the cotton wagon to eat their dinner. Bud was deep in thought while eating a second bologna and cheese sandwich and staring at the ground between his feet. He had spread his empty cotton sack across two rows of cotton stalks that were waist high, and was sitting in the shade underneath the impromptu shelter from the noonday sun. The temperature was in the low nineties. It was very hot for the time of year.

Bud was engaged in a daydream without notable merit, when the younger of the two Milligan sisters, Sherry, eased in beside him, munching an apple. Bud thought Sherry was the prettier of the two sisters. She was kind of cute in her jeans, blue cotton shirt and straw hat. She was a year older than Bud, with black hair, and high cheekbones and a prominent nose with a slight hook. She reminded Bud of a chicken hawk. *There's some Cherokee blood in there somewhere,* Bud thought.

Bud's mind was suddenly in turmoil. What would she say? What would he say? He wasn't around many girls except at school, and there they could be avoided for the most part. He didn't like talking to girls, and he didn't like being cornered by one under a cotton sack.

"A penny for your thoughts," said Sherry.

"I'd have to give you change," replied Bud, suddenly energized by the close proximity of one of the characters in his mental film, and immensely delighted with himself for what he considered to be a completely spontaneous and witty remark.

Sherry chuckled. "So you were not thinking about much then?" she said, taking another bite of apple.

"Well, I was pursuing a particular train of thought," replied Bud.

"Was I on that train?" asked Sherry, with a demureness that was ageless.

"Yep," blurted out Bud, suddenly embarrassed.

"Was Maxine on that train?" asked Sherry.

"It was crowded," replied Bud, his mind searching for the reason behind this line of questioning.

"Was the Taylor girls on that train?" continued Sherry, relentlessly.

"I was the engineer," replied Bud. "I didn't see who all got on." *Now*, Bud thought, *let's see her get around that.*

A deafening silence followed.

"You like to swim?" ventured Sherry.

Bud's mental train had suddenly braked without warning.

"Some," he countered warily, wondering at this sudden change of conversational direction. Could she read his mind?

"Me and Maxine and the Taylor girls are goin' swimmin' down behind our camp next Sunday evenin'. Why don't you come down? There hain't much warm weather left. Hit'll be fun."

Bud's mental train had now derailed, and was rolling down a steep embankment. His vision of viewing naked girls on a sandbar had suddenly been washed away in a flood of despair. He had been invited to be a part of what he had hoped to view from afar. Surely a coed participation would create a need for some kind of attire, and that would just ruin everything. Joel was going to be mad as hell!

"I ain't got no bathin' suit," replied Bud weakly.

"That's OK. We hain't got no bathin' suits neither," responded Sherry.

The ball was now in Bud's court, and it didn't have any air in it. His mind was racing as to what his next response would be.

"Let's go Bud. Time to get with it!" yelled out Ellis Scott.

Saved by the bell, thought Bud, as he jumped up, and without a word, grabbed his cotton sack and ran to catch up with the rest of the group, as the Scott, Adkins and Milligan families moved off toward the end of the field to begin the evening's work. He needed an intermission to think things over and to discuss Sherry's proposal with Joel. Joel would think of something.

"Well, if yore a-goin', then I'm a-goin'," Joel had responded, when apprised of the noonday conversation, and then he had continued, "I wouldn't mind a-goin' swimmin' with a bunch of nekkid wimmin'," and laughed at his own joke.

A diversion in the form of Rabid Robert Ryder came down off the ditch bank late in the afternoon, and out into the field toward the nearest group of pickers that included Ellis Scott. Rabid Robert was a legendary character in the "bottoms." He had acquired his name because he had survived being bitten by a mad dog, when he was twenty years old, and having contracted rabies, or hydrophobia, as some people called it.

His family home was on the bank of Cache River Ditch near Sedgwick. His father had tied him to a bed when he showed the first signs of going mad. There was no doctor for them to call, no medication to give, other than a washing detergent that came in small blue cakes, generically referred to as, "bluing."

Bluing was often given to dogs that had the "fits", and resulted in blue foam coming out of their mouths. There was no scientific way to determine if bluing was effective, and no one seemed to know how the application of detergent got started, as a treatment for the "fits," which later became known as distemper. Bud didn't think it worked because he had helped his dad bury too many dogs with blue heads.

It was said that Rabid Robert had howled for three or four days and great beads of bloody sweat had poured out of him. His family gave him water with the bluing cakes broken up in it. He had blue foam coming out of his ears, mouth and nose, but he had survived, and that was ten years past. However, Rabid Robert had not survived with all of his mental processes intact. Rabid Robert had traveled many a county road the past ten years, all paved with criminal intentions. They eventually converged into one road that led to the state penitentiary.

He had been arrested by the Lawrence County Sheriff for stealing gasoline from a gas station at Sedgwick, and had been sent to the Tucker Prison Farm near Little Rock. Tucker Prison was notorious for the treatment of inmates. Prisoners were subjected to the Tucker Telephone, which was the old fashioned crank telephone that was still seeing limited use in nineteen forty-three. The crank-handled telephone was sometimes used by fishermen to shock fish in the ditch. A short-piece of telephone line, attached to the phone box, with the copper wires bared, was placed in a good fishing hole, usually out of a boat. The operator would then turn the crank on the telephone box, discharging a strong electrical current into the water that momentarily stunned the fish. The fish would go belly-up and float to the surface where the best could be scooped off the top of the water.

The Tucker Telephone was used as a punishment for inmates that had behaved in a way inconsistent with prison behavioral policy, and it was said that sadistic prison guards used it as a diversionary tool, to help them get through the boring routine of another day on the farm. The victim was strapped down and the telephone wire was clamped to the prisoner's privates. The handle was then cranked to shoot electrical current into the groin area. It was said that after a treatment of the Tucker Telephone, the production of the prisoner was increased dramatically, and usually he was much better behaved than before.

The other form of punishment was the razor strop often seen hanging in barber shops and used by barbers to sharpen their straight razors. It was a heavy black cowhide leather strop, three-feet in length, and four-inches in width that was attached to a wooden handle. It was called the "Black Betty." Inmates who needed quick motivation to increase their capacity for work, were given a certain number of licks, dependent, it was said, on the amount of increased production needed, and the energy level of the administrator, on any given day.

Sharecropper children had all been warned about Tucker Prison Farm, and Bud was just one of many kids that had been told the stories, and threatened with incarceration by their parents, for an attitude that was considered to be in need of adjustment.

"If you don't straighten up, I'm going to send you to Tucker," was a familiar refrain.

Bud had spotted the slim, sparse figure coming through the field and had alerted his dad a few yards away. Ellis Scott stood up and stared for a moment, and then he said, "I'll be damned if it ain't Rabid Robert Ryder." Bud and Joel knew about Rabid Robert, but other than the Scotts and the Adkins family, no one else in the field had heard his story.

"Howdy Ellis," said Rabid Robert, as he walked up close enough to recognize Ellis Scott. Rabid Robert was dressed in prison garb, which appeared to be white flannel pajamas, and he was bareheaded and barefoot.

"Howdy Rabid," replied Ellis. "What brings you to these parts? The last I heard, you was down at Tucker, helping them ole' boys git their crops out."

"I walked outta there, three or four days ago, I fergit," said Rabid.

"So you escaped, then?" said Ellis.

"I like to think I took an unapproved furlough," replied Rabid. "I've walked all the way following the ditch. Y'all got anything to eat? I'm pert near starved to death."

"Bud, go down to the wagon and see if there ain't some baloney and bread left from dinner," Ellis called out.

Bud, thankful for any diversion, stepped out of his sack strap, and started trotting down the cotton middle toward the wagon.

"Rabid, you know that they're goin' to have the sheriff after you?" said Ellis.

"Yep, I know it. I expect they already got my folks house staked out up at Sedgwick. I wouldn't mind stayin' 'round here fer a spell, and pickin' some cotton, till things cool down a mite," responded Rabid.

"I didn't know of you ever pickin' cotton," said Ellis.

"They learnt me that skill at Tucker. I'm pretty good," said Rabid.

"Well, how did they go about learnin' you to pick cotton?" asked Ellis barely concealing his amusement.

"Well, when they got me down there in the middle of August, the cotton was already open. You know they're earlier down there, than here. It's well over a hundred miles further south. So the second day, I was there, they asked me if I had ever picked cotton, and I said I ain't, that I had always worked in timber. Well, the fellow said, we don't have no timber here, but we got cotton and lots of it, so you're goin' to be a cotton picker from now on. I said, well how long am I in fer, since I stole only five gallons of gas, about a dollar's worth? The fellow said, we'll keep you till the cotton has been picked, and if you behave yourself, and don't give us no trouble, we'll consider lettin' you git home by Christmas.

They gave me a nine-foot cotton sack and tole' me to go out and pick one hundred and twenty-five pounds of cotton. Well, I did make an effort, but I could only git about one hundred pounds. So that night, they took me in a little room where they spread-eagled me over a heavy wooden table, and fastened my arms with leather straps, then they whupped my nekkid ass with that black leather strop, that I'd heerd so much about. It hurt like hell.

Well the feller says, tomorrow we want you to pick one hundred and fifty pounds. Well, I did make a monstrous effort, but I come up short again. So that night they took me back in that room and whupped my ass again, except this time they gave me a few more whacks. Now the feller says to me, tomorrow we want you to pick one hundred and seventy-five pounds. Do you think you can get it? So I said, by God if it's out there, I'll damned sure git it, and I did, too. I was in the shower later, and one of the other inmates sez to me that he could read the words, 'genuine cowhide' on my ass from clean across the room."

Bud appeared with a slice of bologna between two slices of white bread, and handed it to Rabid. Rabid began to wolf it down. Ellis had turned away, chuckling to himself, thinking about Rabid's cotton-picking training program.

"Rabid," said Ellis, having gained his composure, "if you want to pick cotton, I'll provide you with a pick sack and an old pair of overalls of mine, but you can't stay on this farm. I don't want to be accused of harborin' a convict. You can cross the foot-log back up the ditch apiece, and stay over at the abandoned Claxton house. The house still has some furniture in it, and it's got a nice pitcher pump. I'll give you a little advance on your wages, and you can go up to Turner's Store, and git you some vittles. You just leave your sack on the wagon at night, and ever mornin' come over into the field to wherever we're pickin' and git your sack and go to work. I'll settle with you at the end of each day, and whenever you decide to go on up the ditch, just go ahead. I'd just as soon not know."

Ellis reached in his overalls vest pocket and pulled out a small roll of one-dollar bills. He peeled off five and handed them to Rabid. "Where'd you say that footlog is?" said Rabid.

On Saturday morning, Ellis told all the hands that he expected that they would have a load of cotton picked by middle of the evening. He said he was going to take the cotton to the Egypt gin and anyone that wanted to, could ride in the cotton wagon and go to the stores or whatever in Egypt while he was getting the cotton ginned. He said he would move the other wagon into the field and if anyone wanted to continue picking, then they could.

It had been a good week. They had picked over a bale a day, and would actually produce eight bales during the six-day workweek. Rabid Robert Ryder was contributing over two hundred pounds per day since joining the crew. Everything looked good in the way of the weather.

The Milligan sisters and brother Cody immediately asked their father, Vaughn Milligan, if they could go to town on the wagon. He said they could, and he would come along himself, and maybe buy a few necessities that were not available at Turner's Store. The other Milligan family members said that they would stay in camp. The women said they would take the rest of the day to wash clothes, and Cauly Milligan, Vaughn's brother said he would help draw the wash water and get the fire started, and then he would walk up the ditch to Turner's Store for some groceries. Rabid Robert Ryder said he would just stay out of sight.

Joel and Hazel Adkins said they would ride to Egypt on the wagon, and Dovie Adkins said she had some washing to do. She said that she would keep Little Claude with her. Little Claude wanted to go in the worst way, and immediately pitched a fit right in the field. He began to scream at the top of his lungs. He didn't stop, until Hazel pulled up a four-foot cotton plant by the roots and began thrashing him with it. Leaves, cotton and stems were flying everywhere. It was more noisy than it was painful. Little Claude made a dive under the wagon and came out on the other side, and then he had a runaway to the other end of the field where he stayed until the noon meal.

Inez Scott, who had complained about not feeling well for the past few days, asked Ellis to see if someone around Egypt might suggest something for her stomach. She knew that one of the stores had a section dedicated solely to apothecaries. She said she would stay at home and rest a bit.

The wagon-load of cotton was finished by middle of the evening. Ellis hooked a team of mules to the wagon and started toward the Scott house. He said he would be leaving for Egypt in an hour. An hour would give everyone enough time to clean up a bit, and make it to the Scott house for the departure.

Bud heard the mother of the Milligan sisters admonish them, and Cody, to hurry to the camp and wash up and put on some clean clothes. Joel and Hazel Adkins climbed on into the cotton wagon to ride up to the Scott house. Joel said riding a cotton wagon to Egypt was not any reason to take a bath, as far as he could see, and evidently Hazel Adkins agreed.

Inez, thought differently, however. She made Bud fill a number three washtub full of water on the back porch, and take a full bath. Afterward, she soaped his hair and then she brought him into the kitchen where there was a pitcher pump that had been sunk through the floor and pumped water into a heavy cast-iron sink, that drained out under the floor and into a drainage ditch dug across the yard. Inez rinsed his hair under the pump.

Bud had thick red hair that Inez cut periodically with just horse shears and a comb. Bud dried his hair with a heavy towel, and then he went into his parents' bedroom where he found a bottle of his father's shaving lotion and he applied a liberal dose to his face and neck. Then he spotted a bottle of Rose Hair Oil, and poured a generous amount on his hair and combed it in, finally parting his plastered-down hair in the middle. Bud felt good after the bath and head washing, but most importantly, he knew he looked good. He was ready for town.

Ellis started the mules and wagon toward the Egypt gin at 3:30 p.m., the iron-shod hooves of the mules and the iron-rimmed wheels of the cotton wagon clacking on the gravel road. It would take an hour or better to make the five-mile trip. It would very likely be dark when they got back home, depending upon how many farmers brought their cotton to the gin that evening. The weather was warm; the fresh picked cotton felt warm and clean and had the pungent smell that could never be mistaken for anything else.

Everyone climbed aboard and settled down in the cotton for the ride to the little town of Egypt, named by some early settler, as the story went, who, upon arriving in the area, had called it "the promised land," which somehow had gotten translated to "Egypt." Someone had noted that the town with a population of three hundred or so had as many cotton gins as churches.

Bud and Joel had moved to the back of the wagon and were snuggled down in the cotton close together, with their backs against the tailgate, in preparation for a hushed discussion about what tomorrow might bring, when Sherry and Maxine Milligan moved right in with them. Sherry actually pushed in between the two boys, and Maxine pushed up against Bud on the other side, so that he ended up being sandwiched between two freshly washed girls, that reeked of cheap perfume, talcum powder, and something else, that he couldn't put his finger on. Both girls had put on lipstick, which Bud thought was incredible, considering the occasion.

Bud cast a wary eye toward Vaughn Milligan, who was sitting on the seatboard with Ellis Scott. But Vaughn wasn't paying any particular attention to what was going on in the back of the wagon. Cody Milligan and Hazel Adkins were nodding off to sleep, induced by the slow-rocking motion of the cotton wagon. Cody Milligan, Bud thought, never did look real healthy. Cody always looked a little drawn and pallid. *Maybe, he really is wormy*, thought Bud.

Sherry nudged Bud in the ribs, and in a hushed voice that didn't carry past the end of the wagon, said, "Well, are you comin' to the swimmin' party tomorrow evenin'?" She was the bolder of the two sisters, Bud thought, and she didn't waste any time.

"Well, I suppose so, and Joel is comin', too," replied Bud emphatically, with a slightly belligerent tone that said, either take it or leave it.

"Well, bring your weenies," deadpanned Sherry. Bud had excellent peripheral vision. He caught a smile on Maxine's face without turning his head. *Now what?* he thought.

"How's zat?" interjected a startled Joel.

"We're gonna have a weenie roast, silly," continued Sherry, not breaking stride. "And we're gonna roast marshmallows, too. Me and Maxine is gonna buy some marshmallows today, and the Taylor girls are bringin' some bread and stuff. You fellers will have to build us a fire on the sandbar, and cut us some roastin' sticks. We'll swim and roast weenies and marshmallow all at the same time. We'll swim some, and then we'll eat some. Hit'll be fun."

Bud suddenly had a vision of eight naked teenagers sitting around a campfire on a sandbar in the middle of Cache River Ditch. He and Joel had skinny-dipped many times in the ditch, but to bring skinny-dipping girls into the picture, well, that took some thinking about.

"How about water?" said Joel, who was not having any problem with the idea, and who had been blessed with little inhibition.

"There's a good spring comin' outta the bank. All we need is a cup," said Maxine.

"How many weenies?" asked Bud, contemplating what he had planned for the two dollars he had in his pocket, and which did not include a weenie purchase.

Maxine made a quick mental estimate. "Three dozen," she said.

Joel was doing some mental calculations, too. He had no idea what three-dozen wieners cost, and he didn't expect Bud did either. He had two dollars and some change, and he knew he would be obliged to split the cost of the wieners with Bud. He had planned on eating several ice cream cones, a few chocolate candy bars, and washing it all down with two or three big orange drinks and maybe an R.C. Cola or two. Weiners had not been included in the equation.

A pregnant silence followed, out of which was born a message from Sherry: "Hit'll be so much fun, you'll see."

Sunday dawned warm and clear. There were two weeks of summer left. Fall would arrive on the twenty-third day of September. Weather fronts would bring cold, dewy mornings, hot afternoons, and temperatures that would drop into the lower fifties during the night.

The skin on the fingers would begin to crack from the extremes of temperature and moisture. Every field hand would have their own bottle of a clear glycerin mixture that included camphor, named, "Cotton Pickers Friend," patented and bottled in the little town of Lepanto, Arkansas, thirty miles east of Jonesboro. Liberal applications of the mixture would be applied to the tips of the fingers and around the fingernails throughout the workday.

The entire Milligan clan arrived at the Scott house for a ride to church, on Sunday morning, having been thoughtfully invited by Inez. The Milligans were all Methodists, but no one could really define the difference between a Methodist and a Baptist. It was not uncommon for different members of a mountain family to belong to both churches.

Methodism had a strong hold on the hill people, probably as a result of the early circuit-riding preachers who had been sent into the mountains as missionaries by the Methodist Ministerial Board, to preach the gospel to the heathen. The preachers traveled uncharted roads on horseback, sometimes in a buggy, and toting the King James Bible in their saddlebags. They preached sermons, sometimes standing on a stump or wagon bed, to anyone who would listen. Often they were invited to preach in one of the local churches. They survived on handouts and slept in barns or out in the open, but they left a lot of Methodist church members scattered through the hills.

Inez Scott told Bud that it was the getting to heaven that counted, not the road taken. "Good intentions," she said, "don't get you nowhere in this life or the hereafter. It's the doin' that counts." Bud remembered that saying of his mother, when he was pondering the coming evening activities down at the swimming hole. He wondered just what category of intentions skinny-dipping would fall in.

Bud had a reasonably clear conscious, though, because he had already explained the large paper sack full of wieners that he had brought home from Egypt, and had put in the icebox. When informed of the size and makeup of the group, Inez had formed the opinion that it was an innocent enough gathering, and would provide a healthy diversion from the routine of the cotton harvest. Bud had somehow neglected to mention that they all planned to skinny-dip in the swimming hole.

Inez didn't know the Taylor sisters personally, but she knew they all went to school at Egypt. She had heard that Pearl Taylor, the oldest, was known to dip snuff and chew tobacco in her classroom at Egypt High School, and that she had kept a spit can at her desk, until some parents complained. The teacher then moved Pearl next to a window. Someone said you could always tell where Pearl sat inside the classroom, because of the tobacco stains running down the wall outside her window.

Inez couldn't fault the girl for using tobacco, though. That was the teacher's fault to allow that sort of thing, as sinful as it was. Anyway, swallowing a little tobacco now and then was known to help in ridding a person of stomach worms.

Inez was feeling better now, since Ellis had brought home a quart jar of a chalky-peppermint-tasting liquid from Egypt. The person that ran the apothecary shop had told Ellis that it sounded like Inez had stomach ulcers. He prescribed a bland diet with no salt, nor pork fat, and instructed Ellis that she should take a tablespoon of the medicine before each meal. Inez' stomach pains had diminished, and she was in better spirits, and was smiling more. Bud was happy about that, because he hated it when his mama got sick. It made him feel bad, too.

Before setting out for church, Ellis had thoughtfully placed four straight-backed, cane-bottomed chairs in the wagon, for the adult women to sit on, and he threw in a half-dozen fifty-pound burlap bags of cottonseed for the rest. The first thing that Cody Milligan did was to find a spot in the middle of the wooden wagon bed, sit flat down with his legs spread and begin to flip his open pocket knife, sticking it in the floorboard of the wagon between his legs.

"You wanna play mumbly-peg?" asked Cody, looking at Bud.

"No, I don't believe so," replied Bud, trying to be civil, while secretly hoping that the wagon would lurch suddenly causing Cody to make a miscue, and stick the knife in his own privates. Bud chuckled to himself, thinking about the possibility.

Inez chose to sit in one of the chairs with the women, and Vaughn Milligan sat on the driver's seat with Ellis. As the wagon ground along the gravel road toward the church, the Milligan women began to sing a hymn. Inez joined in, and Bud, who sat with his back to a sideboard directly across from the sisters, thought it might be the prettiest music he had ever heard. Could the angels sing any better?

It was amazing to Bud that the Milligans seemed to know all the verses of every song. Bud reckoned that he only knew two tunes. One was "My Darling Clementine," and the other wasn't. Bud, according to Ellis Scott, "couldn't carry a tune in a water bucket." Ellis said he couldn't imagine an Irishman who couldn't sing a tune or dance a jig.

They were still singing when Ellis, beaming with pride at his wagonload of lyrical feminine pulchritude, pulled the mules up to the hitching post in the churchyard. The usual groups of pre-service gossips looked on in amazement, and broke out into spontaneous applause, as the singing wagon began to unload.

Once inside the church, Sherry Milligan squeezed in on one side of Bud on a church bench, and Maxine squeezed in on the other. Bud, wasn't prepared for this. He had the feeling of grape jelly squeezed between two highly spiced pieces of French toast. He was swamped by the dueling aromas of cheap perfume, talcum powder, hairdressing, lipstick, nail polish, baking powder, flour, vanilla flavoring and mothballs.

It had been just a few weeks before, when he had found himself in this same predicament, when he was hemmed in by Betty Adkins, and the harlot, Mary Margaret Miller. He still hadn't forgotten that experience, and probably never would.

He knew that the other members of the congregation, being naturally curious about the strangers in their midst, would be staring in his direction, and here he was unexpectedly sitting right in the middle of them. Bud clasped his hands together in his lap and looked straight ahead. Sherry, with an innocent air of nonchalance, laid one of her hands on top of his. He thought about moving his hand, but he didn't want to be too obvious. He thought about scratching his ear. That would be an innocent enough gesture, and would require that Sherry move her hand in order to release his.

Maxine, thankfully, had kept her hands to herself—so far. Bud, thought that the Milligan girls must be hurting for affection, but he wasn't about to become their first-aid station while sitting in the middle of a church. He pulled at his left hand to reach up to scratch his ear, only to have Sherry temporarily move her right hand and then to let it drop into his unprotected lap. She immediately began drumming her fingers against the inside of his left thigh against the taut fabric of his overalls. Bud scratched his ear for a long time trying to determine his next move, while Sherry's nimble fingers continued roll call.

Sherry leaned her head over toward Bud and in a hushed voice said, "I see that you have brought your lunch."

"My lunch!" replied a puzzled Bud, in a shocked whisper, a little to loud.

"Yep! Two boiled eggs, and a pickle," replied Sherry.

Maxine sniggered. Bud felt himself turning a bright red and without further hesitation, decided his ear had received its proper quota of scratching, and quickly joined it up with the other, squeezing it with some difficulty back under Sherry's fingers that had not ceased their steady drumming. He wondered if his mother was watching these tactical maneuvers.

The Milligan clan, who had not heard of Homer Adkins, was shocked beyond belief, when the self-appointed prophet and holy man entered the church through the deacon hole. Homer took his customary chair to the left side of the pulpit facing the congregation. Homer was dressed in his prophet's best, a gray woolen robe, and car tire sandals with leather thongs. His head was bared and his flaxen white hair hung straight to his shoulders; his pink eyes glowed in the light from the side windows. "Good God Almighty!" whispered Maxine. Sherry suddenly removed her hands from Bud's lap, and covered her mouth with her right.

The Right Reverend Roscoe Gilmore followed in his usual unsteady Sunday morning gait, and took his customary seat to the right side of the pulpit. Abe Turner stood up and offered a prayer. Bud was praying, too, but he veered off of Abe's spiritual path, and solicited God, Jesus, the Arch Angel Gabriel, or just anybody that might be handy, to help keep Sherry Milligan's hands to herself for the rest of the service.

Bud's prayers were answered, if only temporarily, when Abe called on the Milligan family to come up front and sing a few hymns. This solicitation was met with a few amens from members of the congregation, who were bored to tears with the customary Sunday morning dirges. Any change from the customary routine, would be more than welcome.

All of the Milligan women, without hesitation, stood up and gathered in front of the pulpit. It was fairly obvious that they were used to singing in public. Bud was amazed at the ease in which they performed. He would have been scared to death to do something like that. They sang three hymns that Bud had never heard. Probably came out of a Methodist Hymnal, he thought. He knew they weren't in the Baptist Hymnal.

The thought about the hymnal gave Bud a brilliant idea. He picked up one of the hymnals that were scattered around on the benches, and placed it in his lap, and then placed his hands on top. That, he thought, ought to put a stop to anymore of Sherry's shenanigans.

The rest of the service went forward as usual. The Milligan clan listened attentively to Roscoe's sermon, but kept their eyes on Homer. Homer just sat straight in his chair with his hands in his lap and his feet more or less together. He turned his head occasionally toward Roscoe, and then back toward the congregation. Roscoe finished his sermon with his usual flourish, and then said, "Now it's time to hear from the prophet."

Roscoe took his seat, and Homer, without hesitation, stepped to the podium. Homer spoke without notes, which is usually a grave mistake. No exception was made in this case.

"Children of God, lend me your ears,
From this time forth, you will hear new things.
You have heard them before, but never like this,
So listen up.
Come down and sit in the gumbo clods,
O you children of Satan.
For you shall be called tender to the devil's pitchfork.
And to the clouds of skeeters.
Pass the Calamine Lotion.
Let yore nekkidness be uncovered.
There will be no shame in Eden.
Depart. Depart, stay clear of sheep.
Do not touch unclean things.

159

What are those thangs that fly like a cloud,
And like buzzards to yore windows?
A multitude of skeeters shall cover you,
And there will be fiery chariots from above.
And the Son of Man will be betrayed,
When the frost is on the pumpkin.
And lastly: tomorrow will be a beautiful day.
Lord, it's hot in here."

On the way home, there had been a period of quiet meditation, when Sherry asked in general terms and to no one in particular, just what Homer had said.

"He didn't say nothin' that made any sense," replied Inez.

"He was speaking in parables," said Bud.

"What's a parable exactly?" asked Maxine.

"It's when you talk in riddles, so that no one can pin anything on you," interjected Inez, and continued, "If you read the old-time prophets, you'll find that none of them ever made any sense. They go on forever talkin' complete nonsense, and good Christians for the past two thousand years have set aroun' and argued 'bout what it was they said. And what it boils down too, is that they ain't said nothin'. Homer Adkins is real good at saying nothin', which makes him a real good prophet. I'll give him that much."

"Well, I wish we had the prophet in our church at home," said Sherry.

"Honey," replied Inez. "I wish you had him, too."

"Amen," said Ellis from the drivers seat.

After arriving at the Scott house, Ellis turned the mules through the lot gate and he and Inez got out of the wagon. "Bud, you drive the Milligans on down to their camp. When you get back, I'll help you unharness the team," said Ellis.

Bud moved up to the power position in the driver's seat. He took the reins with an air of superiority and confidence. "Giddy-up," he said.

Upon arriving at the Milligan camp, Sherry lagged behind as the family climbed down out of the wagon, and entered into their campsite at the Thompson barn lot. "Don't fergit, two-thirty sharp, and don't fergit your weenies," she said in a whisper, with just the slightest giggle, and a twinkle in her eyes. Bud flicked the reins, a signal for the mules to head for home.

Bud debated whether he should turn to look back when he reached a point a hundred yards or so down the road, just to see if Sherry was watching his departure. Perhaps she would give him a little wave. He debated: Should he turn? Shouldn't he turn? Should he turn? Shouldn't he turn? After all, he didn't want to create the illusion that he liked this girl, but as a courtesy he could turn, like a cowboy riding into the sunset, and give a perfunctionary wave. Would Hopalong Cassidy turn? Would Wild Bill Elliott turn? His curiosity got the best of him. He turned to look back. Cody Milligan, sitting atop the barn lot gate, was the only Milligan in sight. Cody waved.

Bud ate a smaller dinner than normal. He wanted to save room for roasted wieners, and marshmallows. If there was a deficit in fulfillment, he could always make it up at supper. After dinner he took his sack of wieners and headed for Joel's house, arriving about one-thirty in the evening. Bud was wearing an old pair of blue overalls and nothing else, no hat, no shoes, no shirt and no underwear. He didn't want undressing and dressing to be a complicated and lengthy chore. He would just slip in and out of his overalls, and that would be it. Joel adopted the same mode of dress.

Bud convinced Joel that they needed to go on down to the swimming hole and get the wood out onto the sandbar and get ready to start the fire once the girls arrived. Bud said he thought that once everything was in place that they should go ahead and get out of their overalls and into the water.

Bud was not looking forward to getting undressed in front of a bunch of strange girls. Joel had some advantage in this regard. He had at least been raised with an older sister. Bud thought everything would be all right, once everyone was all naked alike and in the water. He still hadn't worked out in his mind just how he was going to get to the roasted wieners and marshmallows. Hopefully, he would just have Sherry feed him while he stayed in the water.

Bud and Joel went on down to the sandbar which had been created and smoothed by the spring flood and summer current. A sandy pool had been created when the current had pushed the sand out into a bar that very nearly blocked the channel. Two streams only about six-feet across and no more than knee deep flowed out of the pool and around either side of the sandbar, and then the river gradually deepened to about waist deep beyond.

The water in the deepest part of the swimming hole only came up to Bud and Joel's armpits. If you could stand up you wouldn't drown. The washed out pool was round in shape and was about thirty-feet across. The water level in the ditch was down and there were occasional springs flowing out of both banks through blue-clay just above the water line all along the ditch. The clear-water springs, with the sandy bottom of the pool, produced a pool of clean, cool water even on the hottest of days. The greenish color of the

161

swimming hole contrasted sharply with the murky brown of the rest of the water in the ditch.

The boys set about cutting brush and tree limbs for the fire. Joel had brought a small hatchet from his house and was doing a good execution on low hanging limbs, when there was a rustle in the brush on the other side of the ditch. It was too early for the girls to arrive. Bud, slightly alarmed, conducted a visual search of the brush and trees along the east bank of the ditch. Finally, a squirrel could be seen moving through the branches of a tree. *So that's all it was,* he thought. Bud's nerves were on edge. He took a deep breath, and wondered if his father was listening to a St. Louis Cardinal baseball game on the radio. He wished he was.

When a sufficient amount of brush was piled on the sandbar and a good supply of extra wood was gathered, it was time to shuck their overalls and get into the water. Joel had the foresight to leave a box of matches near the brush and wood. That way they could have the girls light the fire when they arrived on the scene.

They had no sooner hung their overalls on a limb on the west bank and dived into the pool, than what sounded like a heard of cattle began moving through the brush down the east bank, and in single file, down a trail through the brush, marched the Taylor sisters single file, led by Pearl, the oldest, and followed by the Milligan sisters. Two of the girls were carrying paper sacks. The girls were all dressed in an assortment of cut-off jeans, shorts, and halter-tops. It was immediately evident that the Milligan sisters had already been to the ditch and had crossed to meet the Taylor sisters on the other side. The girls had been watching all along.

The girls all came down to the water's edge and lined up along the bank. "Why don't you boys show us how to swim on your back," said Pearl. The girls all giggled. "I'd like to see another good run down the bank and a dive in the water," said Maxine Milligan, with more giggles following. *The older girls were more mischievous, and worldly,* Bud thought to himself. "What a mess this is," said Joel, under his breath.

"Well, are you boys going to light our fire?" asked Sherry, the bold.

"Light it yourself," said Joel. "There's a box of matches close to the wood. Strike one or two and throw them in on the brush, it'll catch."

Pearl led the way, and all the girls moved over to the sandbar, and Maxine Milligan took matches from the box and soon had a good fire going.

"Well, girls let's go swimmin'," said Pearl, and the girls all waded into the pool wearing the same attire that they had arrived in. Sherry eased over toward Bud, who was standing with Joel in the deepest part of the pool. "I thought you didn't have a bathin' suit," said Bud, in hushed tones edged with antipathy.

"Silly, this hain't a bathin' suit," replied Sherry.

"Girls, I believe it's time to induct these two fellers into the Snapping Turtle Society," announced Pearl, which was followed by several girlish acclamations. The girls had begun to move into a circle around the two boys who were still standing in the deepest part of the pool. Pearl Taylor, who had a pinch of snuff between her cheek and gum, spit into the water. Bud watched the reddish blob spread and follow the rippling water around the sandbar. He wished he was under it.

"What's a Snapping Turtle Society exactly?" asked Joel, slightly apprehensive.

Pearl Taylor moved in front of the boys, and got their attention by expounding on what she called a secret society. Pearl said, "There is a big snapping turtle that lives under the bank of the ditch just over there." She pointed to the nearby bank. "We believe he will weigh in at over a hundred pounds."

That's one big turtle, but it could be true, Bud thought. He had seen one, once, that came out of this very ditch that weighed one hundred-twenty pounds. Some men had it down at Turner's Store, and had weighed it on Abe's produce scales. It took two men to lift it into the back of a pick-up truck. It had walked upright like a dog through the store, and when one of the men stuck a mop handle in its mouth, the turtle had bit it clean in to with one snap.

Pearl continued, "Snappy, has took a likin' to us girls, and we've been feedin' him fer some time. We give him dough balls, and sometimes a weenie. We aim to give him a weenie today, maybe two." Bud and Joel involuntarily covered their privates with both hands. "We thought we would introduce you boys to old Snappy and let him get to know you," continued Pearl.

Sherry Milligan had moved in behind Bud, and Willene Taylor was in Joel's rear. "I will now call Snappy forth," said Pearl. "Now everyone hold their hands in the air. You too, boys, while I do the snapping turtle chant."

The girls all immediately raised their arms skyward. Bud and Joel were both hesitant with a big turtle around, but with a stern look from Pearl, they reluctantly raised both hands above their heads. Pearl looked up into the treetops along the bank, and began to intone:

"Oh, snapping turtle come and see,
What your daughters have brought to thee.
Oh, snapping turtle have no fear,
Only your daughters, and their friends are here."

It was during the last stanza, that Willene and Sherry had slowly lowered themselves under water and had begun to move around the legs of Bud and Joel, to their front. It was at this point that Pearl said in a loud voice, while looking down into the water, "He's here!"

The girls had evidently practiced this maneuver because the timing was perfect. When Pearl had said, "He's here!" Bud and Joel felt the water swirl around their legs and Willene moved into position and with her left hand cupped Joel's privates and gave a healthy squeeze. Sherry did the same thing to Bud with her right hand.

Bud and Joel were lifted to a buoyant stage, so that they lost all traction with the sandy bottom, and both screamed in terror as the two girls squeezed and lifted. It was at this moment of panic that both girls surfaced right in the face of the boys and yelled, "Snapping Turtle!" The boys squalled out again.

The girls lifted and pushed the boys away, and let them fall back and under the water. Without hesitation, the boys, as soon as they surfaced and regained their footing, made for the west bank and their overalls. They scrambled stark naked up the bank. Bud grabbed his overalls that he had left hanging on a bush and kept running. Joel followed. Shrieks of girlish laughter echoed up from the swimming hole.

The boys ran over the bank and out into the cotton patch on the other side, and as they stopped long enough to don their overalls, Joel said, "Them girls near skeered tha' shit outta me. You got any money? I'm hungry."

Bud fished a finger down into the watch pocket of his overalls. "I gotta quarter," he said.

"I gotta quarter, too," said Joel, fishing the coin out of his pocket. "Let's go up to the store and get some real food."

Bud, already visualizing a big orange drink and a package of salted peanuts, replied, "I'm with you on that."

CHAPTER 16

The atmosphere between Bud and Joel, and the Milligan sisters was chilly on Monday. It got even colder when a weather front blew in at noon, dropping the temperature by twenty degrees, bringing a light, cold rain that delayed picking for an hour. Fall, had arrived. There would be no more skinny-dipping in the swimming hole until next summer. Bud thought that if it were not for bad luck, he wouldn't have any luck at all.

Sherry tried to make a cordial overture to Bud, which he rebuffed.

"How come you boys didn't stay for the weenie and marshmallow roast?" she asked, with an air of innocence.

"Me and Joel decided we wanted some real food, so we went up to Turner's. Besides the water was too cold. It shore woulda been a pity, if someone had choked to death on a weenie, particularly ole' Snappy," Bud replied and walked away, letting her know that the conversation was over.

It didn't help matters, either, when Cody Milligan eased up behind Bud in the field, and unexpectedly yelled, "Snapping turtle!" as loud as he could, causing Bud to involuntarily jump over two cotton rows. Bud, turned and bristled. "How'd you like me to whup yore skinny ass?"

"You hit me, and I'll tell your daddy," yelped Cody.

Bud couldn't do anything right then, because he knew the value of the hill people in getting the cotton out, and he didn't want to cause any strained relations. Besides, Cody could outpick him, which rankled Bud to no end. Bud thought that someday when the situation was just right, though, that he would get even with that little wormy bastard.

Airplanes were dog fighting over the fields more than ever. Bud and Joel kept looking for another one to crash, but it never happened, not where they could see, anyway.

According to an article that Bud read in a local newspaper, the war was going full blast in Italy. A big allied campaign that had started about the middle of September, was unfolding at Salerno, and a U.S. Army Ranger unit led by Lt. Colonel William Darby, called, "Darby's Rangers" was in the thick of the fighting. After reading the article, Bud decided then and there, that if he ever went into the army, he wanted to be a member of Darby's Rangers.

Rabid Robert Ryder had not shown up to pick cotton on the Monday, following Bud and Joel's Sunday afternoon debacle at the swimming hole. Evidently, a few days of cotton picking was enough for him. Ellis Scott thought it was just as well, as he was uneasy about having an escaped convict in the field, even though he thought that being sent to Tucker Prison Farm for stealing a dollar's worth of gasoline, and getting whipped to boot, was a little excessive. Ellis would miss Rabid Robert's daily contribution of over two hundred pounds of picked cotton.

Abe Turner said Rabid Robert had passed by his store that Monday morning and had bought a loaf of bread and a pound of bologna and a pound of cheese. He had continued on foot up the east bank of Cache River Ditch toward Sedgwick.

About the third week in September some troubling news was brought to Abe Turner from Mr. Wilson regarding Blue Duck and his child bride. Mr. Wilson said he had been down near the peckerwood sawmill camp and he had seen Blue Duck beating the little girl outside, in front of the sawmill shack. Mr. Wilson asked Abe, if there was something that could be done about it. Sometimes in domestic difficulties, the local preacher would try to intervene. Perhaps this was the time for Roscoe Gilmore to get involved. It was Roscoe's whiskey that was agitating old Blue Duck into this domestic strife, or so said Mr. Wilson.

Abe took Mr. Wilson's solicitation under advisement, and made the determination that the next encounter he had with Roscoe that he would ask him to go to the sawmill shack and see if he might provide some relief for the little Cherokee girl. Abe knew, too, that she was being beaten regularly, as the couple came to the store once or twice a week, and Abe always observed fresh bruises around the girl's cheeks and eyes. Mr. Wilson had also noted that the beatings were taking place when the big hound was in the woods running game. Evidently, Blue Duck could not lay a hand on the girl when the hound was near.

It was late in the week, when Roscoe Gilmore came up to the store for supplies. Abe decided that it was time to confront Roscoe about the Cherokee problem. "You've been supplyin' moonshine to that drunken Indian. It seems to me that you bear the brunt of the responsibility for him beatin' that little girl. You need to go down to their camp and see if you can't help rectify that situation. He's killin' that child, he calls his wife," said Abe.

Roscoe sat down on an orange crate, and put his head in his hands. He sat staring at the floor. It took considerably longer for Roscoe to digest what he had just heard, than it did for Abe to dictate it. During the considerable lull in the conversation, which had been one-way to that point, Harvey Winkles came into the store. He had not been advised of the Cherokee situation. He just caught the tail end of Abe's statement, and asked to what Abe was referring. Abe laid out for Harvey a short, concise history of the Cherokee couple and the fact that the young girl-wife of Blue Duck Smith was being beaten on a regular basis.

"Is she a big nagger," inquired Harvey, trying to find some justifiable reason for the beatings, "nagging" being considered a strong provocation.

"No," replied Roscoe, in a classic case of misunderstanding. "She's just a little bitty Indian girl."

"That's not exactly what I meant," sniggered Harvey.

"Roscoe, you need to go on down there now, while that hound is out trailin'. He's way back in the woods. I heard him from off the front porch just a while ago," said Abe.

"Maybe I could go with you," said Harvey.

"Would you?" asked a brightening Roscoe.

"Yep," said Harvey.

"Nope," said Abe.

"Nope?" stated Roscoe.

"Nope," reiterated Abe. "I don't want Harvey to git involved. He's not a member of this community and it's not his place to git involved. Besides, if you should git delayed for some reason, Harvey might not git back in time to show the movie tonight."

"Well, it's the possibility of the delay, that concerns me," countered Roscoe. "It sounds like a legal matter to me. Maybe you ought to call the county sheriff."

"Already have," responded Abe, neatly blocking Roscoe's counter. "He said he was not gettin' into no domestic dispute of itinerant Cherokee cotton pickers. You need to go down there. Do you want the possibility of blood on your conscience?"

"Well," said a laconic Roscoe, "if I had my druthers, I druther have it on my conscience than on me."

"Well, you're not goin' then?" said Abe.

"Didn't say that," responded Roscoe, suddenly rising to his feet, having received a sudden flash of inspiration. "Give me a couple of cold bottles of that brew out of the sody case, and a bag to put em' in."

"What are ya goin' to do?" asked Harvey, who had taken up residence on top of a nail keg.

"I'm a-goin' to get on my mule, and take them drinks down there to the shack, and try to get inside. I'll just have to play it by ear from there," said Roscoe.

There are in times of trial and tribulation and during the darkest hour of dread and fear when man may encounter one of life's little unexpected rewards. This was one of those times. Stepping up on the porch at that very moment was the synthetic figure of Homer Adkins.

"Hot damn! The prophet is here," exclaimed Roscoe, as Homer came through the door. Homer was dressed in prophet garb: robe and rubber tire sandals, topped with a planter's hat to complete the ensemble.

"What's up?" inquired Homer, sensing a certain adulation being sent his way.

"I've got a project for you my boy," said Roscoe, with obvious relief.

"What's up?" inquired Homer, a second time.

"Marriage counseling training, son," said Roscoe. "I'm afraid I've neglected that portion of your apprenticeship, but we now have a situation here in the neighborhood that is ripe with possibilities for personal gain and satisfaction on your part, and for a delegation of authority on my part, which all preachers must exercise from time to time."

"Cut the bullshit, Roscoe, and get to the point," stated Homer.

"It's no BS my boy," said Roscoe. "There is believed to be a domestic crisis down at the Cherokee camp."

"What kind of domestic crisis?" asked Homer.

"That little Cherokee gal is gettin' the shit kicked outta her on a regular basis," interjected Harvey from his nail keg perch.

"Roscoe, do you really thank Homer is man enough for the job?" asked Abe from back of the meat counter.

"Whadda ya mean, man enough?" exclaimed Homer, bristling at the insensitivity of what he perceived to be a disparaging remark regarding his manhood. "Hell, I've been in the 82nd Airborne, and while yore back there fix me a baloney sandwich. I wanna slice of baloney a half-inch thick, with mustard and a slice of white onion."

"He's been in the army, Abe," said Roscoe. "He ought to be able to handle a little domestic dispute."

"OK, but it's your decision," said Abe.

"Easiest decision, I've ever made," said Roscoe.

Homer left the store for the Cherokee camp about an hour before sundown. He could hear the Cherokee Devil Hound a mile or so back in the woods. He did not want to go into that camp with that dog anywhere near. Homer was carrying a sack with two bottles of home-brew beer and two baloney sandwiches for the Cherokee couple as sort of a peace offering and icebreaker.

When he reached the gate in the wire fence that separated the Wilson's cotton field from the woods and the peckerwood sawmill camp, he heard the sound of yelling and crying coming from inside the shack. Evidently, Blue Duck was doing what he did best. Homer reached the gate and stopped.

"Hal-loo, the camp!" called out Homer.

There was silence immediately following Homer's call, then came a muffled sound of sobbing.

"Hal-loo, the camp!" called Homer again. The single door to the shack, visible to Homer at the gate, eased open and Blue Duck emerged blinking against the fading light of day.

"Whatcha want white man?" responded Blue Duck.

Homer had a sudden inspiration. He had been born and raised in Izard County, where he had encountered several Cherokee families. He made the immediate decision not to approach this encounter head-on. He would attempt an oblique tactful way to get acquainted with an evidently belligerent savage.

"I'm from Izard County," offered Homer. "I was a missionary among the tribes there."

"Well, hit's a good place to be from," responded Blue Duck. "And what tribes? Hell, there hain't no tribes up there, only some half-breed families scattered here and yon. I said whacha want?"

A change of tactics was suddenly called for. "What do your friends call you?" asked Homer. "Blue Duck, Blue, Duck, or Mr. Smith?"

"I hain't got no friends," said Blue Duck.

"Whaddaya want me to call you?" asked Homer, now hearing more sobs coming from inside the shack.

"I wancha to call me from thet county road back up yonder, and get yore lilly-white ass outta here, I'm busy," said Blue Duck.

It was time to shift to plan-B. "I've brought baloney sandwiches, and some brew, compliments of Mr. Abe Turner, for you and the missus," said Homer.

"Well, whyn't you say so in the first place? Come on in," said a suddenly affable Blue Duck.

"That dog ain't aroun', is he?" asked Homer, looking intently around the shack and into the woods beyond, because he hadn't heard the dog trailing since he had arrived at the camp.

"Nah, he'll be back dreckly, but he won't hurt ya, lessen I sic him on ya," said Blue Duck, in a voice edged with malice.

Homer entered through the gate, but not without some trepidation as to what the next few minutes might bring. He was offered entry into the one-room shack, which was lit with a single candle sitting on a wall shelf. He noted the single door of the shack was hinged with leather strips cut from worn-out mule harness. He scanned the walls for weapons of any kind. The only thing visible was a three-foot steel rod leaning in the corner close to the stove, obviously used as a poker. The stench of unwashed bodies, spoiled food, wood smoke and tobacco, hit Homer full in the face as he entered the shack, bringing tears to his eyes, and very nearly tripping his gag reflex.

On the shelf by the candle was a half-empty quart jar of Roscoe's moonshine. The shack also contained a small wood burning, pot-bellied stove, and two chairs and a small wooden table made from sawmill scrap lumber. Cotton stuffed burlap bags were strewn in the corner, evidently serving as bedding. Blue Duck's wife reclined on a pile of the cotton-stuffed bags in a corner, holding her head in her hands. She suddenly became alert to Homer's pink gaze that was surveying the interior of the shack. She looked straight into his face with hollow eyes. It was evident from her tear-streaked cheeks, that she had been crying, and there was a trickle of blood from her nose collecting on her upper lip. She was barefoot and dressed in ragged jeans and a long-sleeve shirt. Her long black hair was hanging loose. Homer's albino features provided such a sharp contrast to the dimly lit shack and the dark and morose features off the occupants, that a staring match immediately issued.

"Howdy, Miss Smith," said Homer brightly, reaching out to her with the brown paper bag of sandwiches and drinks. Blue Duck stepped forward and intercepted the handout.

"My wife don't talk much," said Blue Duck.

Blue Duck took the two sandwiches out of the paper bag, and handed one to the woman, who without hesitation, began to eat ravenously. *She's starving to death,* Homer thought. Blue Duck did not offer any of the brew to the woman, but kept both bottles for himself. He sat down in one of the camp chairs and opened one of the home-brew bottles and began to eat his sandwich. Homer sat down in the other chair, without invite. Blue Duck looked straight at Homer's shoulder-length white flaxen hair, in obvious admiration. His tongue was thick from having been in the shine. *He's drunk as a skunk,* thought Homer.

"You know in the old days, yore scalp would be hangin' outside my teepee by now," said Blue Duck.

Homer ignored the comment. "Mr. Turner, makes a pretty fair country sandwich, don't he?" asked Homer.

"Tolerable," said Blue Duck. "you hain't come down hyar jist ta pass gas."

Blue Duck had passed the ball to Homer. He caught it and ran with it.

"I come down here because some people in the community believe you are beatin' that little gurl over there," said Homer, pointing to Blue Duck's wife.

"What if I am?" said Blue Duck. "She's bought and paid fer. I've owned her for going on four years now."

"Well, ownin' people went out with the abolishment of slavery back durin' the Civil War," said Homer.

"She hain't no slave, she's my wife," responded Blue Duck.

As in most white man and Indian counsels throughout the history of the United States, this one was not getting anywhere. Homer sat for a moment trying to think of a verbal challenge that would be difficult for Blue Duck to dodge or counter. Homer leaned forward for emphasis and looked Blue Duck square in the eyes for emphasis.

"Well, you could git yore smoky ass hung from one of them trees out there," said Homer, motioning toward the woods. There was a pause in the proceedings, and then Blue Duck responded, "And…who's to do it?"

Homer had come into this session with minimal marriage counseling skills, and so far he hadn't made any progress that he could see. A different tactic was called for, something from the 82nd Airborne perhaps.

"I don't believe I have got your attention," said Homer, as he suddenly stood and reaching across the table, slapped Blue Duck full in the face, knocking him backward out of his chair. Blue Duck rolled into the corner behind him, and came up brandishing the steel poker in his right hand. "Yore a wiry little bastard, ain'tcha?" said Homer, as he grabbed the chair he had been sitting in and prepared to defend himself. They stood staring at one another, neither saying a word. Blue Duck's wife had gotten to her feet. She stepped to Homer's side of the table, opposite Blue Duck.

"Take me with you. He'll kill me now fer shore," she said in a pleading little girl's voice, taking a step toward Homer.

It was at this moment that Blue Duck stepped forward toward his wife, swinging the heavy metal poker, and caught her just above the right eye, fracturing her skull. She was dead by the time she hit the floor. As her body thumped facedown on the floor, a low roar was heard just outside the door. Suddenly, there was a crashing sound as the leather hinges were ripped off the doorframe. The thin cypress door fell into the shack with the Cherokee Devil Hound standing on top of it. Homer leaped to the side and was now blocked from the door, trapped in a corner by the giant hound. Homer could feel every hair on his body stand straight out. But the hound was not paying any attention to Homer. His enormous teeth were barred and he was looking straight at Blue Duck, who still held the lethal poker.

Blue Duck, suddenly cold sober, lunged toward the hound and hit the dog a mighty blow with the poker right between the ears on the crown of his skull. The big dog faltered and seemed momentarily dazed. Blue Duck struck again, and this time the dog went down.

Homer saw his opening and lunged over the dazed dog and through the open door. He spun around the corner of the shack and headed for the fence gate that thankfully he had left open. He was through the gate in a flash, and into the field road that led up to Turner's Store. He glanced over his left shoulder, but there was no sign of Blue Duck, or the hound.

When Homer reached a point up the road at a distance of about one hundred yards, a sudden roar and tremendous crashing sound caused him to stop and look back. The shack was shaking as if blown in a heavy wind. Then he heard an inhuman long drawn out scream, then another, shorter this time, then another, shorter still, then nothing. Homer turned toward the store and ran with all the speed he could muster.

Ruth Turner was hanging clothes on a line tied between two trees at the rear of the store. She saw Homer coming fast up through the field, little spirals of dust kicking up under his heels. She moved toward the road that ran by the store as if to intercept him. As Homer raced by, Ruth called out, "Why're you runnin', Homer?"

"I'm runnin' cause I can't fly!" Homer yelled back over his shoulder.

Homer spun around the corner of the store, onto the front porch, and plunged through the front door, barefoot and out of breath. He had lost his planters hat and both sandals. Abe, Roscoe and Harvey were all still in the store.

"He's killed her!" Homer blubbered, out of breath.

"He's what?" asked Abe, coming around from behind the meat counter.

"Son, what are you sayin'?" asked Roscoe, getting up from off the counter.

"You gotta be shittin' me," said Harvey, still sitting on the nail keg.

"He killed her right in front of my eyes. Hit her with a poker," said Homer. "And he may be coming after me."

"We'd better get down there," said Abe.

"Whaddaya mean...we?" said Roscoe.

"Yeh," said Harvey.

"Don't go down there without no gun, thet hound is there, and the last thing I saw of him, he was mad as hell. Blue Duck hit him twice on the head with that poker, but I don't thank it fazed him much," said Homer. "You'd better call the sheriff."

"Well, I ain't callin' nobody, til I kin go down there and see for myself what the situation is," responded Abe, not putting a lot of faith in Homer's excited tale.

"Then go git Ellis Scott, and have him bring his deer rifle. Yore pro'bly goin' to have to kill thet dog," said Homer.

"Good idee," said Abe. "In the meantime, Roscoe, you and Homer go on home and stay outta sight for the next few days. I don't thank either of you wants to get involved with the sheriff, considerin' your activities. I'll handle this."

Abe went to the back of the store and called to Ruth. He explained the situation to her and told her to watch the store, as he was going to be busy for a while. The sun had dropped behind the horizon. Ellis and Bud had finished the barn chores after coming in from the field. They had just sat down to supper, when Abe pulled up in his pick-up truck in front of the Scott house. He came up on the porch and looked in through the screen door. He could see through the front room and into the kitchen where the Scott family members were eating supper.

Without getting up from the supper table, Ellis called for Abe to come in. Abe entered through the screen door and went on back to the kitchen. "Have a cup of coffee," said Ellis, as Abe came into the kitchen. "It's already been saucered and blowed."

Inez asked Abe if he wanted supper, which he declined, but he sat down at the supper table and sipped a cup of hot coffee while describing the late afternoon events.

Bud was fascinated at the possibility of having a murder on Horse Island, practically in his backyard, but inwardly he hoped it wasn't the little Indian girl. Blue Duck, though, wouldn't be much of a loss.

"Ellis," Abe said. "I need you to bring that heavy deer rifle of yours and let me have your shotgun. I've got some heavy twelve-gauge number-ought buckshot at the store; I'll pick up on the way by. If that dog is down there at that shack, he's probably gonna be guardin' that girl, and we'll have to kill him, to get to her."

"Can I come, too?" asked Bud. Inez shook her head – no – at Ellis. But Abe, who saw Inez's gesture, softened the rejection.

"Bud," said Abe. "Me and Ellis is goin' to have enough to watch out for in the dark without havin' to watch out for you. Why don't you come down to the store and wait there. You can help Ruth wait on customers, while me and your daddy go down to the woods and look around."

Inez did not object to Bud going no farther than the store. So after a hurried supper, Bud and Ellis, with his Remington 30.06 deer rifle, and Greener shotgun, and a box of ammunition for the rifle, loaded in the truck and headed for Abe's store.

"We'll need to keep this quite, until we can see what the situation is. Bud, you don't say nothin' about this to anyone in that store while you're there, because you don't know nothin', and we don't know nothin'. Nobody knows nothin', yet!" said Abe. "And at any rate, don't ever tell nobody that Homer Adkins was involved."

They arrived at the store, and Abe ran inside to inform Ruth that Ellis and him were on their way to investigate the sawmill shack. He picked up a box of twelve-gauge buckshot shells for the shotgun, two carbide miners hats and a large flashlight. He told Ruth to let Bud help sack groceries, that he and Ellis would be back directly, and he also told her to stay quiet about the situation. Abe and Ellis loaded back into Abe's pick-up. Abe drove the pick-up down the field road to within a hundred yards of the shack, stopped the truck and shut off the engine.

"Ellis, let's git these lanterns lit and guns loaded. We'd better go on foot from here," said Abe.

"Yeh, if thet dog comes at us, it'll be better to be in the open," said Ellis. "You back me up with that shotgun. Stand to my left, and let me have the first shot with this rifle. I'll shoot at seventy-five yards. If I don't stop him, shoot him full in the face with one barrel at thirty yards. That should knock him down, but give him the second barrel for good measure. I'll shoot again, if we ain't stopped him by then."

There was no sound from the shack. Owls deep in the woods could be heard calling to one another. A fox "yipped" in the edge of the cotton field. He was looking for quail nests and mice. A screech owl squalled out in the edge of the woods. Ellis saw Abe flinch out of the corner of his eye. Ellis felt the hair stand up on the back of his neck. "Damn!" he said, under his breath.

They were now within fifty yards of the gate. If there was shooting now, it was going to be up close and personal. In the lantern light, they could see that the gate was open. The dog would come through the gate, if it came. Ellis cocked the hammer on the rifle. The Remington lever-action 30.06, held five cartridges in the magazine and one in the barrel. He could stop a deer in flight at one hundred yards, but the dog would probably be coming head-on and low to the ground. He would aim low for the chest area. An audible click could be heard as Abe cocked the external hammer of the right barrel of the old Greener shotgun.

The two men moved slowly through the gate. "Abe move ten yards to my left," whispered Ellis, "the dog will be blinded by our lights, and he can only go for one of us. The other will have a side shot."

Abe moved to the left, and they continued to inch forward, weapons at the ready. They stopped at the open gate to the fence, within thirty yards of the shack that was now bathed in yellow light from the lanterns. Part of the interior sidewall, and back wall of the shack was visible through the open door; the broken door was clearly visible lying just inside the doorway. *Well, Homer was correct on that score*, thought Abe.

"Anybody home?" called Abe, in a low voice.

"Blue Duck, are you there?" called Ellis, louder.

There was no response. They moved up to the door. Ellis turned to watch the tree line of the forest. Abe looked inside. "Good Gawd Almighty!" he exclaimed. "It's just like Homer said."

Abe took up a position to the side of the door where he could watch the tree line and also look inside the shack. It was obvious that the dog was not there, so it had to be in the woods somewhere, and Blue Duck was missing.

Ellis went into the shack over the broken door and knelt down beside the little Cherokee girl who was lying on her face. He reached down with his right hand and put a finger on her throat, feeling for a pulse. "She's graveyard dead," he said matter-of-factly.

"Ellis, look there on the floor and the walls, what is that?" asked Abe.

Ellis stood up and began to shine his lantern around the interior. "That's fresh blood, and it ain't that little girl's. She ain't bled none, except just a little at the hairline. My guess is that used to belong to Blue Duck," said Ellis.

Ellis spotted a trail of blood smeared over the broken door and upon close examination, he could see blood on the ground, intermingled with drag marks, heading toward the woods. "Look here," said Ellis, pointing along the ground. "Thet dog has got Blue Duck and has drug him in the woods yonder."

Abe moved into the interior of the shack and started picking up some of the cotton stuffed bags and covering the girl with them. "Ellis, let's go call the sheriff. We can't do nothin' more in the dark."

The two men sidled away from the shack and through the gate, keeping alert for any movement along the tree line, expecting the dog to come at them at any moment. There was a crashing sound out in the woods. "Is thet the dog?" asked Abe, ever nerve in his body flashing electricity.

Ellis stood listening for a moment. There was nothing but silence. "Just a limb fallin'," said Ellis. "It's funny how a big limb will just suddenly turn loose and fall off a tree. It happens a lot when we're out huntin'. It always scares the hell out of me in the dark."

When they got in the truck, Abe started the motor, and turned the lights on. The lights shone at an oblique angle away from the shack to the edge of the woods about one hundred fifty yards away.

"Look there," said Abe pointing to two large red orbs low to the ground, just visible in the light. Is that him?"

Ellis stared intently toward the tree line. "That's him," he said.

The Democratic Party had elected Al Gunner to the office of sheriff, for a third term, by a handsome margin over his Republican challenger. Sheriff Gunner was a local hero. He was one of the few men in the county that had seen action in World War I. He had enlisted when he was eighteen years old, in nineteen seventeen, and had been a member of the famed Rainbow Division led by General Black Jack Pershing. He had returned home when he was twenty-one, sporting several medals, including the Purple Heart. He had been shot and gassed. Sheriff Gunner had been in the same Regiment as Sergeant Alvin York of Tennessee. Sergeant York had gained a lot of publicity because of his exploits and had won the Congressional Medal of Honor.

Sheriff Gunner said he had killed as many or more "heinies" as York had.

The difference, he said, was that York had brought back a bunch of prisoners. Sheriff Gunner said he took no prisoners. It was this kind of tough talk that made him popular with the voters. Some said he might run for Congress or governor, when he got tired of being sheriff.

Sheriff Gunner told a story on himself that was often repeated in the Walnut Ridge area. He said that the first time he ran for sheriff, he went canvassing for votes back up into the hills above Black Rock, near the Randolph County line, and had walked up a steep hill to a house, inaccessible by car, and had found an old couple sitting side by side on the front porch in their rocking chairs. An earthen jug, which the sheriff assumed contained moonshine, was sitting between the two chairs in easy reach of either occupant.

Sitting on the porch that spanned the front of the house, sat ten young men, all sons of the old couple, ranging in age from eighteen to thirty-two. There were two sets of twins. "What a fine looking family," exclaimed Sheriff Gunner, directing his remarks to the old gentleman. "And I'll bet they're all good democrats, too."

"Well, we tried to raise 'em right," replied the old man. "They're all good Christian boys, and they all vote democratic, too, except for old Sam down there on the end, but thet rascal larned how to read."

It was Sheriff Al Gunner, and two of his deputies, Lester Harris, and Ollie Little, and the Lawrence County Coroner, who was also a Walnut Ridge funeral home director, that showed up at Turner's Store at 9:00 p.m., after receiving Abe Turner's phone call about finding a body at the sawmill shack.

"Who found the body?" asked Sheriff Gunner, directing his comments to Abe Turner. Ellis Scott was sitting on a keg of nails with a soft drink. Abe had lent his truck to Ellis, to take Bud home, over Bud's severe objections, and Ellis had come back with his two coon dogs in case they might be needed. He had arrived back at the store just ahead of the sheriff's party.

"Me and Ellis Scott over there," replied Abe. He wasn't going to implicate anyone else if he could help it.

"How come you to go down there?" asked the sheriff.

"Well, after I called you the other day – remember? – about that old Cherokee beatin' his wife, and you said that you were not goin' to get involved in a domestic dispute...I hadn't seen or heard of those two people since I made that call, so I thought somebody ought to check up on 'em. I got Ellis to go with me and bring his guns, because of that animal they got down there."

"What animal?" asked the sheriff.

"Big dog," said Abe.

177

"Big dog?" said the sheriff.

"Big dog," reiterated Abe.

"How big?" asked the sheriff.

"You got any more of them drinks, we had the last time we was in here?" interjected Deputy Little, referring to Roscoe Gilmore's malt liquor that Abe kept in the soda box. Thankfully, he was out of it.

"Nah! fresh out," said Abe. "Have a big orange drink."

"Shoot!" said the deputy, in disgust. "I don't want no shittin' orange drink."

"Go out in the car and get a drink of water out'n your canteen then, and shut up!" said the sheriff. "Now about that dog, just how big is it, and what is it?"

"He some kind of mix breed, probably Bull Mastiff and maybe Irish Wolfhound. There's nothin' like him in this whole country. Probably go one hundred eighty pounds. Very dangerous. We believe he has killed old Blue Duck, after Blue Duck killed his missus. That dog was very particular about that little Cherokee gal," said Abe.

Abe stayed at the store, while Ellis Scott, driving Abe's truck, with his two hounds in the back led the way down through the field to the sawmill shack. Ellis had warned the authorities that they had better have their guns loaded and ready, because the hound would be nearby in the woods and might charge the group when they went to remove the girl's body.

They went to the shack, all carrying flashlights and lanterns, shotguns and rifles at the ready. The area around the shack was bathed in light. The girl's body was still lying face down as Abe and Ellis had left it, but the cotton filled burlap bags that Abe had used to cover the body, had been pulled away and were lying scattered around the body.

"The dog has been here," said Ellis. "It's pulled off the bags that we left her covered with."

"You boys be on a sharp lookout," said Sheriff Gunner, to the two deputies stationed just outside the shack door.

"Died from a single blow to the right temple area, I'd say," offered the coroner, after a cursory examination of the body. "And that looks to be the death weapon," he continued, pointing to the metal poker lying by the stove. The coroner picked up the poker and looked at it closely in the lantern light.

"It's got blood on it and some short, coarse black hair, that I don't believe belongs to the victim," said the coroner. "Looks like dog hair, maybe."

Holding a lantern aloft, the coroner, noted an excessive amount of blood on the floor and walls. "That's blood and it don't belong to the woman. She ain't bled much," offered the coroner.

"No sir," said Ellis in confirmation. "Me and Abe thought that the dog must have attacked old Blue Duck, and drug his body into the woods, yonder."

"Boys bring a stretcher and let's get this woman loaded into the coroner's truck," said Sheriff Gunner. "And then we'll go off in the woods aways and look around. If we don't find anything, we'll come back at daylight and continue the search for Mr. Blue Duck Smith, or more'n likely what's left of him."

After the woman's body was loaded into the coroner's truck, the coroner turned around on the field road, and started back to Walnut Ridge. Ellis took his two hounds, and led the sheriff's party into the woods following the trail of drag marks and splotches of blood. "Somethin', sure bled a fair amount," said Deputy Harris, as they edged forward into the woods.

"You boys line up to the left of Mr. Scott, five yards apart, and I'll line up on the right," said the sheriff, "...and what's that clicking noise?"

"Ah, that Lester's teeth," said Deputy Little. "He's skeered shitless."

"I am not!" retorted Deputy Harris. "I'm just a-mite chilled s'all. Shoulda' wore a jacket."

"Hell! It's eighty-five degrees!" said the sheriff. "Keep a sharp lookout now, lock and load."

As the group eased through the woods, at about one hundred yards out, the two coon dogs that had stayed close together on the blood trail, suddenly stopped and began sniffing an object on the ground. Ellis moved up to the spot, and in the light of his miner's lantern, he could see a man's brogan with a foot still inside, gnawed off just above the ankle. The group gathered at the spot.

"Well, cut my legs off, and call me shorty," said Deputy Harris.

"Looks to me," exclaimed Sheriff Gunner, "like that old Blue Duck has been cannibalized by that dog, at least partially, if not altogether."

"I'll be damned," said, Deputy Little. "Cherokee today, dog bone tomorrow."

CHAPTER 17

They never did find what remained, if anything, of Blue Duck Smith. The sheriff returned the next morning and brought the two deputies back, along with two blood hounds and Dr. Willis, a Walnut Ridge dentist, who had hunted lions and water buffalo, among other things on an African safari. The doctor brought his big-bore, double barrel, over and under, heavy caliber rifle, but he never got to use it.

Dr. Willis had hunted and killed two man-eating lions on his last African safari, and he was fascinated at the thought of hunting a man-eating dog this close to home, and so was the editor of the *Walnut Ridge Times Dispatch*. The editor sent a reporter with a camera along on the hunt, but they never saw the Cherokee Devil Hound.

The sheriff showed the bloodhounds the foot in the brogan, and the bloodhounds trailed almost a mile into the woods before stopping at the edge of a deep slough. The trail went cold there. "Went wet", said the sheriff.

That night, just after dark, a deep-throated howling began down at the sawmill shack. Abe Turner went out on the front porch of the store and listened for a while, before calling Ruth out to listen. Ruth listened to the deep rumbling howling, and tears glistened her cheeks. "He's calling for his mistress," was all she said, and she went back inside.

The sheriff returned the next day with two more men from Walnut Ridge. The men carried high-powered rifles, but they never found anything, either, so the sheriff said he was calling off the search for Blue Duck. He said he didn't think that there was anything to look for except dog shit. He said he expected that's all Mr. Blue Duck Smith was by now. But every night for over a week, just after dark, the pitiful howling could be heard coming from the sawmill shack. Then it stopped, and nothing was ever heard of the Cherokee Devil Hound again.

The local cotton planters and sharecroppers were too busy getting their crops out of the field before winter, to worry about dogs and Cherokees. Ellis Scott was still hauling at least a bale of picked cotton to the gin daily. Some days he would take a bale at mid-morning, and there would be another bale picked by sundown. When his fellow farmers at the gin asked him if he was busy, he was apt to say, "I'm busier than a cat covering crap on a marble floor." Or sometimes it was, "I'm busier than a one-armed paper hanger."

In the meantime, Joel Adkins, who seemed to possess a devious trait, through a country-stroke of genius, discovered a way for Bud and him to get back at the Milligan sisters for the prank that the Milligan and Taylor sisters pulled on them at the swimming hole. Joel explained to Bud that they would first deal with the Milligan sisters, and if the opportunity arose, they would use his new discovery on the Taylor sisters.

It was already widely known, that if you found a toad frog sitting still in the sunlight, and particularly late in the afternoon that it was feeding. The toad would sit motionless, and then suddenly flick out its long sticky tongue and catch a passing bug or fly. It was possible during this time, to take a wooden board and place it at an angle, like a short ramp, in front of the frog and roll BB shot down the board toward the frog; the frog would catch the rolling BBs and swallow them as he would a bug.

Joel's idea was to take the rock-like granules of carbide that was used in miner's carbide lamps, which most farm families possessed at the time, and fashion the granules into little balls with his pocket knife so that they would roll down the board in front of the frog like a BB shot.

Carbide gas was produced in the lamps, by filling a container with the carbide granules, and when water was added, a chemical reaction resulted which produced a gas vapor that was released through a small hole. The escaping gas could then be lit with a match, thereby producing a small flame that was reflected off a round metal shield, which would throw a flood of light to a distance of about twenty-five yards.

Joel reasoned that if the frog could be induced to swallow some of the carbide granules that the moisture inside the frog would create a sufficient amount of gas that should result in something, but he was not sure exactly what, so like any budding scientist, he experimented. To his great delight, his first experiment was a complete success.

The toad swallowed the granules just as anticipated. After ingesting a half-dozen granules, the frog began to swell to twice its size, then it tripled in size so that it didn't look like a toad frog anymore. The frog was sitting in some grass and in a short time, the grass could be seen moving at the frog's rear end where gas was now escaping. Joel then took a long cane-fishing pole and tied a piece of paper at the tip and lit a match to it. He then stood back as far as he could and eased the small flame at the tip of the pole up to the frog's butt end. An explosion resulted, and the frog was blown to smithereens. Joel was elated.

True genius is not only in the discovery, but also in the application. Joel now took an empty five-gallon, metal lard-bucket and made a dime-sized hole in the bottom-side of the bucket about level, as he envisioned it, where the frog's butt-end would be if it were sitting inside. He gassed up another frog, and as the frog was swelling, placed it inside the bucket with its rear end backed up to the hole.

Joel found that once distended by gas, the frog would not move, or could not move from any position that it might be placed. When the proper time had elapsed, he again lit a piece of cloth which he had tied around the tip of the cane pole, and pushed the flame up to the hole in the bucket, thereby not only blowing the frog to pieces, but producing a nice booming sound to go with it. After four or five more experiments – toad frogs were plentiful – with no failures, he now considered it time to try it out on the Milligan sisters.

Joel put some of the carbide granules in his pocket, for the purpose of performing a demonstration for Bud, and to form a joint plan on how his exploding frog invention could be used most effectively. Joel explained his discovery to Bud as they worked close together in the field, the next day. They carefully arranged to be off by themselves, late in the afternoon when the frogs would start coming out of their underground burrows to feed. The boys did not want any witnesses. The experiment was performed to perfection again. The frog exploded just as Joel predicted. Bud was elated.

Joel brought the five-gallon can, which he had dubbed, the "frog boomer," and he concealed it in some weeds at the end of the cotton rows where they would be working that day. During the day, Joel and Bud, when around the Milligan sisters, purposely talked about finding and capturing a giant frog, and at quitting time, if the girls wanted –and Cody, too, Bud insisted – they could come down near the ditch bank and see the frog. The trap was set. Timing was critical.

Of course, they would first have to catch a frog, and they especially wanted the biggest toad they could find. So late in the day, a limited and discreet search was made, and a nice toad was found which was placed in a small empty cloth tobacco sack, and tied inside the mouth of Joel's cotton pick-sack. At the appropriate time, Joel moved to the spot where he had concealed the can, and then he set about gassing up the frog. He had thoughtfully brought a lid for the can, to conceal the frog, until it was time for the intended victims to look inside.

The plan was for Bud to lead the Milligan kids up to the can, while priming them about the sight that they were about to see. Joel would stand to the side, and discreetly light a ball of cotton tied around a long pole conveniently placed in readiness. Just as Bud lifted the lid from the can and backed away, Joel would give sufficient time for the Milligan kids to get over the opening while peering down inside, and then he would touch off the frog. It worked to perfection.

"We believe thet this frog must have escaped from a zoo or circus, or somethin'. We ain't never seen nothin' like it," Bud was saying, as he led Sherry, Maxine and Cody Milligan up to the bucket. Joel was sitting idly on the ground a few feet to the side opposite the hole in the bucket smoking a cigarette, his prepared pole with the cotton tip at the ready.

"It could be a Peruvian Tree Frog," offered Cody, not expecting a challenge to his self-proclaimed academic skills– "I've never seen one of course, except in a book."

Bud not wanting to get into a frog debate at the moment of truth, agreed with Cody, because Cody was about to get his comeuppance. Anyway, Bud had no idea what a Peruvian Tree Frog might look like, and could not with any assurance come within twenty thousand miles, of knowing where Peru was.

"Well, you might be right," said Bud as he lifted the lid off the can and revealed the highly inflated body of the toad. "Y'all gather roun' and look down in there and tell me what y'all thank."

The kids eased over the can to get a look down into the dark interior. A large gray blob was sitting at the bottom.

"I smell carbide gas," said Cody, as he stretched his neck over the can for a good look.

"I've noticed that, too," said Bud. "The frog seems to give off a smell similar to carbide."

"Thet don't look like no frog to me," said Maxine.

"Look real close, and you can see its head," said Bud, who had backed away several feet.

Joel had lit the cotton on the tip of the pole, and at the very moment when all three of the Milligan kids were pushing their heads close together, to get a good look at the frog, Joel pushed the flaming cotton up to the hole in the bottom of the can.

The booming explosion sent frog fragments into the face and hair of the Milligan siblings. They all screamed and fell backwards on the ground. A cloud of blue smoke drifted upward. Cody was the first up on his feet, squalling. He began to run towards the cotton wagon where the others were weighing-in, and getting ready to quit for the day. Bud could see the men who were emptying cotton sacks up in the wagon, stop and look in their direction to see what all the commotion was about.

The Milligan sisters, were not quite as emotional as their little brother, and after a moment to get adjusted to what had just happened, began to giggle and pick frog fragments off each other, and out of each other's hair. Bud and Joel were lying on the ground and laughing so hard that they were having some problem in getting their breath. There were tears in Joel's eyes, which resulted in Bud's thinking that it was the first time he had ever seen Joel cry.

The Milligan sisters probably saved Bud and Joel from getting anything more than a scolding from their parents for the prank. The girls took it in good humor and were laughing about it when they went back to the cotton wagon. Cody was still sniffling a bit, but he wasn't injured in any way. He just had a little frog slime in his hair and ears. Cody just didn't like the fact that he had been outwitted by Bud and Joel, whom he considered half-wits, and Bud didn't help the situation when he sidled up to Cody the next morning and said, "Was that a Peruvian Tree Frog, or what?"

CHAPTER 18

It was late on a Saturday afternoon, in late October. Bud and Joel were at Turner's Store. Bud was indulging in his customary big orange drink and nickel bag of salted peanuts, and Joel had his big orange, and a banana moon pie.

Joel had come to the store to check the "postal" box in the store, looking for a letter from Betty, but there was none. Mrs. Adkins was getting more and more concerned. Betty had always been a thoughtful girl, and her mother couldn't understand, why she wouldn't at least send a penny postcard to let the family know where she was.

There was a copy of the *Arkansas Gazette* newspaper lying on the counter that a grocery salesman had left at the store. The two big stories on the front page were that the New York Yankees had won the World Series, beating the St. Louis Cardinals, and the U.S. Marines had won a battle at Tarawa, a little known spot in the Pacific, suffering heavy casualties. Bud sat down on a nail keg and spent some time reading through the paper. Abe Turner noted that Bud read anything that he could get his hands on, while Joel never showed any interest in reading anything at all.

Abe mentioned that Mary Margaret Miller was back up at Roscoe's camp on Horse Island. She had come in the store the day before with Roscoe and Homer, to buy some groceries. Mary Margaret said that she decided to go back to the camp to continue her religious training. According to Abe, she had been terribly embarrassed because of the fiasco of her baptismal ceremony, and thought for a while that she never would go back to the camp, but she finally came to the realization that she had been officially baptized and "saved," and was now a Christian. She said that she had her eye set on starting her own ministry, after she received some more training in sermon presentation, and particularly, the "laying on of hands."

Roscoe told Abe that they had built two more one-room log cabins at the camp, one for Homer and the other for Mary Margaret, plus they had built a communal log kitchen. So now there was Roscoe's two-room log cabin, plus the cabins for Homer and Margaret and the kitchen. There was also a small log storehouse for the makings of the home brew and moonshine with a lean-to for the shelter of Roscoe's mule, and a log smoke house, where they smoked the hams from the occasional slaughter of the wild hogs in the area, and they had built "his" and "her" outhouses.

Roscoe, according to Abe, said that the Horse Island complex was based, as best as he and Homer could determine, on the Essene community in Judea, of Jesus' time; the community, which many bible scholars, according to Homer, believed that John the Baptist, and Jesus were involved, when they first ventured out to begin their public ministry in the wilderness. Roscoe went on to say, "We aim to make it into one of the top religious training centers in the country."

There were plans, according to Roscoe, to build a meeting house, a place where aspiring ministers of the gospel could come on a retreat, to work on their preaching technique, specifically the delivery cadence, that was somewhat peculiar to Baptist preachers at the time. They already had a name for the complex. It was to be called, "THE HORSE ISLAND CHARIOTS OF GLORY RELIGIOUS CENTER." They were in the process, now, of preparing posters and pamphlets to that effect.

When he arrived at the store, Bud could see smoke rising, in the still late afternoon air, from Roscoe's camp. He wondered whether Roscoe was smoking a ham, or making moonshine. Just at sundown, a Lawrence County Sheriff's Department car, with two deputies, Lester Harris and Ollie Little, pulled up in front of Turner's Store. The deputies got out carrying a poster. Both deputies stood outside the car for several minutes and looked north up the east bank of Cache River Ditch where a wisp of smoke could be seen rising above the trees on Horse Island.

Bud recognized immediately the "wanted poster" of Homer Adkins, the one Joel and him had seen in the Walnut Ridge Post Office a few weeks past; the one that had announced a thirty-dollar reward for information leading to the capture of Homer Adkins, for desertion from the U.S. Army.

Joel saw it, too, and he gave a knowing glance at Bud, when one of the deputies said that they had received a letter from a person named Elmo Wilson, from a Chicago, Illinois, post office box address, with information that Homer Adkins was in this community. Elmo had asked that the thirty-dollar reward money be sent to the Chicago post office box address. The deputies wanted to put the poster in the front window of Abe Turner's store. "Maybe it'll smoke him out," said Deputy Harris.

Well, it was good news in a way, mixed with bad news. The good news was that the Adkins family could be fairly assured that Betty was in Chicago. However, the bad news was that the law was close on the trail of Homer Adkins. The over-riding question, though, was why would Elmo Wilson inform on Homer from that far away? The obvious answer was that Elmo and Betty must have run into some kind of financial problem. Otherwise, why would Elmo write a letter like that? Dovie Adkins, upon learning of Elmo's letter to the sheriff, became more worried than ever.

"We have heard," said Deputy Harris, "that the army deserter may be hanging out with a preacher, by the name of Roscoe Gilmore."

Before Abe could respond, Deputy Little asked Abe, "You got any more of them drinks like you had that one day we come in here?"

Abe had, in fact, procured several fresh bottles of Roscoe's malt liquor which was especially potent with a higher than normal alcohol content.

"Yes, I believe I have," said Abe, recognizing quickly a way to divert attention from the deputies' primary intention. "I just got a shipment in today, as matter-of-fact from the Nehi Bottling Company out of Jonesboro."

Abe reached into the back of the soda case and pulled out two ice-cold bottles of malt brew and snapped the caps off, handing one to each deputy. Deputy Little took a long drag on his bottle. "This is monstrous fine!" he said. "Monstrous fine!"

Abe took Homer Adkins' wanted poster from Deputy Harris, and began to look at it intently. The portrait was an artist's drawing of the head and shoulders of Homer, in a U.S. Army uniform, apparently made from a military identification photograph. The picture didn't look much like Homer as he presently appeared, with his shoulder-length hair. In the drawing, Homer had a short-cropped military haircut, and was wearing his U.S. Army service cap. The description was about correct, though, showing Homer to be six-feet, four-inches in height, and weighing one hundred-fifteen pounds.

Abe addressed Deputy Harris. "Deputy, how tall are you?"

"About, six, three," said Harris.

"How much do you weigh?" asked Abe.

"One hundred-seventy-five," said Harris. "why do you ask?"

"Well, because, I believe this poster is wrong," replied Abe. "Do you really thank that someone that is six-feet-four, can weigh only one hundred-fifteen pounds?"

"You know, I was wonderin' about that myself," interjected Deputy Little. "You got any more of that soda?"

Abe reached in the back of the soda case for two more ice-cold bottles of Preacher Gilmore's finest.

"Well, you look at Deputy Harris, here," said Abe. "He looks skinny. Can you imagine him weighing only one hundred-fifteen pounds? I don't think he could stand up. I believe that listed weight on that poster is in error. They probably meant two hundred fifteen pounds, don'cha thank?"

"Yes, I do." answered Deputy Harris. "Have you got a black pencil, we'll change it?"

"Also," said Abe, knowing that the albino could not grow facial hair. "Do you thank, that anyone that had deserted the army would now be clean shaven? My guess is, by this time he has grown a beard."

"Yes, I believe your right on the mark," said Deputy Little. "Les take that pencil and color him in a beard and give him a little mustache, 'cause he would have a mustache, too."

By the time Deputy Harris had gotten through altering the poster, the image and description bore no resemblance to the wanted man, except for the listed height.

"If he had been a paratrooper in the 82nd Airborne, as the poster says, I believe thet makes the height wrong, too," said Abe. "'Cause it is my recollection, that the army wants short people as paratroopers, in order for them to bail out through the small doors of the airplane. I believe they meant to list him at five-foot, four."

"I believe your are right on the money," said Deputy Little. "Les, take that pencil and correct the man's height on the poster."

"OK, "said Abe, now satisfied with the revision. "I believe we are now ready to display that poster in the window. Boys," Abe continued, directing the question to Bud and Joel, who had been sitting quietly by, observing the master of deception in action. "Have you seen anyone around that comes close to resemblin' the description on this poster?"

"Nah! I ain't seen nobody that comes close to lookin' like thet," said the grinning Joel, looking toward Bud.

"Me neither," said Bud, knowing that there was indeed a certain truth in his denial. He didn't know anyone that was five-foot, four-inches tall, weighing two hundred-fifteen pounds, and had a beard and mustache, but he also knew that the sin of omission was just as bad as the sin of commission. *If this keeps up*, he thought, *I'm gonna need baptism by Christmas.*

Deputy Harris stood looking north through the store's front window at the wisp of smoke still rising above the trees from the Gilmore camp. "That looks like a moonshiner's fire to me," he said.

"Nah!" said Abe. "That's Preacher Gilmore smokin' a ham. He smokes some of the best hams in the county. Would you boys like a good ham sandwich to go with your colas? I've got one of his smoked hams in the meat cooler. In addition, to the salt and preservative, he takes dried sassafras leaves and grinds them to a powder and massages that into the ham. It's an old Indian recipe. You ain't tasted nothin' like it."

Abe fished out two more bottles of the special cola and handed one each to the deputies as he moved to the rear and pulled a large ham out of the cooler and cut off two sandwich size slices of ham, a half-inch thick. He got out some white bread, and finished the sandwiches with an ample dose of mustard and a thick slice of white onion. The deputies laid into the sandwiches with the gusto of a hound dog.

"Monstrous fine!" said Deputy Little. "Monstrous fine!"

After finishing the three spirited colas, the two deputies began to totter a bit, and it was getting dark. "We'd better head for home," said Deputy Harris. "We'll be back in the mornin' with our horses. I want to ride up the ditch and see the preacher. I might jist buy a ham off-a-him."

As soon as the deputies had passed over the bridge and were out of sight, Abe took Bud and Joel aside, as there were now other customers that had come into the store, and told them to take a flashlight and go up to Roscoe's camp, and warn Roscoe to expect visitors in the morning. "It won't take you long to git up there and back, and Bud, I'll run you home in my pickup, and explain the situation to your folks."

The trail that ran at the base of the ditch bank was dry. Bud and Joel ran all the way to Gilmore's camp. Upon entering the camp clearing, they were immediately challenged by Roscoe's two coonhounds. The barking brought Roscoe and Homer out of their cabins, both carrying Winchester lever action carbines.

"Who's there?" shouted Roscoe.

"It's Bud and Joel!" shouted Bud, and as they moved into the clearing. Roscoe called in the two coonhounds.

"What's up boys?" asked Roscoe, as Bud and Joel moved into the light from the open door of Roscoe's cabin. Homer sidled over toward the trio.

Bud then relayed the message of the planned visit the following morning by the sheriff, and that they would be riding in on horseback.

"Damn!" said Homer. "Attacked by pagans on a Sunday."

From out of the darkness near the third cabin, came the voice of Mary Margaret Miller, "What are we going to do?"

"We're goin' to ground," said Roscoe, and then he turned to Bud and Joel. "You boys better git on back now, and tell Abe, that me and Homer won't be to church tomorrow, and thet I'm much obliged for the warnin', and fer you two fellers to come runnin' up here to deliver it. Be careful now, goin' back."

It may have been a coincidence, or it may have been through some divine providence that not only was the Lawrence County Sheriff's Deputies going to be moving up the ditch on Sunday morning to Roscoe's camp, but at the same time, the Craighead County Sheriff was sending two deputies with dogs in an attempt to run down Rabid Robert Ryder, the escaped convict from Tucker Prison Farm. Rabid Robert had been seen at his folk's house, which was between the town of Sedgwick and the Cache River Ditch, and about four miles due north of Preacher Gilmore's newly christened, The Horse Island Chariots of Glory Religious Center.

The Little Brown Freewill Baptist Church was only a quarter-mile from Cache River Ditch, on the west side, and very nearly parallel with Gilmore's camp on the east side. Heavy caliber gunfire erupted near the Gilmore camp at 10:45 a.m., just as Abe was getting ready to lead the 11:00 a.m. morning worship service. Abe had explained to the congregation that Roscoe and Homer had come down with something and wouldn't be present. He hadn't anticipated that it might be lead poisoning.

There seemed to be at least one and maybe two rifles firing from the camp and two or more rifles firing from north of the camp as well two firing south of the camp. The sound of dogs barking, and shouting, could be heard along with the gunfire. Abe went out into the church yard followed by most of the congregation, for most of the adult members of the church knew, either directly or by innuendo, of Roscoe's nefarious part-time job.

"I don't understand it," Abe said to Ellis Scott, who had moved up beside him to listen, and who was aware the sheriff's planned visit. "I thought Roscoe and Homer would have better sense than to fire on a sheriff's posse."

"Thet gun firin' from the camp don't sound like Roscoe," said Ellis. "Thet gun sounds to heavy for a carbine; it sounds like an old fashioned fifty-caliber Sharps rifle. My Grandpa Scott had one, when I was a boy. Sounds like a cannon goin' off."

"Ain't no point in tryin' to have church today, with that racket," said Abe.

"And anyway, if they happen to come across, on this side of the ditch, bullets could be flying all around here. I think we all oughta get outta here."

Ellis agreed, and Abe quickly moved to dismiss the congregation, and admonished anyone that might be tempted, to stay away from the ditch. "You folks go on home now," shouted Abe. "And make sure to keep away from thet ditch until we can figure out what's goin' on."

Ellis quickly loaded his family in the wagon, along with the Milligan family, and headed for home. Everyone was quiet, as the occupants of the wagon sat facing back toward the ditch, listening intently to the gunfire. Cody Milligan, even, had foregone playing mumbly-peg in the wagon bed. Bud was thinking of what might be happening to Roscoe and Homer, and too, the harlot, Mary Margaret Miller. He wondered if she had a gun and was one of the shooters.

"Somethin's on fire over there," said Cody Milligan, as he stood up in the wagon and stared intently toward the ditch.

First, it was a single spiral of black smoke that rose above the tree line. Then there were two more spirals spaced closely together.

"They must be burnin' the camp," said Ellis Scott from the wagon seat, and he turned and slapped the reins against the mule's backs. "Giddy yap," he said, as the mules broke into a more spirited gait.

After delivering everyone home, Ellis told Inez that he was taking Bud and was going to Turner's Store. "Bud might be needed to help Ruth, if me and Abe have to go up to the camp. We'll be back as soon as we can find out somethin'."

The two Milligan men sent their families to their camp, and got in the wagon with Ellis and Bud. They would go, too, out of curiosity, if nothing else.

Ellis turned the wagon toward the store, slapped the reins, and the mules started off in a slow trot, with the wagon bouncing over the rutted gravel road. In twenty minutes they crossed the bridge over the ditch and were at the store. Ellis tied the mules to a tree beside the movie tent on the east side of the store. Harvey Winkles was scheduled to show the last movie of the season that night. On Monday, his people would come down from Missouri and bring a big truck, to load the tent and all of the movie equipment and take it and Harvey to the orange groves of Florida, for the winter. Inez had told Bud, that he could attend this last movie of the season. It was to be a western, starring Lash LaRue. Bud liked Lash and the way he could use his bullwhip, jerking the bad guys off their horses, and snapping their shooting irons out of their hands. Bud had taken some old leather reins from some mule harness hanging in the barn and had fashioned himself a whip about eight feet long.

He had some problems getting the hang of it, though. He got a good pop or two in on one of the cats, but he did more damage to his own head and ears than anything else, and was just about to give up on it. He was looking forward to seeing Lash in this last movie of the season, to see if he couldn't find something in watching Lash, to improve his own bullwhipping technique.

Ellis bought sodas for Bud, Cauly and Vaughn Milligan, and himself, and he also bought Bud a package of salted peanuts, and moon pies for the Milligan brothers and himself. There had been no gunfire for the past forty-five minutes. Heavy smoke columns were towering above Preacher Gilmore's camp. They all went out on the store porch and sat down watching the smoke, saying little.

Finally, in about an hour after they had arrived at the store, two horses with riders could be seen coming down the east bank of the ditch toward the store. "That'd be the deputies, I guess," said Abe. As they drew closer, Bud could see that something was draped across the pommel, in front of the rider of each horse. "Have them fools, killed somebody?" Abe said.

"What happened up there?" asked Abe, to the lead rider, Deputy Lester Harris, as he reined in his bay horse in front of the store porch. Deputy Ollie Little was a few yards behind, riding a little black mule.

"Well, we had us a little shoot out, I'd say," said Deputy Harris. "Didn't expect that, didn't plan on anybody bein' there. We thought a preacher ought to be in church on Sunday mornin'."

"Was anybody hurt?" asked Ellis Scott.

"Well, not me and Ollie," said Deputy Harris, and chuckling continued. "Ole' Ollie took a bullet through his hat. Damn near shit his pants, too."

"Like hell, I did!" blustered Deputy Little, as he rode up in time to hear the condemnation.

"Whatcha' got in them bags?" asked Abe, motioning toward the burlap bags that was tied across the front of the saddle of each horse, "Looks like hams."

"Hams, it is," said Deputy Little.

"Hams?" replied a perplexed Abe.

"Yep," said Deputy Little. "The smokehouse caught on fire, but we saved the bacon. Thought we was goin' to have to fight them ole' boys from Jonesboro fer 'em though."

"Jonesboro?" said an equally perplexed Ellis.

"Yep," said Deputy Lester. "The Craighead County Sheriff's boys was runnin' an escaped convict down the ditch, from up towards Sedgwick, and he must have got into the camp about the time we did. Thet boy was armed with something like I ain't heerd the like. He was shootin' outta the smokehouse. It was a rifle, but it sounded like a shotgun. He missed hitting me in the head by a hair and shot a four-inch sapling clean in too with that thang. One of them Jonesboro boys eased around to the side of the smokehouse and set it a-far'. The far' was goin' pretty good, when I managed to git the door open. That ole' boy was down over in a corner, and looked like he'd been gut-shot. The far' was pretty hot, but Ollie came in behind me, and we managed to save them four hams thet was hangin' up to cure. Couldn't git thet ole' boy out, though."

"There was another shooter up there, too," said Deputy Little. "He was shootin' outta thet two-room log cabin, but we burnt it down on him, and then we went 'round and burnt all the other buildins down, made hell of a far'."

"Well, we gotta load up and go git our coroner. Thet camp is in Lawrence County. We'll be back this evenin'. Far' ought to be died down by then," said Deputy Harris. "We got to get these hams home—boy, am I hungry. They ain't nothin' like a good shootout to whet the appetite."

"I'm with you on that," said Deputy Little. "Mr. Turner, you got any more of them good colas?"

"Nah, you boys cleaned me out yesterday," replied Abe, and as an afterthought continued. "And I don't know when I'll get in another shipment."

"Well, crap!" said Deputy Little, in disgust, clearly disappointed.

The deputies quickly loaded their animals into a trailer that was hooked to a county pickup truck, and they left for Walnut Ridge. Abe Turner, Ellis Scott and the two Milligan brothers decided to walk up to Gilmore's camp and look around.

Abe suddenly realized that Harvey Winkles was conspicuous by his absence. He had not seen anything of Harvey since coming back from Church, and it was Harvey's usual habit to be lounging around the store somewhere. He went over to the movie tent beside the store and looked inside.

"Harvey ain't here," said Abe. "My guess is…he went up to that camp this mornin' lookin' for some fresh brew and got caught in that shootout. There just might not be a movie tonight."

It took a half-hour for Abe, Ellis Scott and the two Milligan brothers, to reach the camp on foot. All of the buildings had been reduced to ashes and hot coals. Dense smoke hung like a smoky shroud in the moist swamp air. Nothing was left standing upright, including Roscoe's little gray saddle mule, which was lying dead just inside the camp clearing. "They even burned the outhouses," said Ellis in dismay. "And they'd a come in handy huntin' up here this winter."

The hog pen was empty, and there was no sign of any human or animal activity, including Roscoe's two coonhounds. Ellis Scott walked out to the edge of the swamp that surrounded the camp, and called out Roscoe and Homer's name. He never got an answer. The men walked around each one of the building fires and stared intently into the glowing embers, but the fires were still to hot, and the smoke to thick, to get in close.

"Well, we better be goin' on back," said Abe. "We oughten to bother anythang anyway, till the authorities get back here."

The men started back down beside the ditch bank toward the store and walked several yards with neither of them saying a word. Each man was deep in his own thoughts, thinking how they might have reacted if they had been caught in the morning's firefight. Would they have given up, or went down fighting and died in the flames?

"Hell of a way to die," said Cauly Milligan.

"Hell of a way," said brother Vaughn.

Ellis Scott spoke out in general terms to those present, "Abe, Roscoe told me once that he always had some barrels of sour mash workin' off up here," and turning to the Milligan brothers. "Did you men see anythang that looked like a barrel?"

Cauly and Vaughn Milligan looked at one-another for some type of recognition gesture. Finding none, they shook their heads—no while Cauly replied, "I ain't seen nothin' that looked like no barrel."

Sheriff Gunner, the two deputies, and the Lawrence County Coroner, returned about middle of the evening, in two county pickup trucks, pulling two horse trailers. They brought four saddle horses with them, and one pack mule, but they didn't need the pack mule. They never found anything in the ashes to haul out. The cypress logs of the camp buildings burned so hot, that everything was consumed. There was not a trace of a human or animal to be found. The coroner said he had seen some bad house fires, but there was always some bones or part of a limb to be found, but not here.

They tied ropes onto Roscoe's little gray mule and with two of the horses, dragged its carcass onto the hottest remaining fire. They added some brush from around the camp, completing the incineration. About an hour before sundown, the sheriff's party returned to Turner's Store, loaded their animals into the trailers, and returned to Walnut Ridge.

The sheriff came into the store while the animals were being loaded, and said that they had found no evidence of any moonshining activity, no barrels or anything. Abe said that perhaps the barrels had been wooden, if there were any, and had burned in the fire. But wooden barrels had wide iron rings to hold the barrel staves together, and nothing like that was found.

The sheriff said he hated that the camp got burned down, but then whoever was in there shouldn't have been shooting at the law, so it was justified. At least two people were believed to have died in the fires. The sheriff said he was pretty sure, one was Rabid Robert Ryder, the escapee from Tucker Prison Farm. He would have been all right, the sheriff said, if he had just made up his mind to help them boys down at Tucker get their cotton out. They would have let him come home by Christmas.

As to the other one, perhaps it was Harvey Winkles, since Abe let it be known that he was missing and possibly had gone up to the camp. Or maybe it was the preacher, but if he was a real preacher, said the sheriff, he should have been in church, performing his Christian duty, which he wasn't. And where was the albino that was supposed to be hanging around the preacher? Perhaps they were all burned up in the fire. The sheriff left on a positive note, though. He said all-in-all, it had been a successful operation; nobody got hurt that shouldn't, and that he was coming up for re-election in November, and that he would appreciate everyone's vote.

CHAPTER 19

There had not been a sighting of Roscoe Gilmore, Homer Adkins, or Mary Margaret Miller during the two weeks following the shootout at Roscoe's camp. They were presumed dead in the conflagration, even though no physical evidence was found to that effect. Ellis Scott and Hazel Adkins, with Bud and Joel, tagging along, had returned to the camp a week after the shootout and had poked around through the ashes. They did find the warped barrels of two rifles. One was a lever-action carbine, and the other was a breech-loading .fifty-caliber Sharps. "An old buffalo gun," Ellis Scott said, as the fished the barrel out of the ashes. "I'll take this thing home and clean it up and see if I can straighten the barrel. I can carve a stock for it. It won't never shoot agin, but it'll make a nice conversation piece."

"You know it is strange," said Hazel Adkins, in a moment of introspection, after they had poked around though the building fires for a while, "that nothin' that I kin see belongs to a human, no bones, no scrap of clothin', no nothin'."

"Them fires must have been hotter'n the fires o' hell," said Ellis.

Abe Turner conducted church services, at the Little Brown Freewill Baptist Church, the two Sundays following the firing of Roscoe's camp. He recommended to the congregation that a search be made for a new preacher. Abe said that he would scout around Bono, and possibly Jonesboro, for a Baptist preacher that wasn't committed to a church. He said he didn't expect having a problem finding someone as there seemed to be an abundance of Baptist preachers and not that many churches. Abe said that some young man was always getting the "call," and it was possible that they could get someone to drive out from as far as Jonesboro to pastor the church.

Bud would not allow himself to believe that Roscoe, Homer and Mary Margaret were dead. Roscoe was too "country-smart" to get caught like that, especially after having been warned about the sheriff's intended visit.

Homer, on the other hand, was a different story. Bud didn't know Mary Margaret well enough to speculate on her intelligence level.

The company that owned the movie tent came down from Missouri and packed up the tent and all the equipment for transportation to the orange groves of Florida. Harvey Winkles had disappeared, and was presumed dead, burned up on Horse Island.

The movie company people were disappointed in losing Harvey. He had become a skilled projectionist and now they were going to have to find and train a replacement. Bud wished he could go. Joel said that he would go, and went so far as to inquire about the possibility with the movie company people, but they said – no – he was too young. Joel decided, then and there that he would work in the fields until he was sixteen, which was a year-and-a-half away, and then if the war was still going on, he would lie about his age and join the marines, or maybe he would go to Chicago and look for Betty, but whatever he did, he would soon be out of the cotton patch. He wasn't going to spend all of his life working on a cotton farm and end up like his old man, a dollar-a-day field hand.

However, at the current time, Bud and Joel had a problem that required immediate attention. They had to figure out what to do about Halloween, which was the last day of October, and only three days away. They wanted to do some "trick and treating," that had not been done before. Something that, as Joel said, "would scare the hell out of them Milligan kids." But what? The Milligan family would be leaving the first week of November, returning home to Cord, to go back to school for the winter session.

Usually, on Halloween night, weather permitting, a number of kids – boys and girls – from around the Horse Island community, would gather at Turner's Store, where Abe Turner would provide candy treats and Halloween masks. That was his backhanded way of bribing the kids to leave his property alone during their "tricking." It usually worked, but not every time. Most of the youngsters would usually partake of Abe's "treats," and then venture out along the county road to conduct some nefarious Halloween mischief.

Bud and Joel had already witnessed some pretty special Halloween tricks. They had seen a wire fence, complete with fence posts, strung across the county road, that blocked traffic for an hour until the sheriff was called, and a deputy sheriff showed up with fence cutters.

The two boys had been involved just the past year, in cutting down willow trees across the county road near the bridge over Cache River Ditch. They effectively blocked traffic for over an hour. They and some other kids hid out in the cotton field next to the road and threw green, unopened, cotton bolls at the drivers, whom had gotten out of their vehicles and was trying to move the trees out of the way. One of the blocked drivers, in a fit of exasperation, fired on them with a shotgun. He didn't hit anyone, but Bud heard the pellets falling among the cotton leaves near his hiding place. It had been extremely exciting.

Two years before some kids near Egypt, disassembled a cotton wagon belonging to Jim Fortson, and by use of a ladder and ropes, had hoisted the wagon parts on top of Jim's barn and reassembled it. In Bud's book, that was one of the top Halloween tricks of all time. And then, there was the trick someone had played on Abe Turner. Some said it was the Wilson boys, but it was never proven, and they never publicly claimed it, and for good reason.

It seems that Abe took his nightly constitutional – when he was "regular" – about 8:00 p.m., in his outhouse that he had constructed on the ditch bank about twenty-five yards from the side door of his store. The heavy oak, two-holer had been placed in a rather precarious position. It was backed up to a sharp ten-foot drop-off in the bank.

The general public had become aware of Abe's routine and personal habits by the simple fact that if you were in the store at the appropriate hour, and asked Ruth Turner where Abe was, "In the outhouse," was her usual reply.

Some devious mind figured out that if a rope was tied to the top of the outhouse and then strung down the bank near the water that once Abe got inside and into his comfort zone, it would be a simple matter, with a slight tug on the rope, to topple the outhouse and its' occupant, ten feet down to the next level of the ditch bank, and that is exactly what someone did.

Abe wasn't hurt much. He had a few bruises and scrapes, but nothing serious. His feelings were hurt more than anything. He felt betrayed. He was embarrassed, too, especially when he had to call on Ellis Scott to bring a team of mules up to the store and help him pull the heavy outhouse back up to its original position.

Abe's pride remained intact, however, when he found that the outhouse he had built himself out of heavy oak planking had held together, after the ten-foot drop. "That thing would probably stand up under a tornado or an earthquake," said Ellis Scott, in admiration.

Abe was pleased at the offhanded compliment. Abe took the precaution of securing the outhouse in place with heavy half-inch steel cables firmly attached to several surrounding trees. It was going to take a super-human effort to topple it again, but after the incident, he always took a flashlight with him, when he visited his throne after dark. Before he settled in, he always conducted a thorough visual search for an attached rope or any other suspicious activity along the ditch bank.

Bud and Joel had originally been accused of the prank. Ellis had asked Bud about it. He hadn't even been near the place, he told his father, and tears had come into his eyes as he vehemently denied it. Bud was severely disappointed in the accusation, not so much that he had not been involved, but, more so, by the fact that he had not even thought about the possibility of doing something as devious as that. Was it to be his station in life to always take the moral highroad, to always be good? He hoped not, and that was why he was wracking his brain to come up with something this Halloween that would be significant, and would be talked about for years to come, something for which to be remembered, perhaps something involving a graveyard.

The Taylor family graveyard was the nearest burial ground to the Scott farm. It was across Cache River Ditch not far from the Adkins house. The little graveyard was on a slight knoll close to heavy woods and a swamp, and a quarter-mile north of the Taylor house. The graveyard had been the burial ground for the Taylor family for one hundred years. The knoll was high enough to escape most floodwaters except for the great Arkansas flood of nineteen twenty-seven. Floodwaters had washed over the knoll then, and had left the graveyard in disarray with many of the wooden markers washed away and a number of sunken empty graves.

After the floodwaters receded, some of the more sturdy homemade cypress-board caskets had been found scattered around the surrounding farmland. Some were never found. The Taylor family gathered up the cypress boxes that they found and reburied them, but they didn't know who was buried where.

Because of this massed disinterment, it was said that there were many agitated souls of deceased Taylor family members in constant movement around the graveyard and were often seen by people passing by in daylight as well as after dark.

Bud and Joel had been to the graveyard only once before, when Bud was ten years old, and Joel was eleven. They didn't go in search of ghosts; Joel said there was no such thing, anyway. They had heard that there was a very old and large Black Walnut tree, and an English Walnut tree – a rarity for that part of the country – and several Pecan trees on the knoll, that produced an abundant crop of nuts.

The ancient members of the Taylor family had planted the trees, and it was also rumored that the Black Walnut tree had been planted in the first grave dug on the knoll, in eighteen forty-three. The old tree still produced a large quantity of the hard black walnuts. The English walnut tree was about past bearing and produced few walnuts, but the Pecan trees still produced large quantities of "paper shell" pecans that could be cracked by simply squeezing two of them together in your hands.

Bud and Joel did not ask their folks or anyone else about going over to the graveyard. It had not occurred to them that perhaps the Taylor family wanted all of the walnuts and pecans for themselves. So when it was time for the nuts to begin falling, one fine sunny Sunday afternoon, in late autumn, they took two large brown paper bags and headed for the Taylor graveyard. It was the first time either boy had met Bull Taylor up close.

The boys filled both bags with a combination of black walnuts, pecans and a few English Walnuts. They sat down under the black walnut tree, and began cracking some of the pecans, enjoying the fruits of their labor.

"I see you boys have picked me up some nuts," said a sonorous voice resonating from somewhere in their rear. Bud first thought it was the voice of God. What was God doing in a graveyard? Suddenly, all six feet four inches, and two hundred seventy-five pounds of Bull Taylor loomed over them. They leaped to their feet. Bud had the sensation of actually being suspended in mid-air, his legs were churning like he was going someplace in a hurry, but he was actually standing still. He had suddenly become paralyzed, and had lost the power of speech. Joel had reacted more decisively and was quickly astride one of the big lower limbs of the black walnut tree. He was looking wide-eyed down on the activities below, like unto a possum. Neither boy could remember later Joel actually climbing the tree.

"Brang yore scrawny ass down from there," boomed Bull, looking up at Joel, who was poised to go higher, if necessary. "I ain't gonna hurt you'ins none, but y'all oughta know thet y'all are trespassin' on private property."

Trespassing, Bud thought. *That's in the Bible, in the Lord's Prayer. Wonder if Mr. Taylor knows he's supposed to forgive that sort of thing.* He wasn't about to mention it, however, not right then, anyway. Joel began a slow descent that belied the speed in which he had previously exhibited, in going in the opposite direction.

"I'll take possession of these here nuts," said Bull, as he picked up a large brown paper sack of walnuts and pecans in each hand. "Now, y'all get yore raggedy-asses offen my land, and get back acrost' that ditch yonder, where y'all belong, and don't let me ketch you'inses in amongst' my nut trees agin."

Bud would never forget the fear he had experienced in that encounter with Bull Taylor, and now he felt the need to duplicate that fear, but somehow direct it toward the Milligan kids. He had a plan, but he would need an accomplice. He went to find Joel.

It was three days until Halloween, still plenty of time to put a good plan into action. The first thing that needed to be done was to convince the Milligan siblings that there were ghosts in the Taylor family graveyard, and on Halloween night, according to *The Old Farmer's Almanac*, there was to be a full-moon, an ideal climate for ghosts.

"There hain't no sich thangs' as ghosts," Cody Milligan stated in a derisive tone.

"Don't you believe in the Holy Ghost?" asked Bud, falling back on his religious training, thinking it would be a difficult question for Cody to get around.

"I don't believe in nothin' I can't see nor feel," replied Cody, who was obviously not as religious as Bud had thought. Maxine and Sherry sat quietly noncommittal, smiling at the bantering back and forth.

"What about you girls?" asked Bud, seeking reinforcement. "If you go to church, you know there is a Holy Ghost, and if there is a Holy Ghost, then there has to be ghosts, less holy."

"Bull shit!" exclaimed Cody.

"Is Joel goin', too?" asked Maxine, suspecting treachery.

"Nah, Joel is gonna have to go with his folks to Turner's Store for groceries on Halloween night. Neither one can read. He has to read the labels for 'em," replied Bud. "They won't get back home till late."

"Ain't you afeered?" asked Sherry.

"Nah, I've been over there lots of times," replied Bud. "Seen plenty of ghosts, too."

"Bull shit!" said Cody.

"What do they look like?" asked Maxine.

"Kinda like little white clouds," responded Bud, in a quite, introspective serious vein. "Vapors, really."

"Bull shit!" exclaimed Cody.

Ignoring Cody, Bud continued. "I'll come down to your camp at dusky-dark, with a lantern. We'll cross the footlog over the ditch, and head for the Taylor place. The graveyard is back this side of the Taylor's, and over by the woods, on a little rise. We can walk over there in thirty minutes."

"Well, I'd like to see a real live ghost," said Sherry.

"Well, I guess so," said Maxine.

"Bull shit!" said Cody.

"Well, if you're afraid you can't take it," said Bud, directing a challenge at Cody, "you can stay in your camp, with the covers pulled up over your head, because the goblins will be out. That's for sure."

"Bull shit!" replied Cody. "Whadda ya mean, take it? I can take that."

"See y'all at dark-thirty, then," said Bud, satisfied that he had set the trap, now to spring it.

Maxine Milligan smelled a rat, so without telling brother Cody, late that same afternoon after Bud's Halloween challenge, she and sister Sherry headed for the ditch, to pick muscadines, they said.

Maxine had carried a flashlight hidden in her clothes, and at about sundown, she and Sherry crossed the ditch on the footlog, and found the now familiar well-worn trail through the field to the Taylor house. They had been there before.

Bud had lied of course, about Joel going to Turner's Store, on Halloween night. Instead, Joel was going to tailor an old worn-out nine-foot cotton pick sack, so that when he slipped the mouth of the sack down over his head, it would just touch the ground. He cut two eyeholes in the bottom of the sack to see through, and slit the side of the sack to give him a little legroom for walking. In the darkness, it would make a perfect, albeit tailored, ghostly shroud.

The plan was for Joel to position himself on the west bank of the ditch near the footlog, and watched for Bud's approach to the Milligan camp. Once Bud reached the Milligan camp, Joel would race over to the Taylor graveyard so as to have ample time to find the best spot to hide, before Bud and the Milligan kids arrived on the scene.

When Bud's group arrived at the graveyard, Joel was supposed to give out a few ghostly moans from his hiding place, and then rise up, revealing himself in ghostly attire. He would then move ominously toward the group, moaning all the while. Bud would yell something about a ghost, and head for the ditch. This action should – thought the boys – cause a general stampede. At least, that was the way it was suppose to work.

The sun had set when Bud arrived at the Milligan camp, to gather up Maxine, Sherry and Cody. "This better be good," said Cody, as they made for the ditch and the footlog.

Bud was carrying a kerosene lantern. The weather was a cool sixty degrees. The sky was clear except for a few fluffy thunderheads that reflected the last rays of the setting sun. Bud was wearing an old pair of khaki pants, handed down from his father, and altered by his mother. He had on his St. Louis Cardinal baseball cap and a long-sleeve dingy yellow cotton shirt, an old pair of brogans, and no socks. The Milligan siblings all wore new denim jumpers that they had bought at Egypt, with their cotton-picking earnings, and they all had on old work trousers and shoes, to complete their ensemble. Maxine Milligan had secreted a two-D-cell flashlight on the inside pocket of her jumper. Joel was dressed similar to Bud, except he was barefoot, as usual.

After crossing the footlog without incident, the ghost hunters emerged from the undergrowth along the east ditch bank and out into Bull Taylor's patchwork fields of cotton and corn that lay between the Cache River Ditch and the woodlands a little over a quarter-mile to the east. Bud looked to his right—south—down the ditch bank, toward the old Claxton house. It had been vacant ever since Irene Claxton's untimely death, except for the short period when it was occupied by the escaped convict, Rabid Robert Ryder, who now, for all intents and purposes, was dead. The thought of two dead people having once occupied the same house was enough to give one pause. Bud paused.

There was a light flickering in the window of the house, *either a candle or coal oil* lamp, Bud thought. "Wonder who that is?" Bud said aloud, more to himself, than anyone else. He hoped that it wasn't Joel, who for some reason might have gotten sidetracked. Joel should be at the Taylor graveyard by now, waiting in his cotton sack shroud.

"Who do ya reckon that is?" asked Sherry.

"I don't know," said Bud. "But it could be Irene Claxton's ghost."

"Bull shit," said Cody. "Let's just go find out."

"Nah," said Bud. "We need to git on over to the graveyard. We can check it out on the way back."

Bud moved the group along at a good pace, but he got to thinking about what he had just said. What if it was the ghost of Irene Claxton or Rabid Robert Ryder? Bud suddenly realized that he didn't like the idea of having ghosts in his rear that could possibly block the way back to the footlog crossing over the ditch. No one was saying anything, and there were few sounds except for the sound of feet shuffling along the dirt track across the field. In a few minutes they were in close proximity to the graveyard. The lights of the Taylor house were clearly visible less than a half-mile to the south. A full moon was rising over the woodlands behind the graveyard. The woodland extended north towards Turner's Store, and south well beyond the Taylor homestead. The old sawmill camp where Blue Duck had killed his wife and then met his gruesome end was three-quarters of a mile northeast.

Bud thought about that a minute, so he thought he would add to the spooky conditions by pointing that out. Pointing toward the northeast, he said, "Over yonder aways is the sawmill camp where old Blue Duck killed his wife. They say her ghost can still be seen in the edge of the woods." Bud felt the hair rise up on his neck as soon as he uttered the statement.

In addition to the possibility of ghosts in their rear, a number of other unwanted possibilities began trespassing on Bud's mind, namely: there was a full-moon that always brought out the worst in animals and people, where was the Cherokee Devil Hound, and what if Bull Taylor happened to see the light from the lantern Bud was carrying across his field, and who was in the Claxton house? Bud suddenly stopped two hundred yards short of the graveyard.

"What is it?" asked Maxine.

"I thought I heard somethin'," replied Bud. He was now having second thoughts about this whole escapade. He began to wish he hadn't thought of it.

"Well, what?" said Cody. "I ain't heerd nothin'."

"You reckon we ought to go back?" asked Bud. He would explain to Joel that the Milligans chickened out, and since he had the lantern, he had to take them home. Maxine, of course, had not revealed the fact that she had a flashlight in her jumper pocket.

"We want to see a ghost," said Sherry. "And we ain't goin' back till we do."

"Yeh, you ain't got scared on us, have ya?" asked a scornful Cody.

"Nah, I ain't afraid," answered Bud. "I just remembered about that Cherokee Devil Hound, and the way he 'et up old Blue Duck. He runs in them woods yonder."

"I heerd he left the country. Hain't nobody seen nor heered him in a while," stated Sherry.

"Well, I wouldn't want to bet my life on it," said Bud.

The full moon had cleared the tree line to the east, and if by signal, the woods came alive with the sound of woodland music. Hoot owls began to talk to one another. A screech owl screamed out. Coyotes and foxes were heard yipping along the edge of the field next to the woods. Bud could clearly hear two bobcats calling, and then from way down in the swamp, a woman's scream, not once but twice, in quick succession. "That's a panther," said Bud, quietly. "I heerd it last winter, coon huntin' down in there with my daddy."

The Milligans were now beginning to have second thoughts. All that would be needed now was to hear the deep baying voice of the Cherokee Devil Hound, and it would be a foot race for the footlog over the Cache River Ditch.

What Bud, Cody and Joel didn't know, but Sherry and Maxine did, was that the Taylor sisters had secreted themselves in the edge of the corn field that bordered the south side of the graveyard, and had for some time been watching Joel's movements. So while Joel was easing into position to spring his ghostly surprise on Bud's group, the Taylor sisters were easing into position to spring their ghostlier surprise on the whole kit and caboodle. Each girl had brought her own sheet.

The old black walnut tree was in the very center of the graveyard, and Joel had chosen this tree as his hiding place. He had hunkered down in among the enormous roots on the south side of the tree. The old pecan trees and the equally large English walnut tree were scattered across the graveyard. The Taylor sisters had moved into position behind four of these trees in Joel's rear.

Joel watched the bobbing lantern as Bud's group crossed the field. When the full moon cleared the tree line of the woods, east of the graveyard, he, too, noticed the increased activity of the forest creatures. Joel felt the hair rise up on the back of his neck when the panther screamed, and he had involuntarily stood up behind his tree. Now the lantern movement stopped, and in the pale moonlight, Joel could barely make out Bud and the Milligan kids clustered in a knot, as if discussing something. *Now what*, he thought.

But, in a moment, the lantern came on, and Joel moved to the south side of the tree and slipped the cotton sack over his head. The Taylor sisters were ready behind their trees and had completed wrapping themselves in their sheets. The great Halloween double-cross was now set.

Bud and the Milligan siblings now moved into the edge of the graveyard. The group stood quietly, looking up the gentle slope of the knoll. Head stones, old wooden crosses, and other ancient grave markers were in various states of disarray. "Evidently, the Taylors ain't much for graveyard cleanin'," Bud said quietly.

Joel, down on his knees, peeped from behind the big black walnut tree. He cupped his hands to his mouth and in the lowest vocal register that a fourteen-year-old boy could muster, issued a low, quavering moan. Bud said quietly,

"There it is and pointed toward the darkness under the overhanging branches of the big tree. Cody Milligan, for all his previous bluster, had involuntarily taken two steps backward, and had turned as if ready to depart for home.

Slowly, a ghostly white apparition emerged from behind the tree. Another low quavering moan was heard, as the apparition now appeared to float toward the group. Then, suddenly, from off to the left was heard a higher-pitched quavering moan. The apparition under the tree seemed to hesitate. Then from the far right, came another moan. Then there were two more moans that came from positions in between the first two. The visible apparition was now clearly confused and had appeared to turn and look behind it.

"My God!" exclaimed Maxine. "Hit's a family reunion. I feel faint."

"Me, too," said Sherry, and both girls collapsed in a pile at Bud's feet. Bud looked around for Cody. He needed help, but Cody was long gone.

The four white apparitions seemed to rise up out of the ground; two of them were directly behind Joel, and there was one on either side. They advanced with terrible sobbing moans. Joel was heard to distinctly to utter, "Oh, m'God!"

Joel had made a critical mistake when he altered the sack that he now wore down over his head. He had made eyeholes to look through, and he had cut a slit up one side to give his legs some freedom of movement, but he had forgotten holes for his arms, which were now pinned to his sides under the sack.

He was struggling to get the tight sack off over his head, but at the same time he felt a tremendous need to run. He wasn't going to be able to do both in what he considered to be the time allowed before the ghosts were upon him. He chose option number two and headed for the Cache River Ditch as fast as his partially confined legs would allow. Bud had already departed and was a good fifty yards behind Cody, but was gaining.

It was at this time that one of the thunderheads floated in front of the moon, turning what had previously been a golden yellow-lighted night, with good visibility, to one of murky gray, with little visibility. Bud, now completely terrified, was in full flight. He dropped his lantern and darkness came over the land.

Bud had run almost a quarter-of-a-mile and was nearing the ditch before he chanced looking back. He could barely make out Joel's shrouded figure, struggling inside the cotton sack, kicking up dust and coming hard. "Is that you, Joel?" Bud called, but the only answer he got was the sound of raspy breathing coming out of the eyeholes of the shroud, and the sound of bare feet slapping the earth. "Is that you, Joel?" Bud, called again. Still no answer. The gasping apparition was within twenty yards, but Bud was not going to wait any longer. He turned and streaked for the ditch and the footlog to safety.

Meanwhile the Taylor sisters, still wrapped in their sheets, came up to where the Milligan sisters lay in a heap giggling. "I don't know when I've had more fun," exclaimed Pearl Taylor, as she spat out a wad of chewing tobacco, and began to unwrap her sheet. "I thought about chasin' after 'em some, but they ain't no way we couda caught 'em."

The other three Taylor sisters came up and began to unshroud. All of the girls were laughing and talking at the same time. Maxine and Sherry Milligan were on their feet and dusting off each other. Maxine produced a flashlight from her inside jumper pocket. "Let's all go up to the store," she said.

"OK girls," said Pearl. "We'll leave our sheets hangin' here on a bush and collect 'em on the way back." The girls started walking up the field road toward Turner's Store. It was time for Halloween treats.

Cody, with Bud close on his heels, was out of breath and near collapse, when he finally reached the east bank of Cache River Ditch. He plunged into the brush along the bank, and headed for where he hoped to find the footlog.

Joel, following behind Bud, tripped and fell headlong. He was unable to break his fall because his arms were pinioned by his side under the sack. He landed flat on his face, in a patch of weeds, driving the wind out of his lungs. He lay gasping for breath inside the cotton sack, unable to move, trying desperately to get air back into his lungs.

The moon eased out from behind the thunderhead; golden light returned to the fields. Bud reached the ditch bank, paused momentarily to look back for his pursuer, but there was nothing in sight. How could that thing have disappeared? The gasping sounds coming from the white shrouded figure, combined with the slapping sounds of bare feet hitting the ground, and the refusal to answer the simple question, "Is that you, Joel?" had scared Bud, witless. If that thing had vanished so quickly, where and when would it reappear? Bud, would not feel safe until he was across the ditch and in the field road on the way home. Bud dove headlong into the brush along the ditch bank.

As Bud, neared the top of the bank, he heard a loud splash. Cody Milligan had either fallen off the footlog or had jumped in the ditch. Bud could barely make out the footlog in the dimness of the tree-shrouded ditch. He began to cross. When he was halfway across, he heard moaning and sobbing coming from below. He looked down from the footlog to see Cody Milligan standing waist deep in water, in the middle of the ditch.

"Is that you, Bud?" sobbed Cody.

"It's me, I reckon," answered Bud.

"Help me, Bud," pleaded Cody.

"I've got to be goin'," said Bud. "An' I ain't got no time to waste. You ain't fer from yore camp."

"Where are my sisters at?" asked Cody, in a pitiful little child's voice.

"Don't know," replied Bud, who had now safely reached the west end of the footlog. "Ghosts gottem, I reckon."

A long wailing sob rose up from Cody, who was struggling in the water to reach the bank. Bud plunged up and over the west bank of the ditch. He was soon in the field road that led past the Milligan encampment at the old Thompson barn, and on to his house. Bud felt an immense sense of relief at being on familiar ground. He stopped in the moonlight to take inventory. He had lost his lantern somewhere; he was barefoot, having thrown both shoes; and he now became aware of a warm wet sensation down his right leg and the front of his pants. He had not been in water. How did the water get on the front of his pants? Then the horrible truth dawned. Bud had wet himself.

CHAPTER 20

Bud was elated. He had just heard from his mother, that the family was going to buy Abe Turner's black, nineteen thirty-six model Ford pick-up truck. The way it came about was that Mr. Houston Johnson, the absentee owner of the farm the Scotts sharecropped, had made one of his periodic visits to the farm, this time, to pick up his checks from Ellis Scott, for his share of the cotton sales, to date. Mr. Johnston received a one-fourth share of all cotton sold, and Ellis Scott received the rest. However, Ellis, out of his share, had to pay back the bank for his spring farm loan. He used the loan funds for the day-to-day operational expenses of getting the cotton planted in the spring, and then out of the field in the fall, plus family living expenses. He hoped to clear five hundred dollars, to seven hundred dollars, for the year, after expenses. That amount would tide the family over until spring, when he could go to the bank and get his spring farm loan and start the farming cycle all over again.

Ellis hoped to have an extra one hundred dollars so that Inez could get her teeth fixed. Ellis knew he also needed some dental work. He had two lower jaw teeth that had been bothering him since late summer. He had been getting some relief by crushing aspirin tablets into a fine powder and packing the powder into the bad teeth. However, he knew that they were decayed to the point that they couldn't be saved so he planned to have them pulled for fifty-cents apiece.

He didn't need all those teeth, anyway. Pulling them, he reasoned, would leave him with three good bottom teeth on the left side of his jaw, and one on the right. That was surely enough teeth to do any chewing required. He probably would have Bud's teeth looked at as well. Some of Bud's teeth were already showing signs of decay. When Bud overheard his parents discussing the proposed dental work, which included his teeth, he had become physically ill and had gone to bed early.

While Mr. Johnston was at the farm, he dropped what best could be described as a "bombshell." It gave such a jolt to Ellis' senses, that after Mr. Johnston left, and without the aid of a spirited beverage, he took the old fiddle down from off the wall, and played a snappy rendition of "Sally Gooden" while dancing a little Irish jig at the same time. Bud thought that he had never seen his father so happy.

Mr. Johnston had gotten involved in one of President Roosevelt's government programs, named Works Projects Administration, or W.P.A., for short.

Mr. Johnson said that the federal government was furnishing grant money to various States to revitalize the economy, in an attempt to get the country out from under the Great Depression.

Mr. Johnston said that he had been authorized to hire a crew that would be working east of Jonesboro, around Leachville, Monette, Bay and Trumann. The crew would cut right-of-way, for power lines, using axes and cross-cut saws, and he wanted to know if Ellis, and Hazel Adkins, too, wanted to work during the winter on his crew. He said the pay would be good, and that they could make as much as one hundred dollars, a month, working only five days each week.

Ellis jumped at the chance for winter work, but before he had time to say anything to Hazel, and after the elation died away, he began to have second thoughts, because Mr. Johnston said that they would have to meet him at Bono every morning at 6:00 a.m. Bono was five miles east down the county road, and that road, a combination of gravel and gumbo mud, could be almost impassable during the winter months.

Ellis and Hazel would have to get out of bed by 3:00 a.m., and either ride two of the mules or walk the five miles to Bono, in the dark. If they each took a mule, they would have to find some place to leave them until they returned to Bono, at the end of the workday. That meant that the mules would have to be tied outside in the weather all day. That did not bode well for the mules. It would be dark by the time they could get back to Bono and start for home, and they would have to ride the mules, or walk home, in the dark, and that did not bode well for men or mules. There were no good choices.

Ellis had about given up on the idea of working on the W.P.A. crew, and thought he would probably have to fall back on his normal winter routine of hunting raccoons and possums, with Hazel, for the Jonesboro fur market. First, he couldn't afford to get his mules hurt, and second, he didn't need to get Hazel and himself hurt traveling ten miles round-trip every day in all kinds of weather, which usually included snow and ice, particularly in January and

210

February.

He was discussing the situation with Abe Turner the day after Mr. Johnston's visit.

"Why don'cha buy my truck?" asked Abe.

"How's zat?" Ellis replied, not sure what he had just heard.

"Buy my truck," replied Abe. "Now hear me out. I've got this deal I'm workin' on to buy a nineteen forty-two, Ford Sedan, out of Memphis. I know some people over there that's involved in what they call the black market. Those people can get things like batteries, gas, tires, shoes, sugar and other rationed goods, and other things in short supply, because of the war – like cars. As a matter of fact, I'm goin' over to Memphis within the week to pick up the car that I ordered last summer. After I git it, you kin have my truck for two hundred dollars."

"Abe, I ain't got no extra two hunnerd dollars," said Ellis.

"Don't worry bout it," said Abe, cheerfully. "I'll just put it on your grocery bill here at the store, and you kin pay me so much a month, or by the quarter. Anyway, your goin' to be makin' some extra money this winter with the W.P.A. The old truck is still in good shape. It starts and runs good. The battery and tires are still good, and I got two spares, and—Abe paused for emphasis—its got a good heater in it."

Ellis sat for a moment, slightly shocked at what he had just been offered. He thought that someday, he might own a motor vehicle, but he didn't expect it this soon. He silently considered the possibilities. He would be able to take the family to town and to the doctor. With sideboards, he knew that a pick-up truck would hold a bale of picked cotton. The truck had a trailer hitch on the bumper and he knew he could rig up a hitch on his cotton wagon, which meant he could haul two bales of cotton to the gin at more than twice the speed that he was hauling one behind a team of mules. Inez could take the truck to church and she and Bud could go comfortably in the rain and cold. Of course, Inez would first have to learn to drive and use the gearshift. But she could learn to do that in the field behind the house.

"Well?" asked Abe, breaking in on Ellis' daydream.

"Abe, I've got to do it," responded Ellis. "They ain't no reason not to."

And so it was by a simple stroke of fate, and good fortune, not to mention a good friend that Ellis Scott became the first, in a long line of Scotts, to own a motor vehicle. Ellis made it a point to go to church the following Sunday. He silently joined in the prayer offered by Abe Turner, and made a special effort to recognize President Roosevelt and the W.P.A., and when the collection basket was passed, he dropped in a crisp one-dollar bill. Bud was amazed at his father's unusual display of benevolence.

The Milligan family was going home Sunday evening after church. Ellis would borrow the soon to be his truck, from Abe, and take them home to the little town of Cord, Arkansas, nestled in the foothills west of Black River. The family was leaving a couple of days before their scheduled departure because Cody Milligan was sick. "My baby is real sick," his mother said to Inez Scott. "I think hit' might be the newmony'."

Cody had been shaking off and on with chills since coming home Halloween night, soaking wet, after falling off the footlog in Cache River Ditch. His skin had taken on a yellow hue, reminding Bud of a lemon. Cody's mother had related to Inez Scott that she had not received a satisfactory answer from Cody, nor the girls as to how Cody happened to be by himself when he fell in the ditch. Inez Scott had questioned Bud about it.

"What do you know about this Mister?"

"Nothin'."

"Nothin'?"

"Nope!"

"Did you see him Halloween night?"

"I'm hungry, is there any biscuits left over from breakfast?"

"Answer my question."

"Briefly."

"Briefly, what?"

"I'd like a slice of onion, too."

"There ain't gonna be no biscuit nor onion nor anything else until I get some answers."

"Whaddaya wanna know?"

"Did you see Cody Milligan, Halloween night, and I better not have to repeat myself, again?"

"Well, he was with me and Joel and his sisters for a while. We all crossed the footlog up by Joel's house and went over to the field road that runs from the Taylor's house to Turner's Store. We got over to the road, but Cody said he didn't feel good, and he went back."

Bud thought that was a pretty good explanation. At least they had been in the field road, and he had heard from Joel that the Milligan sisters had gone up to Turner's Store, and the Taylor sisters had been there, too. Bud occasionally allowed himself a little white lie. He didn't think that a thirteen-year-old, would be sent to the lower depths of hell for that. Hopefully, just to one of the warmer upper chambers, and anyway, his planned baptism would wipe out all previous sins, or at least, that was the way he understood it.

"Cody went home in the dark by hisself?"

"There was a full moon."

"Well, you come home early. You didn't have time to go to the store."

"I wasn't feelin' good neither."

"Well, you seemed alright when you left the house. You 'et half a fried chicken, and near half a bowl of creamed taters, plus a soup bowl full of turnips, plus cornbread and buttermilk, and two slices of punkin' pie. You didn't seem sick to me."

"Musta been somethin' I 'et."

Ellis offered Bud the opportunity to ride along with him when he took the Milligan family home, but Bud declined. There had been a certain chill in the air, between him and the Milligan sisters. Part of the problem was that he was in charge of the expedition that had resulted in Cody falling in the ditch and getting sick, and too, Sherry had insinuated that he was a coward for leaving her and Maxine to the "witches and ghosts" that came out of the graveyard.

"A brave warrior would stand up to any demon, for damsels in distress," she had taunted.

Joel wasn't to happy with Bud either, for running off and leaving him out of breath and near suffocation inside the cotton sack. Joel had finally struggled free, and had crossed the ditch. He had walked up to Turner's Store, but on the west side of the ditch, away from Bull Taylor's field.

Bud thought, too, that if that wasn't bad enough, wait until the whole world found out that he had refused to help Cody Milligan out of the ditch, and had run off and left the little wormy thing to struggle out of the water by himself. Evidently, Cody hadn't talked yet, and Bud didn't want to be around when he did.

However, Bud had another ulterior motive for not riding with Ellis to the hills. While Ellis was gone, Bud would find the time to go back across the ditch and try to find his shoes and the lantern. The shoes and the lantern ought to be along the trail that led across the field from the ditch to Taylor's graveyard, but he couldn't be sure because he had no recollection of when and where he lost them. Neither of his parents had yet noticed the missing items.

Ellis Scott, with his pick-up truck loaded with the Milligan family and all their camp equipment, drove to the side of the Scott house and parked in the orchard near the barn. Inez Scott came out of the house to say goodbye to the families. She carried two large brown paper sacks, and one smaller sack, filled with freshly-baked yeast rolls. She handed the two large sacks to Maxine Milligan in the back of the truck, and the smaller one to Ellis, for the people in the cab.

The unmistakable sweet aroma of yeast rolls hung in the still air of the orchard, and Bud, who had ambled up behind the truck, began having second thoughts about riding along. However, he had already eaten three of the chewy rolls with blackberry jam, and his plan was to eat two or three more, but this time with honey and cow butter, or perhaps apple butter. Bud liked to eat his rolls in a variety of ways.

"Y'all kin have somethin' to eat on the way," said Inez. And then noticing Bud, behind the truck with his mouth still smeared with blackberry jam said, "My goodness, Teddy Bud, you've got jam all over your face."

The statement by Inez triggered a reaction from Sherry Milligan, who was waiting for an invitation for mischief. She suddenly vaulted over the end gate of the truck and was upon Bud, before he could react. She grabbed him, head-on, by the shoulders, saying, "Teddy Bud, let me have a taste of that," and planted a kiss flush on Bud's lips. Bud was frozen in his tracks. He had never, to his recollection, been kissed on the mouth before, not even by his mother.

"Yummy, yum-yum!" exclaimed Sherry, as Bud pulled away and staggered backwards. "Thet tasted like blackberry. Can I have another?" She made a feint toward Bud, but this time his legs worked. He made a run to the barn lot fence and leaped astride of the gate.

The whole crowd had a good laugh at Bud's expense, including his mother. Ellis put the truck in gear and pulled out into the county road, heading west. The occupants in the back of the truck all waved, and Inez waved back until the truck went out of sight west of the house and garden.

"Well, Teddy Bud, wasn't that a sweet kiss? How did you like it?" Inez said to Bud, who was still perched on the gate.

"I didn't like it none, I reckon. I just come out here to wave goodbye," he replied.

Bud's immediate plan was to head for Cache River Ditch, to find his lost shoes and lantern, but he needed a good reason to run down there this late in the day. He was suddenly inspired.

"Mama, I gotta run down to Joel's house. I pulled my work shoes off down there Halloween night, 'cause they was hurtin' my feet, and I went off and fergot 'em."

"Well, don't stay long. You got to feed and water the stock a-fore dark, and I want you to do the milkin' tonight."

With that admonition, Bud was off on a run down through the field. He noted that there was still a lot of cotton in the fields to be picked, and there was going to be far less people to pick it with the Milligans gone.

The Scotts and the Adkins families would continue picking cotton and pulling corn through the months of November and December, and in all probability would be pulling the half-open cotton bolls through January.

Bud hated that part of the harvest, when you were out in the field in the dead of winter, wearing a heavy winter coat, hat and cotton gloves, and wearing all the socks you could get on, under rubber knee boots, freezing from daylight until dark.

The water table was shallow under the bottom land, so that even in dry weather, ice crystals would form on the ground, when the temperature dropped below freezing, which was a continuous occurrence during January, and when it rained, sleeted or snowed, pools of ice froze in the middles between the rows, which made for slippery footing, but it did lead to the welcome result of making it easier to pull a heavy laden cotton sack over the ground.

There was money still on the stalks, but you couldn't spend it, until you collected it in a cotton sack and got it onto a wagon and to the gin. The quality of the cotton was poor in winter, and the gins didn't pay as much for it as for the early cotton, so the boll-pullers only got a dollar per hundred pounds instead of the usual three. But, with gloves, it was easy to strip the stalks of the bolls, so that you could pull a couple of hundred pounds more a day than you could normally pick, and whatever you could make was better than nothing. Bud hated every minute of it.

Bud was soon across the footlog and facing the current reality of being in Bull Taylor's field. The overriding question that he had bantered back and forth on his way to the ditch: what would his story be to his mother, if he couldn't find the shoes and the lantern, and what was he going to do, and say, if he encountered Bull Taylor?

Immediately, he noticed the smell of smoke in the air, and he detected a slight blue haze drifting from down the east ditch bank, coming from the stovepipe protruding through the roof of the formerly vacant Claxton house. Someone was in the house, but who? He went on about the business at hand, which was finding his shoes and the lantern. He started on across the field toward the Taylor graveyard. He had not gone ten yards until he found both shoes with the lantern sitting in between. *Now how did this happen?* he thought. You don't run out of your shoes and lose your lantern all in one place. Someone or some thing had set the shoes and lantern in the middle of the path leading from the ditch; someone, who knew he would be back for them, but he wasn't going to question his good fortune, not for long anyway.

Bud, gathered up his shoes and the lantern and with an elated sense of relief, turned back toward the ditch. He kept his eye on the Claxton house to see if he could discern any movement. He considered going to the house to see if the Claxton's had returned, but then he thought better of it, because if it were the Claxtons, they would have already been across the ditch looking for work.

Just before entering the trail through the cordon of brush along the ditch bank, he paused momentarily in the field and stood watching the house for a moment. He noted movement inside. The shadowy outline of a figure appeared through a side window, and appeared to be looking at him. The possibility of it being Irene Claxton's ghost suddenly crossed his mind. But would she start a fire?

Bud had his fill of shadowy figures in Bull Taylor's field, and he wasn't about to hang around any longer to try and figure out who or what was in the Claxton house. He quickly exited the field, and was soon across the footlog and over the ditch, and into the field road leading home. When he reached the Thompson barn, he stopped long enough to put on his shoes, and then swinging his lantern, and stepping smartly along toward the setting sun, began to whistle, "My Darling Clementine."

CHAPTER 21

It was 9:30 a.m., the first Monday in November. Abe Turner had just received the latest issue of the weekly newspaper from Walnut Ridge, dropped off at his store by a produce salesman. There was a lengthy article prominently displayed on the front page reporting the latest escapade of Sheriff Al Gunner, World War I hero and lawman extraordinaire. Abe noted that the timing of the article closely preceded election day the following Friday. There was a head and shoulders photograph in a political advertisement on the same page with the article, promoting Sheriff Gunner for re-election.

The article described how Sheriff Gunner and two of his deputies had "busted" up a moonshining operation in the Horse Island community, on Cache River Ditch, four miles south of Sedgwick. The article stated that the moonshiner's camp had been accidentally burned to the ground after a deadly exchange of gunfire that had left two men dead, and burned beyond recognition. One of the dead was believed to have been the escaped convict Rabid Robert Ryder, recently discovered hiding out on Cache River Ditch near the town of Sedgwick. The other fatality was believed to be the moonshiner and sometime preacher, Roscoe Gilmore, who had a sordid history of moonshining in Izard County, prior to moving his operation to Lawrence County. The fire was believed to have started from sparks caused by bullets hitting the copper works of the whiskey still. However, there was no explanation as to how all of the buildings in the camp, separated from one another by several yards, were also burned to the ground.

Abe noted that the article was also remiss in failing to note the involvement by the Craighead County Sheriff's Office. It was the Craighead County authorities, who had actually spooked Rabid Robert from cover, and had chased him down the ditch into Roscoe's camp. The article also failed to mention the missing movie projectionist, Harvey Winkles. Abe was fairly certain in his own mind, that the second known fatality, was Harvey, but where was Roscoe and Homer, and, too, Mary Margaret Miller, who Abe knew to have been in Roscoe's camp the day prior to the shoot-out? Those three had disappeared completely from view.

A deep rumbling sound of an unfamiliar motor, sending vibrations through the store, broke Abe's concentration on the newspaper article. He looked out of the front window and saw a uniformed police officer dismounting from a motorcycle. *Now what?* he thought.

The officer released the kickstand of the cycle and pulled off his helmet and goggles and laid them on the seat. The officer stood a moment surveying his surroundings, stretching his arms and legs, and then he turned and entered the front door.

"Howdy," said the officer.

"Howdy-do."

"Lookin' for the Wilson family."

"Which Wilson?"

"The one with the boy named Elmo."

"How is Elmo?"

"Not good."

"Sick?"

"Dead!"

According to a police report from Chicago, Elmo Wilson had killed himself by diving head first, through a tenth-floor window, of a south side apartment building.

The report stated that Elmo's body was being shipped by train to a funeral home in Jonesboro, Arkansas; a Miss Betty Adkins would accompany the body.

Abe gave the officer directions to the Wilson home, and told him he would notify the parents of Betty Adkins. Abe noted that the report had referred to Betty by her maiden name and he wondered what that meant. He thought Elmo and Betty would have been married.

Two days later, Dovey Adkins, walked up through the field along the west side of Cache River Ditch to Turner's Store. She wore her best cotton print dress under an old gray woolen coat, and brown high top shoes with brown laces. She and Abe, in Abe's pickup truck, drove to Jonesboro, and met the noon train from Chicago. Hazel and Joel Adkins had stayed behind. There was still a lot of cotton to be picked, and the season was growing short.

The parents of the deceased Elmo Wilson were at the train depot when Abe and Dovie arrived. The Wilsons recognized Abe of course, but neither had ever seen Dovie Adkins or her daughter, Betty. Abe and Dovey approached the Wilsons, who were sitting on a wooden bench on the platform outside the depot.

"I am sorry to hear about Elmo," said Abe, as he and Dovey drew up in front of the seated couple. "This here is Dovey Adkins, Betty's mama."

"Please to me y'all, I'm shore'," said an ashened faced Mrs. Wilson, as she stood and took Dovey by the hand. Mrs. Wilson had on a new black wool overcoat and was wearing black shoes. Her hair was covered with a black silk headscarf. Mr. Wilson sat noncommittal, wearing a heavy short coat over his overalls and brogans. He was bareheaded and sat staring north up the railroad tracks, watching and listening for some signal from the expected train.

"We never did meet Betty," said Mrs. Wilson.

"We met Elmo some," said Dovie. "He used to come over the ditch on a footlog. He come to the house, sometimes for supper."

"Elmo, never said," replied Mrs. Wilson.

"We never heard from Betty or nobody about their whereabouts," said Dovie. "We wouldn't have knowed they was in Chicago, for sure, but for the Lawrence County Sheriff getting a letter from your boy, turnin' in the army deserter, Homer Adkins, and askin' fer that thirty-dollar reward."

"Thet was a shameful thing fer Elmo to have done," replied Mrs. Wilson. "Specially when he run off from the draft like he done."

The conversation was interrupted by the rumbling sound of an approaching train that suddenly appeared around a bend in the tracks a quarter mile from the station. Then in quick succession came a long blast of an air horn, followed by two shorter blasts. With air brakes hissing steam, a twelve-car passenger train slowed to a stop in front of the depot, a final blast of steam billowed out across the platform. As soon as the train came to a halt, the conductor came down the steps off the rear platform of the last car and walked over to where Abe and Dovey Adkins were standing with the Wilsons.

"Is the Wilson family here?" he asked.

Mr. Wilson had risen and had taken his wife by the hand. "We're the Wilsons," he said.

"Come with me, please."

The conductor and the Wilsons then walked back to the last car on the train and mounted the steps to the car's rear platform. A long black hearse from the Jonesboro Funeral Home pulled up to the end of the depot platform and two young men in black suits got out and walked toward the train. They walked up the steps to the platform, past the conductor and Mr. and Mrs. Wilson, and entered the car.

Abe and Dovey Adkins remained back on the depot platform and watched for any sign of Betty. The police report had indicated that Betty would be accompanying Elmo's body, but Abe didn't know if that meant she would be in the same car.

"There she is!" exclaimed an obviously relieved Dovey Adkins, as she spotted Betty, following the men from the funeral home, as they rolled a plain metal shipping casket resting on a gurney, out onto the rear platform of the car. Mrs. Wilson stood by as Mr. Wilson made a half-hearted attempt to help the men from the funeral home manage the casket gurney down the steps of the train car to the platform.

Mrs. Wilson watched the unloading of the casket for a moment, while Betty stood in the open doorway of the car until the steps were clear. Then Mrs. Wilson turned to Betty and looked at her a moment and went over to her and said something in the way of introduction and took Betty's hand momentarily. She then turned away and followed the gurney into the station house. It was a very pregnant Betty Adkins that departed the train car, holding onto the platform rail while gingerly easing down the steps onto the depot platform. "Hi Mama," she said.

CHAPTER 22

Bud started back to school for the winter session on the first Monday in November. Joel would not be going back. The Adkins family had to have all the help they could muster, especially with Betty back home and pregnant. Bud had a feeling of loneliness, as he waited on his front porch for the bus to arrive.

Ellis and Inez Scott were on their way to the field when Bud caught the school bus that morning, and they would still be there when he came home that evening. Bud would come in from school, grab a biscuit from the warming compartment on back of the kitchen cook stove, and hopefully find some leftover bacon or sausage from breakfast, but more than likely he would eat his biscuit with a slice of bologna and a slice of onion. He would get to the field late in the day, but still in time to pick a sixty to seventy pound sack of cotton.

By the second week in November, Ellis and Inez were going to the field in style – in Abe's old pickup truck that he had sold to Ellis. Abe had added the two hundred dollar cost for: "truck", to the Scott's grocery bill just below a five pound bag of flour and a pound of cheese.

Farmers were able to acquire extra gas ration coupons, so Ellis would be able to buy gas in limited quantities when he went to Egypt. The gas was currently priced at twenty-two cents per gallon, and Abe had said the nineteen thirty-six Ford pickup, was getting about fifteen miles per gallon. Ellis figured that he could make a round-trip to Walnut Ridge for less than fifty cents worth of gas.

Ellis was now using the truck to haul a double load of cotton to the gin. He could put one bale on the truck and pull the wagon behind with another bale. Since a number of his fall pickers had left, leaving just Inez, himself, and the three members of the Adkins family, he would only be making one trip to the gin each week, weather permitting.

Usually, though, as surrounding farms finished their cotton, their workers would be looking for other places to pick. Ellis didn't expect any problem with getting the cotton out, and now he had to think of getting in the corn crop. Once, he and Hazel started work for the W.P.A., the first of December, there wouldn't be anytime except weekends to gather in the corn, but what they didn't get in would be cleaned up by the mules and hogs that would be turned loose in late January, to winter in the open fields until spring.

Betty Adkins was slowly gaining weight and strength. She had returned from Chicago, emaciated and weak. Things had not gone well for Elmo and her in the Windy City. They arrived without proper clothing for one thing. It had been warm in early fall when they caught the bus at Bono, but when they arrived in Chicago, the winds off Lake Michigan cut through them like a knife.

Betty woke up nauseated every morning, and finally one day while washing clothes at a laundrymat, she met a young woman about her age who was six-months pregnant. In the ensuing conversation, Betty mentioned her morning sickness, and her companion said that she, too, had morning sickness after she became pregnant.

Betty was stunned. The full realization hit her like a dead weight, and her knees buckled. She had to sit down for a moment on a bench in the laundrymat to recover her wits. Betty did not tell Elmo right away. Elmo was having enough problems coping with Chicago.

The couple had not legally married. Elmo told Betty that she was his common-law wife. Both of them had heard the term, but neither knew what it meant. Betty thought she remembered someone saying that when a woman brought a stove into the house, she and the man were considered to be married under common law, and when the woman moved out and took the stove with her, the marriage was terminated. Betty didn't have a stove.

Elmo and Betty had not brought much money with them. Elmo had planned on getting a job in one of the many defense-related plants in the Chicago area. Elmo soon discovered that the problem was not getting a job; the problem was getting to the job. Elmo's tenth-grade education at Bono High School, had ill-prepared him for the reality of life in a big city. He didn't know the first thing about streetcar and bus routes. He had boarded a bus once and rode several miles without the foggiest idea of where he was or where he was going, when finally the driver told him he was going to have to get off. He was forced off the bus at what he took to be the outskirts of the city. He went to a nearby grocery store and used a pay phone to call a cab. The cab ride back to his apartment had cost him considerably more than he could afford at the time. Elmo had learned his lesson. He would never again get on a city bus.

The first major challenge for the young couple was finding a place to live. They got off the Greyhound Bus at the station in downtown Chicago, carrying all of their possessions in two suitcases. The first establishment that they entered was an Italian restaurant. While there, Elmo mentioned to the waitress that they were looking for a place to stay. Fortunately, there was a two-room apartment that had just become vacant above the restaurant.

Elmo was required to sign a six-month lease for seven-dollars per week, with the owner of the restaurant, who also owned the apartment. Elmo or Betty didn't know what a lease was. Neither one could remember ever hearing the word. The next day they went for lunch in the same restaurant, and Elmo asked a waitress what it meant. It meant, she said, that legally you are obligated to live there and make payments for six months, and if you move, you are still obligated to make the agreed-upon payments until the end of the lease.

The young couple had become effectively trapped in their new environment within twenty minutes after getting off the bus. They were in downtown Chicago, with limited funds, no personal transportation, no job and no job skills, a limited education, and a tendency to get lost if they ventured more than five blocks from their apartment. They couldn't sleep at all during the first week in their new apartment, because of the constant roar and grind of the street traffic passing below, punctuated by occasional gun fire and the sound of ambulance and police car sirens.

Elmo finally found a job as a night janitor, paying twelve dollars per week, in a twenty-story apartment building across the street from where they lived. "Hell," said Elmo. "I kin make a lot more'n twelve dollars a week, at home, pickin' cotton or cuttin' timber." Many of the buildings in downtown Chicago were taller than any trees that Betty and Elmo had ever seen. They spent a good deal of the time when outside of the apartment, looking skyward.

"I'm trapped like a rat," Elmo was in the habit of saying, when he came home from work at six o'clock in the morning. Betty would try to get past her nausea, and have something on the table for him to eat. She always had a pot of coffee. She was good at making coffee, and she could scramble eggs and make toast, and fry bacon. Elmo would then try to sleep after breakfast, usually unsuccessfully, in a cacophony of Chicago morning sounds.

Betty filled her days by reading a Chicago newspaper that she usually found downstairs in the restaurant, or she sometimes walked a few blocks to .

a nearby park where she watched the pigeons. Some of the pigeons seemed to stare at her and she thought they, too, looked familiar. She wondered if any of them had ever visited the Thompson barn.

Betty tried to make Elmo as comfortable as she thought a common-law wife should. She wasn't much of a cook, but she could make potato soup like her mother had taught her. However, she never learned how to make the big fluffy cathead biscuits. The couple often ate sliced bread, toasted or plain. She couldn't bake, but she knew how to take light bread and spread butter on it and then sprinkle it with brown sugar for a nice dessert. Betty was good at opening cans of sardines, soup, pork and beans, and Vienna sausages, and she could make grilled cheese sandwiches. The couple discovered a number of new foods. Neither had ever eaten pizza, spaghetti, salami or pretzels, prior to coming to Chicago. There was a pretzel maker who set up his cooker on the corner below their apartment. They both liked the twisted, hard, salty, crusty treats, and they were filling. Elmo and Betty ate a lot of pretzels.

After a few weeks, Betty thought that it was time to reveal her pregnancy to Elmo. Elmo was stunned. The possibility of fatherhood had not crossed his mind. His plans were to stay where they were until the lease expired, and by that time he would learn the ropes and maybe they could move out close to one of the steel foundries. There was good money to be made there or so he had been told by some of the janitorial personnel that he worked with, but they could never satisfactorily explain why they were working as janitors rather than in the steel mills. Maybe someday soon, he and Betty would be living in one of those little row houses that they had seen as the bus passed on the way to the downtown station. He had seen people through the windows of the houses as they passed. He wondered who they were. Were they from Arkansas, too? His plan was to become rich while working in the steel mills and eventually own a house, with a car, maybe two, parked in the driveway. His plan had been currently parked in fate's driveway.

Elmo went into a blue funk for a week, after learning that Betty was pregnant and that the baby would probably be born by winter. Elmo did some mental calculations and wondered how that was possible.

Elmo came into the apartment one Saturday with a quart of strawberry wine. He sat sipping glass after glass while staring out the window at the place of his employment across the street. That was the first time that Betty had ever seen Elmo drink anything stronger than an R.C. Cola. Elmo decided to challenge Betty about who was responsible for her pregnancy.

"When did you say that baby was due?"

"Didn't say, cause I don't know."

"Well, when did you get knocked up?"

"I don't know. I didn't know I was until I talked to a girl down at the laundrymat."

"You don't know much, do ya?"

"No. Reckon not."

"I don't believe that's my baby."

"Well, whose is it then?"

"How the hell should I know?"

"You don't know much do you?"

"Well, I think I know it can't be mine."

"If it ain't yours, then I don't know whose it is."

"Well, we'll damned sure know when it gets here. I bet it won't favor me none."

"Well, I hope it's a girl and it favors me."

"I don't want no girl. It damned well better be a boy."

"We'll see."

"Yeh. We'll see."

Sooner'n we're ready, I expect."

Betty, also, was having doubts that Elmo was the baby's father. Her pregnancy was too far advanced, and the way she counted, it might not be Elmo's child. Betty had a secret she hadn't told anyone, and she sure wasn't about to tell Elmo now.

In late summer, Elmo told Betty that he remembered seeing a wanted poster in the post office at Walnut Ridge, for the army deserter, Homer Adkins, and against Betty's wishes and tears, he had gone to the downtown Chicago Post Office and rented a box by the month. He had sent off a letter to the Lawrence County Sheriff, telling what he knew of the location of the albino, Homer Adkins, and requesting the thirty-dollar reward be sent to his Chicago post office box. He said to hurry with the payment, as he needed the money.

Elmo had taken to strong drink. Betty began to notice during the summer that he had fallen into the habit of buying a quart of strawberry wine every Friday – payday – from a liquor store a few blocks from the apartment. He had progressively increased his drinking. Soon he was buying two quarts a week, and by the first of October, he was up to a quart a day. Elmo left for his night shift in a muddled state of mind, and it was soon apparent that he was drinking on the job.

Finally, on October thirty first, Halloween night, everything came to a head. The maintenance supervisor for the apartment building, who had been forced into ever increasing confrontations with Elmo about his indifferent attitude, had made up his mind to fire the Arkansas farm boy, if he had to confront him one more time, and he had told him so.

The supervisor found Elmo sitting on the floor in a tenth-floor hallway with a half-empty bottle of red wine between his legs. The supervisor looked down on the sorry sight.

"Elmo, go down to the office in the morning and see the secretary. Tell her to close out your work file, and give you your pay, to date. We can't afford you no more. You're fired!"

Elmo looked up through blurry eyes. Fired! He hadn't ever been fired. He had worked as long as he could remember in a cotton patch or a peckerwood sawmill from daylight till dark, and he had never heard the word. Elmo got to his feet blinking back tears.

"I'm sorry boy," said the supervisor. "But you just ain't cuttin' it."

"Cuttin' it!" exclaimed Elmo, "I'll show you, cuttin' it!"

There was a large plate glass window at the end of the hallway facing to the south. Elmo had often stood at the south windows looking toward Arkansas, hoping to see some part of it, if nothing but the shadowy outline of the Ozarks, to the southwest. He had wanted to go home for a long time now, but he didn't know how. He had a lease, and he had a pregnant wife. There would be hospital bills when the baby came and extra stuff to buy. They would need a car, and where was the money coming from? And then the supervisor said, "You're fired," just like that, and now he was going to have to start all over, and he didn't want to start over. He wanted to go home.

"I'm head'n south!" shouted Elmo, and with those words he raced down the hallway, lowered his head, and launched himself through the window, and for a brief moment, into the Chicago skyline.

The maintenance supervisor stood momentarily stunned, trying to comprehend what he had just witnessed. He stared at the shattered glass, and then his sense of responsibility surfaced. He had an unsafe condition on his hands that needed immediate attention, and he made a mental note to talk to the building operations supervisor about the poor quality of safety glass supplied by the contractor.

Betty didn't go to the funeral. She had mixed emotions about Elmo. She didn't love him when she agreed to go to Chicago with him, and she didn't love him after he was dead. She felt as if an enormous burden had been lifted from her shoulders; part of the load was Elmo, the other part, Chicago. However, she was grateful to Elmo for at least making the attempt to get her out of the cotton patch – but Chicago? They should have gone to California or Florida; it was warm there, and they had farms.

When Inez got her first good look at Betty after her return from Chicago, she immediately became concerned at her haggard appearance. Inez made a point of sending Bud down to the Adkins house several times a week with a variety of pies and candies. Fresh sweet potatoes were in season, and Inez often sent her specialty, sweet potato pie, with melted marshmallows on top. After three weeks of the pie diet, Bud noted that Betty's cheeks had begun to fill out, and that Little Claude, who was staying home with Betty, had swollen up like a toad.

Betty had reported hearing sounds in the night, and thought that someone was coming up around the house. Joel and Hazel discovered strange footprints in the yard and around the window of the bedroom where Betty and Little Claude slept. Occasionally, the sounds of dogs barking could be heard coming from the direction of the Claxton house across the ditch. Hazel said he thought it was probably some of Bull Taylor's field hands that might be hungry and were looking to steal food. He said he did not expect any trouble as long as Betty was home, but he told Betty to keep the doors latched from the inside while the rest of the family was in the field.

CHAPTER 23

It was going to be a white Christmas. Bud could only remember one other. Not that the Arkansas delta didn't have snow, but it normally fell in January or February. One of the heaviest snowfalls in recent memory fell on March 25, 1937.

It was Christmas Eve. Ellis Scott and Hazel Adkins had been working for the W.P.A. since the first of December. Both had drawn one hundred dollars in one paycheck for two weeks work. Ellis had brought home one hundred crisp new one-dollar bills wrapped tight with a brown paper band. Ellis let Bud take the bundle and count the money. Bud took out his Barlow pocket knife and carefully slipped it under the paper band holding the bills and cut it. He slowly counted out ten stacks of ten one-dollar bills. It was the first time Bud or Inez had ever seen that much money at one time.

The W.P.A. shut down their crews for the holidays the middle of December. They would start back to work the first week in January, weather permitting. Ellis and Hazel had been driving the truck to Bono, and leaving it in the parking lot behind the post office, where they met other men from the Bono area. Mr. Houston Johnston arrived at a little after 5:00 a.m. with a large truck covered by a tarpaulin. He transported the crew to work points east of Jonesboro. Currently the crew was cutting right-of-way for the new electrical poles and wires in the Monette, Leachville and Caraway areas. They would probably work in those areas until spring.

It had been snowing since midnight. Ellis came in from the barn stomping his boots free of snow on the back porch. "Already a foot deep," he said, as he came through the kitchen door and headed for the coffee pot on the cook stove. He poured out a steaming hot cup of very black coffee and immediately began to sip it. Bud was never ceased to be amazed that his father could drink boiling coffee straight from the pot; coffee so strong that Ellis said, "would float a horseshoe."

Bud had more than once commented to his father about his ability to drink boiling coffee, because it usually prompted a remark from Ellis, which usually was, "I like my coffee, like my women, strong, hot and black." This remark usually got a chuckle and a witty aside from Mama Inez. Bud once had been embarrassed by his father's salty remarks, but he was now thirteen, and little his father said embarrassed him anymore.

"Bud, I brought the scoop shovel up from the barn. It's leanin' outside by the back steps. You need to get your boots on, and go clean the snow off the woodpile. Cut some kindlin' for the cook stove and chop some wood for the heatin' stove. I'll be out dreckly' to help you carry it in. Looks like this snow is goin' to keep on for sometime, so the more wood we get in today, out of the wet, the better."

Bud was reluctant to get out into the cold. He had been sitting in the warmth of the kitchen, drinking hot cocoa and reading the latest edition of the weekly *Grit Newspaper* that the Smith boy had dropped off the day before.

Ellis had agreed with Adam Smith to take the weekly newspaper for ten cents a copy. Adam would send seven cents for each copy sold back to the publisher and he would keep three cents.

Adam Smith was in the same class as Bud at Egypt Elementary. He was the son of a sharecropper that farmed about two miles west of the Scott home, on the Egypt-Bono road, just where it intersected with the Egypt-Hoxie road. He usually made his newspaper deliveries on a new, red Schwinn bicycle, a bicycle greatly admired by Bud.

Adam rode a route of eight to ten miles delivering the *Grit* to over 30 families. His average profit was a dollar a week. He always seemed to have money in his pocket all year round, and he even bought Bud a big orange soda pop one time down at Turner's Store when he had passed through on his route, and found Bud sitting on the store porch, out of funds, and with no prospects. Someday Bud hoped to be able to return the favor.

Bud and Inez had spent the day before and most of the morning trimming a cedar tree that Bud had found down on the Cache River Ditch bank and had cut down with an ax. Cedar trees were rare in cotton country, but a few of varying shapes and sizes could be found along the ditch bank and sometimes in a fencerow. Inez had saved the decorations from the year before and she had an assortment of silver tinsel and glass bulbs. She even had a star for the top with a little angel, which Bud always found a challenge to keep upright.

Today, Inez was baking. She had already baked a dried apple pie, a pumpkin pie, and a chess pie. She was in the process of baking a fat duck and two guinea fowls. Bud had a real time trying to corral the half-wild guineas. They were birds that originally came from Africa, and somehow got to Arkansas. Mr. Johnston had left a flock of them on the farm. Guineas didn't seem to belong to anyone, and didn't take well to living in captivity. They could fly for long distances, roosted in trees and it seemed that they liked to be out in the road in front of the house better than anything. They kept up a very loud chatter and people often said that they were better than dogs to let you know when strangers were around. They were extremely wary, and it was a very difficult proposition to catch one.

Bud took some crushed corn and scattered a heavy corn trail from out in the orchard in through the door of the chicken house. Following a corn trail was the only way you would ever get a guinea to go inside a building. Bud waited patiently and quietly out of sight beside the chicken house while the guineas followed the corn trail inside. After several had gone inside, he made a lunge and slammed the door trapping them.

Bud finally caught two inside the chicken house, and tied their feet together. He hung them upside down on a nail. Inez would come out later, wring their necks and clean them. Bud was not that fond of eating guinea or duck. The meat of the guinea was dark and dry and the duck was fat and greasy, but they were passable with his mother's cornbread dressing, and bowls of green snap beans and hominy grits.

Inez asked Ellis to get the sled ready because she needed to go to the Adkins house and carry several containers of food and a gallon of milk. Dovey Adkins had come to see Inez the day before. She told Inez that Betty could deliver at any time, but she was pretty sure it would be Christmas Eve.

Dovey said she didn't know what to expect and she might need some help. She had "mid-wifed" some and had delivered all three of her own children at home, mostly by herself, but Betty had returned from Chicago emaciated and mal-nourished and that couldn't have been good for the baby, even though, Betty had gained back most of the weight.

It was middle of the evening and the snowfall was still heavy. Ellis measured a depth of two feet in the back yard, and there were drifts against the barnyard fence of three feet. Bud and Ellis had spent over four hours since mid-morning keeping the woodpile clear and cutting wood.

They stacked wood on the back porch, in the front room and the kitchen for both the heating stove in the front room and the cook stove in the kitchen. Now, they called a halt and went into the kitchen for hot coffee and chess pie. It was time to load the sled and get ready for the trip to the Adkins house.

"I wish there was a doctor handy," said Inez. "But they ain't no way one could git here anyway from Walnut Ridge, and wishin' ain't gonna make it so. We'll just have to make do with what we got."

Using the truck was out of the question. Ellis had parked it under an overhang at the barn. He had originally intended to harness one mule to pull the sled, but as the day wore on, and with the snow accumulation, he changed his mind and decided to use a team. The sled was the same one that they had used in the spring to haul stumps while clearing new ground. It was nothing more than a heavy five-foot by seven-foot oak planked platform nailed to two runners, which was originally the trunk of a twelve inch tree that had been halved and the ends beveled, to cut through the dirt and mud of the new ground. There wouldn't be any problem with the mules pulling it through the snow, particularly if they weighted it toward the rear and kept the nose of the sled elevated.

Everything was finally ready. The food was protected inside a large wooden box and loaded to the rear of the sled. Bud was to sit on the box and make sure it didn't fall off. Ellis had shelled two large buckets of corn for the mules and set them back against the box of food. All of the barn animals, chickens, dogs and cats had been fed and watered, and the old jersey cow milked. The animals had settled down for what would be a premature nightfall behind heavy overcast, snow-laden skies. The Scotts would need a lantern and a back-up flashlight.

Bud made a last minute addition to the mission. He remembered an old copper cowbell hanging in the barn. He wanted to hear sleigh bells in the snow. Inez and Ellis were pleased at his idea. After all, it was Christmas Eve and it should be a festive occasion.

It was an early dark when they finally got underway at four o'clock. Ellis lit the kerosene lantern and Inez and him sat flat down on a rolled up tarpaulin in the middle of the sled, while Bud sat directly behind on the box of food. Bud would ring the cowbell.

Inez turned to Bud. "Do you know what day it is tomorrow?"

"Of course. It's Christmas."

"I mean, the significance?"

"Jesus was born on Christmas Day."

"Yes, the Christ Child was born on Christmas Day, and we may have another little Christmas baby tomorrow."

Inez was clearly excited with the prospect. It was a rare occurrence for someone to have a birthday on December twenty-fifth. A quick poll was taken, to see if anyone on the sled knew of anyone that was born on Christmas Day, to include Bud's classmates. None of the Scotts could think of anyone.

The mules moved through the snow at a fast clip and the sled rode well, slipping through the snow with minimum drag. The hot breath of the mules could be seen puffing out in the outer reaches of the lantern light, steam was rising from their backs.

As they passed the Thompson barn and neared the Cache River Ditch where they would turn south along the west ditch bank to the Adkins house, hoot owls could be heard calling in the timber along the banks of the ditch. Bud quit ringing the cowbell and listened to the night sounds. Off in the distance a fox barked, and he heard the unmistakable sounds of dogs barking across the river, in the direction of the Claxton house.

In the outer perimeter of the lantern light, a figure suddenly emerged coming toward them through the falling snow. It was Joel Adkins bundled in a heavy winter coat and cap, wearing rubber knee boots. Ellis reined in the mules as Joel came along side. The lantern light revealed serious concern in his eyes.

"Miz Scott," said Joel. "Mama sent me to git you. It's Betty. She's been havin' an awful time."

Joel got aboard the sled and, within 20 minutes, Ellis reined in the mules in front of the Adkins house. He tied the mules to a tree in the front yard. Inez immediately left the sled and went inside leaving Ellis, Bud and Joel to bring in the food. Joel and Bud began to unload the food, while Ellis began to unroll the tarpaulin, and with the boys' help draped it over the mules just leaving their necks and heads bare. He placed a bucket of shelled corn in front of each mule. The mule's body heat would keep them fairly warm under the tarp, and the corn would hold their attention for a while.

A strong odor of tobacco greeted all who entered the Adkins house. Hazel Adkins found that he could grow a few rows of the tobacco weed along the base of the ditch bank. He dried the broad leaves inside the house by hanging them in bundles around the walls of the kitchen and the front room, of the aged four-room cypress log cabin. The only other buildings in the clearing were a log smoke house and a cypress-planked outhouse. Hazel used the smokehouse to cure rabbits, possums, coons, and an occasional wild-hog over a hickory wood fire.

Hazel ground some of the cured leaves of tobacco into fine fibers for smoking, and used some other leaves to roll into cigars. Additionally, he stacked other tobacco leaves, after coating both sides of each leaf with either wild honey or sorghum molasses. He used heavy slabs of wood to compress the stacks into a one-inch thickness. After a few days of bonding, he cut the stacks into two-inch squares. Both Hazel and Joel carried cuts of the flavored tobacco in the bib pocket of their overalls the year round.

Inez didn't expect the Adkins family to have any pain killing drugs, so she brought a few tablets that a dentist had once given her for the toothache. She reasoned that although the pain of childbirth was not the same as a toothache, a painkiller for any purpose is better than nothing.

Ellis, Bud, Joel, Hazel and Little Claude gathered around the kitchen table. Ellis chuckled at the pudgy face of Little Claude peering across the kitchen table at him.

"Hazel, he ain't missed to many meals lately, has he?" he asked.

"No, not many," Hazel answered with a chuckle in his voice. "He's et' more'uv them sweets that Inez has been sending to Betty, than Betty has."

Inez and Dovey Adkins had gone into the bedroom just off the kitchen, to minister to Betty.

"Her water broke about two this evenin'," said Dovey. "And she seems to be havin' more trouble than I ever did, but she ain't as strong as I was when I had my babies. She got soft in Chicago. She shoulda been here workin' in the field. She could handle it better."

"I brought some pain killer," said Inez. "I got six tablets. I'm gonna give her two now and save the rest for later."

There was a large cast iron pot full of water boiling on the stove. Joel and Hazel would take turns feeding the fire. There was a fire also going in the heating stove in the front room, but the old house was drafty, and Bud could feel a slight breeze coming from somewhere and finally realized the air was coming up through the cracks in the floor boards underneath his feet.

Soft moans could be heard coming out of the bedroom. The door had been left ajar in order to let in heat from the kitchen. The moans would increase in intensity and frequency. Hazel Adkins had tried to drown out the sounds of Betty's labor with an old battery radio, but all he could get was static, so he stopped trying.

Bud looked around the kitchen. He had been in the house often, since the Adkins family had occupied it, and each time his attention was always drawn to the colorful strings of peppers, garlic and onions that Dovie Adkins hung from the walls beside the door facings. He liked the sweet scents of the dried vegetables mixing with the stronger aroma of tobacco. The smell helped to mask the aroma of unwashed bodies and spoiled food. Inez didn't hang such things in her kitchen, and her kitchen smelled like flour, baking powder, vanilla flavoring and yeast. Bud suddenly realized that it was suppertime, and that he had not eaten in two hours.

Bud turned slightly to look at the wall behind him, at a calendar hanging on the wall. The individual month pages had been torn off, leaving nothing but the sunny scene of what appeared to be a tropical forest.

"Why cha'all still got thet ole' calendar hangin' up?" asked Bud, to no one in particular.

"Mama, likes the picture," answered Joel. "Says it makes her warm to look at it."

It must be hell, being poor, Bud thought, and then he suddenly came to the realization that he was poor, too.

The Adkins were poor people, but poorer than most and that was saying a lot. Joel had said that about all his family had to eat the past winter was potatoes, turnips and swamp rabbit. The big swampers were very nearly as large as Texas jackrabbits, and they were plentiful around the ditch, woods and swamps. Joel, in jest, said that his family had eaten so much rabbit last winter that if they were outside and a dog barked, they all ran under the house. Bud grinned and chuckled to himself, thinking about it.

There were no Christmas decorations in the house or any sign of the Christmas season anywhere. Bud started to say something, but thought better of it. He didn't know what affect it might have on Little Claude, who was sitting in a cane-bottomed rocking chair near the cook stove, and was nodding off to sleep.

Dovey Adkins came out of the bedroom with an aluminum dishpan full of bloody rags. Bud was shocked at the sight of so much blood, but he didn't say anything. However, he suddenly wasn't hungry anymore.

"Joel, take these and dump 'em in the kettle outside," said Dovey. "And throw in a couple more of them bluin' tablets."

That was the first time that Bud realized that there was a large fire burning behind the house with a wash pot full of boiling water hanging above the fire.

"C'mon Bud," said Joel. "Let's go outside a while. I need to put some more wood on the fire."

The boys put on their coats and wool toboggans. They stepped through the back door and directly to the ground as the Adkins cabin had neither porch or steps, front or back. The snow had melted in a large circle around the kettle from the heat of the fire leaving a circular pool of glistening earth, wet on top but still frozen underneath.

"There's some footprints here thet I don't believe's mine," stated Joel, and he looked around the yard. "Well maybe Daddy and Little Claude came out and I didn't know it."

Joel dumped the pan of bloody cloths into the boiling pot, and he and Bud went over to a nearby woodpile and brought several sticks of wood and leaned them up around the kettle. The wood was wet with snow, but it would dry and catch fire quickly in the extreme heat from the hot coals of the fire. Joel took the empty dishpan and went over to dip several pans full of snow that he added to the kettle.

It was ten o'clock, and the snow had stopped falling. There was a hint of stars through the cloud cover. A full moon had risen and the snow-covered landscape began to take on a ghostly glow. The boys stood momentarily listening to the sounds of the night. A dog barked across the ditch, not far from the Adkins' house.

"Somebody's over there in that Claxton house," said Joel.

"Been there since Halloween, I reckon," said Bud. "I seen a light in the window that night."

"Whoever it is don't wanna be seen," said Joel. "I know, cause I tried more'n once. I went over the footlog and slipped down the bank behind the house, but I ain't never seen a soul inside. And iffin you git in smellin' distance, them dogs'll open up and then the lights go out, and you just know somebody is watchin' you. I don't need gettin' shot, so I quit goin' over there. I'll tell you somethin' else. Somebody's been comin' up round our house at night. I've seen fresh footprints more'n' once round the house and specially outside the room where Betty sleeps."

"Well, Daddy says, whoever it is ain't got no business in that Claxton house," said Bud. "He says, far as he knows that house and the forty acre homestead still belongs to the Claxton family. Bull Taylor wants it, though."

The boys took a long last look at the fire. The cloths had boiled out white in the bluing detergent. "Wonder where the blood goes?" said Joel. The boys re-entered the backdoor to hear Hazel and Ellis talking in hushed tones.

"You know what puzzles me?" Hazel was saying, "in order for her to be havin' thet baby now, means she wouldda had to be with thet Wilson boy back in March, and as fur as I know, she ain't never laid eyes on him till summer. That's when he cut that footlog across the ditch and started comin' over here."

"Well, if it ain't him whose the Daddy?" replied Ellis. "Who is it?"

"Damned if I know," said Hazel. "Maybe it's one of them freaky things."

Inez and Dovey came out of the bedroom and left the door open. Dovey was carrying another pan of soiled rags. "Gotta get some heat in thet bedroom, freezin' in there," she said.

"Well, we got her quite," said Inez. "I give her three of them painkillers. Hope it ain't too many, but she's in an awful lot of pain."

An hour passed and the house had been quiet. Joel had gone back outside and fished the cloths out of the boiling water, and stoked the fire. He brought them inside for Dovey and Inez to wring out and hang on nails in the kitchen to dry.

Little Claude was sound asleep in the rocking chair, sitting up, his head fallen on his chest, bushy dirty blonde hair in disarray.

"Boy needs a haircut," said Hazel, as he looked over at the sleeping boy. "Maybe tomorrow."

Bud was sitting on a straight-backed caned-bottom chair in the front room trying to read a nineteen-forty edition of *The Old Farmer's Almanac* by the light of a kerosene lamp. Joel was sitting on the floor, leaned back against the wall sipping hot coffee from a tin cup. Inez, Ellis, Hazel and Dovey were sitting in chairs around the kitchen table.

"Anybody hungry?" Dovey asked in a hushed voice. Nobody answered. "Guess not," she said.

Hazel fished a chrome plated railroad watch out of the bib of his overall. "Twelve o'clock, I thought so," he said.

"It's Christmas," said Dovey. "We're gonna have a Christmas baby." Her eyes glistened with tears. "I wish it's Daddy was here."

Inez got up from the table and went into the front room and leaned over to Bud still sitting with the almanac. "It's Christmas, Teddy Bud," she whispered tenderly.

"Yep. I know."

"You and Dad can go home at daylight, even if I can't. Maybe Santa's been there. Maybe he's left a surprise."

"Mama, you know there ain't no Santa Claus."

"No, I don't know that. Santa is a spirit like God. You believe in God don't you?"

"Yessum, I guess so."

"Well, God is a spirit. Santa is a spirit. They're all spirits alike. They reside in the center of our soul."

"I ain't never laid eyes on neither one."

236

"You can't see spirits. You can only feel 'em, like now. I feel somethin' close."

"Maa-maaaaah!" Betty cried out from the bedroom.

Inez and Dovey rushed into the bedroom. "I wish to God, thet baby'd come," said Dovey.

"Mama, I'm so tired," said Betty, her face contorted in pain.

"I know baby," said Dovey. "But you ain't got fer to go. You're gonna have to be brave and help us git that baby on this side of creation."

Hazel came to the door of the bedroom. Dovey spotted him out of the corner of her eye. "Go on and git out, ole' man. You ain't needed here," she snapped.

Hazel slumped back over to the kitchen table and sat down. "Thet woman shore gits snappish come birthin' time," he said. "And I don't need none of this."

A series of loud moans in quick succession could be heard as birthing spasms racked Betty. Bud thought about going outside so he couldn't hear, but he wondered just how far he would have to get from the house, and it was cold outside and he was comfortable and warm where he was. He shut his eyes, and put a finger in each ear in an effort to block out Betty's suffering.

"Push!" exclaimed Dovey, louder than usual. "Push, dammit!"

"I see it's head," Bud heard his mother say.

Bud had shut his eyelids together as tight as he could and he had pushed a finger as far as he could into each ear. Then there was a quiet moment. Bud opened his eyes, and eased the fingers out of his ears. From where he sat in the front room, Bud could see through the door and into the kitchen. He could see his father and Hazel Adkins sitting upright and staring toward the bedroom door in tense anticipation.

Then Bud heard a cat mewing. It sounded like it came from outside the house. Joel stood up by the stove. He cocked his head to listen.

"Y'all got a cat?" asked Bud.

"Not as fur as I know," answered Joel.

Then the mewing got progressively louder, and it was coming from the bedroom. The boys looked at one another in simultaneous recognition.

"It's the Christmas baby," said Bud.

"Here, I'll cut the cord," Bud heard Dovey say.

Bud and Joel walked into the kitchen, just as Dovey emerged from the · bedroom with a dishpan full of soiled cloths. She handed the pan to Joel. "You know what to do," she said.

Bud looked through the bedroom door. He couldn't see Betty, but he could see enough of his mother to make out that she was wrapping up the whimpering baby in a large white cloth.

Dovey came out of the bedroom and stood for a moment wiping her hands on her apron, looking toward Hazel and Ellis sitting at the table. "Well, ole' man, yore a grandpa of the longest and whitest baby boy, I ever saw," she said. Then they were jolted by an exclamation from Inez in the bedroom. "My God! It's an albino!"

Dovey walked over to the bedroom doorway where Inez cradled the baby and pulled the swaddling clothes back for a closer look. Hazel and Ellis got to their feet. Bud and Joel edged forward for a look at the newborn child. Bud had seen farm animals shortly after birth, but not a newborn human baby. Dovey looked at Hazel. "This is Homer's baby," she said. There was a soft knock at the front door.

"Who in the world, could that be?" exclaimed Hazel. Everyone, but Inez moved forward and stared intently at the door as Joel opened it. Joel turned his head and smiled, announcing, "It's Roscoe, Homer and Mary Margaret."

Hazel went to the door. "Well, come on in and get the door closed," he said. The trio filed in. Homer was carrying a large stuffed canvas bag. "We brought some gifts and things," said Roscoe. Little Claude had awakened from the commotion. He eased up behind Dovey, wrapping his arms around her legs and peeked around at the visitors, rubbing the sleep out of his eyes and trying to focus on the scene before him.

"We thought you boys were done for back in October, when your camp got raided," said Ellis.

"Well, to make a long story, short," replied Roscoe, "we went into an underground shelter that I had built in a briar patch out in the edge of the swamp, where I kept my still. We took the dogs in there with us. I wish I coulda got my little mule in there too, because it didn't survive. Boy, I hated to lose that mule. Anyway, we waited until after dark, and then we carried what we could up here to the Claxton house on a little two-wheel cart. We've been livin' over there across the ditch, and only coming out at night. We've been pulling the cart over to Egypt for supplies. We always wait till dark, and me and Homer stay out of sight and send Mary Margaret to do the shoppin' cause she's not as well known there as up this way."

"That Lawrence County Sheriff'll wantta kill us fer shore now," interjected Homer. "Since he has made his brag in the newspaper. We've been waitin' for the right time to get outta the country."

"We've brought cha'all some things, toys and heavy clothes, and baby things," said Mary Margaret.

"How'd you know we had a baby?" asked Dovey.

"We knowed it was comin' fer some time. We've seen Betty a few times outside the house, and we've kind of kept up with things," replied Mary Margaret. "And we've been outside tonight watchin' some, thru the window."

"Well, for goodness sakes," exclaimed Inez. "Why'nt y'all come on in?"

"You had a crowd in here and you've been awful busy, so we just thought we'd stay outta the way," replied Roscoe. "We stayed out by the fire, and when Joel came out we just went around behind the smokehouse. We didn't want to be no bother."

"Is Betty, OK?" asked Homer.

Then they all, except Inez, realized that Betty had been forgotten since the baby came. "She's all right," said Inez. "She's awful weak and tared, and she needs to eat somethin' – Dovey, make her some potato soup – and she's got to feed the baby, but she's got the milk to do it."

The three visitors crowded around Inez to view the squirming child who was trying to suck his fingers.

"Pore little guy," said Inez. "He's hungry." And then she pushed the baby toward Homer. "Here Homer, hold your son."

Homer, without surprise or hesitation, gathered the baby into his arms, and with a growing mist in his eyes, looked down into the tiny face. He said softly, "It's the only miracle I was ever able to perform."

CHAPTER 24

"There's nothin' more to be done here," said Inez, looking toward Bud and Ellis. "We can go home now."

Bud was more than ready. It was two o'clock on Christmas morning. A special day was still ahead for Bud. The Scotts were soon on their way, under a star-filled sky and a full moon that lit the landscape bright as day. When they passed by the Thompson barn, their house and outbuildings were clearly visible from half-mile away.

No one had said anything since boarding the sled, and leaving the Adkins house. The night was still except for the sloshing of the mule's hooves through the deep snow, and the creaking of leather harness. Finally Bud broke the silence, "How in the world did Homer get to be the daddy of that baby?"

"God works in mysterious ways, " said Inez.

"Very mysterious, " Ellis concurred.

The house was cold when they got home. There were only embers left in the kitchen cook stove and in the heating stove in the front room. Ellis, with Bud's help got the mules put away in a barn stall with a manger full of hay, and while they were doing that, Inez put wood in both stoves and stoked the fire, soon both were roaring hot.

It wasn't long until Ellis and Bud came in on the back porch and stomped the snow off of their boots. Bud removed his boots and padded into the front room in his red sawmill socks, and took a quick look around. Everything was just as they had left it earlier in the afternoon. The two big, knee-length, red hunting socks were hanging limp where he had secured them to the wall with thumbtacks, and there was not one present of any kind under the tree. "It's past two o'clock in the mornin' and Santa ain't here, yet," said Bud.

"Don't worry about it, hon," replied Inez, as she placed two large red bricks on top of the heating stove. "He's probably delayed some because of the heavy snow. Go on to bed. Soon as the bricks get hot enough, I'll put a couple by yore feet."

Bud was too tired just then to worry about Santa's travel plans, but he did wonder to himself, as he crawled under several layers of blankets and quilts, just how someone who supposedly drove a sleigh and eight reindeer through the air, could possibly be delayed by heavy snow. He lay shivering under the heavy covers thinking about Santa and the Christmas baby until Inez came into his bedroom and slipped two hot bricks wrapped in an old blanket, next to his feet. That did the trick. He was soon warm all over and fell into a sound asleep.

Bud was awakened at mid-morning on Christmas Day, by the thumping sound of sheets of snow slipping off the tin roof of the house, and thudding into a snowdrift piling up just outside his bedroom window. He was drowsy and warm under the pile of blankets and quilts, but he could see his breath in the cold bedroom, and he knew that the temperature on the other side of the quilts was below freezing. He was reluctant to get out of bed, but then he thought about what he might find under the tree in the front room.

"Merry Christmas!" exclaimed Inez, as Bud padded out of the bedroom into the kitchen in his longhandle underwear and his heavy sawmill socks, and still wearing his toboggan. He was greeted with a cornucopia of smells. His ultra sensitive nose detected cocoa boiling on the stove, coffee, salty ham, cathead biscuits and sawmill gravy.

Ellis was sitting at the kitchen table drinking coffee. Bud thought he noted a little smile on his father's face, as he sat staring through the kitchen window at the whiteness beyond, seemingly oblivious to Bud's presence. Bud would want a cup of that hot cocoa later with perhaps a marshmallow melted on top, but first thing's first. He headed for the front room. The first things to greet his eyes were two bulging red hunting socks. That would be oranges, apples, English walnuts, Brazil nuts and pecans. He would tend to those later.

Then his eyes caught the glitter of green and white metal reflecting light from behind the Christmas tree. It was the Schwinn, green with white trim. It had an adjustable seat and handlebars, a green chain guard with a white design on it that made the bike look like it was moving when it was standing still. It had green fenders front and back, a battery-powered headlight, and a push-button horn that also operated with two D-cell batteries.

Bud stood in the middle of the room and marveled at the prize, and then he went over and pulled it out from behind the tree, and straddled the seat. He turned on the headlight and beeped the horn a couple of times. He sat a moment looking into the future when he would be able to get this work of art outside. He would leave it where it was for the time being. He would have to wait for the snow to melt and the ground to freeze, before he took the bike out for a test ride. He wasn't about to put this beauty out in the mud.

Bud never noticed his mother, who had eased up to the door leading from the kitchen, and his father peeking in over her shoulder. Bud stood a moment, thinking about the activities of the previous night, the birth of the Christmas baby; the three midnight visitors, bearing gifts, and one of them – the daddy of the baby. It seemed like a dream, like something that happened a long time ago. He thought about being thirteen years old, and it being Christmas Day, nineteen forty-three. It was a day that he would always want to remember.

CHAPTER 25

It was early January, and a Saturday. The giant Christmas snow still covered the ground. The temperature had fallen below zero for eight days in a row. The hard freeze had made the gravel roads passable, but extremely rough with frozen ruts. Abe Turner drove his new car up to the Scott's house to ask a favor. He asked that Ellis and Bud help him load some boxes of canned goods onto Ellis' truck and haul them to the Greyhound Bus Station at Bono for shipment.

Ellis was glad to oblige, but first he had to get the truck out from under the barn overhang, through the heavy snow in the barnyard and out into the gravel road. There had not been much traffic on the road since Christmas, but a few vehicles had passed and packed the snow enough to make it possible to drive the road. Ellis hooked a team of mules to the pickup and with Bud behind the wheel guiding, pulled the truck out onto the county road.

The battery wouldn't turn the engine over until Ellis removed it and brought it into the house and warmed it by sitting it on top of the stove. He had drained the radiator, so after he got the truck to start, he poured hot water into the radiator, reset the radiator cap and it wasn't long until he had the old truck warmed up and the heater coil putting out heat. He and Bud loaded up and headed down the county road to the store.

They arrived in time to find Abe completing the packing of a half-dozen heavy cardboard boxes with a variety of food items. Neither Bud nor Ellis asked any questions, but Bud noted that some of the can goods had contents with strange names. There was a can of Matzoh Balls, another of Gefilte Fish, two bottles of dark grape colored Mogen-David Wine, and a five-pound bag of Matzoh Meal that Abe was packing into the last box. Bud eased around to look at the other sealed boxes and noted that they all had the same Jackson, Mississippi, address written on them with a heavy black marker of some kind. Noting Bud's inquisitive gaze, Abe volunteered, "I got some family in Jackson. I try to send them some things that I can get through my wholesaler in Memphis. They ain't able to git much in Jackson, with the war on and all."

They loaded the truck, and with Ellis driving, Bud in the middle and Abe on the right, eased along over the bad road, taking the better part of an hour to travel the five miles to Bono. They arrived at the bus station with a few minutes to spare before the St. Louis, to New Orleans bus passed through. After a stop at Walnut Ridge, the bus would be stopping next at Bono. After departing Bono, the bus would make stops in Arkansas at Jonesboro, Trumann, Marked Tree and West Memphis, cross the Mississippi River into Memphis, Tennessee, then continue on to Jackson, Mississippi, and points south, terminating its run in New Orleans.

Ellis and Bud helped Abe carry the boxes of canned goods into the office of the ticket agent. While Abe was making the shipping arrangements, the sound of familiar voices were heard coming from the adjoining waiting room. Bud stuck his head through the door, and there gathered around a coal-burning potbellied cast iron stove were Roscoe Gilmore, Homer Adkins, Mary Margaret Miller and Betty Adkins who was breast-feeding her baby.

Bud turned to Ellis and Abe. "Y'all come on in here. The gang's all here," said a jubilant Bud. Bud then eased over to take a closer look at the baby. It made little mewing sounds, as it slurped at his mother's breast. It reminded Bud of a little white pig feeding. He suddenly remembered that it had been two hours since he ate breakfast, and he started thinking about how long it would be until dinnertime.

Ellis and Abe entered the waiting room just as the ticket agent pushed past them and addressed the group huddled near the fire. "Mr. and Mrs. Gilmore, Mr. and Mrs. Adkins, I just wanted you to know that the bus is on time. It has departed Walnut Ridge and will be arriving any minute. You should be in New Orleans by tomorrow night."

"Mr. and Mrs. Gilmore, Mr. and Mrs. Adkins," said Abe. "How'd that happen?"

"Well, we're both ministers of the Gospel," replied Homer. "I married them, and Roscoe married us."

"Ain't that a caution?" said a bemused Roscoe.

"You're goin' to New Orleans, then?" asked Bud.

"You just ain't a rooster pootin'," said a jocular Homer.

"We're a-goin' where they ain't none of this durned snow," said Mary Margaret.

"We hear that there's a mess of sinners in the swamps of Louisiana, and we aim to save some," exclaimed Roscoe.

At that moment, the big blue and silver bus with the racing greyhound on the side, pulled up in view through the front window of the station. "And here is our ride now," exclaimed Roscoe, and turning to Homer and the women, sang out,

"OK folks, sinners are awaitin',
Let there be no hesitatin',
All aboard the Chariot of Glory."

THE END

Printed in the United States
18988LVS00005B/64-72